C000170744

History and Cultural Memory in Neo-Victorian Fiction

History and Cultural Memory in Neo-Victorian Fiction

Victorian Afterimages

Kate Mitchell
Lecturer in English Literature, Australian National University, Australia

© Kate Mitchell 2010

All rights reserved. No reproduction, copy or transmission of this publication may be made without written permission.

No portion of this publication may be reproduced, copied or transmitted save with written permission or in accordance with the provisions of the Copyright, Designs and Patents Act 1988, or under the terms of any licence permitting limited copying issued by the Copyright Licensing Agency, Saffron House, 6–10 Kirby Street, London EC1N 8TS.

Any person who does any unauthorized act in relation to this publication may be liable to criminal prosecution and civil claims for damages.

The author has asserted her right to be identified as the author of this work in accordance with the Copyright, Designs and Patents Act 1988.

First published 2010 by
PALGRAVE MACMILLAN

Palgrave Macmillan in the UK is an imprint of Macmillan Publishers Limited, registered in England, company number 785998, of Houndmills, Basingstoke, Hampshire RG21 6XS.

Palgrave Macmillan in the US is a division of St Martin's Press LLC, 175 Fifth Avenue, New York, NY 10010.

Palgrave Macmillan is the global academic imprint of the above companies and has companies and representatives throughout the world.

Palgrave® and Macmillan® are registered trademarks in the United States, the United Kingdom, Europe and other countries.

ISBN 978–0–230–22858–0   hardback

This book is printed on paper suitable for recycling and made from fully managed and sustained forest sources. Logging, pulping and manufacturing processes are expected to conform to the environmental regulations of the country of origin.

A catalogue record for this book is available from the British Library.

A catalog record for this book is available from the Library of Congress.

10 9 8 7 6 5 4 3 2 1
19 18 17 16 15 14 13 12 11 10

Printed and bound in Great Britain by
CPI Antony Rowe, Chippenham and Eastbourne

For Adam, and for Ella, Grace and James

Contents

Acknowledgements

I am grateful to a number of institutions and individuals for their support, advice and assistance as I wrote this book. The University of Melbourne provided an intellectually engaging research environment. I would especially like to thank Clara Tuite whose judicious advice, warm encouragement and ongoing enthusiasm were invaluable. I am also indebted to Ken Gelder whose astute advice helped to shape this project in its early stages.

I am grateful for the research support I've received from an Australian Postgraduate Award, the English Department and School of Graduate Studies at the University of Melbourne, the School of Humanities and Social Sciences at the University of New South Wales (ADFA), and the National Europe Centre at the Australian National University. I am particularly grateful to the intellectual community at the National Europe Centre for providing both practical support and a stimulating and enjoyable research environment.

This book would not have been possible without the friendship, forbearance and practical support of my colleagues, friends and family. I am grateful to a number of individuals who counselled, challenged, and assisted me in a variety of ways as I wrote this book: Nicola Parsons, Julie Thorpe, Amanda Crawford, Branka van der Linden, Adam Berryman, Paul Pickering and Simon Bronitt. I am profoundly indebted to my parents, John and Jean, for their faith in me and their practical support, and particularly for their generosity in caring for my children. Thanks go also to my brother, Chris, who has always shown great interest in this project and has been willing to discuss it at length and in detail over several years, and to Peter, Jeanette, Kristy, Jez, Tanya and Brett who have provided warm encouragement and support. Most importantly, I could never have undertaken nor completed this book without the boundless support of my partner, Adam. He has spared no energy in assisting me from the beginning of this process to its end. To Adam, and to Ella, Grace and James, I owe a huge debt of gratitude for their love and patience during what I know seemed at times like a never-ending process.

An early version of the arguments presented in Chapter 3 appeared as '(Feeling It) As it Actually Happened' in *Literature Sensation* (Newcastle, UK: Cambridge Scholars Publishing, 2009), pp. 266–79. An early version of Chapter 6 appeared as 'Ghostly Histories and Embodied Memories' in *Neo-Victorian Studies* 1:1 (2008), pp. 81–109. Finally, I would like to thank Lee Jackson, creator of the Victorian London website (www. victorianlondon.org), for generously providing the photograph of London Bridge that appears on the cover of this book.

Introduction: 'I told you we'd been invaded by Victoriana'

> I told you we'd been invaded by Victoriana.
>
> (Liz Jensen, *Ark Baby*, 1998)

In 1918 Ezra Pound coined the term 'Victoriana' as a way of pejoratively characterising the Victorian past: 'For most of us, the odour of defunct Victoriana is so unpleasant ... that we are content to leave the past where we find it' (cited in Gardiner, 2004: 168). In stark contrast to Pound's confident marginalisation of the Victorian past at the outset of the twentieth century, a steady interest in things Victorian gained momentum in the second half of the same century until, in the final decades, a fascination with the period invaded film, television, trends in interior decoration, fashion, genealogy, advertising, museums, histori-cal re-enactments, politics and scholarship about the Victorian period. Far from an unpleasant odour detected and quickly left behind, the literature and culture of the Victorian period have been courted, sought and summoned across many facets of contemporary culture for more than three decades. If we are indeed invaded by Victoriana, we welcome the incursion and insist upon it. The sense of reiteration, of repetition and re-assertion that characterises our fascination with the Victorians is captured in the epigraph above: '*I told you* we'd been invaded by Victoriana' (Jensen, 1998: 165).

A seemingly ever-increasing number of authors participate in, and contribute to, this fascination by recreating the Victorian period in their fiction using a range of narrative strategies. Some novelists, such as A. S. Byatt in *Possession: A Romance* (1990) and Graham Swift in *Ever After* (1992), critically engage this straddling of two historical moments by creating dual storylines that, read together, dramatise the process of reconstructing an earlier time. Others, like Gail Jones in *Sixty Lights*

(2004) and William Gibson and Bruce Sterling in *The Difference Engine* (1991), create a Victorian period that is overtly informed by their twentieth-century knowledge without dramatising this in the story itself. And still others, such as Beryl Bainbridge in *Master Georgie* (1997) and Sheri Holman in *The Dress Lodger* (1999), recreate a Victorian world by suppressing all reference to their own historical perspective.

For their reconstructions of the Victorian period, novelists mine features of its history such as the cholera epidemic, the Crimean war, the invention of photography, the Anglo-Franco race to control the Nile, colonialism and the discovery of fossils, as well as the Victorian interest in spiritualism, the crisis of faith engendered by science, the emergent discipline of psychiatry, the experience of the expanding city, and burgeoning consumerism.[1] Additionally, some novelists choose to ventriloquise Victorian writers, such as Peter Ackroyd's *The Last Testament of Oscar Wilde* (1983) and Colm Tóibín's *The Master* (2004), which narrativises the life of Henry James. Others reinvent not writers but their characters, such as Peter Carey's *Jack Maggs* (1997), which explores the character of Magwitch from Charles Dickens' *Great Expectations* (1860–1), and Emma Tennant's *Tess* (1993), which imagines a lineage for Thomas Hardy's Tess, from *Tess of the D'Urbervilles* (1891). Still others rewrite Victorian novels, such as Valerie Martin's *Mary Reilly* (1990) which reworks *The Strange Case of Dr Jekyll and Mr Hyde* (1886) from the perspective of a housemaid, and Carlo Fruttero and Franco Lucentini's novel *The D Case: The Truth About The Mystery of Edwin Drood* (1989), in which fictional detectives, such as Sherlock Holmes, attempt to solve the mystery of Charles Dickens' unfinished novel *The Mystery of Edwin Drood*. Sometimes contemporary reworkings of Victorian novels take the form of a prequel, sequel or paralellquel, in which novelists explore tangential, marginal or background events and/or characters, as in Jean Rhys's *Wide Sargasso Sea* (1966) which explores the shadowy figure of Bertha Mason, both central to and marginalised in Charlotte Brontë's *Jane Eyre* (1847), and Emma Tennant's *Adele* (2003) which shifts the narrative focus to Rochester's daughter.

Growing in popularity and in sheer number throughout the last decades of the twentieth century and into the twenty-first, this sub-genre has embraced every literary genre, from the collection of detective fictions by Anne Perry to the science fictions of William Gibson and Bruce Sterling, as well as novels conventionally considered more 'literary', such as the Man-Booker Award-winning novels of A. S. Byatt and Peter Carey.[2] The Victorian period has also captured the imagination of writers of many nationalities, from African-American writer Toni Morrison and

Australian writer Richard Flanagan, to Canadian Helen Humphreys and Egyptian Ahdaf Soueif.

Neo-Victorian fiction prompts authors, readers and critics to confront the problem of historical recollection. These novels grapple with the issue of how to package the Victorian past for the tastes and demands of contemporary readers, how to make 'retro' accessible and, for that matter, commercially successful. Moreover, they struggle, too, with the issue of what is involved in this re-creation of history, what it means to fashion the past for consumption in the present. The issue turns upon the question of whether history is equated, in fiction, with superficial detail; an accumulation of references to clothing, furniture, décor and the like, that produces the past in terms of its objects, as a series of clichés, without engaging its complexities as a unique historical moment that is now produced in a particular relationship to the present. In its very form historical fiction poses the question of whether we, unavoidably influenced by our own historical moment, can know the past, and if so, whether we can do so through the medium of fiction. Can these novels recreate the past in a meaningful way or are they playing nineteenth-century dress-ups?

History and Cultural Memory in Neo-Victorian Fiction explores the ways in which contemporary historical fictions that return to the Victorian era stylistically and/or thematically critically engage the past. It opens up the question of what claims neo-Victorian novels make to history in general and the Victorian past in particular: what attitudes toward historical recollection are manifest in these novels and what particular versions of the Victorian past do they invoke? I suggest that these novels, while demonstrating a vivid awareness of the problematics involved in seeking and achieving historical knowledge, remain nonetheless committed to the possibility and the value of striving for that knowledge. They are more concerned with the ways in which fiction *can* lay claim to the past, provisionally and partially, rather than the ways that it can not. This argument is a departure from much scholarship on contemporary historical fiction which has, following Linda Hutcheon's influential model of historiographic metafiction, focused upon the ways such fiction problematises the representation of the past and foregrounds the difficulty of attaining historical knowledge.

The present study seeks, then, to draw a wider context for historiographic metafiction itself and considers some of the ways neo-Victorian fiction might extend and transform this category. Approaching neo-Victorian fiction as a subgenre of historical fiction, it reconnects contemporary historical fiction with the tradition of the historical novel, a category to which Hutcheon opposes historiographic metafiction. It suggests that the historical novel has always been invested in historical recollection *and* aware of the partial, provisional nature of such representations. It also links contemporary historical fiction to the burgeoning interest in a broadly conceived 'historical imaginary' (DeGroot, 2009) in order to disrupt a hierarchical approach that privileges history and marginalises historical fiction. I suggest that the emergence of memory discourse in the late twentieth century, and the increasing interest in non-academic forms of history, enables us to think through the contribution neo-Victorian fiction makes to the way we remember the nineteenth-century past in ways that resist privileging history's non-fictional discourse, on the one hand, and postmodernism's problematisation of representation on the other. Approaching neo-Victorian fiction as memory texts provides a larger framework for examining the sheer diversity of modes, motivations and effects of their engagement with the past, particularly one which moves beyond dismissing affect. As Mieke Bal suggests, 'the memorial presence of the past takes many forms and serves many purposes, ranging from conscious recall to unreflected re-emergence, from nostalgic longing for what was lost to polemical use of the past to shape the present' (Bal, 1999: vii). And, I would suggest, these multiple forms and purposes are often simultaneously present in the one text. Moreover, 'memory is active and it is situated in the present' (ibid.: viii). Positioning neo-Victorian novels as acts of memory provides a means to critically evaluate their investment in historical recollection as an act in the present; as a means to address the needs or speak to the desires of particular groups now.

I resist a popular and academically persuasive use of 'nostalgia' as the opposite of critical historical inquiry, This opposition is evident in Hutcheon's suggestion that in *The French Lieutenant's Women* 'the past is always placed critically – and not nostalgically – in relation to the present' (Hutcheon, 1988: 45). Indeed she is at pains to distinguish postmodernism's approach to the past from 'recuperation or nostalgia or revivalism' (ibid.: 93). Nostalgia is, for Hutcheon, an encumbrance from which postmodernism, and its historiographic metafictions, frees itself for its 'critical, dialogical reviewing of the forms, contexts, and values of the past' (ibid.: 89). Here, a conservative, even naïve, nostalgia is contrasted with a somehow more authentic, because critical, attitude toward the past. David Lowenthal, too, asserts that 'nostalgic dreams' of retrieving the past 'have become almost habitual, if not epidemic' in recent years. He finds nostalgia expressive of 'modern malaise', calling it today's 'universal catchword for looking back' (Lowenthal, 1985: 4).

This 'looking back' seeks not to engage with the past but is 'eager', rather, 'to collect its relics and celebrate its virtues' (ibid.: 7). Similarly, Frederic Jameson has charged postmodernity with an inability to think historically. He says 'it is safest to grasp the concept of the postmodern as an attempt to think the present historically in an age that has forgotten how to think historically in the first place' (Jameson, 1991: 9). For Jameson, the current trend for retro is characterised by the swift recycling of past styles as an aesthetic, without any understanding of, or reference to, the broader historical context in which they emerged. Indeed, contemporary historical fictions are 'historical novels in appearance only ... we seem condemned to seek the historical past through our own pop images and stereotypes about that past, which itself remains forever out of reach' (Jameson, 1985: 118).

This dichotomisation of nostalgia and critical engagement with the past structures Christian Gutleben's account of neo-Victorian fiction in *Nostalgic Postmodernism* (2001). Much of his critique rests upon an invocation of nostalgia as a conservative, negative term. Thus, 'because the contemporary novels celebrate to some extent the Victorian tradition, they *cannot* be deemed radically subversive' (Gutleben, 2001: 218, original emphasis). Furthermore, their success in the marketplace, stemming from the 'exploitation' of Victorian celebrity, further marks them as complicit in postmodernism, not seditious (ibid.). However, the complexity of our present relationship to the Victorian past cannot be simply dismissed as nostalgic and neo-Victorian fiction is informed, in part, by Jameson's own challenge, to art and critical thought, to 'think the present historically' (Jameson, 1991: ix). Undoubtedly individual texts engage the nostalgic moment in their process of reaching back to the past, in the sense that they invoke affect as a means toward historical recollection. However, this does not preclude sustained, critical engagement with the past. Moreover, nostalgia might be productive, giving voice to the desire for cultural memory to which these novels bear witness. In the last decade or two scholars working in a range of disciplines have reworked the notion of nostalgia, claiming for it a more positive and productive role in recalling the past, a project that seems important, even necessary, in a culture that multiplies historical narratives in a variety of media (see, for example, De Groot, 2009; Colley, 1998; Chase and Shaw, 1989). Michael Pickering and Emma Keightley argue that nostalgia 'can only be properly conceptualized as a contradictory phenomenon ... it is not a singular or fixed condition' but rather it 'covers a range of ways of orienting to and engaging with the past' (Pickering and Keightley, 2006: 926). And Ann C. Colley re-examines the idea of nostalgia 'to consider its idiosyncrasies and frequently unacknowledged complexities' (Colley, 1998: 1). Writing about nostalgia in the work of Victorian writers she suggests that their homesickness disrupts the conventional understanding of nostalgia as 'a response that primarily trivializes, simplifies, and misrepresents a former time'. Rather, nostalgia becomes a creative tool for remembering the past and mapping present identities (ibid.: 4–5). Svetlana Boym suggests that nostalgia implicitly critiques the very history that is its ostensible object of desire:

> there is in fact a tradition of critical reflection on the modern condition that incorporates nostalgia, which I will call *off-modern*. The adverb *off* confuses our sense of direction; it makes us explore sideshadows and back alleys rather than the straight road of progress; it allows us to take a detour from the deterministic narrative of twentieth-century history ... In the off-modern tradition, reflection and longing, estrangement and affection go together. (Boym, 2001: xvii)

Here nostalgia is granted a subversive function, disrupting and diverting the gaze of traditional histories. Rather than falsify and trivialise the past it produces multiple stories, at least some of which challenge and critique official historiographies and other dominant images of the past. Thus, rather than consider nostalgia as 'History's negativized other' (Pickering and Keightley, 2006: 934), we can understand it as standing in a complex relationship with both history and memory. Indeed, insofar as it always involves an 'act of recollection' (Colley, 1998: 1) nostalgia is inveterately linked to both history and memory as a mode of reaching back into the past. Whereas nostalgia and memory are often opposed to history as affective, and therefore critically suspect, in Boym's analysis nostalgia plays an important role in negotiating the relationship between what we might call memory and history. Nostalgia, she argues, 'is about the relationship ... between personal and collective memory' (Boym, 2001: xvi).

My aim is to explore the ways in which contemporary historical fictions remember the Victorian past, to examine which aspects of that past they choose to memorialise, and to consider what the implications of these memorialisations are, both for the historical period in which they are written and read, and for the Victorian era that they represent. I open up the question, pertinently phrased by Jennifer Green-Lewis: 'why, when we want to reinvent and revisit the past, do we choose the nineteenth century as the place to get off the train? What is it about the look of this past that appeals to the late-twentieth-century passenger?' (Green-Lewis, 2000: 30).[3] Neo-Victorian fiction ensures that the Victorian period continues to exist as a series of afterimages, still visible, in altered forms, despite its irrevocable past-ness, its disappearance. They couple a contemporary scepticism about our ability to know the past with a strong sense of the past's inherence in the present, often in non-textual forms and repetitions. The neo-Victorian novels examined here expand 'history' beyond textual, representational apparatuses, to include other, non-textual modes of memory and retrieval. These include oral histories, geographies, cartographies, paintings, photographs and bodies, all of which join diaries, letters, poems, novels and historical archives as means through which aspects of the past can be remembered and, often, repeated. Thus, while Frederick Holmes suggests that 'the [historical] novel emphasizes the efficacy of the imagination in providing us with provisional structures with which to make sense of the past' (Holmes, 1994: 331), I argue that, in many ways, these fictions are less concerned with *making sense* of the Victorian past, than with offering it as a cultural memory, to be re-membered, and imaginatively re-created, not revised or understood. They remember the period not only in the usual sense, of recollecting it, but also in the sense that they re-embody, that is, re-member, or reconstruct it. As we shall see, the dis(re)membered pieces of the past are reconstituted in and by the text, and also in the reader's imagination. The reader thus literally embodies (re-members) the reimagined past. In *History as an Art of Memory* (1993), Patrick Hutton contends that today historians 'speak less of invoking the past, and more of using it' (Hutton, 1993: xxii). I suggest that for contemporary novelists this is not true; novelists today are still interested in invoking the Victorian past.

My analysis of the significance of the Victorian era for contemporary novelists and their readers begins by examining what it means to rework the past in fiction. Chapter 1 discusses the protean forms of history, fiction and historical fiction as tools for historical knowledge. It traces the reception of the historical novel from the late-eighteenth century to the present, exploring how the relationship between history and fiction has been constructed, and how this has impacted upon critical approaches to the historical novel. Its title, 'Memory Texts', is taken from Gail Jones's reference to her novel *Sixty Lights* as a 'memory text' (Jones, 2005). It then turns to the recent critical interest in a more broadly conceived 'historical imaginary', which attempts to account for the multitude and variety of ways in which we think historically today across a range of media. I suggest that approaching neo-Victorian novels as memory texts enables us to critically account for the variety of historical modes they enact, without automatically privileging ironic distance and dismissing nostalgic revival. Moreover, it opens up a range of questions beyond historical fidelity on the one hand, and the problematisation of representation on the other. Using memory as a framework for approaching historical fiction also shifts focus toward reception; how do readers participate in making historical meaning? Finally, this chapter suggests that these novels are haunted not by the desire for history, or the past itself, since they know that the past is, indeed, passed. Rather, they are haunted by the desire for the act of historical recollection, the process of remembering.

Chapter 2 situates these novels in relation to other twentieth-century evocations of the Victorian period, including those in scholarship and politics. It opens up the question of which characteristics, attributes and ideals have been considered Victorian since the period ended and asks what attitudes toward the past have coloured twentieth-century representations of the era. First, this chapter provides a brief history of the way the Victorian period has been used throughout the twentieth century as an 'other' against which modernity might establish its identity, ranging from the modernist rejection of the period typified by Pound, to the celebration of the period by neo-conservatives like Margaret Thatcher and Gertrude Himmelfarb, each of whom, at least rhetorically, promotes the virtues of the era as the panacea for contemporary malaise. The focus then turns to contemporary historians and cultural critics who identify the origins of several current cultural features in the Victorian era and establish continuities between Victorian culture and our own. The chapter's title, 'Contemporary Victorian(isms)', reworks Charles Taylor's discussion of 'our Victorian contemporaries'. He argues that we are 'close' to the Victorians because we still employ their Enlightenment and Romantic vocabularies and still experience the legacy of their faith in science, progress and the moral exceptionalism these underpin (see Taylor, 1989: 393ff and Krueger, 2002). It is my contention that while these novels posit the inherence of the Victorian past in the late twentieth and early twenty-first centuries, this takes the form not of seamless continuity but of a series of flashes and repetitions that suggest the alterity of the past, its difference, while also, paradoxically, producing a shock of recognition. Their attempt to forge a middle ground between alteritism and continuism in (re)presenting the Victorian era can be understood in terms similar to those Valerie Traub uses to describe the approach to the past she adopts for her own work, 'assuming neither that we will find in the past a mirror image of ourselves nor that the past is so utterly alien that we will find nothing usable in its fragmentary traces' (Traub, 2001: 262).

The remaining chapters are devoted to close analysis of several contemporary historical novels with reference to their contexts of production, including their own historical moment of emergence, and the representations of the Victorian era they each produce. In my choice of novels I have attempted to examine texts from the earliest explosion of this sub-genre in the 1980s through to recent examples of neo-Victorian fiction. I have included two, *Waterland* (1983) and *Possession* (1990), which are generally cited as examples of Hutcheon's historiographic metafiction and typify many of its traits. I will also point out the ways in which they extend or simply exceed the terms of Hutcheon's categorisation. Sarah Waters' *Affinity* (1999) and *Fingersmith* (2002) represent a more marked shift away from the overtly metafictional techniques of the earlier examples. As a result, scholarly attention has been more divided about the relationship to history they embody and represent, and as to whether they are examples of historiographic metafiction. Gail Jones' *Sixty Lights* (2004) and Helen Humphreys' *Afterimage* (2001) have yet to receive much scholarly attention but their reviews do not identify them with Hutcheon's category, reflecting, perhaps, their privileging of memory as a mode of historical recollection.

Chapter 3 discusses Graham Swift's *Waterland*, in which the Victorian era is made to illustrate conventional history-making and the accompanying notion of historical impetus and design. In its history-teacher protagonist, the novel confronts the late twentieth-century crisis of this historiography, exploring the narrativity of history and positing the uncertainty of historical knowledge. In Tom Crick's meandering narrative, history *becomes* memory as the French Revolution, the First and Second World Wars and Fenland regional history are subsumed within his own memories. History is depicted here as excessive, eluding the representations that attempt to circumscribe it so that complete knowledge is always beyond reach. Yet even as it undermines the possibility of historical knowledge, the novel is infused also with a sense of the inescapability of history. The very excess of history is recast as fecundity, and the desire to know the past is celebrated as the guarantee that stories, including those about the past, will continue to be told, and meanings will continue to be made, even if those meanings are provisional and incomplete.

Chapter 4 turns to A. S. Byatt's *Possession: A Romance*. At first this novel seems implicated in the reductive opposition between nostalgia and historical inquiry because it contrasts a cult of nostalgia, which centres upon possessing the dead relics of the past, with the literary text as living artefact and efficacious medium of the past. However, its own complex relationship to the Victorian period complicates this apparent distinction between nostalgia and historical knowledge. The novel's Victorian period is the natural home of the ideal reader, one whose relationship to the text is one not of appropriation, but of mutual possession, characterised primarily by desire. Byatt establishes the metaphor of romance, the relationship of lovers, to explicate this model of knowledge. The 'Romance' of her subtitle refers not only to the affairs between her two pairs of central characters, it refers also to the romance between the text and reader. Here any opposition between nostalgia and historical inquiry breaks down. Indeed the ideal reader must cultivate an affective relationship to the past, a certain nostalgic longing, in order for historical inquiry to be productive.

In Chapter 5 a discussion of Sarah Waters' critically acclaimed novels *Affinity* (1999) and *Fingersmith* enables an examination of the revisionist impulse of neo-Victorian fiction. I position these texts as examples of 'faux' Victorian fiction; novels written in the Victorian tradition that refuse to self-reflexively mark their difference from it in the characteristic mode of historiographic metafiction. Dubbed 'Vic Lit', these novels revive Victorian novelistic traditions. Specifically, they invoke Victorian gothic and sensation novels, two genres that were associated with transgressive femininity. In these novels, Waters bypasses history altogether, as a masculine mode in which a genealogy of lesbian desire is invisible. Instead, she speaks with the language of Victorian fiction in order to invent a tradition of nineteenth-century female homosexuality, writing it into our cultural memory of the Victorian literary tradition by a fictional sleight of hand.

Chapter 6 turns to the Victorian visual technology of photography, with a discussion of Gail Jones' *Sixty Lights* and Helen Humphreys' *Afterimage*. These recent novels differ from *Waterland* and *Possession* in that, for each, the entire novel occupies the same temporal plane: like *Affinity* and *Fingersmith* they are set wholly within the Victorian period and do not switch between it and a contemporary present. In contrast to the earlier novels, these do not dramatise a scholarly pursuit of historical knowledge via academic history or literary criticism. Their exploration of historical knowledge in general, and the Victorian period in particular, is refracted through memory. Their portrayal of the longing for, and pursuit of, history, proceeds via the metaphor of yearning to be returned to the dead mother's body. Whereas for Hutcheon the past is only available via its textual traces, these novels suggest that the past inheres in the present, often unnoticed, in the form of embodied memory, as a repertoire of shared cultural images, and as a series of repetitions. Exploring the efficacy of words and images as memorials, or attempts at reparation, *Sixty Lights* and *Afterimage* suggest that imaginative re-creations of the past enable us to embody it, to siphon into ourselves the experience of another time. Together, these textual analyses suggest the variety of narrative strategies and diversity of Victorian images that characterise neo-Victorian fiction's engagement with the past, and demonstrate the sub-genre's commitment to exploring its own creative role in historical recollection.

1
Memory Texts: History, Fiction and the Historical Imaginary

> The very term 'historical fiction' is a kind of oxymoron, joining 'history' (what is 'true'/'fact') with 'fiction' (what is 'untrue'/'invented', but may aim at a different kind of truth).
>
> (Diana Wallace, *The Woman's Historical Novel*, 2005)

> ... my starting point is the way we actively engage with the past using various media and methods, rather than some abstract notion of 'history' as sleeping-beauty object waiting for the professional kiss to arouse it.
>
> (Ann Rigney, 'Being an Improper Historian', 2007)

It is, perhaps, no coincidence that neo-Victorian fiction achieves momentum at around the time when personal memory of the Victorians was slipping away. By the 1980s there could be few, if any, Victorians left; at least, very few who were born early enough to have any personal memory of the period itself. A number of neo-Victorian novelists describe their work in relation to memory, rather than history, and further neo-Victorian novels invoke memory as a category of historical recollection within their pages. Yet in critical accounts, neo-Victorian fiction is most often situated in relation to a postmodern problematisation of historical knowledge, rather than as an act of recall. In the first systematic treatment of the sub-genre, Christian Gutleben focuses on the formal properties of neo-Victorian fiction in order to situate it in relation to aesthetic postmodernism. The novels are primarily assessed in relation to their imitation or subversion of Victorian literary techniques, not as attempts to contribute to historical understanding. Indeed, Gutleben does not specifically address their generic heritage as historical fictions, a genre with a complicated relationship to history and historiography, making it difficult for his analysis to consider the novels' engagement with history generally and with the Victorian past in particular.

This chapter situates my scrutiny of neo-Victorian novels in relation to their broader generic categorisation as part of the tradition of the historical novel in order to foreground their investment in re-membering the Victorian past. Rather than chart the history of historical fiction, which has been done excellently elsewhere (see Fleishman, 1971 and Wesseling, 1991), this chapter begins by mapping the intersections of the historical novel with its two components, history and fiction, since the eighteenth century, making the question of reference central. To this end, I am not concerned with primary analysis of historical fictions so much as with tracing the reception and perception of the genre itself in relation to its ability to produce historical meaning. I suggest that at the very moment when postmodern challenges to the traditional authority of history seemed to open up new possibilities for the role of fiction in historical recollection, freeing it from questions of accuracy and authenticity, scholarly debates equated non-ironic recuperation of the past with critical naiveté: historical fiction must self-reflexively problematise representation or be deemed nostalgically uncritical. I aim to move debates about contemporary historical fiction on from this reductive opposition by turning to cultural memory as a field of enquiry, and to broader notions of mnemonic practices, to propose an alternative framework for understanding the ways in which neo-Victorian novels *do* lay claim to historical recollection, one which opens up a range of questions beyond historical fidelity on the one hand, and the problematisation of representation on the other: why does the text invokes this aspect of the past, in this way and in this form, now? How does it function as a technology of cultural memory, shaping our historical consciousness? And how does it enable us, as readers, to conceptualise the *relationship* between the Victorian past and our present? I situate the historical novel as an act of memory which, as Mieke Bal argues, is 'an activity occurring in the present, in which the past is continuously modified and redescribed even as it continues to shape the future' (Bal, 1999: vii). Approaching neo-Victorian novels as memory texts enables us to critically account for the variety of historical modes they enact, without automatically privileging ironic distance and dismissing nostalgic revival. It posits nostalgia as a more complicated and multiple mode of recollection. Moreover, understanding the neo-Victorian novel as a present act of recollection foregrounds the role of the reader in producing historical meaning. It furthers our understanding of how the relationship between present and past is conceptualised in multiple ways in a culture that is, paradoxically, obsessed with history and yet charged with the inability to think historically.

I

In an introductory essay for a 2005 special edition of the journal *Rethinking History*, Hayden White asserts that 'the conjuring up of the past requires art as well as information' (White, 2005: 1949). It is a polemical statement which invokes a series of contentious and complex issues that can largely be resolved into the question of the difference between history and fiction and the value and use of each for understanding the past. Another way to frame these questions would be to ask, as Ina Ferris does in her discussion of the impact of Sir Walter Scott's *Waverley* novels, 'what will count as history?' (Ferris, 1991: 137). Ferris notes the peculiar status of the referent in historical discourse. History represents 'that which no longer is', so that 'history as a genre has a special dependence on absence and on discourse that makes the referent of history highly vulnerable, threatening it with indeterminacy, fictionality, specularity' (ibid.: 152–3). Indeed, 'history' has always been slippery, and defining what constitutes the 'historical', whether for the purpose of historiography or historical fiction, has been an object of debate at least since the eighteenth century. This is particularly true of its relationship to fiction.

The distinction between history and fiction has long been a disputed and contentious one while also, paradoxically, appearing 'commonsensical'. As Louis O. Mink suggests, '"everyone knows" … that history claims to be a true representation of the past while fiction does not, even when it purports to describe actions and events locatable in particular times and places' (Mink, 1978: 129). And yet, so trammelled is this purportedly transparent, or natural, distinction that Suzanne Gearhart argues that the boundary between them 'is more open than closed, more often displaced than fixed, as much within each field as at the limits of each' (Gearhart, 1984: 3). She claims that theories of history and theories of fiction alike have always been uneasy with this porousness:

> they have consistently sought to fix the boundary between them and to establish once and for all the specificity of the fields in one of two ways: democratically, in that each accepts a mutually agreed

upon boundary which grants to each its own identity and integrity; or, just as often, imperialistically, in that each tries to extend its own boundary and to invade, engulf, or encompass the other. In the first case history and fiction exist side by side as uncommunicating opposites; in the second, one dominates the other – as when history makes fiction into its subject and treats it as just another historical document, or when fiction makes history into one form of fictional narrative among many possible forms. (ibid.: 4)

The contest turns upon the issue of truth. While Mink's common-sense knows that history purports to be 'true', it is unclear what, in this formulation, fiction purports to be. Fiction is constructed negatively, as the opposite of history's claim to truth. The distinction, presumably, is between an 'actual' past and an imagined one. And it is to the actual past that authority accrues. History is valorised as true, or real, while 'made-up' fiction is reserved for entertainment.

While the opposition between history and fiction is, paradoxically, commonsensical *and* fiercely contested, Hayden White has famously observed that history did not always demand the excision of fiction. In the eighteenth century, prior to the disciplinisation of knowledge, he argues, fictional techniques and literary devices were considered necessary for historical representation (see White, 1978b). Historians such as François-Marie Arouet de Voltaire, Charles-Louis de Secondat, Baron de La Brède et de Montesquieu and Edward Gibbon saw their task as discovering the meaning of past events, and this meaning might best surface through a combination of what actually happened – what is generally considered 'fact' – and what could have happened – details lost to the historical record but which do not obviously contradict it. History's meaning was deeply embedded in rhetoric. It had a firmly philosophical purpose, functioning to enlighten and instruct the present. Thus, James Chandler argues that, far from striving for objec-tivity, much of the history written during the romantic period had a political motive, seeking to 'state *the case of the nation* – and to do so in such a ways as to alter its case ... [these writings] take on the national cause' (Chandler, 1998: 6).

This mingling of historical narrative and fictional techniques was accepted, in part, because the disciplines had yet to separate as distinct forms of knowledge. History formed part of a broad category of litera-ture in the eighteenth century, which, in addition to history, included philosophy and political philosophy, as well as the poetry and novels that make up the category today (Gearhart, 1984: 10). Historians, artists and scientists were designated as such because of their subject matter, not their methodologies and 'were united in a *common* effort to comprehend the experiences of the French Revolution' (White, 1978a: 42). Gradually this common effort was undermined by a suspicion toward myth and an acute awareness of the dangers of misreading history and misunderstanding historical process (White, 1978b: 124). 'Truth' became equated with 'fact' and the opposition between 'truth' and 'error' was redrawn as an opposition of 'truth' and 'fiction'. Importantly, in this shift, the underlying assumption that the past can be known and represented remains, although the emphasis is transferred to the means of representation. Fiction, White observes, thus became seen 'as a hindrance to the understanding of reality rather than as a way of apprehending it' (ibid.: 123). Indeed Linda Orr suggests that 'it is as if history awakes in the nineteenth century surprised and even horrified to see how closely it is coupled with fiction. It seeks thereafter to widen a difference within its very self, in order not to be engulfed by that other self' (Orr, 1986: 3). Attempting to escape association with fiction, it is the separate discipline of science, and its increasing authority as a mode of knowledge, to which history attaches itself.

In the context of a growing faith in scientific methodologies as the means to truth (see Knight, 1986: 5), some historians recast their efforts as a science, adopting the 'heroic image of an unprejudiced, dispassionate, all-seeing scientific investigator', who is pitted, with the scientist, against 'superstition, fanaticism, and all other forms of intellectual and political absolutism' (Appleby et al. 1994: 89). Leopold von Ranke, whose name has become virtually synonymous with the scientific model of history, sought to sever history from contemporary politics and philosophies and to achieve impartiality and scientific objectivity. History was no longer to judge the past nor instruct the present, but strive to show only 'what actually happened' through a meticulous use of primary sources (See Ranke, 1973). The historian should chart a course from particular detail to general historical principles. The fundamental tenets of scientific empiricist history are usefully summarised as follows: 'the rigorous examination and knowledge of historical evidence, verified by references; Impartial research, devoid of *a priori* beliefs and prejudices; And an inductive method of reasoning, from the particular to the general' (Green and Troup, 1999: 3). No longer amateur rhetoricians, nineteenth-century historians professionalised themselves, cultivating objective detachment in the assessment of evidence and dispassionate narration of the facts in order to withstand the scientific test: to 'tell a truth that would be acceptable to any other researcher who had seen the same evidence and applied the same rules' (Appleby et al. 1994: 73).

The identification of history as a science necessitated its demarcation from fiction, 'especially', White argues, 'from the kind of prose fiction represented by the romance and the novel' (White, 1987b: 65). For science is, in the nineteenth century, increasingly aligned with knowledge, objectivity, rationalism and empiricism, while literature is defined in opposition to these, as pertaining to value (spiritual and moral), subjectivity and inspiration. Literature's emotion and passion are opposed to science's cool rationality and impersonality (Cordle, 2000: 21). However, far from firmly establishing history as distinct from fiction, the assertion of history as a science had to be reiterated and insisted upon. Even in 1902 J. B. Bury, in his inaugural address as Lord Acton in the Regius Chair at Cambridge, found it necessary to exhort historians to remember that:

> it has not yet become superfluous to insist that history is a science, no less and no more ... History has really been enthroned and ensphered among the sciences ... but the particular nature of her influence, her time-honoured association with literature, and other circumstances, have acted as a sort of vague cloud, half concealing from men's eyes her new position in the heavens ... (Bury, 1956: 214)

Indeed Ann Curthoys and John Docker argue that throughout the nineteenth century the claim that history was a science met with dissent and criticism within the profession and was never universally accepted: 'the notion of history as art and the view of history as science have jostled against one another ever since the 1820s, unresolved, often within the one author' (Curthoys and Docker, 2005: 71). Perhaps this is in part due to the fact that fiction, too, was impacted by empiricist epistemology and the dominance of science in the nineteenth-century, an impact observable in the dominance of realism as a mode for fiction. Realism shared Rankean history's faith in the past's availability for factual representation. Realist texts detail the particularities of a life or lives within a broader, recognisable context, seeking to convey the experience of living in a particular space and at a particular time, while also implying 'truth claims of a more universal philosophical or ethical nature' (see Morris, 2003: 9, 101). Pam Morris calls this their 'truth effect' (ibid.: 109). Alison Lee suggests that some writers were explicitly influenced by the scientific method, 'and sought to make the novel as objective as they perceived science to be' (Lee, 1990: 12). Indeed, their shared preference for realism as the narrative mode with which to represent the past, and the shared, empiricist assumptions that underpin this preference, draw history and fiction closer together on the boundary line that attempts to separate them. This is not to suggest that realist literature saw itself as coterminous with history. As Lee points out, 'lying' literature and 'true' history were still distinguished from each other for the realist aesthetic. 'History was seen as accessible as pure fact, independent of individual perception, ideology, or the process of selection necessitated simply by creating a written narrative' (ibid.: 29).

II

If history is viewed, here, as the authoritative discourse, it is also, paradoxically, the more vulnerable, 'always under threat', as Ferris suggests, 'from the nonrational, oddly aggressive power of fiction' (Ferris, 1991: 138). Fiction is thought to have a greater affective power and, divorced from the rigorous research and scholarship of history, might powerfully mislead its readers (ibid.: 146-7). These fears about fiction are nowhere more apparent than in debates about historical fiction, which is often called to account for the liberties it takes with historical fact. Historical fiction is usually described as a hybrid of its component parts, history and fiction (see Wesseling, 1991: 49 and Wallace, 2005: 3). Ferris observes that 'while all generic hybrids constitute what [Mikhail] Bakhtin calls "border violations," historical fiction violates an especially sensitive border' (Ferris, 1991: 139). The hybrid draws attention to its problematic status so the effort to define historical fiction illuminates the difficulty of defining both history and fiction. This has been reflected in reviews of historical novels but rarely in definitions of the genre. For Avrom Fleishman, who produced one of the first systematic studies of the genre, the central questions for defining historical fiction are how much time needs to have passed before an event or person is considered 'historical' (sixty years) and, what type of events can be considered 'historical' (war, politics, economic change etc) (Fleishman, 1971: 3). He concedes that readers will also require truth, 'if only to praise or blame on the grounds of "accuracy," or faithful recording of presumably established facts' (ibid.: 4). In Fleishman's account, then, history is conceived as a knowable space available to representation, in this case, in fiction. History is the authoritative element of the hybrid, the real that fiction must truthfully reflect.

Most accounts of the genre position it as intervening in the field of historiography, rather than that of fiction. Thus, observing that 'the [traditional] historical novelist intervenes in a field that already exists as an authoritative discourse, no matter how contested portions of this discourse might be' (Ferris, 1991: 200),[1] Ferris describes the distinction between historical fiction and history in terms of generic authority and propriety so that the novel, whose purpose is 'amusement', is secondary to history, whose object is 'truth' (ibid.: 148). She argues that Sir Walter Scott's historical fictions are structured around a deference for history (although this asserted deference was often undermined by other narrative elements), establishing a relationship between history and historical fiction that is 'tangential' rather than 'tangled'. Scott's imaginative activity was to fill the gaps left by the historical record, rather than displace it (see Ferris, 1991: 203–7). Georg Lukács and Elizabeth Wesseling also discuss the emergence of Scott's *Waverley* novels in these terms, as supplementing official history. Wesseling argues that prior to the nineteenth century's professionalisation of history, the task of historical inquiry was divided in two and undertaken by different bodies of people: the antiquarians, who collected and managed archival materials, and the historians, who created narratives that would be interesting and entertaining enough to preserve the history that the antiquarian divulged (Wesseling, 1991: 44). The historian could, therefore, include certain speeches or add particular details to make the narrative fuller and more pleasing, since, as we have seen, it was assumed that their work involved some use of rhetoric and imagination. Wesseling argues that historical fiction stepped into the space left by these historians when they adopted scientific methodologies and the previously separate roles of research and writing were conjoined. The task of the historical novelist, as Scott and his peers conceived it, was to instruct the reader in the manners and customs of the past in an entertaining manner (ibid.: 44).

If Scott's work supplements official historiography, by providing colour, it does so on official history's own terms, by reproducing the same interests and emphases. Scott identifies, and is identified, with a model of history based upon the centrality of political events, great men and their deeds. Interestingly, this focus on the political and great events of history is reproduced in criticism of the historical novel that places Scott at the genre's centre. As we have seen, White makes the French Revolution and Napoleonic wars a pivotal moment in the separation of the disciplines of philosophy, literature, history and science. Lukács, in his influential account of the genre, cites the tumult of the French Revolution and Napoleonic wars as prompting the beginning of the historical novel as he locates it, with Sir Walter Scott's fiction. He, too, suggests that these events established a new concept of history, providing 'the concrete possibilities for men to comprehend their own existence as something historically conditioned, for them to see in history something which deeply affects their daily lives and immediately concerns them' (Lukács, 1962: 24). The accelerated social and economic change heralded by the French Revolution and Napoleonic wars prompted new attempts at understanding 'ordinary man' and how he was affected by the evolutionary clash of civilisations (see ibid.: 27, 53). Here, the focus remains upon the great, political events of history, with only a minor shift to address the effect of these upon 'the broadest masses' (ibid.: 25). In Lukács' Marxist account the historical novel steps in to rewrite feudal history to fit the emergent bourgeoisie's sense of itself and its place in that history.

The redistribution of historical value toward experience and process suggests an interest in the effects of large-scale, public events on the private, ordinary individual and the evocation not only of these events but of the broader cultural sphere in and from which they occurred. This brings the concerns of history-writing closer to the conventional concerns of literature since the private and the individual were considered the domain of fiction with its vivid evocation of detail and its focus on 'ordinary' people whose lives are not recorded in historical records. Indeed, fiction was considered superior to history in representing particular kinds of historical experience. Ferris notes that Francis Jeffrey, one of the early reviewers of *Waverley*, judged that '*because* it was a novel it offered historical insight and valid if implicit critique of history writing' (Ferris, 1991: 197). By attributing to the historical novel a greater capacity to meaningfully represent the experience of everyday life amidst the tumult of historical events, Ferris argues, Jeffrey 'authorizes for historical fiction a critical space vis-à-vis standard [political] history' (ibid.: 199). Historical fiction could share, perhaps even trump, history's privileged relationship to the real when it came to the private and personal. Yet rather than change the terms of the contest between history and fiction over access to the real, the assertion of fiction's superior claim to representing the past only reverses the terms and makes history the problematic category while naturalising fiction, instead of examining the functions of both forms of representation.

Whereas Lukács, Wesseling and Ferris situate historical fiction, as a hybrid of fiction and history, primarily in a complementary relationship to historiography, Barbara Foley defines and examines historical fiction primarily in its relationship to fiction. She situates it among a broader category of documentary novels, comprising the 'pseudofactual' novel of the seventeenth and eighteenth centuries, the historical novel of the nineteenth century and the fictional biography and the meta-historical novel of the twentieth century. The documentary novel overlaps with what Foley calls 'the mainstream tradition of the novel'; it is not an insignificant or small subgenre of the novel. However, she distinguishes it from this larger, mainstream, tradition because it fore-grounds the problem of reference in a particular way, 'insist[ing] that it contains some kind of specific and verifiable link to the historical world' and 'implicitly claim[ing] to replicate certain features of actu-ality in a relatively direct and unmediated fashion' (Foley, 1986: 26). Foley maintains history and fiction as discrete categories and identi-fies the historical novel as fiction. Here, historical fiction is not a hybrid but a particular form of fiction that is located near the border between fact and fiction, but which does not eradicate or even seri-ously challenge it. 'Rather, it purports to represent reality by means of agreed-upon conventions of fictionality, while grafting onto its fictive pact some kind of additional claim to empirical validation' (ibid.: 25). According to this account, rather than offering itself as access to the historical real, the historical novel seeks to propagate a particular moral and simply 'borrows' history's special relationship to the past to pull this off. Rather than supplement history it simply uses the past for its own purposes. In this account of historical fiction, as in those accounts that make it supplementary, history is an unproblematic and authorita-tive category.

Historical fiction's very hybridity seemed to make it unviable as either history or fiction by the end of the nineteenth century. The re-evaluation of historicism in the late nineteenth- and early twentieth-centuries by perspectivist historians like Benedetto Croce and R. G. Collingwood challenged history's authoritative relationship to the past. Their claim was that the historian could not escape his or her preju-dices and preconceptions, the structures of which shaped any historical account. For historical fiction, perspectivist historicism clashed with the demand for moral commentary upon characters' actions charac-teristic of the nineteenth-century realist novel, since any judgement would stem from the novelist's own values and ethics, not those of past figures, and would be a kind of psychological anachronism. 'In this situation', observes Wesseling, 'authors of historical fiction can hardly avoid incurring the censure of either the novelist or the historian.' By the end of the nineteenth century critics such as Leslie Stephen and writers such as Henry James declared the historical novel to be impossible (Wesseling, 1991: 58).[2] For Wesseling and others who make Scott's *Waverley* novels normative, the historical novel all but disappears in the twentieth century until after the Second World War. For these accounts of the genre, the classical historical novel was 'designed for the telling of a thrilling tale of high adventure within a historical setting, which was to entertain the reading public and to rouse their curiosity, and certainly not for the tackling of intricate epistemological issues', for which purpose it was 'fundamentally unsuited' (ibid.: 73).

However, Diana Wallace's *The Woman's Historical Novel* (2005) is devoted to women's historical fiction from 1900–2000 and includes many examples of historical fiction published in the early twentieth century (see Wallace, 2005: 25–52). Indeed, she persuasively argues that the impact of the First World War transformed historical consciousness as the Napoleonic wars had done a century earlier, forcing upon the individual an awareness of living within history, intimately affected by it. Quoting Lukács, she suggests that history was again, visibly, a 'mass experience', with the key difference being that 'this consciousness of existence within history includes *women* for the first time' (ibid.: 25). As the Napoleonic wars had done, the First World War transformed literature, not least in its galvanising effect upon historical fiction. Newly enfranchised and with experience of the workforce and of university education, women turned to the genre and renovated it. While Wallace's argument, that women turned to the genre at a time when male writers were abandoning it, supports Wesseling's claim in some respects, it suggests, too, that rather than disappear, the historical novel becomes invisible to a generic definition built upon the *Waverley* model. Indeed, this critical invisibility works retrospectively to include examples of women's historical fiction written both prior to *Waverley* and since. The dominance of Lukács' definition of 'classical historical fiction', modelled upon Scott's fiction, 'actually worked to exclude many forms of the woman's historical novel from critical attention' (ibid.: 3). Contrary to the suggestion that the historical novel was unsuited to questions about the nature and possibility of historical knowledge, Wallace's focus upon a maternal genealogy for the historical novel enables her to suggest the ways in which the unique properties of historical fiction have always raised questions regarding the epistemological issues associated with knowing the past. Wallace gives the example of Sophia Lee's *The Recess, or A Tale of Other Times* (1783), set during the reign of Elizabeth I. Upon its reception, this novel, which invents twin daughters for Mary Queen of Scots who must live, hidden, in an underground, labyrinthine series of passages and rooms, or the 'recess', was criticised for its lack of historical truth, its failure to adhere to the facts of history. Yet these criticisms are predicated upon a particular notion of historical truth. Wallace argues that Lee's use of invented characters in a factual historical setting enabled her to posit a truth lost to the official historical record: 'the very excesses for which the text is criticised – the lack of probability, the disregard for agreed chronology, the excessive sentiment of the heroines – all work to disturb accepted accounts of 'history' and suggest that what it offers as 'truth' is in fact equally fictional, and damaging to women' (ibid.: 16–17). This would suggest that the late twentieth-century feminist challenge to historical method and historiography has its eighteenth-century antecedents. The woman's historical novel was already addressing official history's neglect of women and already telling the 'untold story of women and everyday life' that, for Linda Hutcheon, is a focus of historiographic metafiction (See Hutcheon, 1988: 95).

III

It is issues such as these, which Wallace credits women's historical novels with raising several centuries ago, that become a central focus in the late-twentieth century. The 'postmodern' challenge to history's authority turns upon the issue of reference in history and fiction, and particularly upon the distinction between the events of the past and the meaning attributed to them in narrative. Or, as Hutcheon observes, postmodernism's problematisation of history brings 'a new self-consciousness about the distinction between the brute events of the past and the historical *facts* we construct out of them' (Hutcheon, 1989: 54). Distinguishing between the events of the past and our accounts of them enables Hutcheon to formulate the problem of reference in a productive way: 'is the referent of historiography, then, the fact or the event, the textualized trace or the experience itself?' (Hutcheon, 1988: 153). The 'linguistic turn' in historiography has focused history's dependence upon language and narrative both as the source of its evidence and in its communication as a story. For example, Roland Barthes analyses history's conventional rhetoric to highlight the way that history naturalises itself, producing its narrative as authoritative discourse by eliding the presence of the historian as author, and creating the appearance of unmediated access to the past (see Barthes (1957) 1986). And Hayden White identifies the tropes and narrative devices common to history and fiction, their shared source in language, and argues that the imposition of narrative lends the past the shape of a story, imbuing the events of the past a 'coherence, integrity, fullness, and closure ... that is and can only be imaginary' (White, 1987a: 24).

If language and narrative are the 'other sources' of history and fiction alike, and if history's referent is not 'out there' waiting to be discovered and recorded, but is rather constructed, the notion that historical narratives have privileged access to the real is undermined. Indeed, no longer guaranteeing unproblematic access to the past, the historian's narrative is at a double remove from the past 'as it really happened'. The primary sources have not simply mediated the past but have always already interpreted it, and the historian's narrative, constructed from these textual remains, is itself an interpretation of them. History is no longer a stable entity, the assurance of an extra-textual reality or context against which literature can be understood. Nor is it a stable context against which historical fiction can be judged as true or false. As Paul Hamilton observes, the new historicism 'recasts history as a battle over fictions' (Hamilton, 1996: 171).

Indeed, the reconfigured relationship between history and fiction forged by the new historicist emphasis upon the historicity of texts and the textuality of history seems to suggest that the writer of fiction can share the role of the historian. Martha Tuck Rozett links the publication of Umberto Eco's *The Name of the Rose* (1984) to the influence of the new historicist school of literary criticism. She claims that 'this dazzling mixture of thick historical research and popular detective fiction invited its readers to view historical fiction as an academically respectable genre and a vehicle for recovering and reimagining the past in unconventional ways' (Rozett, 1995: 145). In his *Postscript to The Name of the Rose* (1988), Umberto Eco emphasises the importance of historical research in the construction of a detailed world, and in the creation of characters that truly belong to that time and place. More specifically, he suggests that the novelist can present a past 'that history books have never told us so clearly [and] make history, what happened, more comprehensible ... identify in the past the causes of what came later, but also trace the process through which those causes began slowly to produce their effects' (Eco, 1984: 75, 76). The delineation of the postmodern historical novelist's task in this way recalls that which Ferris attributes to Scott, in writing his fiction. His or her role is to illuminate history, including making the pattern of history comprehensible. Whereas for Scott this meant the depiction of a Hegelian dialectical development, or evolution, effected by the clash of civilisations, for Eco it means a Foucauldian genealogy or archaeological descent, the process of historical inquiry, not a process of purposive history.[3] What is significant about Eco's account of his own project as a postmodern historical novelist is that he still foregrounds a strong engagement with the past as a reality that once existed, although now only traceable through texts. In Hutcheon's categorisation of the postmodern histori-cal novel, which she terms 'historiographic metafiction', engagement with the past, Eco's reconstruction of a detailed world, is firmly subju-gated to foregrounding the process of construction, the mechanics of representation.

Hutcheon's *A Poetics of Postmodernism* (1988) remains the most influ-ential account of historical fiction in its specific, late twentieth-century manifestation. In her account of historiographic metafiction she fore-grounds the problematisation of representation, arguing that historio-graphic metafiction refutes history's authority by challenging the 'implied assumptions of historical statements: objectivity, neutrality, impersonality, and transparency of representation'. This contestation erodes 'any sure ground upon which to base representation and narration', although, she argues, historiographic metafiction first inscribes and subsequently subverts that ground (Hutcheon, 1988: 92). For historiographic metafic-tion the shared referent of history and fiction is never an extra-textual reality, only other texts. History can be known only in its traces, which are always already ideologically and discursively encoded and 'always already interpreted' (ibid.: 143).

In a sense the question for historiographic metafiction and post-modern historiography remains the same as for the traditional histori-cal novel and nineteenth-century historiography. 'The past really did exist. The question is: *how* can we know that past today – and *what* can we know of it?' (ibid.: 92). Yet nineteenth-century historiography and historical fiction were driven by a confidence that the past could in fact be known, while for historiographic metafiction that assurance has faded. Indeed, Hutcheon places historiographic metafiction in an oppositional relationship to the traditional historical novel, suggesting that it 'problematiz[es] almost everything the historical novel once took for granted ... [it] destabilizes received notions of both history and fic-tion' (ibid.: 120). It destabilises them, but does not eradicate them, 'for it refuses to recuperate or dissolve either side of the dichotomy, yet it is more than willing to exploit both' (ibid.: 106). This is the structur-ing pattern characteristic of historiographic metafiction as Hutcheon conceives it: the non-dialectical inscription and then subversion of the grounding principles it seeks to contest (ibid.: 92). The genre, like the postmodernism of which Hutcheon makes it representative, foregrounds problematisation and paradox, in contrast to the traditional historical novel's resolution and completion (ibid.: xi). As its label suggests, his-toriographic metafiction focuses the production of texts, the way they construct their meaning. Intensely self-reflexive, these novels are, for Hutcheon, more interested in exploring how the past is constructed by texts than in engaging in their own 'recuperation' or 'revival' of history (ibid.: 93). This expectation, that contemporary historical fiction should privilege a problematisation of representation over the portrayal of history, is evident in other writers who utilise Hutcheon's formulation. Thus, in her discussion of the postmodern historical novel, Wesseling, too, argues that 'postmodernist writers do not consider it their task to propagate historical knowledge, but to inquire into the very possibility, nature, and use of historical knowledge from an epistemological or a political perspective' (Wesseling, 1991: 73).

Hutcheon's account has proven very useful for understanding those texts that do foreground the problematics of representation, deploying an ironic playfulness that undermines even their own attempt to depict the past. However it is limited for understanding texts that eschew this mode, or which combine it with a range of other attitudes towards the past, ranging from ironic distance to affective identification. As we shall see, Sarah Waters' faux-Victorian novels, for example, do reflect upon the way history is constructed, but this is firmly embedded within the novels as a thematic concern; they are more earnest and affectionate than ironic and parodic in their representation of the Victorian past. As Brian McHale argues, in making the genre representative of her particular description of postmodernism as 'complicity and critique' (see Hutcheon, 1989: 11) Hutcheon fails to account for the unique resonances of individual texts: 'what strikes one sooner or later is the *sameness* of many of [her] readings. Can all of these very diverse novels, one begins to wonder, really mean so nearly the same thing?' (McHale, 1992: 22). Similarly, Suzanne Keen's fascinating study of 'romances of the archive' suggest that these novels evince historiographical views, like presentism and antiquarianism, that 'predate postmodernism' and pose a broader range of historiographical questions than Hutcheon's category accounts for (Keen, 2001: 61). Del Ivan Janik, too, argues, 'the new type of historical novel ... is not merely a subspecies of the postmodern' (Janik, 1995: 161).[4] And Amy J. Elias, writing in the wake of postcolonial theory, opens up Hutcheon's category to describe a variety of positions characteristic of what she calls metahistorical romance, ranging from 'ironic, even nihilistic deconstruction' to 'a reconstructed secular-sacred belief' (Elias, 2001: 143). More recently, Jerome De Groot argues that the historical novel 'articulates within it a complex of ambiguous imperatives towards the past – an attempt at authenticity, at real(ist) representation, at memorialisation, at demonstrating the otherness of history, working within the confines of the web of fact' (De Groot, 2009: 218).

Since defining a genre does, to a certain extent, necessitate focusing upon the similarities between texts, and since Hutcheon does not disqualify further discussion of these novels, the 'sameness' of her readings is perhaps not as problematic as McHale suggests. However, a potential problem of Hutcheon's making historiographic metafiction coextensive with her postmodernism is that it effectively makes the pattern of inscription and subversion, together with an emphasis upon the problematisation of historical reference indicative of, a critical distance. Built into her analysis is an opposition between a critical engagement with the past (exemplified by the experimental, self-conscious narrative of historiographic metafiction) and a critically suspect 'recuperation or nostalgia or revivalism', usually associated with some form of narrative realism, which becomes the opposite of historical inquiry (see, for example, Hutcheon, 1988: 45, 93). A conservative, even naïve, nostalgia is contrasted with a somehow more authentic, because critical, attitude toward the past. Her contention that historiographic metafictions embody a history of representation, rather than representing history (Hutcheon, 1989: 55), makes it difficult to discuss and assess the claim contemporary historical fictions might also make to representing, or in Hutcheon's terminology, 'reviving' the past. For novels that attempt revisionist histories this is particularly problematic. For example, if historical fiction provides a space for women to enter history, women writers of historical fiction might have a greater investment in representing history than Hutcheon's model of ironic inscription and subversion pattern allows for. Women's historical novels have never been interested in recuperating history as unproblematic presence, they have always been aware that it only tells a partial truth. Nonetheless, their recovery of women's history suggests some optimism about, and political commitment to, producing meaningful accounts of past actuality, however provisional, partial and plural those accounts might be (see Wallace, 2005).

Nor does Hutcheon's focus upon irony, problematisation and complicitous critique seem the most useful terms with which to think about a novel like Toni Morrison's *Beloved* (1987), which explores slavery from the silenced perspective of the slave. As Caroline Rody observes, 'though touched by the prevailing postmodern irony toward questions of truth and representation, fiction and history, *Beloved* and most contemporary novels of slavery are not "historiographic metafictions" denying the possibility of historical "Truth"' (Rody, 1995: 94). While the novel indeed makes use of the white history it seeks to rewrite, its introduction of the notion of 'rememory', which posits an intimate, if often unconscious, connection between past and present, appeals to a stronger sense of historical reference than Hutcheon's historiographic metafiction accounts for.[5] It is not that Morrison offers her novel as *the* correct version of this traumatic history, but it does invoke or reconstruct *a version* of it as true to experience, and as a way to meaningfully remember this dark aspect of America's past.

In fact, Morrison calls her neo-Victorian novel *Beloved* a 'memorial' to lives lost to slavery. Her magical realist novel self-consciously eschews historical representation in favour of memory, or in the novel's lexicon, 'rememory', as a means to honour the past, to understand its reverberation in the present, and to find a way to move forward. She writes 'there is no suitable memorial ... And because such a place doesn't exist that *I* know of, the book had to' (Morrison, 1991 qtd. in Rody, 1995: 98). By suggesting that her novel is a memorial Morrison implicitly positions historical fictions among other modes of historical recollection outside of academic history, and clearly foregrounds a purpose for her novel beyond reflecting on the problematic nature of representation. Morrison offers her novel as an act of re-membrance.

'Memory' recurs, too, in what other late-twentieth and early twenty-first century historical novelists say about their craft. Gail Jones' reference to *Sixty Lights* (2004) as a 'memory text' (Jones, 2005) signals the novel's preoccupation with ways to achieve permanence or recover loss, and with the persistence of the past in the present as a series of repetitions. It invokes the Victorian period as a cultural memory that continues to resonate and have meaning because it endures, today, in a repertoire of shared images. Graham Swift, in an unpublished interview, says of the use of time-shift in his work that it 'possibly imitates more accurately the way *memory* does work ... So it seems to me that my way of doing things is objectively quite accurate' (Swift, 1988 qtd. in Janik, 1995: 162, italics mine). As we shall see, the narrative of *Waterland* meanders between the present and several historical moments. History, both personal and public, is re-presented according to the working of Tom Crick's memory, both of what he has personally experienced and of what he has read or heard about via histories and stories. In effect, history is rewritten in, and as, memory.

One reason for these references to memory might be that the emergence of memory in historical discourse seems also to invoke an affective aspect of historiography, excised from disciplinised histories. Rody suggests that particular theoretical approaches to historical fiction, such as Hutcheon's, are not illuminative, or are only partially so, 'because they view historical writing solely in terms of ideologies of representation, without considering the affective aspect of historical writing, insofar as the historiographic project enacts a relationship of desire, an emotional implication of present and past' (Rody, 1995: 94).

In the following section I position the historical novel generally, and the neo-Victorian novel in particular, in relation to recent critical interest in the range of practices that informs our current 'historical imaginary' (De Groot, 2009: 249), as a way of thinking about the neo-Victorian novel's investment in representing history. Positioning neo-Victorian novels as historical fictions, and historical fictions as 'memory texts', helps to account for the multifariousness and complexity of their approaches to the past. It shifts focus from the production of an accurate, objective account of past events to the always-unfinished *process* of remembering. It foregrounds the historical novel as an act of recollection that is firmly grounded in the ways we remember in the present. Whereas historical fiction is often evaluated in terms of its faithfulness to history's account of past events, and historiographic metafiction is expected to privilege the problematisation of representation over historical recollection, the memory text can incorporate a variety of historical modes, including the affective. Indeed, a number of these modes may compete within one text.

IV

Invoking 'memory', rather than 'history', does not offer a simple way out of the definitional knots associated with 'history' and 'fiction' but introduces another set of terms often defined in opposition to each other. Conventionally history and memory, like history and fiction, colonise each other. Indeed, echoing Gearhart's claim about the open boundary between history and fiction, quoted earlier in this chapter, David Lowenthal asserts of history and memory that 'each involves components of the other, and their boundaries are shadowy' (Lowenthal, 1985: 187). Critiquing the emergence of memory in historical discourse, Kerwin Klein suggests that 'memory is replacing old favourites – *nature, culture, language* – as the word most commonly paired with history, and that shift is remaking historical imagination' (Klein, 2000: 128). As we have seen, as a concept against which it has been defined and redefined, we could add fiction to this list of pairings with history. In the opposition of history and memory that Raphael Samuel describes as a legacy of Romanticism, the demarcation is strikingly similar to the conventional one between history and fiction, with memory standing in the place of the latter. Memory is associated with the subjective, the anecdotal and the imaginative, but in this discursive economy these become the guarantee of authenticity (Samuel, 1994: ix). Just as at certain times these very qualities have led to the privileging of fiction as an historical mode, so, too, is memory sometimes privileged over history for understanding the present in its relationship to the past. In Pierre Nora's account of *lieux de mémoire,* history and memory remain antinomies. Memory, which is valorised as 'life', the 'affective' and the 'magical', is associated with unbidden repetition, while history is 'the reconstruction, always problematic and incomplete, of what is no longer' (Nora, 1989: 8). History becomes artificial while memory is naturalised. Here, once again, the past is conceptualised as unproblematic presence, directly accessible in the present if the right tool is deployed. In this case memory replaces history as the authority about the past. Promising immediacy, memory becomes a replacement for a history that can no longer promise access to the real: 'Memory appeals to us partly because it projects an immediacy we feel has been lost from history ... memory promises auratic returns' (Klein, 2000: 129). Klein argues that, deployed by recent formulations of the new historicism and the new cultural history, for which it is a key word, 'memory' has become a 'quasi-religious' term that is used to 'supplement', or, more frequently, replace, history as a mode of historical thought: 'In contrast with history, memory fairly vibrates with the fullness of Being' (ibid.: 130). Memory restores the authenticity, and accessibility, of past reality, history's conventional referent. It is asked to 're-enchant our relation with the world and pour presence back into the past' (ibid.: 145).

Nora's opposition of history and memory has been complicated by scholars who seem to reverse what Nora claims about 'the conquest and eradication of memory by history' (Nora, 1989: 8). They elide the opposition of history and memory, so that history becomes a type of memory, most often associated with willed recollection. Thus, Paul Ricoeur identifies two types of *memory* using the distinction made in Greek between *mnēmē* and *anamnēsis. Mnēmē* is 'memory as appearing, ultimately passively, to the point of characterizing as an affection – *pathos* – the popping into the mind of a memory', while *anamnēsis* is 'memory as an object of a search ordinarily named recall, recollection' (Ricoeur, 2004: 4). For Patrick Hutton, this would appear to align *anamnēsis* with history. In *History as an Art of Memory* (1993), he traces two different 'moments' of memory and, in effect, subsumes history into the category of memory. The first moment of memory is repetition, which 'concerns the presence of the past. It is the moment of memory through which we bear forward images of the past that continue to shape our present understanding in unreflective ways. One might call them habits of mind' (Hutton, 1993: xx–xxi). As such it is largely unconscious. The second moment of memory is recollection, which is a more conscious, willed attempt to retrieve memory. This leads Hutton to assert that history is an art of memory 'because it mediates the encounter between two moments of memory: repetition and recollection' (ibid.). History is reconstituted as a facet of memory, which 'concerns our present efforts to evoke the past. It is the moment of memory with which we consciously reconstruct images of the past in the selective way that suits the needs of our present situation' (ibid.: xxi, emphasis mine).

One effect of subsuming history into memory is that it emphasises the range of memorial practices that constitute the ways in which we engage with the past today, making history – academic, disciplinised history – only one of many approaches to historical knowledge. Whereas historians seek the best, most valid and documentable story about the past, to discover as closely as possible what 'actually happened', memory may have a number of different goals:

> It is important to recognize that certain things are remembered not because they are actually true of the past (which may or may not be the case), but because they are somehow meaningful in the present. In other words, 'authenticity' may not always be relevant to memorial dynamics, and certain things may be recalled because they are meaningful to those doing the recalling rather than because, from the historian's perspective, they are actually true. (Rigney, 2004: 381)

There is a growing body of work that acknowledges and celebrates the 'matrix' (Rigney, 2007: 53) formed by history, historical fiction, film, memory, memorials and material heritage, all of which contribute to the way we, in the twenty-first century, think about ourselves historically. The aim of this work is to understand the ways in which the community participates in memorial dynamics. Variously described this way, as 'memorial dynamics', or as 'collective', 'public', 'social' or 'cultural' memory, 'historical consciousness' or the 'historical imaginary', this work avoids romanticising memory as an involuntary and unmediated form of historical recollection that guarantees authenticity. Instead, it formulates public or cultural memory as constructed and mediated; its relationship to history is '*entangled* rather than oppositional' (Sturken, 1997: 5). The multiplying literature on memory, drawing from philosophy, psychology and a range of other disciplines, has rendered the field diverse and complex. Here I want to suggest the value of memory discourse to discussions of historical fiction because this broader sense of cultural memory incorporates history as one way in which we understand the past, but it also departs from historians' narratives to consider the role that a wide range of other media play in shaping our beliefs about the past. These different media, including novels, are structured by different goals, issues and concerns. Memory discourse offers a framework for examining what these media *do* with the past and evaluating the ways in which they contribute to our historical imaginary, that resists privileging the 'factual', which is not the primary goal of some mnemonic practices.

As we shall see in more detail in Chapters 5 and 6, I argue that historical fictions can be understood not as corrupted history but as 'memory texts': constructed accounts of the past that emerge from and participate in contemporary memorial practices. For Paul Connerton, memory objects perform 'acts of transfer'; they are the means by which memory is transmitted within the community (Connerton, 1989: 39). Or, as James Young puts it, they function as 'received history', that is, 'the combined study of both what happened *and how it is passed down to us*' (Young, 1997, 41, emphasis mine). Memory texts function as 'acts of memory' in the sense that they are 'acts of performance, representation, and interpretation' (Hirsch and Smith, 2002: 5). Hirsch and Smith's formulation of memory foregrounds its production in and through the objects that convey it. The literary text does not simply communicate or transmit memory but actively shapes it. Similarly, Marita Sturken argues that '[c]ultural memory is produced through objects, images, and representations. These are technologies of memory, not vessels of memory in which memory passively resides so much as objects through which memories are shared, produced, and given meaning' (Sturken, 1997: 9). Here I am suggesting that as memory texts, historical novels both communicate memory – that which is already know through a variety of media about the Victorian era, for example – and offer themselves *as* memory; as we shall see in the following chapters, neo-Victorian novels reinterpret our memory of the Victorian period and transform it.

Recently, Lena Steveker has positioned A. S. Byatt's novel as a 'memorial novel' since 'it is engaged in exploring the cultural present within the context of the cultural past of the Victorian Age' (Steveker, 2009: 122). This suggests the emphasis I have been arguing for, of the historical novel as an act in the present designed to communicate and construct cultural memory. However, positioning historical fiction as memory texts, in relation to memory discourse as a trans-disciplinary framework that aims to understand the multiple ways in which we remember the past, also has the advantage of highlighting the ways in which memorial practices perform a number of functions, including to discover and communicate the past; to recognise the ways in which the past continues to impact the present; to revise our knowledge of the past in light of new theories and evidence; to unite a community in the present through the vision of a shared past; to entertain; to produce commodities that revive a past aesthetic and many more. More often than not memorial practices address manifold purposes and produce multiple effects, not all of which were intended in the act, or object, itself. That is, acts of memory achieve new meanings in their reception and redeployment by the community. I noted above that one problem with Hutcheon's account of historiographic metafiction is that it privileges those texts that focus on the constructedness of representation and renders any attempt to non-ironically revive the past as nostalgic, and critically suspect. This focus on the text's production, upon its representation of representation, elides the role of the reader in producing historical meaning. In fact, Michael Pickering and Emily Keightley argue that in postmodernist accounts of meaning-making processes generally, the agency of the reader – or audience – is denied, '[a]s if particular texts are inevitably tied to specific responses' (Pickering and Keightley, 2006: 929). They argue that postmodernist conceptions of nostalgia, such as Hutcheon's, assume that the 'reduction of meaning' in certain media representations is 'passively accepted by the audience, resulting in loss of meaning at the site of reception' (ibid.). This effectively reduces the audience to 'an unthinking collectivity who passively absorb the meanings communicated to them via the media, thus deny them a role in meaning-making processes' (ibid.: 933). Linking historical fiction to a more broadly conceived historical imaginary, to a range of memorial practices, enables us to consider the role of the reader in new ways. Rigney writes: 'As the term "practice" itself suggests, my starting point is the way we actively engage with the past using various media and methods, rather than some abstract notion of "history" as a sleeping-beauty object waiting for the professional kiss to arouse it' (Rigney, 2007: 152). Her notion of memorial practices incorporates the idea that history is constructed, rather than simply told, and it foregrounds our engagement with and participation in this process. De Groot, too, in describing the broad range of practices that constitute the contemporary historical imaginary, argues against the assumed passivity of readers of historical novels. He describes them as 'participatory, involved, active, part of, employed, and connected' (De Groot, 2009: 248) and assigns them a dynamic role in the production of historical meaning. Whereas traditionally histories strive to be closed texts, to demonstrate for the reader that the past should be interpreted in a specific way, historical fictions are usually more open, inviting a variety of responses and interpretations. As I suggest throughout this book, neo-Victorian novels are particularly concerned with the role of the reader as the bodily means through which the past is mediated, or revived.

While one of the important criticisms about the emergence of memory discourse in the late twentieth century is that it attempts to circumvent the contemporary problematisation of historiography and re-enchant our relationship to the past (see Klein, 2000), much work in the field of memory discourse also retains a sense of fragmentation and partiality, the impression that the remembered past could look entirely different, and accrue different meanings, from another perspective. It retains the conventional sense of memory as subjective, fragmentary, slanted and personal. The foregrounding, in memory discourse, of the anecdotal, the subjective and the personal, may enable these novelists to move beyond exploring the history of representation, which Hutcheon attributes to historiographic metafiction, to 'a concern', as Del Ivan Janik writes, 'with the ways in which past and present intersect and the ways in which those incidents of intersection can influence and illuminate human experience (Janik, 1995: 176). This is not the positing of a seamless continuation of the Victorian into the late twentieth and early twenty-first centuries. Nor is it an uncritical return to a past that is celebrated at the expense of the present. Rather it is an exploration of the necessity of looking back, of remembering, as well as the recognition of the uncanny repetition of various Victorian cultural features in a contemporary context.

Indeed the temporal logic of textuality obstructs the reification of history as Presence, as John Frow suggests when he makes the logic of textuality a figure of memory. This logic 'is predicated on the non-existence of the past, with the consequence that memory, rather than being the repetition of the physical traces of the past, is a construction of it under conditions and constraints determined by the present' (Frow, 1997: 119). The logic of textuality defies the ownership of the past by one body or another, whether historian or novelist and suggests, moreover, that there is no one, final truth: 'rather than having a meaning and a truth determined once and for all by its status as event, its meaning and its truth are constituted retroactively and repeatedly' (ibid.: 154). Memory is not *retrieved* for 'the time of textuality is not the linear, before-and-after, cause-and-effect time embedded in the logic of the archive but the time of a continuous analeptic and proleptic shaping' (ibid.: 154). Here, again, memory is inextricably bound to the very fabric of the present as the means by which present and past make and remake each other. And, understood this way, memory resists identifying a singular origin but mimics instead a series of fragments and repetitions.

Throughout *History and Cultural Memory in Neo-Victorian Fiction* I explore the ways in which the reworking of the Victorian period in neo-Victorian novels embody its uncanny repetition, so that the period is both shaped by and shapes our twenty-first century present. The re-presentation of the past entailed is not the assertion of historical Truth but is simply the 'weirdness of a ghost' (Rody, 1995: 104). In a similar vein, Cora Kaplan argues that we should understand 'Victoriana' as 'what we might call history out of place, something atemporal and almost spooky in its effects, yet busily at work constituting this time – yours and mine – of late Capitalist modernity' (Kaplan, 2007: 6). As we shall see, a great many contemporary historical fictions that return to the Victorian era are preoccupied with images of ghosts and metaphors of haunting, especially positioning the fictional text as medium of the past.[6] The materiality of the ghost is illusory and always already under erasure. The ghost is an evocative metaphor for the past, as 'the *nothing-and-yet-not-nothing* and the *neither-nowhere-nor-not-nowhere* that nonetheless leaves a trace in passing and which has such a material effect' (Wolfreys, 2002: 140). Embedded in the figure of the spectre is indeterminacy and incompletion. As Nick Peim argues, 'the authenticity of the spectre is always questionable – a function of the gap between its partial nature and the full version it claims to represent' (Peim, 2005: 77).

The ghost becomes a useful metaphor for charting a position for these novels between the positing of history as Presence, a locus of univocal meaning, and the ironic subversion or negation of the very possibility of historical knowledge. Yet while Rody identifies the ghost with 'a fearful claim of the past upon the present' (Rody, 1995: 104), a phrase that grants the past agency, the ability to make demands upon the present, I would suggest that the ghost signals rather the uncanny repetition of the past in the present. The ghost speaks with the voice of flesh and spirit, and adopts its look, but, in its very essence, or 'inessence', as Jacques Derrida would have it, it is departed. Its very disappearance is held always before it: 'There is something disappeared, departed in the apparition itself as reapparition of the departed' (Derrida, 1994: 6). These texts exploit the ghostliness of textuality to foreground the non-presence of history, its disappearance, and to suggest that its meaning is fleeting, or flickering; in fact, more than this, its meaning only exists as it is created, and recreated afresh. In this sense it is like the text itself, the meaning of which is configured and reconfigured with each reading, and by each reader. Similarly, the past is configured and reconfigured, and attributed different and multifarious meanings in each act of historical recall. Julian Wolfreys writes: 'recognizing the signs of haunting it must be concluded that whether one speaks of the experience of reading or the experience of the materiality of history, one witnesses and responds to ghosts' (Wolfreys, 2002: 11). Indeed, he explores the ways in which texts, because of our tendency to anthropomorphise them, can themselves be considered ghostly, 'are neither dead nor alive, yet they hover at the very limits between living and dying' (ibid.: xxii). This ghostliness is part of what separates the historical novel from the objectives, and assumed objectivity of history, and aligns it with the functions of memory: 'To the extent that memory "reincarnates", "resurrects", "re-cycles", and makes the past "reappear" and live again in the present, it cannot perform historically since it refuses to keep the past in the past, to draw the line, as it were, that is constitutive of the modern enterprise of historiography' (Spiegal, 162).

The contemporary proliferation of historical fictions, and their commercial success, registers a persistent desire for cultural memory. Stemming from this continuing desire for stories about the past, historical fiction might extend and elaborate our versions of the past, offering different ways of seeing it, without asserting finality or Truth. In the earliest identification of the neo-Victorian subgenre, Dana Shiller observes, the 'neo-Victorian novel ... attest[s] to the unflagging desire for knowledge of the past, a desire not extinguished by doubts as to how accessible it really is' (Shiller, 1997: 557). This could be reformulated as an unflagging desire for historical recollection, the act of remembrance, which is privileged over historical knowledge itself. In her discussion of collecting in Susan Sontag's historical novel *The Volcano Lover*, Julie C. Hayes suggests that it is desire that ensures the past will continue to be interpreted, that its stories will continue to be told. Indeed, far from erasing historical difference and distance, she argues that the collector's desire for the object, his or her passion and the resulting fear of its loss, 'assures [the object's] status as unique, as having belonged to a specific, punctual place and time. The pastiche-collection is thus not so much critical or ironic, as paradoxical and complex, less bent on unmasking or contesting than on extending and elaborating. Desire's elaborations elude closure' (Hayes, 1998: 29).

Privileging their own texts as mediums of the Victorian past, writers such as A. S. Byatt and Gail Jones reverse the trajectory of the ghost. That is, it is not the non-presence of the ghost that reaches out to us as its future. Rather, it is we who reach for historical recollection, desirous to re-member the past and to ensure it continues to have meaning. The desire for cultural memory that these novels both dramatise and invoke is cast as a desire not for a univocal truth, or finality of meaning. It is not a seeking after the past 'as it happened'. Nor is it the conceptualisation of history as a fixed point and locus of meaning. Rather, it is a re-membering of the past which is partial, fragmentary and always open to further re-membering. The past only exists in our re-creations of it. Its meaning is produced in and by our very accounts of it. Historical inquiry is recast as desire in these novels, and remembrance is naturalised as a necessary human action.

While I trace a shared preoccupation, in neo-Victorian fiction, with the need for historical recollection, the six texts that I have chosen for close readings were selected as much for their differences as for their similarities. The representation, in these fictions, of diverse aspects of the Victorian period, from the commitment to progress, to the wide-ranging intellectual endeavour, and from the introduction of photography to the production of pornography, demonstrates something of the range and breadth of possible depictions of the era, and suggests that competing narratives such as these each have a role to play in furthering our recollection of the past. Moreover, in the selection of texts from each decade since the explosion of interest in the Victorian era, and the postmodern problematisation of historiography, in the late 1970s and early 1980s, it is possible to trace a series of shifts and restructurations in fictional responses to the recent challenges posed to narrative histories; shifts that mark the progressive opening up of history to the field of fiction. In *Waterland*, the incorporation of contemporary challenges to history as memory, is restructured a decade later, in *Possession*, as a re-centring of literature as a mode of historical recollection. By the turn of the twenty-first century, faux-Victorian novels like *Affinity* and *Fingersmith* focus on conjuring forgotten histories into our memory of the corpus of Victorian literature, while in the last few years memory becomes the focus of both *Sixty Lights* and *Afterimage*, and literature is accorded a key role in establishing a series of connections between past and present, and in tendering images of the Victorian period as shared, cultural memory. Exploiting the very indeterminacy of their generic boundaries, these memory texts explore different territory in the opening up of history to fiction, and confront the contemporary historiographical crisis in unique ways. Nonetheless, each seeks to re-present the past, to explore its intersections with the present, and to help ensure that the Victorian era will continue to have meaning today.

2
Contemporary Victorian(ism)s

> The jumble brick and stone of the city's landscape is
> a medley of style in which centuries and decades rub
> shoulders in a disorder that denies the sequence of
> time ...
>> (Penelope Lively, *City of the Mind*, 1991)

> the Victorians have been made and remade through-
> out the twentieth century, as successive generations
> have used the Victorian past in order to locate them-
> selves in the present.
>> (Miles Taylor, Introduction to
>> *The Victorians since 1901*, 2004)

Even in the twenty-first century we inhabit Victorian urban space. The
streets and buildings are a palimpsest, but these reinscriptions never
effect the full erasure of the past and this, at times, produces a 'shock of
recognition' (Himmelfarb, 1995: 15–16). The past exists in the present
in the shape of buildings and urban spaces and in residual customs,
beliefs, institutions and practices. Since the spatial distance between
the present and the past is negligible, this can sometimes make the
past seem close, as though very little separates it from the present at
all. In spite of this, or perhaps because of it, for much of the twentieth
century and, at times, today, the Victorians and their culture have
been characterised in terms of their absolute otherness. Rather than
the shock of recognition we experience the terror (and sometimes
pleasure) of alterity, the fright (and satisfaction) of estrangement. We
feel keenly, and assert strongly, our indomitable distance from the
Victorians.

Simon Joyce argues that the term 'Victorian' came into use almost immediately upon the Queen's death in 1901, coined by journalists who desired to 'summarize her reign, the century with which she seemed synonymous, or both (Joyce, 2002: 7). However, Miles Taylor notes that the term has been dated to 1851 and suggests that 'certainly by the Jubilee years of 1887 and 1897 it was being used to describe a distinct historical era, with its own poetry, literature and song, military heroes, drama, graphic art, dress and fashion' (Taylor, 2004: 3). This suggests something of the slipperiness of the term, the difficulty of defining the 'Victorian'. It is a term that, since Victoria's death, has accumulated multifarious and often contradictory meanings and which often colonises the several decades both before and after her reign. In their introduction to *Victorian Afterlife*, John Kucich and Dianne F. Sadoff appear to use the term 'Victorian' interchangeably with 'nineteenth century'. This may be, in part, because they wish to argue for what might be called a 'long Victorian' era, suggesting that the contemporary obsession with this period includes the adaptations of E. M. Forster and Jane Austen novels by filmmakers like Merchant and Ivory, Iain Softley, Ang Lee and Patricia Rozema since these '[project] a "Victorian feel" into Regency and early high-modern texts alike' (Kucich and Sadoff, 2000: x, xi). In keeping with this periodisation, in *The Past is a Foreign Country* (1985), David Lowenthal defines the Victorian period as beginning after 1815, asserting that 'the end of the Napoleonic Wars marks a more significant divide than the accession of Victoria' (Lowenthal, 1985: 96).

Writing in 1993, Robin Gilmour draws together the multifarious attitudes with which the Victorian era has been treated throughout the twentieth century, claiming that '[we] look back to our Victorian ancestors with conflicting feelings of envy, resentment, reproach, and nostalgia' (Gilmour, 1993: 1). The fusion of proximity and distance, recognition and unfamiliarity, is manifest in the diverse, and often contradictory, images the era evokes in the contemporary imagination. As Gilmour argues, we still live in the long shadow cast by the nineteenth century, 'in the aftermath of that powerful and seemingly assured civilisation' (Gilmour, 1993: 1) and for us, the term 'Victorian' is dense with signification. It conjures up conflicting images of large, richly decorated drawing rooms and narrow lanes of decrepit slums; tightly laced corsets and dens of ill repute; the thrusting grandeur of empire and the oppression and subjugation of 'savages'. It may even evoke 'images of piano legs modestly sheathed in pantaloons, table legs (as well as human legs) referred to as "limbs," and books by men and women authors dwelling chastely on separate shelves in country-house libraries' (Himmelfarb, 1995: 15–16).[1] The images are diverse and incongruous. Yet the diversity of characterisations of an era spanning some sixty years can hardly be surprising, and perhaps the period is best understood in terms of its contradictions and discrepancies. The difficulty is not to discover which of these images truly represents the Victorian era but to determine which images have prevailed when and to what purposes. As the prevalence of the period in contemporary fiction, film, television, fashion, home furnishings and collectibles suggests, the Victorians continue to have meaning for us today. The question is *what kind* of meaning does it have and how is this affected by the various ways in which the era is represented across a range of media today?

Characterisations of a period are influenced by artistic endeavours and trends in scholarship, by political concerns and by the philosophy of history and historiography that dominates at a given time. As I have argued in the previous chapter, these memorial practices shape Victorian culture and ensure that it shapes our own. If we can understand these practices as 'acts in the present by which individuals and groups constitute their identities by recalling a shared past' (Hirsch and Smith, 2002: 5), we recognise that since the death of Queen Victoria, a variety of attitudes toward the past has impacted the way we have shaped the Victorians and our relationship to them; attitudes ranging from repudiation and disavowal to condescension and affection. Such is the ubiquity and vigour of the contemporary return to things Victorian that John Kucich and Dianne Sadoff suggest that we 'fixat[e] on the nineteenth-century past as the specific site ... in which the present imagines itself to have been born and history forever changed'. For them, the postmodern might better be characterised as the post-Victorian, 'a term that conveys the paradoxes of historical continuity and disruption' (Kucich and Sadoff, 2000: x, xiii). In the same volume Nancy Armstrong presents the Victorian period as a nascent form of sociocultural postmodernity. Or, more to the point, postmodernism becomes here, 'an extension of Victorian culture' (Armstrong, 2000: 313).[2] And Christine L. Krueger, in another collection of essays about the deployment of the 'Victorian' in contemporary culture uses the term 'post-Victorian' to suggest, and then negate, our postmodernity. She argues that 'no matter how vociferously we protest our postmodern condition, we are in many respects post-Victorians, with a complex relationship to the ethics, politics, psychology, and art of our eminent – and obscure – Victorian precursors' (Krueger, 2002: xi). This chapter examines some of the evocations of the Victorian era throughout the twentieth century, in the work of literary critics and historians, and in the rhetoric of politicians, many of whom have attempted to fix a stable identity for the period in order to compare or contrast it with our own.[3] Here and in my discussion of neo-Victorian fiction I am not concerned with judging the appropriation of 'Victorian' according to a set of traits defined as 'Victorian', to determine how faithful, or otherwise, they are to the period. Rather, my interest lies in exploring which characteristics, of people, place and period, are depicted as Victorian in these novels, and to what ends. Thus, I follow John McGowan in his assertion that 'the Victorians as a group characterized by certain shared features do not exist except insofar as they are produced in that similarity by a discourse that has aims on its audience' (McGowan, 2000: 23).

I

Like C. P. Snow, whose rejection of the Victorian period I quoted in the Introduction, many early-twentieth century writers characterised the Victorians in terms of their difference and distance. The Victorian period quickly came to signify the very opposite of modernity: 'in the early years of this century no self-respecting literary or artistic modernist or political liberal would wish to think of him or herself as the child of repression, realism, materialism and *laissez-faire* capitalism' (Bullen, 1997: 1–2). Virginia Woolf, T. S. Eliot, Wyndham Lewis and F. T. Marinetti all repudiated the influence of the Victorians in order to mark out the distinctiveness of their own, 'modernist' writing. Targeting mid-Victorian writers, they conducted what Taylor describes as an 'onslaught against what they saw as the excessive moralism of George Eliot, the journalistic style of Charles Dickens, the insincerity of William Thackeray and the melancholia of Alfred Tennyson' (Taylor, 2004: 4). This anti-Victorian sentiment is perhaps most clearly embodied in Lytton Strachey's iconoclastic *Eminent Victorians* (1918). In contrast to the Victorian tradition of hagiographical, expansive biography, these four, short biographies reinterpreted their prominent Victorian subjects, focusing on character flaws, anxieties and inconsistencies. This early anti-Victorian reaction was exacerbated by economic catastrophe in the 1930s. As Taylor argues, 'unemployment opened up a further gulf between Victorian materialism on the one hand and breadline Britain on the other' (Taylor, 2004: 5).

However, against the notion of a wholesale rejection of the period, Guy Barefoot's study of 1930s screen and stage productions of the Victorian plays *Gas Light* and *East Lynne*, traces a tension, in these productions and their reception, between nostalgia for the period and a rejection of its 'tastelessness, bad art and paraphernalia, misogyny and poverty' (Barefoot, 1994: 101). Amidst the dismissal of the era, and contrary to it, was also a rather condescending attitude toward the era as quaint and charming, 'an explicitly gendered, popular notion of the Victorian that could be contrasted with modern functionalism or austerity' (ibid.: 102). This ambivalence toward the Victorian era was caught up in a growing uneasiness about modernity and its achievements in the wake of war and economic depression. Studies such as G. M. Young's *Portrait of an Age* (1936) made some effort to reassess the Victorian period and to cast off some of the negativity associated with it, but it was not until after the Second World War that a new fascination with the period achieved prevalence.

By the end of the Second World War commentators noted a marked increase of interest in the period in both England and America (House, 1955: 78). Writing in 1948 Humphrey House cites the illustrated articles about the Victorians featured in *Picture Post* and *Illustrated*, the BBC Programmes 'Ideas and Beliefs of the Victorians' and also the talks on the Third Programme and the Home Service as evidence of this new fascination. These and other articles and programmes often explored aspects of Victorian art and architecture that had been unobserved or disregarded (ibid.). House also notes a return to the Victorians in publishing and book purchasing trends, with George Eliot and Alfred Lord Tennyson achieving a certain currency again. Exhibitions mounted by the Victoria and Albert Museum to mark the centenaries of the Great Exhibition (1951) and the opening of the Museum itself (1952) prompted renewed interest in Victorian decorative arts. These exhibitions helped to cast off the idea that Victorian decorative arts were not 'merely unfashionable' but actually 'an immoral monstrosity', establishing them rather as objects worthy of scholarly study (Burton, 2004: 121, 133). However, Anthony Burton notes that '[s]ome of the revivalists took up Victorian art just because it was naughty, while a good deal of the motive power of the revival ... was fuelled by *disapproval* of Victorian art, rather than *liking* for it' (ibid.: 123) so that the revival of Victorian arts provided curios rather than objects of admiration.

The treatment of the era as a curiosity was fostered by the historiographical belief that the past could be researched and discovered once the passing of time provided sufficient distance for objectivity to be attained. This allowed mid-century historians, and the public who took an interest, to feel they could grasp the Victorians and understand them.

Thus, in an introductory talk broadcast on the BBC Third Programme in 1949 G. M. Trevelyan's remarked:

> the BBC has chosen the time for this series well. The period of reaction against the nineteenth century is over; the era of dispassionate historical valuation of it has begun. We can by this time examine without prejudice what we have inherited from the Victorians, what we have improved away, and what we have lost. (Trevelyan, 1949: 15)

With the passing of nearly fifty years sufficient for producing critical distance, the Victorians were then harnessed within the bounds of these 'dispassionate valuations', studies in which they were described in categorical detail under headings such as 'Doubt', 'Art', 'Science' and so on. These neat labels and descriptions meant that the Victorian era and its influence could be controlled and contained and they perpetuated the sense of 'otherness'. Bullen observes that this approach to the Victorian past 'was interesting and comforting, but it made the nineteenth century seem very remote' (Bullen, 1997: 3). House demonstrates this sort of attitude which allows for an interest in the Victorians whilst ensuring that they and their culture remain quaint, oddities, their features and concerns not taken too seriously:

> one may possess and even collect typically interesting Victorian objects without being seriously involved in any major errors of judgment: but there is a real risk that what may seem at first just an 'amusing' fashion (that word has been current in this context on and off for nearly thirty years) may by various means, and even by the disproportionate influence of a few individuals, develop into something more through the failure of alertness and discrimination. (House, 1955: 80)

He urges the use of critical discrimination to prevent a useless, and even dangerous, return to things Victorian, a return characterised, he feels, by a mood of unhealthy nostalgia. He quotes Professor Basil Willey's observation of just such a mood as a response to the war that had just ended. In his talk for the Third Programme Willey contrasted the 'debunking' of the Victorian period after the First World War with the current mood in 1948, when 'we are deferring to it, and even yearning after it nostalgically'. Pointing to the increased demand for Victorian novels and volumes of essays and poetry, he observes: 'In our own unpleasant century we are all displaced persons, and some of us feel tempted to take flight into the nineteenth as into a promised land, and settle there like illegal immigrants for the rest of our lives' (Willey qtd. in ibid.: 83). Whereas early in the century denigrating the Victorians had been a means through which to delineate and praise modernity, by mid-century, in comparison with the Victorian era, the twentieth-century present no longer came off favourably. This was in part due to disenchantment with a modernity that had facilitated two world wars and economic depression. It was also due to a new phase in the representation of the Victorian period by historians and critics.

Shifts in literary and historical theories, methods and interests had coalesced so that Victorian culture had begun to seem more vivid and interesting, more diverse and less straight-laced than had hitherto been imagined. A suspicion grew, Bullen argues, 'that Victorian life was richer, more diverse, and less homogenous than had been supposed, and that gigantic monster called Victorian culture was coming into being'. The intellectual life of the century was rediscovered and 'to the handful of eminent Victorians were added … the philosophers, the scientists, the reformers, the theologians, the politicians, together with the sprawling mass of nineteenth-century art and literature in all its popular and eso-teric forms' (Bullen, 1997: 3).

Studies focused upon intellectual and 'high' culture. This concentra-tion, whilst reflecting the Arnoldian academic and artistic values of the era itself, also served to distance the Victorians from an increasingly populist culture by the 1960s. It was not until that decade and after-wards that the intervention of the discourses of feminism, semiotics, psychoanalysis and materialism all contributed to new representations of the Victorian era, representations that moved away from discus-sions only of high culture and included features previously invisible or excluded: women, the working and criminal classes and non-Europeans, for example (see ibid.: 6). As the title of Steven Marcus's *The Other Victorians* (1964) suggests, his investigation into pornographic literature opened up an underside of Victorian culture, one that he argued was rel-egated to the margins both during the period and by twentieth-century Victorian studies. Part of his professed aim was to contribute to restor-ing the Victorians 'for the first time to their full historical dimensions' (Marcus, 1966: xix). His concept of the 'other Victorians' is built upon the idea of a hidden, silent and repressed sexuality, rendered mute and invisible to history by societal inhibitions and prohibitions. As his and others' scholarship opened new aspects of the Victorian era to scrutiny, twentieth-century notions of the period were necessarily revised and the Victorian era became increasingly identified with sexuality and, more specifically, with its repression.

As Michel Foucault has argued, this narrative of Victorian repression is a pervasive cultural myth that functions to cast the twentieth century in the role of enlightened liberator. For Foucault, histories such as Marcus's tell only part of the story. They participate in the promulgation and perpetuation of what he calls 'the repressive hypothesis', which holds that the Victorians' attitude toward sex and sexuality had been primarily characterised by repression, that sex was shrouded by silence, that it was *the* secret. Against the image of a repressive and oppressive silence, Foucault paints another picture, one that refuses Marcus' characterisation of sex relegated to the margins of society. According to Foucault's account, discourse about sex proliferated in the nineteenth century (Foucault, 1976: 17). Whereas talk about sex may have been eradicated from 'the authorized vocabulary' and 'a whole rhetoric of allusion and metaphor was codified', some words were screened out, and new rules of propriety governed, at another level, there was 'a discursive ferment that gathered momentum from the eighteenth century onward' (ibid.: 18). Not only did the restrictions mean that talk of sex was newly valorised *because* it was indecent, but new techniques for speaking about sex were also produced within and by religious, political and economic institutions. Whereas religious discourse spoke about it with the language of morality, Foucault argues, political and economic discourse deployed the vocabulary of rationality, 'in the form of analysis, stock-taking, classification and specification' (ibid.: 23–24). In each instance, sex became a public issue between the state and the individual and 'a whole web of discourses, special knowledges, analyses, and injunctions settled upon it' (ibid.: 26). Thus, Foucault argues that sex and sexual desire, far from being mute, was transformed by the Victorians into a different, indeed copious, discourse and that it is not the case that power operated primarily in a repressive capacity regarding sex.

Foucault acknowledges that by questioning the repressive hypothesis his argument 'not only runs counter to a well-accepted argument, it goes against the whole economy and all the discursive "interests" that underlie this argument' (ibid.: 8). It is these interests that he wishes to expose by posing new questions: 'why do we say, with so much passion and so much resentment against our most recent past, against our present, and against ourselves, that we are repressed?' (ibid). Or, why has the twentieth century created the cultural myth of repression?

One argument, suggests Foucault, is that conceptualising Victorian sexuality in this way enables the late twentieth century to cast itself as heir to this repressive regime, but a rebellious one; to characterise itself as willing to 'speak out against the powers that be' and free sex from its cloak of silence: 'to utter truths and promise bliss, to link together enlightenment, liberation, and manifold pleasures; to pronounce a discourse that combines the fervor of knowledge, the determination to change the laws, and the longing for the garden of earthly delights' (ibid.: 7).

By casting doubt upon the repressive hypothesis Foucault not only postulates that it functioned as a tool with which the twentieth century could establish a particular identity for itself, but also drew attention to a range of Victorian practices and discourses that suggested that Victorian culture was less homogenous and more diverse than it had previously seemed. His scholarship helped to transform the popular images of Victorian culture and provide a fuller picture of the range of experiences constituted within it. The Victorians and their sexuality were credited with greater complexity than the repressive hypothesis' ascription of silence and prudishness had allowed. More broadly, Foucault's insights also enabled more complex ways of understanding how sexuality is produced in and by representation and different kinds of discursive practices.

The first volume of Foucault's *History of Sexuality* was published in French in 1976 and in the English translation in the USA and Canada in 1978. However, it was not published in England until 1979, making its emergence coincidental with Margaret Thatcher's election victory. The posthumous publication of the second and third volumes of Foucault's *History* in the mid to late eighties, as Thatcher entered her second and third terms of office, meant that his ruminations upon sexuality shared an historical moment with Thatcher's discoursing upon sex and family values. This historical moment was one in which political activism centred upon issues of sex and sexuality, fuelled by the furore surrounding the AIDS crisis, which the media, together with politicians influenced by the New Right, cast as a moral crisis.

II

The 1980s was not the only historical moment Foucault shared with Margaret Thatcher. They shared, too, a revisiting of the Victorian era, with Thatcher urging a return to 'Victorian values'.[4] However, her images of the era, and the agenda of sexual and cultural politics that they served, were diametrically opposed to Foucault's own. Whereas Foucault described the ways in which, since the nineteenth century, sexualities are produced through discourse and labelled normal or deviant, Thatcher reasserted the traditional and naturalised boundaries between normalcy and deviancy, morality and perversity in her campaign for family values. This approach is encapsulated in the (in)famous Clause 28 of the Local Government Act (1986), passed during her third term of office, which sought to prevent local authorities from 'promoting homosexuality', particularly as a 'pretended family relationship' (qtd. in Weeks, 1991: 137). Thatcher's invocation of the Victorian era centred upon her particular re-creation of the Victorian family, with the heterosexual marriage relationship as the permissible locus for sexual activity.

Hers was a return to the type of vision of the Victorian era that the work of scholars like Foucault and Marcus had, since the 1960s, attempted to revise. Indeed, Tristram Hunt, in a 2001 article for *The Australian Financial Review*, explicitly links Thatcher's visions of Victorian England with those of Lytton Strachey as they appeared in *Eminent Victorians*, arguing that together they 'managed to gut the reputation of the Victorian era'. He suggests that Thatcher's 'fond reminiscences of her parsimonious grandmother condemned the 19th century to being considered a time of cloying evangelicalism, repression and illiberalism' (Hunt, 2001: 6). She produced such images of the Victorians as a rhetorical basis for her campaign of family values which was intended to counteract what she saw as the permissiveness that had grown during and since the 1960s. Once again the Victorian era was called upon to provide a contrast with the present and, as in the 1940s and 1950s, the Victorian era was the celebrated period.

Thatcher used the term 'Victorian values' as a measure against which to identify the social ills of her milieu – a regulated economy, welfare dependency and the decline of the family – and to advocate a return to *laissez faire* economics, to a reliance upon individual charity and to strong family discipline. This would, as Gary Day suggests, 'revive Britain's flagging fortunes and restore her place in the world' (Day, 1998: 1–2). She contrasted a corrupt present with an idyllic and highly romanticised past, characterised by stability and strength, constructing the Victorian period as all that was other to contemporary culture.

Thatcher's use of the Victorian period is characterised by an ahistorical nostalgia, in which the 'Victorian' floats free of its temporal location in the nineteenth century and simply stands in for a series of ideals. Raphael Samuel argues:

The past here occupies an allegorical rather than temporal space. It is a testimony to the decline in manners and morals, a mirror to our failings, a measure of absence. It also answers to one of the most universal myths, which has both its left-wing and right-wing variants, the notion that once upon a time things were simpler and the people were at one with themselves. (Samuel, 1992: 18)

Thatcher's Victorian idyll was peopled with industrious, honest and morally upright citizens; hard-working artisans who rose slowly through diligence. The 'Victorian' values she extolled were those of thrift, charity, independence and hard work. In a much-quoted interview with Peter Allen she praised the upbringing she was given by a Victorian grandmother and used it to delineate Victorian values as she wished to exploit them:

> you were taught to work jolly hard, you were taught to improve yourself, you were taught self-reliance, you were taught to live within your income, you were taught that cleanliness is next to godliness, you were taught self-respect, you were taught always to give a hand to your neighbour, you were taught tremendous pride in your country, you were taught to be a good member of your community. (Thatcher, 1983b)

Arguing that Thatcher was highly selective in her invocation of 'Victorian values', Samuel contrasts the Victorian Britain of Thatcher's rhetoric with that described in the oral histories and accounts given by those of her generation and earlier. Rather than focusing upon frugality, hard work and discipline, these accounts emphasise a sense of joy, of fun and of community:

> in working-class accounts of the 'good old days', ... it is the images of sociability that prevail – the sing-songs in the pubs, the funeral processions, the 'knees-up' street parties, the summer outings. The canvas is crowded with characters; street performers will sometimes get a page or two to themselves and there may be a whole chapter for Whitsun or Bank Holiday. Shopping is remembered for its cheapness ... People are forever in and out of each other's houses... (Samuel, 1992: 18)

In these accounts, too, the Victorian era is celebrated in contrast to the present, and painted as an idyllic, simpler time. Yet Thatcher's Victorian idyll is very different to the Eden constructed by these oral histories. Her version, Samuel observes, is 'altogether more severe. Her lost Eden is one where resources were scarce and careful husbandry was needed to ensure survival. She remembers her childhood not for its pleasures but for its lessons in application and self-control' (ibid.: 19). In its focus upon hard work, discipline and their rewards, argues Samuel, Thatcher's Victorian Britain is similar to that of Asa Briggs', 'one of the "new way" social historians who, by their scholarly work, prepared the way for the rehabilitation of Victorian Values'; for both it is the 'age of improvement' (ibid.: 22). Of course, the oral histories with which Samuel debunks Thatcher's image of Victorian Britain are also highly selective, for all that Samuel makes their status as recorded memories the pledge of their authenticity. The details in these oral histories might differ from those of Thatcher's, but in each the Victorian era represents a benchmark from which we have regressed. The period is marked in terms of difference, alterity.

In keeping with their temporal dislocation, Thatcher cast her Victorian values as universal and enduring, claiming that 'all of these things are Victorian values ... They are also perennial values' (Thatcher, 1983b). In this move, as Samuel argues, 'Victorian Values thus passed from the real past of recorded history to timeless "tradition"' (Samuel, 1992: 18). This claim of universality only points to the significance that Thatcher did alight upon a specific piece of Britain's history for its cultural cache; she did not, primarily, promote the values as perennial but rather marketed them as Victorian. Writing in 1987, James Walvin argues:

> Few could deny that late Victorian Britain was one of the world's leading powers, at the peak of economic and imperial achievement. Britannia not only ruled the waves but she ruled vast tracts of the globe's surface, and her industries – pioneering and (as it seemed) unmatched – dominated the markets of the world. (Walvin, 1987: 4)

Rather paradoxically, since it functioned primarily to contrast the Victorian period with a disappointing present, to the extent that her rhetoric aligned Thatcher herself to the image of past industrial, military and economic success, it also suggested a tradition, or a lineage, for the kind of radical politics she was advocating. The Victorian era was at once the inverse of her 1980s present, and its heritage.

Yet if referencing Victorian values allowed her to fashion herself as a traditionalist, then behind that façade even a glimmer of real faith in the Victorian era and its achievements can hardly be discerned. Although she promoted frugality and thrift under the rubric of Victorian values, she did not attempt to curtail consumer credit and household debt actually grew throughout the 1980s. Samuel argues that 'if her precepts had been taken seriously, the economy would have been in ruins ... Frugality and thrift, in short, so far from staging a come-back during Mrs. Thatcher's period of office, all but disappeared' (ibid.: 22–3). While urging a return to Victorian values, Thatcher proceeded to wage war against Britain's traditional industries. Her rhetoric praised and upheld the traditional, but in practice she undertook a far-reaching program of modernisation (ibid.: 10–11). While praising the Victorians and advocating a return to 'their' values, she attacked such Victorian establishments as the public service ethic, the Universities, the Bar, the House of Lords and the Church of England, and she deregulated the City of London. Indeed, as Samuel suggests, even her use of the phrase itself alternated between positive and pejorative: 'Marxism, she liked to say, was a Victorian, or mid-Victorian ideology; and she criticised nineteenth-century paternalism as propounded by Disraeli as anachronistic' (ibid.: 9). Thus, Samuel argues that 'the rhetoric of Victorian Values could be seen as an example of what the post-modernists call "double coding" and sociologists "cognitive dissonance" – i.e of words which say one thing, while meaning another and camouflaging, or concealing, a third' (ibid.: 24). Thatcher's return to Victorian values was a political ploy that enabled her to appear to be protecting stability and tradition when in fact she sought change, transformation and the new. Behind the appearance of a staunch and inflexible traditionalist was a ruthless innovator and behind reference to 'Victorian values' was a programme for vast change.

Thus, Walvin attributes the appeal of Victorian values in Thatcher's Britain to their ephemeral quality. 'Victorian values', as espoused by Thatcher, was a purely rhetorical phenomenon which could metamorphose to include or exclude virtues as deemed desirable in a given situation. 'Roll[ing] easily from the tongue ... It is an idea which has the virtue of defying easy definition, yet people have no trouble knowing exactly what it means. It is a concept which has been divorced from its historical roots, representing instead a simple code of good behaviour and decent ideals' (Walvin, 1987: 6). They functioned this way too for neoconservative historian Gertrude Himmelfarb who, though she eschews the term 'values' itself, also castigates the culture of late twentieth-century Britain by referencing its Victorian past. In contrast to the sanitised, romanticised view of the Victorian era tapped by Thatcher, Himmelfarb's valorisation of Victorian 'virtues' depends upon a characterisation of the period as an endless cycle of poverty, hunger, drudgery and misery; it is the moral strictures of the period that provide a buffer for such experiences. Like Thatcher, she denounces the twentieth century for a regression in values and moral progress. In the Victorian era, she maintains, even if many people did not live the ideals they espoused, they at least still held ideals. She argues that today, we do not espouse any ideals, which is evident in the transmutation of the word 'virtues' into its contemporary corollary, 'values', which can be 'beliefs, opinions, attitudes, feelings, habits, conventions, preferences, prejudices, even idiosyncrasies – whatever an individual, group or society happen to value at any time, for any reason' (Himmelfarb, 1995: 11–12). In contrast to the Victorians, we appear relativistic, without recourse to the authoritative weight of virtues. In a 'relativistic' society, Himmelfarb argues, morals, virtues and judgements become only a matter of individual taste or opinion and do not form a firm foundation against which to measure cultural features or behaviour, undermining the confidence with which such judgements could, in any case, be made (ibid.: 11). Asserting our reluctance to speak in terms of moral absolutes, she produces the Victorian era, in contrast, as a time when 'moral principles and judgments were as much a part of social discourse as of private discourse, and as much a part of public policy as of personal life' (ibid.: 241). Invoking 'Victorian virtues' thus becomes an indispensable means of speaking with the language of morality in contemporary culture. The historian can intervene instructively, Himmelfarb suggests, 'to remind us of a time, not so long ago, when all societies, liberal as well as conservative, affirmed values different from our own' (ibid.: 249). She charges history with the role of 'reminding us of our gains and losses – our considerable gains in material goods, political liberty, social mobility, racial and sexual equality – and our no less considerable losses in moral well-being' (ibid.: 253).

Himmelfarb's Victorian period is more securely tied to its temporal location and she is careful to present a more balanced account of the era than Thatcher's selectivity. Indeed, she catalogues the faults of the Victorian period, in terms of its 'social and sexual discriminations, class rigidities and political inequalities, autocratic men, submissive women, and overly disciplined children, constraints, restrictions, and abuses of all kinds' but goes on to suggest that 'there is also much [in the period] that might appeal to even a modern, liberated spirit … the importance of an ethos that does not denigrate or so thoroughly relativize values as to make them ineffectual and meaningless' (ibid.: 249–50).

Whether she is applauding the period's superior morality or deploring the abuses that somehow coexisted with this morality, as surely as Thatcher's, Himmelfarb's own return to the Victorian period is predicated upon the assertion of absolute difference. Implicit is the idea that there is a break or rupture between present and the past that utterly divides the two, so that scarcely a mark remains, at the present time, of the attitudes, institutions, values and cultural features of the Victorian era. If vestigial remnants persist, they serve only to highlight our 'otherness' and, indeed, our inferiority. Our memories of the Victorians are, therefore, 'rather like an amputated limb that still seems to throb when the weather is bad' (ibid.: 221). For Himmelfarb as for Thatcher, to assert continuities between the Victorian era and contemporary culture would be to destabilise the images of total contrast and undermine its use as an 'other' against which our culture can be denigrated.

III

Culturally, Thatcher's appeal to Victorian values coincided with the boom of the 'heritage industry', a term coined by Robert Hewison to describe the expansion and convergence of a number of cultural institutions to remake the past as entertainment (see Hewison, 1987: 221). It coincided, too, with heated and protracted debates about the historical value of this industry. Indeed, John Gardiner argues that these debates were partly a response to Thatcher's call for a return to Victorian values, 'conflating her suspect use of history with the nostalgia they identified all around them' (Gardiner, 2004: 176). And Suzanne Keen suggests that against the backdrop of the economic slump of the Thatcher years 'an emphasis on a more positive past can seem a natural reflex, an understandable impulse of nostalgia, a calculated program on the part of conservative politicians, or a pernicious evasion of responsibility for the present and future' (Keen, 2001: 103). For the heritage industry is usually associated with the promotion of a celebratory narrative, focusing on elements of the past that the nation can cherish, defend and in which it may take pride. It is not focused on any one aspect of Britain's past; indeed, it has been roundly criticised by some scholars who argue that it promotes a generalised view of the past, in which the particularities of different eras are flattened. Here the specificities of recorded history become 'timeless tradition' (see Samuel, 1994: 139). Gardiner suggests that in some ways it makes no sense to talk about the Victorian period in relation to the heritage industry because here excitement attaches to 'atmosphere', the *frisson* of 'olden times', more than to 'conscious connection with a particular age'. He argues that '[a] stroll around any "Past Times" shop (the chain was founded in 1986) or the large gift shop at the Victoria and Albert Museum will confirm how comfortably imitation Victoriana nestles alongside artefacts from other periods when it is being sold to the public' (Gardiner, 2004: 168).

The 1980s and 1990s were marked by a mania for collecting Victorian artefacts, fostered by the rehabilitation of Victoriana in the 1950s and 1960s (as the last generations of Victorians passed away and the second-hand market flooded with their jewellery, clothing and furniture (see Gardiner, 2004)) and boosted by an increasingly consumer-driven economy. Money from the National Trust was contributed to the restoration of privately owned Victorian terraces and mansions, elevating them to the status of 'period residences', in the name of preserving national heritage. 'Heritage' colours and styles became popular for home furnishings and soon became known as 'the Laura Ashley look', and open-air and industrial museums multiplied. All of these factors, as Samuel suggests, 'had the effect, so far as popular taste was concerned, of rehabilitating the notion of the Victorian and associating it not with squalor and grime, but on the contrary with goodness and beauty, purity and truth' (Samuel, 1992: 14).

This mania for original and replicated Victorian material culture has been associated with uncritical nostalgia for a past that never existed, as Miriam Bailin argues: 'Belonging to another time and to other circumstances, and thus ineluctably value-laden, they also have the talismanic power to evoke whatever we long for as if it were something we've lost ... ' (Bailin, 2002: 44). Bailin contrasts our obsession with Victoriana to the Victorians' own mania for revivalism which she describes as being an adaptation of the old to new uses, with the emphasis being on the new object. Whereas they valued the new object created by the mixture of old and new, she suggests, 'the current mania for reproduction and revival is characterized by a reverent attachment to the past as aura and ideal' (ibid.). Her study of the magazines, newsletters and catalogues that purvey Victoriana suggests their dependence upon a nostalgic invocation of 'a gentler more romantic time' (ibid.: 38).[5]

For its detractors, the heritage industry generally is accused of being ahistorical, of cultivating a depthless desire for the generalised past with little interest in historical understanding; selective, nostalgic and depthless and, as such, is opposed to history. The lines of demarcation in the history-heritage debate thus fall similarly to those of other debates that animate this book, including the opposition of history and memory and, crucially, history and fiction. Keen argues that this debate evinces 'a hierarchy of values in which history (detached, scholarly, dispassionate, accurate) trumps heritage (nostalgic, dysfunctional, inexact)'.

However, just as historical fiction is sometimes privileged over history, sometimes, in a reversal of values, 'heritage (popular, inspiring, authentic, belonging to us all) outdoes history (academic, hyper-specialized, politically correct, irrelevant)' (Keen, 2001: 98).

The last two decades of the twentieth century also saw a shift in historians' construction of the Victorians, participating in and contributing to popular fascination. Like the attitude fostered by the heritage industry, their histories are flavoured by affection for the Victorians. However, an increasing number of historians rejected the characterisation of Victorian culture in terms of its difference and distance, focusing instead upon the connections between the Victorians and ourselves. Indeed, Kucich and Sadoff suggest that one reason for the preponderance of neo-Victorian engagements is the way in which Victorian culture appears in many respects to anticipate our own, 'providing multiple eligible sites for theorizing [cultural] emergence' (Kucich and Sadoff, 2000: xv). Historians Gary Day, Richard Gilmour, Nadine Holdsworth, Matthew Sweet and others highlight similarity more than difference, continuity more than rupture in constructing our relationship to the Victorian past. Their scholarship appears, in part, a response to the absolute alterity posited by politicians such as Thatcher and historians such as Himmelfarb. Sweet and Day, particularly, challenge the particular version of Victorian values promulgated by Thatcher. Day not only argues, along the same lines as Samuel, that Thatcher was necessarily selective in what she chose to represent as Victorian values (state intervention, he suggests, is as Victorian as *lassez faire*), but also that to speak of a 'return' to these values is erroneous: 'the idea of a return to Victorian values assumed that they have faded away into history, requiring a deliberate act to revive them. However, it is possible to argue that Victorian values have never ceased to be a shaping force throughout the twentieth century' (Day, 1998: 2; see also Sweet, 2001). In many ways, then, this approach appears absolutely opposed to that of Thatcher and Himmelfarb. Yet, it, too, makes the Victorians key figures for establishing our identity today. It is simply founded upon similarity instead of difference.

In her article 'Haven't I Seen You Somewhere Before?,' literary critic Nadine Holdsworth makes our consumer culture a product of the Victorian period, arguing that a 'preoccupation with style over substance and an emphasis on pleasure through visual excess is not the sole domain of the contemporary age. The Victorian era also heralded a demand for impressive visual spectacle which rejected the principle of utility … ' (Holdsworth, 1998: 197). Thomas Richards propounds a similar argument in his *The Commodity Culture of Victorian England: Advertising and Spectacle, 1851–1914* (1990). He argues that the Great Exhibition of 1851 heralded the beginning of 'modern' perceptions of the commodity. Tracing the origins of advertising back into the Victorian period, he claims that it was with the Great Exhibition that the appetite for the spectacle began. He argues that at this event, designed to celebrate the dignity of production, the commodity 'came alive' and began to function in society apart from human agency as it is seen to do today. Prior to this time the commodity had been mundane, neutral, only itself, not symbolic. In the second half of the nineteenth century the commodity assumed the central significance it still has today and the cogs of capitalism, and a resultant consumer culture, had already begun to operate: 'In the short space of time between the Great Exhibition of 1851 and the First World War, the commodity became and has remained the one subject of mass culture, the centerpiece of everyday life, the focal point of all representation, the dead center of the modern world' (Richards, 1990: 1). According to Richards, despite its not being held for profit, The Great Exhibition was also the point at which entrepreneurs realised that there was money to be made from representing the commodity. Advertising dominated in this commodity culture, and, as in contemporary culture, it colonised the body through an ever-multiplying number of therapeutic commodities which opened all of the body to marketing. 'The body had become the prevailing icon of commodity culture, and there was no turning back' (Richards, 1990: 205).

   This assertion of continuities between Victorian visual culture and our own can be traced in a number of neo-Victorian novels that link the origins of photography to our own image-obsessed society. Examples of such novels include Lynne Truss' *Tennyson's Gift* (1996), Robert Solé's *The Photographer's Wife* (1999), Ross Gilfillan's *The Edge of the Crowd* (2001), Katie Roiphe's *Still She Haunts Me* (2001), Gail Jones' *Sixty Lights* (2004) and Susan Barrett's *Fixing Shadows* (2005). Fiona Shaw's novel, *The Sweetest Thing* (2003), explores the birth of the iconic image in the Victorian era, stemming from the introduction and popularisation of photography, and dramatises early uses of advertising in the Victorian period. Imitating the style and plot of Victorian sensation fiction, with echoes of Wilkie Collins' *Woman in White* in particular, the novel explores the creation and consumption of various types of images, comparing three ostensibly different types of photographic images: Samuel Ransome's collection of photographs of working-class women, which he keeps in albums in his room, Mr Benbow's pornographic photographs, which are sold to the men who commission them, and the photographs William Ransome uses for his advertisements for cocoa and chocolates. Each of these images circulates and reproduces promiscuously, accruing meanings in excess of their original purpose. Their production and consumption are entwined with a burgeoning capitalism galvanised by the introduction of photography in advertising. William Ransome's rationale for using photographic images of Harriet to sell his chocolates appeals to an increasing public appetite for the visual, and for imagistic invocations of pleasure, instead of information in their consumer choices:

> my plan is a girl. Not an imaginary girl, but a real one. Not only a painted picture, but also a photograph. A real girl. If we put a girl on our boxes, we will sell them faster than we can imagine. She will become the Wetherby's girl and when people look at her, and she is pretty and pure and smiling, like someone they might like to know, they will think of us, and they will buy our cocoa (165) ... [if] when you drank a glass of smooth cocoa, its froth catching in your beard, if you had one, its sweet warmth caressing your throat, you thought of the girl? Would not that be a clever thing? (234)

Here, the commodity, the tin of cocoa or box of chocolates, comes alive, symbolic of something else. The photograph of a girl stands in for the girl herself, becoming 'a girl on our boxes' (165), with the implication being that she is coeval with her image and that consumers will acquire her when they purchase the cocoa or chocolates. Throughout the novel the Victorian era is produced as the origin of our advertising practices and types of image-production and, ultimately, as the foundation for the consumer culture we inhabit today.

Gary Day, too, constructs our relationship to the Victorians in terms of continuity; that of Victorian values and of 'the Victorian condition itself: 'what we understand as modernity and postmodernity can simply be seen as different facets of Victorianism' (Day, 1998: 2). He argues that whereas Jürgen Habermas claimed that the division of substantive reason into science, morality and art, so that each becomes the domain of the expert to the exclusion of others, is characteristic of modernity, this is 'equally the feature of the Victorian period', in which the reform in universities and in technical education had led to increasing specialisation, undermining the 'synthesis' of knowledge (ibid.). And whereas Lyotard distinguished between modernity and postmodernity by identifying the use of metadiscourses to legitimate knowledge with the former, and the suspicion of such metanarratives with the latter, Day argues that both attitudes were manifest in the Victorian era. He cites the legitmising importance of the metanarrative of human progress to the study of the natural world and to technological development on the one hand, and Walter Pater's claim that 'his age was distinguished from the ancient "by its cultivation of the 'relative' in place of the absolute",' on the other (ibid.). Similarly, Gilmour points to the 1870s Vernacular Revival as an example of this cultivation of the relative. The Revival, he claims, was 'part of a larger awakening to the virtues of regional life, of the homely and the local' that can be identified as a reaction to the accelerating change brought about by increasing industrialisation, urbanisation and mass production (Gilmour, 1993: 230). These changes transformed the Victorians' experience of everyday life in ways that can appear quite similar to the impact made by the technological advancements of postmodernity. Just as in contemporary culture the introduction of the information and development of web and web 2.0 technologies continues to transform communication and information systems at a rapid rate, the Victorians were witness to, and participants in, vast developments in their own communication structure. These included the building of an extensive railway system, the development of the efficient 'penny post' and the proliferation of newspapers and journals, all of which produced a saturation of information comparable, in its impact upon everyday life, to the technological developments that have transformed contemporary culture.

This, continuist, approach to constructing the relationship between the Victorians and ourselves is perhaps epitomised by the fascinating work of Matthew Sweet which, he claims, 'aims to expose the Victorian-ness of the world in which we live; to demonstrate that the nineteenth century is still out there, ready to be explored' (Sweet, 2001: xxii). His work 'liberates' the Victorians from the 'utterly false' stories about the period that have stood in place of the truth and argues that these have been perpetuated because we prefer to think of the Victorians as the 'figures against whom we have rebelled', and to suggest otherwise is to undermine one of the 'founding myths of modernity' (ibid.: 230–1). His study persuasively argues that there are connections between the Victorians and ourselves, that 'they built a world for us to live in' (ibid.). He writes poetically about the effect of continuing to live in Victorian urban spaces, suggesting that 'there are places where the Victorian past will rush to meet you', places that are 'luminous with a sense of the 1890s' (ibid.: 222). His is an engaging investigation of some lesser known Victorian figures, such as Blondin the acrobat, and offers alternative approaches to features of the Victorian period that often receive bad press today, such as the freak show. Rather than a study of 'other' Victorians and their practices, however, Sweet argues that these are more typical of the Victorian period than hitherto imagined. Attempting to debunk various stereotypes about the period, Sweet suggests

> that Victorian culture was as rich and difficult and complex and pleasurable as our own; that the Victorians shaped our lives and sensibilities in countless unacknowledged ways; that they are still with us, walking our pavements, drinking in our bars, living in our houses, reading our newspapers, inhabiting our bodies. (ibid.: xxiii)

He argues that the Victorians bequeathed to us many cultural features we think of as uniquely ours, such as the theme park and shopping mall, investigative journalism and political spin-doctoring, free education and pornography (ibid.: xi–xii). However, having convincingly established the manifold similarities between Victorian culture and our own, and the ways in which they have undoubtedly shaped us, he goes further, at least rhetorically, to efface any difference altogether. His assertions, above, that the nineteenth century still exists to be explored, and that the Victorians are still with us, which can still, perhaps, be construed as suggesting that there are elements of the Victorian still visible in our otherwise unique culture today, slide into the final, summarising declaration: 'We are the Victorians. We should love them. We should thank them. We should love them' (ibid.: 232). Here the risk of continuism is clear: it tends to suppress otherness just as alteritism suppresses continuities. Effectively, this final statement papers over the textured Victorian period he has offered us throughout the rest of his book. Not only are the Victorians coextensive with ourselves, but our attitude toward an era which, by Sweet's own contention, was multifariously 'good and bad', should be surprisingly homogenous. The diverse and multi-layered identity bestowed upon the Victorian era in the preceding pages dissolves into a conflation of the period with our own. In the process our own, contemporary culture is also flattened and rendered stable, even static. We are the Victorians and we should be singularly grateful to them and even love them.

While urging the necessity of exploring similarity over difference himself, Day ultimately suggests an approach to the past that lies somewhere between the assertion of absolute continuity or the positing of total rupture: 'too great a stress on discontinuity obscures how the past inheres in the present and, if this is not recognised, we are doomed to repeat it. The task, if we are to move forward instead of marking time, is to understand both continuity and discontinuity' (Day, 1998: 1). This model of history is dependent upon progressive linearity and a didacticism that much contemporary historiography, and, indeed, historical fiction, would contest. However, his suggestion that we should recognise both continuity and discontinuity is useful for exploring other approaches to the relationship between the Victorian past and our present other than positing simple alteritism or continuism, each of which is predicated upon a stable identity for both the Victorians and ourselves. This stable identity does not fully allow for overlaps or restructurations and their impact upon the cultural, political and social features of the present. It glosses over changes such as those generated in and through the media and technology, which produce reconfigured types of public spaces, subjectivities and economic and material realities, and naturalises the processes by which these transformations take place.

William Gibson and Bruce Sterling's cyberpunk novel, *The Difference Engine* (1988), resists this kind of glossing over, or naturalising of, change. An alternative history, it imagines that Charles Babbage's Difference Engine, which was designed but not built in the Victorian era, was in fact completed. In the novel, this early computer is a catalyst for the arrival of the information revolution in the Victorian period, instead of our own. This kind of history, or historical fiction, which explores not what was, but what could plausibly have been, suggests that historical events are contingent, not inevitable. In the case of *The Difference Engine,* it acts as a reminder that the vast technological changes of the late twentieth-century, and their cultural impact, were not 'natural' or inevitable, but the result of processes in which the cultural manifestations and technologies of the Victorian era impacted and were impacted upon by those of the twentieth century, configuring and reconfiguring in new and distorted forms.

This is illustrated further by the fact that in 1991 the Science Museum in London built a machine to Charles Babbage's nineteenth century plans. As Francis Spufford suggests, in doing so, Babbage's machine was given a retrospective history, a place in the history of computer science: 'they possessed the very significant power to name Babbage's enterprise as part of, well, the history of computers, in which his thinking made perfect, retrospective sense' (Spufford, 1996: 268). Part of the problem for Victorian Babbage had been the absence of a language with which to conceptualise and express his ideas, 'he could not refer the intellectual endeavour represented by the Engines to any established context of ideas'. In 1991 the engineers could 'simply refer ... to his hardware and software difficulties' (ibid.: 267–8). When the Science Museum built the Engine, the intervening century had supplied the solutions to these problems and, as Spufford observes, 'supervising the production of several hundred identical metal gears only proved to be interestingly tricky for them' (ibid.: 268). A whole history of computers, of which the Engine is now retrospectively a part, had developed in the meantime and the supporting technologies had become available.

The Difference Engine, as it now stands in the Science Museum, bears tangible witness to the way in which contemporary culture both inhabits and inherits Victorian technologies. Even in computer technology, which seems to epitomise postmodernity, the legacy of the Victorian era, and its continuing influence and impact, is evident. *The Difference Engine* dramatises the impact of technological change, removing it from its familiar context in order to disrupt its seeming naturalness, and suggests certain links between the Victorian period and our own. Yet the Difference Engine is an anachronism, out of place in the Victorian era, because it was not yet built, and not quite belonging to our period either since it was constructed to Victorian plans with technology that is now well outmoded. Rather than imply seamless continuity or smooth evolution between Victorian culture and our own, it is an uncanny presence that somehow produces *both* alterity and recognition.

If alteritism and continuism can be thought to exist on a spectrum of attitudes towards the past, as the excesses at either end, individual neo-Victorian novels can be plotted at various points along the entire spectrum. The contemporary reader might find little continuity between ourselves and the cholera-ridden Victorian period of Matthew Kneale's *Sweet Thames,* and, conversely, might find little to suggest the Victorian in Emma Tennant's exploration of Hardy's character in *Tess.* Most often, however, these texts contain traces of both alterity and continuism. They produce both the shock of recognition and the fright of estrangement. Thus, as we shall see, A. S. Byatt's *Possession* is predicated upon the assertion of alterity between the Victorian past and our own. This difference is both celebratory and censuring of the era. It generates a lively Victorian intellectual climate for our emulation, while at the same time rendering its failures toward women. At the same time the novel also explores the ways in which Victorian culture continues to have a presence in our own, via the text-as-medium and embodied memory. Although it is structured by nostalgia, the text both advocates and promulgates a critical engagement with the past, and produces a textured portrayal which explores both continuities and discontinuities between Victorian culture and our own. As Michael Pickering and

Emily Keightley suggest, 'nostalgia is not all of a piece' and its functions are complex and even contradictory. They argue that nostalgia can map the present and future in productive ways, that it can signal 'retrieval for the future' as much as 'retreat from the present' and that these two functions are not mutually exclusive. Here, 'nostalgia becomes an action rather than an attitude, showing how the politics of nostalgia are realized in its applications rather than being inherent in the affective phenomenon itself' (Pickering and Keightley, 2006: 937). As Jerome De Groot argues, following Pickering and Keightley's reformulation of nostalgia as slippery and mutable, nostalgia has the ability 'to open up multiple spaces for reflection and dissidence'. Looking to the diverse range of practices, objects and media that make up our experience of the historical today, De Groot adds that the value of this multiplicity of engagements lies in its very variance, it ability to 'contain complication, difference, ideology, interrogation, artifice, virtuality, escape and experience' (De Groot, 2009: 250).

Taken together, and alongside the multiple evocations of the 'Victorian' in other media and in a range of practices, the depiction of the era in neo-Victorian fiction does not amount to the attempt to fix a stable identity for the Victorians for emulation or denigration (though it may in individual texts). And the sheer multiplicities of our fascination cannot be simply dismissed as exemplificative of an uncritical reverence for the past. What the prevalence of neo-Victorian novels and their diverse representations primarily suggests is that the Victorians continue to have meaning for us today because we continue to grant them meaning. Indeed, the very contest of meanings attributed to the Victorian era, whether by historians, politicians, entrepreneurs or historical novelists, ensures that the Victorians continue to have (multifarious, contradictory, contested) meaning(s) in our culture. These novels stress the importance of historical recollection itself, of remembering the past in its multiplicity of possible meanings. In unique ways, Graham Swift's *Waterland*, A. S. Byatt's *Possession*, Sarah Waters' *Affinity* and *Fingersmith,* Helen Humphreys' *Afterimage* and Gail Jones' *Sixty Lights* each posit the persistence of the past, and celebrate, promulgate, and give voice to, a continuing desire for cultural memory in an age charged with the inability to think historically.

3
A Fertile Excess: *Waterland,* Desire and the Historical Sublime

> What every world-builder, what every revolutionary
> wants a monopoly in: Reality. Reality made plain.
> Reality with no nonsense. Reality cut down to size.
> Reality minus a few heads – I present to you History,
> the fabrication, the diversion, the reality-obscuring
> drama. History, and its near relative, Historionics ...
> (Graham Swift, *Waterland*)

For Tom Crick, the narrator of Graham Swift's *Waterland* (1983), history's referent does not exist. 'Reality is that nothing happens' (40). Yet histories, stories and 'making things happen' proliferate, circulate and entwine in fecund excess in the novel, indicative of a desire for history that persists, even flourishes, despite its absence. This desire ensures that, paradoxically, the very void of history generates its surfeit. History always exceeds the attempts to represent it, so both hi*stories* and desire for hi*stories* are produced and reproduced excessively. Faced with the excision of his discipline from the school's curriculum, history-teacher Tom abandons lesson plans and embarks upon a narrative that, in its meandering course through a range of historical moments, including many from Tom's own childhood, in an order (or anti-order) determined by his own effort of recall, subsumes history into memory.

Waterland naturalises a desire for history, asserting its necessity and value even as its exploration of the narrativity of history highlights the late twentieth-century crisis of historiography, centering upon the loss of faith in historical pattern and design and, ultimately, in the possibility of historical knowledge. The drive for historical knowledge is recast as a romance, an often urgent desire to return, part of a universalised and essentialised 'human nature'. Following Diane Elam and Catherine

Belsey I examine romance as the excess that conventional history must exclude in its production of itself as the real, as that which exceeds the knowable. Romance and desire are thus positioned as the uncertainty that undermines the assertion of historical narrative's privileged relationship to the real, as those elements that defy the authority of conventional history. I argue that integral to the novel's recasting of history as desire is its embodiment of this relationship of romance to realism, whereby romance appears as the excess elements to be excluded from Tom's wandering and far-reaching narrative, but which nonetheless reappear, disrupting and subverting any attempt at a linear, coherent narrative. These very elements of excess ensure that the model for historical inquiry posed by the novel, an endless questioning prompted by a never-ceasing desire or curiosity, is never finished or complete. The very notion of excess ensures that there are always more elements to consider, more questions to ask.

The novel achieves its characterisation of history and historiography by establishing an opposition between 'artificial' history, including written histories, stories and 'things made to happen', and 'natural' history; that which, supposedly, lies outside of representation, including nature and empty reality itself. This opposition rests heavily upon the novel's evocation of the Victorian era, particularly its association of the period with ideals of historical design and progress and with a view of nature as both sublime and inviting of human effort to control, contain and use it for its own purposes. Moreover, the novel draws upon a concept of nature, conventionalised during the period of Britain's industrialisation, as more authentic, more real than human constructs.

I

Ostensibly a history lesson delivered to students whom Tom will soon no longer teach (history teacher Tom is a victim both of unfortunate personal circumstances and of curricular cut-backs), the novel ranges broadly across many historical periods from AD 695, centring upon the late-eighteenth and nineteenth centuries, the early-and mid-twentieth century and finally the late twentieth-century present. However, incarnated by the Atkinsons, it is the Victorian era that looms large over the twentieth century of the novel's making. The ideas attributed to it are integral to the novel, forming a monolith, albeit an unstable one, against which Tom propounds his alternative vision of history and reality. It is the entrepreneurial Atkinsons who make things happen in the Fens. It is they who build the dykes and sluices that make the river Leem navigable; they who squeeze the water out of the land to grow barley and turn a profit on the reclaimed land sold for farming; they who '[offer] work and a future to a whole region' (16), becoming prominent and revered citizens in the process. The Victorian Atkinsons, entrepreneurial but ostensibly civic minded, galvanised by the twin narratives of Empire and Progress, transform the 'backward and trackless wilderness' (67) of the Fens by 'making things happen'. As Marcel Damon Decoste writes, 'the history of the Atkinson family, as related by Crick, is one, first and foremost, of history as grand narrative, of world-making undertaken under the auspices of a linear, progressive, and purposive theory of history' (Decoste, 2002: 386).

The multiple definition of *historia,* given as an epigraph to the novel, signals at the outset the novel's opening up and expansion of 'history' beyond its conventional meaning. History is treated as a protean form comprising the process of investigating past events, the account given of those events, and also those past events themselves. The epigraph also points to another, less common, use of the term to designate 'any kind of narrative: account, tale, story', which foreshadows the novel's foregrounding of history as narrative.[1]

As this epigraph suggests, the novel explores the crisis of historiography outlined in Chapter 1 of this book. *Waterland* weaves stories conventionally considered fictional together with those considered historical. Their distinction from each other is complicated, their difference elided, in order to focus each of them as narrative constructs. As John Brewer and Stella Tillyard suggest in their review of the novel, it can be read as 'an exposition of the modern critical dictum that every text and every story is problematic – opaque and inscrutable' (Brewer and Tillyard 1985: 49). The narrative of *Waterland* is Tom's attempt to account for his current circumstances, in which he faces early retirement and his wife is being treated in a mental health institution following a baby-snatching incident. As we shall see, the inscrutability of these events plunges Tom further and further into the past, confronting ever more opaque stories. The reader shares with Tom the effort to construct the meaning of these events from what has gone before.

Robert K. Irish identifies the deliberate gaps in Tom's narrative, where he poses unanswered questions, or swerves off into yet another tale, leaving the previous one open-ended, as precisely those moments when the reader is forced into an awareness of his or her own role in the production of meaning, is aware that he or she is constructing a meaning not to be *found* or *discovered* in the text itself.

When my assumptions in reading fail to be satisfied and my ability
to structure meaning into recognizable patterns is thwarted by the
text, I can no longer just 'read' the novel, that is, be absorbed in a
world, but am confronted by the fiction of what is absorbing me and
by the way it is fashioned. (Irish, 1998: 923)

Waterland thus casts doubt upon the possibility of historical knowledge by dramatising the process of interpreting historical documents.
This is compounded by the device of an untrustworthy narrator, or, as
Linda Hutcheon describes Tom, 'an overtly controlling narrator' who
is not 'confident of [his] ability to know the past with any certainty'
(Hutcheon, 1988: 117). Tom allows us to see the way in which narrative
can create from speculation the appearance of incontrovertible fact.
Reconstructing events from the Victorian period, he recites the litany
of reasons his great-grandfather had to be sorrowful, that '(conjectural)
inward sorrowfulness', which is invisible to the historical record,
becomes, 'surely no longer conjectural' (160). Elsewhere, Tom not only
asserts as fact a detail which he had earlier claimed was omitted from
the historical record, but also gives two contradictory interpretations of
this speculative detail:

> *history does not record* whether the day of Thomas's funeral was one
> of those dazzling mid-winter Fenland days in which the sky seems to
> cleanse every outline and make light of distances and the two towers
> of Ely cathedral can not only be seen but their contrasting architec-
> ture plainly descried ... *But such things would have been appropriate.*
> (82, emphasis mine)

Several pages later the sunshine is no longer conjectural and has become
inappropriate: 'compare the *unbefitting* sunshine of old Tom's funeral
day' (98, emphasis mine). In addition to highlighting the usually invisible process of truth-making, these 'mistakes' signal, too, the limitations
of Tom's knowledge. Far from being an omniscient narrator, Tom casts
doubt upon his and all historical narratives, claiming that 'history is
that impossible thing: the attempt to give an account, with incomplete
knowledge, of actions themselves undertaken with incomplete knowledge' (108). His difficulty in interpreting the historical record undermines
its authority and its ability to provide the means to resurrect the past.
When Tom references his sources – 'a day's delving into local archives'
(10), 'a verbatim copy of this brave and doomed speech' (161) – this does
not lend authority to his narrative but suggests that the past is primarily

available to him in the form of texts equally constructed, and in need of interpretation. Tom does not use these sources to *discover* the meaning of history but to *produce* the past in a way that has meaning for him.

Waterland highlights, too, the effect that shaping the past into narrative form has upon historical events, making them appear as a story with a beginning, middle and, importantly, an end. Frank Kermode observes that in every age people have pointed to certain events which appear to indicate the coming of the end, suggesting that 'this anxiety attaches itself to the eschatological means available' (Kermode, 1967: 95). For Kermode the prevalence of apocalyptic imagery in fiction 'reflects our deep need for intelligible ends' (ibid.: 8). He suggests that fictions of endings are an attempt to project the self 'past the End, so as to see the structure of the whole, a thing we cannot do from our spot of time in the middle' (ibid.). The idea of an end satisfies the longing for structure, coherence and meaning. The end is a landmark constructed to support the comforting illusion that history is moving in a particular direction and toward a fixed goal or telos.

Similarly, in her discussion of the use of apocalypse as a metaphor in contemporary fictions, Lois Parkinson Zamora points to the Greek origins of 'apokalypsis' meaning 'to uncover, reveal, disclose' (Zamora, 1989: 10). She, too, suggests that the apocalyptic vision signifies our desire to 'interpret and assign significance to our experience of history' (ibid.: 3). Images of apocalypse permeate *Waterland*, making themselves felt in each of the historical periods to which Tom's narrative returns. Tom's account of the 'Grand Purge' of the French Revolution verges on the apocalyptic, describing the thousands of corpses 'piling up' in the streets and battlefields of Europe (141). Ernest Atkinson employs apocalyptic imagery for his malediction of 1911, telling how 'he foresaw in the years ahead catastrophic consequences ... How civilization ... faced the greatest crisis of its history. How if no one took steps ... an inferno ... ' (161). The First World War is described as that 'catastrophic interval to which such dread words as apocalypse, cataclysm, Armageddon have not unjustly been applied ... ' (201). Tom describes 'with faltering eloquence, [the] gutted cities, refugees, soup kitchens, mass graveyards, bread queues' (119) of the Second World War. And in the narrative present, 1979, it is the Cold War, and in particular what seems the imminence of nuclear war, which evokes the sense of apocalypse and gives Tom's students nightmares about the end of the world (296–7).

It is this prospect that prompts Price to announce that 'the only important thing about history, I think, sir, is that it's got to the point where it's probably about to end' (7). 'What matters', he argues, is the 'Here and Now' (6).[2] And it is in the sense of the end, images of apocalypse, that 'reality', 'history' and the Here and Now' imbricate in the novel. Tom's response to Price reiterates the notion that the end of the world has appeared imminent in every age:

> yes, the end of the world's on the cards again – maybe this time it's for real. But the feeling's not new. Saxon hermits felt it. They felt it when they built the pyramids to try to prove it wasn't true. My father felt it in the mud at Ypres. My grandfather felt it and drowned it with suicidal beer. Mary felt it ... It's the old, old feeling, that everything might amount to nothing. (269)

Apocalypse, in the novel, is a rhetorical device, a story that shapes the wider stories that we construct and that we convince ourselves constitutes our reality. The novel rehearses the end of the world many times over, particularly in connection with the two world wars and with the nuclear threat of the novel's contemporary narrative. It rehearses it, too, by the repeated 'ending' of the many stories that make up Tom's larger narrative, which are continually disrupted, aborted or eclipsed by another story which clamours for attention, asserts its importance. The effect of these continually threatened and yet always deferred endings is to call into question the very notion of the end itself.

II

Through recounting the numerous times that the end of history has appeared imminent, and yet has not come, by beginning his narrative in the middle of a story and ending it, similarly, in the middle, and by disrupting each of his own stories before their closure, Tom rejects the notion of the End, and the linear view of history in which it is entrenched.[3]

Moreover, he connects apocalyptic vision with a glimpse of reality. For against the sense of the End, which is a rhetorical effect rather than a reality, Tom posits an alternative version of reality: 'reality doesn't reside in the sudden hallucination of events. Reality is uneventfulness, vacancy, flatness. Reality is that nothing happens' (40). 'Reality' becomes one of the novel's most slippery terms, defined and re-defined in opposition to other slippery terms, like 'history' (in its multiplicity of meanings) and the 'Here and Now'.

Del Ivan Janik reads Tom's 'reality' as the simple flat existence of everyday life, what he calls 'the empty space of daily life' (Janik, 1989: 85). However, this is closer to headmaster Lewis' notion of the 'real world' than it is to Tom's 'reality'. Lewis rejects academic history in favour of General Studies, with its 'practical relevance to today's *real* world' (22, emphasis mine). For Lewis, history is a 'rag-bag of pointless information' (23) with little to teach about the 'real' world of families, job prospects and economic difficulties in 1979. Tom explicitly expounds his theory of reality in opposition to Lewis' (40).

Tom's theory of an empty reality evacuates history. That is, it rejects the notion of design that fuels many notions of history. Reality exceeds the claims of historical narratives, since, whatever the story proffered, there are always details that resist inclusion. Or, as Damon Marcel Decoste puts it, 'insofar as narrative and history are at odds with the meaninglessness of the real, insofar, then, as they can never be either coincident with or adequate to it, the real constantly exceeds and eludes them (Decoste, 2002: 395). *Waterland* consistently undermines various Grand Narratives and patterns of history, proffering the narratives of progression, regression, circularity and hubris as examples of a human predilection for positing a shape and meaning to the flux of historical events where there is none. The central thesis of the novel intersects with Jean François Lyotard's suggestion of a postmodern crisis in the metanarratives of progress and Enlightenment which have underpinned science and politics in the West. This is the end of history in the sense of historical design, the end of legitimising, overarching patterns (see Lyotard, 1984).

Tom suggests that any pattern 'found' in history is in fact the illusion of narrative. For him, historical events are without design and without discipline: 'it goes in two directions at once. It goes backward as it goes forwards. It loops. It takes detours' (135). When he refers to reality as empty, he means empty of design, purpose and feature, which all exist only as a product of human desire:

> because each one of those numberless non-participants was doubtless concerned with raising in the flatness of his own unsung existence his own personal stage, his own props and scenery ... there's no escaping it: even if we miss the grand repertoire of history, we yet imitate it in miniature and endorse, in miniature, its longing for presence, for feature, for purpose, for content. (41)

In some respects it would seem that *Waterland* supports a view of history as circular rather than erratic, with its fifty-two chapters, its preoccupation with notions of return and the apparent recurrence of events. Decoste suggests that the novel 'follows a circular course, repeating itself at both the macro- and microcosmic level' (Decoste, 2002: 387). Irish, too, argues that 'history's circularity is reinforced everywhere in the narrative (Irish, 1998: 928). However, as Alison Lee suggests, 'it is clear ... that the narrator's choice of language and form is responsible for the circularity in a way the events themselves could not be ... he synthesizes events in such a way that history itself does indeed seem to repeat and foreshadow itself (Lee, 1990: 42). In fact, apparent 'macro- and microcosmic levels' of history and/or extra-textual reality must also be constructs of narrative since this very notion is dependent upon an ability to stand outside the flux of history, to see its shape, or to construct its shape, as would an author. Similarly, the theory of hubris, which Ronald. H. McKinney suggests is the theory of history favoured by Tom, is, I argue, a narrative effect and conveys rather the capacity for stories to exceed their own boundaries, to bleed into other stories and have effects beyond the original intention. Notions of circularity, hubris and return in the novel signify not the pattern or direction to history, but our 'lostness'. Or rather, that even the idea of direction, and therefore lostness, is meaningless since there is no fixed point outside the flux of history and 'no compasses for journeying in time' (135).

Tom's 'reality' is somewhat akin to Amy J. Elias's notion of the postmodern historical sublime, or 'history itself' which 'has no motivation or dialectical movement' (Elias, 2001: 55). Tom's reality is, like Elias' postmodern historical sublime, 'the realm of terror, of chaos'. However, despite her assertion that 'history itself' is always deferred, receding, Elias' references to 'History itself', 'history itself', 'upper-case *H* History' all seem to suggest Presence. Moreover, the sublime is the residence of 'Truth' (ibid.). In contrast, Tom's reality is never 'the realm of potential revelation' (ibid.). The only revelation it gestures toward is that there can be no revelation.[4] Since the very notion of an empty, featureless reality is difficult to conceptualise, is even, in the sense used by Elias for the historical sublime, 'unpresentable' (ibid.: 27), the novel's primary representational strategy is metaphor. It establishes two interrelated metaphors for the elucidation of reality, history and the Here and Now, as they inform its theory of history and historiography. Both metaphors derive from a particular, Victorian, view of nature.

III

The entrepreneurial Atkinsons provide the novel with its central metaphor. The novel's Fenland setting is a watery wasteland which the

Atkinsons' ingenuity reclaims for habitation, water transport and farming via a complex system of dykes, sluices and drainage, but which is ever susceptible to flooding. For Tom, the empty, flat, formless Fens symbolise his version of vacant reality, 'and no one needs telling that the land in that part of the world is flat. Flat, with an unrelieved and monotonous flatness' (2). The dykes, sluices and channels that give the Fens their provisional shape represent history, the stories and 'things made to happen' with which that reality is filled. Just as the land which is reclaimed appears firm and solid, so do the 'fragile islands' (341) built out of the formlessness of reality give the appearance of solidity, truth and actuality.

Initially the novel distinguishes between two means by which chaotic, formless reality is filled, or reclaimed. The first is embodied in the languorous, 'phlegmatic' Cricks who, 'born in the middle of that flatness, fixed in it, glued to it even by the mud in which it abounds', outwit reality by telling stories: 'and there's no saying what meanings, myths, manias we won't imbibe in order to convince ourselves that reality is not an empty vessel' (41).

Stories, told by both his mother and father as well as read in books, infuse Tom's childhood: 'made-up stories, true stories; soothing stories, warning stories; stories with a moral or with no point at all; believable stories and unbelievable stories; stories which were neither one thing nor the other' (2). Since *Waterland* is an assemblage comprising history and fiction, and makes no uncomplicated distinction between these categories, historical narratives are included as story-telling possibilities here. Indeed history-teacher Tom becomes the most prominent embodiment of this method for outwitting reality.

The second means of filling an empty reality is embodied in the 'sanguine' Atkinsons, Crick's maternal ancestors, who, being from the hills of Norfolk, look down and 'see in these level Fens – this nothing-landscape – an Idea, a drawing-board for plans' (17), the opportunity to make things happen:

> and there's no saying what consequences we won't risk, what reactions to our actions, what repercussions, what brick towers built to be knocked down, what chasings of our own tails, what chaos we won't assent to in order to assure ourselves that, none the less, things are happening. (41)

The Atkinsons are associated with the (apparently) solid images of 'civilisation', maps, bricks, buildings and projects. Indeed their New Brewery is a monument to the narrative of Progress, and the description of it, beginning at the bottom, advancing inexorably upward and ending with its crowning glory, encapsulates the same Ideas (90).

Avatars of civilising Progress, the Atkinsons envisage themselves as effecting the advance of not only their own families, but those of their town and country, and so enjoin themselves to the national project of Empire. Indeed, the Atkinson ideology is coterminous with that which informs Britain's imperial thrust (92–3).

However, the distinction Tom initially makes between the 'Atkinsons [who] made history' and the 'Cricks [who] spun yarns' (17) is rendered unstable by the double resonance of 'making history', which signifies both the 'happening' of past events and the recording of them. These are consistently represented in the novel as familial acts: 'I present to you History, the fabrication, the diversion, the reality-obscuring drama. History, and its near relative Histrionics' (40). By employing terms such as 'histrionics', 'theatre' and 'stage' Tom thus suggests that 'making history' is more about performance than 'reality'. The Atkinsons' entrepreneurial zeal is a story, part of a larger narrative of progress, to which they are committed. In fact, insofar as it invokes the idea of drama, or theatrical story, rather than the real, history-making is related ever more closely to telling (hi)stories and opposed to 'reality'.[5] Indeed, the story-telling Cricks 'come to work for [the Atkinsons]. They make their great journey across the Ouse' (16), and 'thr[o]w in their lot with the drainers and land-reclaimers' (12). Moreover, 'some say' that the history-making Atkinsons, too, were 'originally Fenmen' (63). Telling stories bleeds into making things happen. And things made to happen both emerge from and contribute to the production of meaning via stories told. The Atkinsons and the Cricks are each invested, then, in what the novel terms 'artificial history'. While the stories they tell are different, each is committed to evading the flatness of reality with history-making. The key difference between them is not that between the making of history and the telling of stories, for these are familial acts.

Rather, the key difference between the Atkinsons and the Cricks is that the Cricks remember the fictiveness of their stories. That is, they remember that the stories told and the meanings produced are constructs. They are made, not found. It is a difference encapsulated in the dual vision of nature that the metaphor of land reclamation incorporates, centering upon water, that 'liquid form of Nothing'.

In his discussion of the Victorian formulation of, and response to, the 'Arctic Sublime', Chauncey C. Loomis attributes to that period a notion of the 'Natural Sublime' which recognises at once the 'magnitude [and] immensity of creation', and an 'irregularity and natural order that is beyond man's ken'. This produces two contrary responses in the observer: 'part of him goes out to it in rapture; part of him withdraws from it in fear' (Loomis, 1977: 98). The Victorian reaction to the Natural Sublime, he argues, 'began with the desire to conquer it and ended with the knowledge that what is human and finite in us, terrified on the brink of the mysterious abyss of nature, will draw back trembling from the inhuman and the infinite' (ibid.: 99).

The first key element of the metaphor of land reclamation reflects the desire to conquer. It is the human struggle to control, contain and triumph over nature: 'The obstinacy of water. The tenacity of ideas' (69). Here, nature is a vessel to be shaped to human desire, a sentiment most clearly enunciated in the novel by the Victorian Thomas Atkinson who builds an empire upon his ability to shape and mould the Fens. As Decoste puts it, the Atkinsons 'obscure the real by conjuring up universalist narratives which underwrite the active transformation of the Fens to their ends, and which enable the recasting of the real in the image of their own desires' (Decoste, 2002: 386). For the Atkinsons, nature can be modelled by steps taken, actions effected, things made to happen in service of an ever-brighter future, ensured by history's overarching pattern of progress. Finally, Judith Wilt describes the Atkinsons as 'builders and brewers on the rise, in league with progress' for whom 'the things that happen, are done, are made, *are* reality' (Wilt, 1990: 111–12).

A sense of patronage, and of offering a bright future insured by material measures and precautions and bolstered by cheery rhetoric (and by the provision and consumption of alcohol), links the Atkinsons with Lewis, a twentieth-century, like-minded stalwart of Progress. Promoted to headmaster above the older and more experienced Tom, he leads the school community as the Atkinsons led their town: 'a good, a diligent, a persevering man ... He cares; he strives; ... Our school a new ship bound for the Promised Land' (23). As McKinney suggests, Lewis and the Atkinsons share the belief 'that the human imagination can fundamentally change reality for the better'. This is manifested in their faith in 'the science and technology by which we can control reality' (McKinney, 1997: 827). Just as the Atkinsons build elaborate systems of locks, sluices and Relief Channels to guard against the 'perennial' danger of floods (100), so Lewis builds a nuclear fall-out shelter to protect him and his family from what seems to be (at least the physical manifestation of) the threat of his time. 'So it's all right, children. No need to be afraid. Lewis is here. Don't be gloomy. To all these morbid dreams, a simple answer: the nuclear fallout shelter' (154).

The other key element of the metaphor of land reclamation is that nature cannot be controlled, or not for long, the idea 'that, however much you resist them, the waters will return; that the land sinks; silt collects; that something in nature wants to go back' (17). This formulation of nature appeals to the sublime, the sense that nature dwarfs humanity, and is indifferent to it. Nature, in the novel, exists outside of history, typified by the eel which 'doesn't care two hoots about History, or what the history books call history' (195). The river, too, is characterised by a 'continued contempt ... for the efforts of men' and the 'ungovernable desire to flow at its own place and in its own way' (144) despite efforts to channel a new path for it. In fact, representative of natural history, and opposed to the artificial kind, the river is 'true and natural, if wayward' (145), the antithesis of the revolutionaries, prophets, champions of progress who 'can't abide it' (205). Opposed to artificial history, nature becomes another version of the real, so that Tom tells his students: 'if you want to be in the real world, let me tell you ... About the Ouse' (142).[6]

By virtue of their long habitation in the empty, watery and natural Fens, then, the Cricks are linked more closely to nature, and to the knowledge that it is indifferent to human effort. When the Atkinson Lock is opened the Cricks, who have worked upon it, 'do not cheer as heartily as the other spectators ... And though they draw pride from their part in the making of this newly navigable, brightly gleaming river, they know that what water makes, it also unmakes' (73). For despite Tom's claim that in going to work for the Atkinsons his ancestors 'ceased to be water people and became land people, [joining] in the destiny of the Fens, which was to strive not for but against water', he is forced also to acknowledge that 'perhaps they did not cease to be water people. Perhaps they became amphibians. Because if you drain land you are intimately concerned with water; you have to know its ways. Perhaps at heart they always knew, in spite of their land-preserving efforts, that they belonged to the old, prehistoric flood' (13). He makes a 'virtue' (15) of the Crick humour, phlegm, claiming that the reason that the Cricks worked for the Atkinsons, tending pumps and sluices and locks, but rose no further, was because of 'that old watery phlegm which cooled and made sluggish their spirits' and ensured 'they did not forget, in their muddy labours, their swampy origins; that however much you resist them, the waters will return; that the land sinks; silt collects; that something in nature wants to go back' (17).

Analogously, then, the Atkinsons believe their own stories. They mistake their history-making for reality, while the Cricks remember that they are only stories, able to be re-written. This distinction emerges most clearly in the novel in relation to paternity. For the Atkinsons, invested in empire and progress, paternity is related to the desire to control reality, to shape the future. Wilt argues: 'the Atkinson vision thus privileges paternity as the ultimate sign of reality: Atkinsons will seek fatherhood, invest it with godhood, be unable to relinquish it' (Wilt, 1990: 113). In contrast, the Cricks are not so heavily invested in Progress. They are willing to work on Atkinson projects but they are not passionate about Empire, they do not see themselves as servants of the future so much as doing their job in the present and, as Wilt suggests, they do not share the Atkinson obsession with paternity: 'for the Cricks, fatherhood is what it was to primitive peoples, man's hallucination his favourite fiction ... A Crick will not believe his own fatherhood nor insist upon it, nor, on the other hand, will he be destroyed by it or by its lack' (ibid). Thus, Tom's father, Henry Crick, accepts Dick, fathered by his wife's own father and passed off, to the general public, as Henry's own. His final words to Dick confirm this sense that fatherhood is performance, a tale to be written, a story that can be made true: 'Dick, it's all right! Dick. *I'll be* your father' (356, italics mine). The Cricks do not invest fatherhood with the same significance as the Atkinsons, they do not mistake paternity for the building of empires, and nor do they mistake the building of empires, the narrative of progress, with its linear shape, its beginning and end, its continual advance, for reality itself. Paradoxically, the stories told to relieve the vacancy of reality must be believable enough to fulfil their task, but at the same time, in a kind of negative capability, as McKinney suggests, 'we should acknowledge the fictiveness of our fictions' (McKinney, 1997: 826).

This second element of the metaphor, nature's refusal to be contained for long by human effort, its indifference to human initiative and history, places excess at the centre of its meaning. Specifically, it depicts an encounter with the excess of nature, which always exceeds the boundaries that human inventiveness builds for it. Just as the waters break their banks and cause flooding, forcing a confrontation with the limits of human ingenuity, so the effects of history, stories and things made to happen exceed their boundaries: they come to the limits of their power to explain.

For the stories that are created in order to fill reality are fertile, they exceed their own boundaries and produce unforeseen effects. Things made to happen, and the stories that both beget and are begotten by those happenings, reproduce promiscuously, with unanticipated and unimagined consequences:

> the dissemination of Christian tenets over a supposedly barbarous world has been ... one of the prime causes of wars, butcheries, inquisitions and other forms of barbarity ... the discovery of the printing press led, likewise, as well as to the spreading of knowledge, to propaganda, mendacity, contention and strife ... the invention of the steam-engine led to the miseries of industrial exploitation ... the invention of the aeroplane led to the widespread destruction of European cities along with their civilian populations ... And as for the splitting of the atom – (135–6).[7]

Stories are, like phlegm, of 'equivocal comfort', of 'ambiguous substance' (344). Indeed a host of ambiguous substances become metaphors for story-making and its effects. Phlegm is 'benign' yet 'disagreeable' (344); the East Wind is 'twins, and one twin kills and the other ripens' (290); and importantly, silt 'obstructs as it builds; unmakes as it makes' (11). The cumulative effect of the multitudinous history-making undertaken to fill reality is as silt in the drained waterways of the Fens:

> every so often there are these attempts to jettison the impedimenta of history, to do without that ever-frustrating weight. And because history accumulates, because it gets always heavier and the frustration greater, so the attempts to throw it off ... become more violent and drastic. (136–7)

This is Tom's explanation for the prevalence of apocalyptic visions throughout the historical record; that the weight of our history-making, and its unforeseen effects, bring us to the limits of our powers to explain, our abilities to tell stories. As history and stories are wound together and then tied to making things happen, they also form a complex link to the Here and Now. For despite what appears a radical separation between history (and stories) and the Here and Now – 'life is one-tenth Here and Now, nine-tenths a history lesson' (61) – the boundary between the two, like that between history and fiction, is porous. They are not discrete categories, but rather leak into each other, forming a substance as ambiguous as the Fens.

The Here and Now is an intense experience with 'more than one face'. Bringing 'both joy and terror', it is encountered, in the novel, via such diverse experiences as the discovery of Freddie Parr's body, which 'pinioned [Tom] with fear' so that 'he ceased to be a babe' (61); sexual discovery, 'which unlocked for [him] realms of candour and rapture' (61); and the blow to the head which commits Sarah Atkinson to a waking coma: 'horror. Confusion. Plenty of Here and Now' (77).

Those moments described as an encounter with the Here and Now are confrontations with the limitations of stories. They are proof that history is a 'thin garment easily punctured by a knife blade called Now' (36). For, strangely enough, though they are the effects of history-making, these moments are 'tense with the present tense ... fraught with the here and now' (207). While the Here and Now results from history it is also, conceptually, opposed to it, as in Price's rejection of history: 'what matters is the here and now' (60). The vexed nature of this term, its grasping of a present that is continually slipping away, prompts Crick to wonder: 'what is this much-adduced Here and Now? What is this indefinable zone between what is past and what is to come?' (60).

The Here and Now can be understood as what Linda Hutcheon calls 'brute reality' (Hutcheon, 1988: 155); it is present experience in that fleeting moment before it becomes the past, narrativised and emplotted. Or, as Janik puts it, the Here and Now is 'direct, unmediated, unintellectualized experience' (Janik, 1995: 178. See also Janik, 1989: 84–6). It is an encounter with the limits of our powers to explain. That is, it is that moment when we confront an event which seems inexplicable, for which we have no contextualising, explanatory story. For this reason, the Here and Now is also an aperture where, very briefly, reality, in Tom's sense of 'emptiness', is glimpsed.[8] This evanescent experience is the closest we come to non-narration, to being 'outside' story and meaning. It is the moment when history is made 'nonsense by that sensation in the pit of your stomach ... the feeling that all is nothing' (270). It is the reminder that there is no guiding purpose, or over-arching pattern and meaning to history; meaning is (provisionally) provided only by the stories we tell. Thus, an encounter with the Here and Now is always a more or less bloody apocalypse, an encounter with the end; the end of meaning, the end of a particular story which has framed and filled reality. Thus when Price proclaims the end of history just as Tom is confronting the limits of his power to explain Mary's baby-snatching actions, it prompts Tom to launch himself into the past, to break away from teaching the French Revolution and try to come to terms, instead, with his own sense of the end and to elucidate the moments of crisis in his life which elude meaning and defy explanation. 'There are a thousand million ways', he reflects, 'in which the world comes to an end' (155).

Situated on the cusp of reality and history, the Here and Now forms the knife's edge separating, but also linking, these in the novel. If the Here and Now constitutes an aperture through which reality, as the absence of meaning, might be glimpsed, this encounter is fleeting and the chasm quickly closes, rewritten in and as story. Tom's example is Marie Antoinette who, during her famous return from Varennes to Paris, 'was aware not only of the Here and Now but that History had engulfed her' (61).

If, as Elias suggests, metahistorical romance 'gestures toward the sublime and attempts to enunciate the boundary or limit where lived human experience meets the past' (Elias, 2001: 53), then for *Waterland* this limit exists as the Here and Now, the point at which an event defies understanding. It is pure experience that cannot yet be spoken and therefore textualised, but which also, paradoxically, throws one into history. No sooner does the encounter with the Here and Now produce a glimpse of meaninglessness than the mind performs its work of nar- rativisation, the experience is again harnessed by story and ascribed meaning. 'The reality of things – be thankful – only visits us for a brief while' (33). The moment passes and all that is left is the telling of it. Tom observes that 'so often it is precisely these surprise attacks of the Here and Now which, far from launching us into the present tense, which they do, it is true, for a brief and giddy interval, announce that time has taken us prisoner' (61). The Here and Now is an encounter with meaningless reality but also, always, an encounter with history, for the intensity of the Here and Now incites the demand for explanation, and that explanation incites the demand for more explanation until, as Tom puts it, 'that incessant question Whywhywhy has become like a siren wailing in our heads' (107).

IV

Decoste makes this endless questioning central to his discussion of *Waterland*. He pertinently identifies the tendency of Swift scholarship to focus upon *Waterland's* treatment of history as narrative, and to 'elide', therefore, 'the text's own unease with such endorsements of history as narrative (including the inextricable textuality of both its sources and its form) and leave relatively unexamined the tension obtaining between *historia* as narrative and *historia* as inquiry' (Decoste, 2002: 379). He rightly argues that, for the novel, the narratives that are used to regulate and shape a chaotic and destructive reality themselves become danger- ous if they seek finality and are not themselves subjected to further inquiry. Once naturalised, they 'become as senseless and threatening as the reality they are meant to ward off' (ibid).

Ernest Atkinson's engulfment by a story of his own making is a case in point. Ernest is the late-Victorian, doubting figure, schooled, as no Atkinson has been before him, at Cambridge in 'European socialism, Fabianism, the writings of Marx' (156). It is through Ernest's fingers that the Atkinson empire slips when he doubts the future of humanity and the narratives of empire and progress on which this future has been built. Typically, Crick offers two explanations for Ernest's being 'a renegade, a rebel' (156). The first, 'realist' version, is that he assumes his 'inescapable' role as director of the Atkinson empire during what Crick calls 'a period of economic deterioration from which we have never recovered' (157), as the first Atkinson 'to assume his legacy without the assurance of its inevitable expansion, without the incentive of Progress, without the knowledge that in his latter days he would be a richer and more influential man than in his youth' (157). The second explanation Crick offers is a more symbolic one, drawing upon the novel's leitmotif of water, natural history, as that which counters and undermines 'the artificial stuff'. Crick suggests that since Ernest was born during the notorious floods of 1874, 'affected by the watery circumstances of his birth, he wished that he might return to the former days of the untamed swamps, when all was yet to be done, when something was still to be made from nothing' (158). Born amidst watery chaos his affinities are not those of his father, 'who was not a master of the present but a servant of the future' (157) and who greeted the economic downturn by becoming more politically active, 'a staunch advocate of forward imperial policies (for here, after all, expansion was still possible)' (157). Ernest returns, instead, to the origins of the Atkinson empire and focuses upon brewing beer. 'What finer cause could there be to labour in than the supplying of this harsh world with a means of merriment' (158). Selling off the Water Transport Company and retaining only the Gildsey Pleasure Boat company, Ernest wishes, its seems 'for nothing more than to be an honest and unambitious purveyor of barrels of happiness' (158). This is figured in the novel as a retreat from the vision of reality upon which the Atkinson empire was built. Tom describes drunkenness as 'a let-out for the march of history' (236).

'And that is another difference between the Cricks and the Atkinsons. That whereas the Cricks emerged from water, the Atkinsons emerged from beer' (64). Beer is another symbol of making things happen, of filling and forming a chaotic reality. The Atkinson company motto, Tom notes, 'does indeed mean, simply "Out of Water, Ale",' and can even be construed, as perhaps Thomas intended, 'Out of Water, Activity' (86).

For reclaimed land is highly fertile, and Atkinson beer, brewed from its yield, is expected to 'cause a new flooding of the Fens, but not a flooding of water – a flooding of beer' (90). And also of good cheer. For drunkenness 'makes reality seem not so really real' (236), not so very empty. It also, like the Here and Now, 'occurs in many sudden and wonderful forms' (172), and has diverse effects; more than one face: 'pleasure, satisfaction, well-being, elation, light-headedness, hot-headedness, befuddlement, distraction, delirium, irascibility, pugnaciousness, imbalance, incapacity … ' (171). Indeed, drunkenness is the summoning up of the Here and Now. It erases meaning.

The townspeople disapprove of Ernest's rejection of politics, this 'unpatriotic shirking … in this time of arms-racing and gunboat-sending' (159). However, despite his watery origins, Ernest is an Atkinson and thoughts of the future do infect his sought-after jollity. When Ernest announces his return to the political sphere, spurred by his conscience and fears for the future, it is as a Liberal candidate in the general election, criticising the Conservative tradition that has long influenced the town. 'He did not shrink from accusing his own father (muttered protests), for berating him as one of those who had fed the people with dreams of inflated and no longer tenable grandeur, who had intoxicated them with visions of Empire … thus diverting their minds from matters nearer home' (161).

The novel would, perhaps, approve, thus far, Ernest's questioning of the narrative of progress into which he has been born. However, outcast by the town he retreats to Kessling Hall with his daughter and becomes immersed in another story, a fairy tale. 'Can it be that he too has succumbed to that old Atkinson malaise and caught Ideas? And not just any old idea, but Beauty – the most platonic of the lot?' (219). Having seen the power of his daughter's beauty to disrupt a military recruitment parade (218), and, symbolically, the future-destroying war, he inscribes Helen as Beauty itself, and his worship of his daughter increases in proportion to his disgust with humanity as the war goes on. He 'starts to believe that only from out of this beauty will come a Saviour of the World' (220). Not only would this double, or reinforce Ernest's paternity (as father of both child and mother), it would bestow godhood indeed; as father of the saviour Ernest would be the Origin and, according to the Christian narrative invoked, the End. For the Christian narrative the Saviour of the World *is* the author of history, is *history itself*, its origin and end. The Saviour of the World is the original, non-produced, meaning.

Engulfed in this story and mistaking it for reality, Ernest's attempt to exclude all that does not 'fit' his particular vision of reality – including the marriage of his daughter to Henry Crick – ends in his own, miniature, endorsement of apocalyptic conflagration.[9] First comes the creation of Coronation Ale, which quickly and spectacularly inebriates the entire town and ends in the fiery destruction of the Atkinson brewery. Then, the end for Ernest himself comes early when, having written a letter to his future son, and after drinking his potent Coronation Ale all day, Ernest suicides. Finally, his son, born to his daughter, is Dick Crick, a 'potato head', with 'clumsy mental faculties' (38) who murders a schoolboy before killing himself. The narrative in which Ernest becomes engulfed and fails to question, indeed, the reality of which he rigorously asserts, produces effects in excess of his own envisioning.

This more dangerous aspect of the excesses of history-making (both as story-telling and making things happen) is prefigured in Tom Crick's childhood dreams when, feverish with the flu:

> the stories which his mother told him, in her inimitable fashion, to soothe and console him, failed to perform their normal office. For, far from issuing from his mother to confer on him their balm, they seemed instead to be rising up to envelop and overwhelm her, casting round her their menacing miasmas, so that through his hours of fever he strove to cleave a passage through to a mother who was becoming less and less real, more and more besieged by fiction. (272)

As Tom suggests, 'there was prophesy in little Tom's dreams' (273), because his mother catches his flu whilst telling these stories and dies as a result. His dreams also prefigure Mary's engulfment by fiction. As Mary becomes lost in her story, Tom 'is constrained to hug his wife as though to confirm she is still there. For in the twilight it seems that, without moving, she is receding, fading, becoming ghostly' (148). As with his mother in his dream, he must strive to reach her.

For Mary, too, exemplifies the need for, in Decoste's terms, '*historia* as inquiry, not just narrative' (ibid.: 378). Mary's curiosity, 'which drove her, beyond all restraint, to want to touch, witness, experience whatever was unknown and hidden from her' (51), comes to an abrupt end with the death of Freddie Parr. Her abortion, which disrupts teleological history, marks too her rejection of history, stories and things made to happen and the meaning that accrues to them. Mary determines to live without stories and without making things happen, to embrace reality, 'to make do ... with nothing. Not believing either in looking back or in looking forward, she learnt how to mark time. To withstand … the empty space of reality' (126). Although they move together to historical Greenwich, Tom tells us that 'in her heart she'll always remain in the flat fens' (341).

Yet Tom has already claimed that 'there are very few of us who can be, for any length of time, merely realistic' (41). That is, he asserts again our inability to accept the emptiness of reality, the absence of overarching, explanatory meaning. If Mary appears to live most of her life incurious about the stories and things made to happen amidst the nothingness of reality, she does, at a decisive moment, return to the realms of story, and of making things happen.

Invoking the narrative of the religion with which she grew up, she suddenly announces 'I'm going to have a baby. Because God said I will' (130). And in fact she does, though it is one she takes from someone at the supermarket, convinced it is from God. It is as though her long residence in the realms of the merely real produces in her the need to retreat into a story large enough to fill a big emptiness. As a result she becomes trapped in the story, because 'sometimes the happening won't stop and let itself be turned into memory' (329), into a story with a beginning and, importantly, an end: 'so she's still in the midst of events (a supermarket adventure, something in her arms, a courtroom in which she calls God as a witness) which haven't ceased' (329).

Mary has been engulfed by her own story and by making things happen because of that story. And yet, because she cannot tell the story again, because she cannot accept that it is simply a story, she cannot relieve herself of its burden. Or, more importantly, her inability to submit her chosen narrative to questioning, to subject it to the question 'why?' leaves her embedded in it as a version of reality.

Mary's story makes curiosity vital to the novel's depiction of historical knowledge, and this adds an important dimension to inquiry, which Decoste's account does not fully apprehend. The novel does indeed stress the importance of *historia* as inquiry, not simply narrative. Yet Decoste seems to place the questioning of narratives outside of narrative itself, a reading that the novel, with its assertion of the ubiquity of textuality and meaning-production, does not support. Just as history cannot exist as a fixed point outside the flux of historical time and events, nor can we stand outside these narratives to pose our questions. We cannot cross over the (even linguistic) boundary to extra-textual, empty reality. The endless 'whywhywhy' that Tom describes is provoked by crisis, at those times when far from standing outside of history, we realise we are deeply entangled in it. As Tom puts it, 'the past gets in the way; it trips us up, bogs us down; it complicates, makes difficult' (108). For the novel, historical inquiry is not a detached questioning because of a 'responsibility' (ibid.: 398) to do so. Rather it is a desperate yearning for history as meaning, the desire for explanation, 'knowing', Tom suggests, 'it is not a complete explanation' (107–8).

V

Thus, a model of historical inquiry is re-configured, in the novel, as desire, around the 'vital force' (51) of curiosity: 'which doesn't want to push ahead, which always wants to say, hey, that's interesting, let's stop awhile, let's take a look-see, let's retrace – let's take a different turn? What's the hurry, What's the rush? Let's *explore*' (194, emphasis in original). Curiosity does not want to leave the past behind in an effort to push forward to the future. It is thus opposed to a more conventional notion of historical inquiry that seeks

> to uncover the mysteries of cause and effect. To show that to every action there is a reaction. To show that Y is a consequence because X preceded. To shut stable doors, so that next time, at least, the horse – To know that what we are is what we are because our past has determined it. (107)

Historical inquiry as curiosity is embodied by Tom's narrative itself, which, although fuelled by the question 'why', digresses into tales of beer bottles, winds, floods, the French Revolution, the reproductive life of eels, and so on. Although it scurries into the past it does not mark out a straight trajectory, but stops, ponders, considers, pursues the desire to be ' sniff-sniffing things out' (194). The novel mimics its own lauding of historical inquiry as curiosity by sparking the reader's own.

Similarly, endless curiosity is inscribed in Stan Booth's words at the end of the novel: 'someone best explain' (338). While Geoffrey Lord observes, rightly, that the answer to this question, the explanation, lies in what has gone before, that 'the reader is thrown back into the text' (Lord, 1997: 148), it is also true that the answer *does not* lie in what has gone before: the explanation exceeds the stories that are meant to achieve it. And whereas DeCoste describes this moment as one that emphasises 'the exploration of, and exhortation to, *historia* as inquiry and not just as narrative' (Decoste, 2002: 378), I argue that its significance is, additionally, that it installs in the reader the *desire* for explanation. Even though we know that explanation is impossible, we are curious.

The novel's repeated elicitation of desire for its narratives, which end at a point of climax, unresolved, marks it as romance. For whereas realist narratives court, and ultimately (appear to) achieve, final explanation, closure and coherence, romance narratives, like *Waterland*, court the desire for narrative, the 'seditious' force of curiosity that refuses to arrive at the end of itself but, rather, exists as excess. The model for historical inquiry advocated by the novel, which resists a unitary history, 'reality cut down to size' (206), is recast as romance.

Again, the Fenland setting provides an illustration for the disruption of unitary, realist history by the excess of romance. As Pamela Cooper suggests, it is both the 'story-teller's realm of free imaginative play ... and the site of the historian's exact, disciplined investigations' (Cooper, 1996: 371). It could equally be construed as the setting of both romance and realism. Indeed, in its opening pages the novel enacts postmodernism's displacement of realism as Diane Elam conceives it, 'shifting the site of the representation of historical events to romance' (Elam, 1992: 14). Tom observes that it is, perhaps, 'only logical' that 'the bare and empty Fens yield so readily to the imaginary – and the supernatural' (18). The Fenlanders see marsh sprites and will-o'-the-wisps and observe 'a catechism of obscure rites' (18) cultivated by their swampy surrounds. In this 'fairy-tale place ... Far away from the wide world' (1), the explanations offered by myths are as crucial for comprehending experience as those offered by discourses conventionally considered factual. While Mary's abortion at the hands of the local 'witch' Martha Clay is one probable cause of her infertility in later life, the Fenland superstition stating that a live fish in a woman's lap will make her barren (18) is offered as at least as important to understanding her inability to conceive as any other more 'rational', 'real' or 'historical' reason.[10] Elam argues that 'realism, as far as postmodern romance is concerned, ceases to be the privileged form of representation for the 'real', for historical reality' (ibid.: 14).

Yet while romance precedes, exceeds and displaces realism for a time, Tom also locates this romantic place with an increasingly detailed, realist, precision. It is a lock-keeper's cottage at the Atkinson Lock 'on the River Leem, two miles from where it empties into the Ouse' (3) in the middle of the Fens, 'which are a low-lying region of eastern England, over 1,200 square miles in area, bounded to the west by the limestone hills of the Midlands, to the south and east by the chalk hills of Cambridgeshire, Suffolk and Norfolk' (8).[11] Tom persistently, although rather ironically, marginalises and attempts to discredit romance, urging his students to 'avoid illusion and make-believe, to lay aside dreams, moonshine, cure-alls, wonder-workings, pie-in-the-sky – to be realistic' (108). However, in the form of myths, fairy-tales and alternative histories that continually interrupt the flow of Tom's narrative, romance repeatedly erupts into, and disrupts, the realist account of Tom's personal history. As Elam observes, if

> romance-writing appears as an excess to be cut out, this excess simply cannot be regulated. Excess is in the nature of the genre: romance returns even at the point where it is most violently excluded in the name of realism, making even a clear distinction between realism and romance impossible. (Elam, 1992: 7)

The excess of romance is, for Elam, its political value. Romance 'exceeds' realism's nostalgia, claiming 'because we can never fully come to terms with the past, we can never justly represent it' (ibid.: 15). While realism desires closure, romance delights in the pleasure of curiosity. Indeed, to return to Elam's claim, cited at the beginning of this chapter, if romance is indeed disruptive and subversive, a 'counter-discourse on history and the real which modernism must repress in order to establish itself as the statement of the real' (ibid.: 3) then curiosity can be considered *as* romance. In fact Tom does name it as 'an ingredient of love' (51). For, in the depiction of historical inquiry as desire, curiosity – which *is* 'our insatiable and feverish desire to know about things' (194) – is 'complex and unpredictable' and, therefore, 'is the true and rightful subverter and defeats even our impulse for historical progression' (194). Curiosity, like romance, does not want to discover the univocal meaning of history. Never satisfied, its desire is always in excess of itself. It wants to explore, digress, and uncover multiple meanings, myriad stories. Itself characterised by excess, the romance that is curiosity 'contaminate[s] history' (ibid.: 14) with this excess, and thereby ensures that history-making is endlessly productive, a ceaseless inquiry, not a seeking toward finality and closure.

Therefore, alongside Tom's depiction of land reclamation and, by virtue of his metaphor, historical inquiry, as 'a dogged, vigilant business. A dull yet valuable business. A hard, inglorious business' (336), he also depicts history-making not as a carefully considered process of questioning narratives, but as a far less ordered process, 'anarchic, seditious' because governed by our 'love of life' (205). For as curiosity begets stories, it also 'begets love. It weds us to the world. It's part of our perverse, madcap love for this impossible planet we inhabit. People die when curiosity goes' (206). History, in this transaction, becomes desire.

Elias, too, makes the desire for history essential to human nature, writing, 'people are inquisitive animals and they will always ask wh-questions, and the key one that they ask is 'Why?'' This question, she asserts, is 'hardwired' into us (Elias, 2005: 159). She argues that meta-historical romances like *Waterland* are driven by the 'construction of, or desire for, the historical sublime, which is a kind of warmed-up or negative idealism; it is a weak hope and desire that history, the space of ontological order, exists somewhere, but also the belief that human history will never reach it' (ibid.: 160). Yet she also describes this weak hope, rather paradoxically, as that obsession which is characteristic of postmodernism in the arts, an 'obsession with history and a desperate desire for the comforting self-awareness that is supposed to come from historical knowledge', coupled with a scepticism about the possibility of such knowledge (Elias, 2001: xvii).

In *Waterland*, the desire for history is more akin to obsession than a weak hope. It is an urgent and unremitting longing: 'can I deny that what I wanted all along was not some golden nugget that history would at last yield up, but History itself: the Grand Narrative, the filler of vacuums, the dispeller of fears of the dark?' (62), asks Tom. The novel, like Elias, installs and naturalises a desire for history. Tom teaches his students:

> children, only animals live entirely in the Here and Now. Only nature knows neither memory nor history. But man – let me offer you a definition – is the story-telling animal. Wherever he goes he wants to leave behind not a chaotic wake, not an empty space, but the comforting marker-buoys and trail-signs of stories. He has to go on telling stories, he has to keep on making them up. As long as there's a story, it's all right. (62–3)

The novel achieves this essentialising and universalising move[12] by situating human nature within its rubric of natural history. They are aligned in the novel as 'those weird and wonderful commodities, those unsolved mysteries of mysteries' (205). Specifically, it is pubescent sexuality that belongs to the same articulation of the real which the novel accords nature, belonging, with the river, to what Elias calls a 'mythic, spatialized time that preceded Western, scientific time' (Elias, 2001: 57). Thus, in their childhood, 'in prehistorical, pubescent times', Tom and Mary drift to the windmill 'instinctively, without the need for prior arrangement' (52). They are barely conscious of the bombers that fly overhead, the intimation of the world of linear time and history.

Sexuality is naturalised here and is opposed to textuality, to the imposition of historical, linear time. Desire is grafted onto the opposition
between natural history and its artificial counterpart, so that it is somehow most authentic before it is channelled and contained or, in Tom
and Mary's case, inhibited by the imposition of time and history, when
they must meet by appointment (48–9).

The novel's second metaphor for history and reality accommodates
this expanded notion of historical inquiry as desire. The female body,
like the empty fens, is 'equipped with a miniature model of reality:
an empty but fillable vessel. A vessel in which much can be made to
happen, and to issue in consequence. In which dramas can be brewed,
things can be hatched out of nothing' (42). This metaphor reiterates the
notion of reality as a blank canvas upon which meaning can be etched.
Woman here is as nature, so that this thought intersects with what
Genevieve Lloyd calls the 'long-standing antipathy between femaleness
and active, "male" Culture' in Western philosophical thought. Rational
knowledge, she suggests, has been associated with maleness; 'construed
as a transcending, transformation or control of natural forces; and the
feminine has been associated with what rational knowledge transcends,
dominates or simply leaves behind' (Lloyd, 1993: 2).

This has particular resonance in the novel because Mary, Helen
and Sarah are all linked as those who '[offer] companionship to those
whose lives have stopped though they must go on living' (118). Mary
and Sarah are further linked by their association with madness. Mary
takes her place 'amongst the senile' (123), first by working with them,
then, at the close of the novel, by joining them; those for whom 'life
has come to a kind of stop' (122), though, like Mary, they must go on
living. Sarah is reputedly placed in the asylum that her family builds
in her honour (95). They are a strange version of that image, popular in
Victorian poetry, of the embowered woman. However, in contrast
to Tennyson's Lady of Shalott, who looks down to Camelot, they
each adopt 'the paradoxical pose of one who keeps watch – but over
nothing' (78).

Obsessively desired by the men who surround them in the novel,
each of the key women becomes symbolically over-determined by the
stories that attach to them. Helen Atkinson personifies Beauty itself,
which marks her, her father thinks, as the mother of the next Saviour
of the World (219), and is associated, by Tom, as 'the Brewer's Daughter
of Gildsey', with 'ghosts and earnestly recounted legends' that inhabit
the villages along the Leem (18). Mary Metcalf, too, is re-written as the
Madonna, first by her father (46) and then by Tom Crick (48), in whose

mind she is also the restoration of his dead mother (48). Tom also inscribes her, in her exile, or vigil, as Saint Gunnhilda (118), a princess awaiting rescue (120), his own dead mother (283) and as his maternal forebear Sarah Atkinson (118).[13] Meanwhile, Sarah is 'Guardian Angel, Holy Mother, Saint Gunnhild-come-again ... [and] an intrepid Britannia' (94). She is alternately a benevolent and prophetic goddess credited with safe-guarding the prosperity of the region (83–8), and a 'stark raving' lunatic (95) blamed for floods, fires, riots and inability to conceive (88).

Written and rewritten by and as male desire, the meanings that accrue to them make the women slippery, so that Mary appears 'ghostly' to Tom (148), and reports abound after her death of a ghostly Sarah watching over her own grave (102), seeking admittance to Kessling Hall (101) and to the maltings (104) and diving 'like a very mermaid' into the Ouse (104). The effect of the many and wondrous stories with which these women are inscribed is such that the women seem to haunt the novel, both marginal to it and, equally, filling it. Characterised by desire, which Catherine Belsey describes as 'the irrational, arbitrary, inexplicable residue which exceeds or defies the category of the knowable' (Belsey, 1994a: 11), women disrupt history-making.

Sarah Atkinson impedes the onward and upward march of the Atkinson dynasty, and by extension, of Progress, indeed history itself, by subverting her husband's energies for expansion and redirecting them toward herself. When she is injured by a blow to the head from a jealous Thomas, 'he no longer attends to the expanding affairs of Atkinson and Sons. He no longer reads his newspaper ... History has stopped for him' (80). Patriarchy, which is implicated in notions of Progress and Empire, is also disrupted, for although Sarah bears Thomas two sons, these become the first Atkinsons to have difficulty in begetting heirs, 'inhibited by that woman up there in that upper room' (88).

Helen Atkinson is, as we have seen, similarly disruptive of history, making a mockery of progress in a way her father, for all his diatribes, could not: 'once upon a time there was a beautiful girl at a parade of soldiers, and the silly soldiers with their rifles bumped into each other and forgot how to march because they all wanted to look at the beautiful girl' (218). And it is in her relationship with Ernest, her father, that Helen further disrupts and subverts the centrifugal, expansionist tendencies of the Atkinson dynasty, so that the outward thrust of progress turns back upon itself, and history, instead of 'marching unswervingly into the future' (135), is similarly redirected, 'because when fathers love daughters and daughters love fathers it's like tying up into a knot the thread that runs into the future, it's like a stream wanting to flow backwards' (228).[14]

Mary's abortion is the consummate disruption of a linear and tele-ological notion of history. As Judith Wilt argues, 'the novel dramatizes neither birth nor death but abortion – the disruption of the teleologi-cal narrative of beginnings and ends, the biological-historical fable of centred structure (Wilt, 1990: 390). The abortion subverts the one-directional flow of history as 'what the future's made of' (308) is not allowed to develop, but is instead cast into the river. Moreover, Mary's disruption is represented as an attempt to abort history itself. Mary's empty vessel has been filled, things have been made to happen inside her, just as history is made to happen within an empty reality. When Mary decides to abort the baby she makes an attempt to discard history (including things made to happen), and embrace the vacancy of reality. She is waiting for 'Nothing to happen. For something to unhappen' (295). The abortion is thus associated with other attempts to cast off the burden of history, perhaps the most violent yet. She literally takes Tom out of historical time by leading him to Martha Clay's mud hut: 'children, have you ever stepped into another world? Have you ever turned a corner to where Now and Long Ago are the same and time seems to be going on in some other place?' (303).

Women are thus associated with the excessive, subversive elements that disrupt history-making as it is conceived in the novel. As objects of male desire, women represent the romance element of the novel. Associated with many and fantastic stories, they communicate and embody the notion of history as desire because, as the traditional 'other' of rational, realist history, they are the disruptive excess that realist his-tory attempts to exclude. They are, therefore, part of natural history, 'which doesn't go anywhere. Which cleaves to itself. Which perpetually travels back to where it came from' and which is 'always getting the better of the artificial stuff' (205).[15]

Furthermore, the use of metaphor to equate the desire for woman with that for history enables the novel to naturalise its characterisa-tion of historical inquiry as desire. For the novel, desire for history is, paradoxically, an ahistorical given, separate from and impervious to history-making and its effects. Understood this way, the emptiness of reality is actually always-already inscribed. And, indeed, Tom's central metaphor for this empty reality, the Fens, is an imperfect one. In the mind of the young Tom, the Fens is always already a 'filled' reality, an ordered realm, so that he can only imagine its emptiness: 'and yet this land, so regular, so prostrate, so tamed and cultivated, would transform itself, in my five- or six-year old mind, into an empty wilderness' (3). By analogy, even the space that we imagine belongs to 'reality' is always already mapped. It is unavoidable.

The novel's attempt to represent the unpresentable, an empty reality, devoid of overarching pattern and meaning is therefore undermined or countered by the category of natural history, which naturalises the human condition and makes a continued desire for history, in the face of the problematisation of historical knowledge, a universal and time-less quality. Tom's installation of natural history as a category of the real suggests that his empty reality does posit Truth, that of nature, in much the same way as Elias cannot avoid her metaphysical idea of 'History' as that which is beyond what we live (the present) and remember (the past). Yet, whereas for Elias, the Truth that constitutes the historical sublime is 'opposed to or other to, the materiality of lived history' (Elias, 2001: 53) the novel attempts to avoid a metaphysical positing of truth by making it material. Desire is the fundamental truth of human nature, just as the desire to return is the fundamental truth of natural history. Both these truths are firmly housed not in a metaphysical concept, however, but in the materiality of bodies and of nature.

Committed to representing the late-twentieth century crisis of histo-riography, the novel nonetheless posits the continuing value of seek-ing historical knowledge, even if that knowledge is provisional. For reclaimed land is highly fertile. The Fens yield 'fifteen tons of potatoes or nineteen sacks of wheat an acre' (16). Similarly, the emptiness of reality, the absence of over-arching pattern and meaning, invites inscrip-tion, proliferates stories, which produce a multiplicity of meanings. These meanings are not guaranteed by a perspective outside of the stories themselves and, as such, are always open to revision, to new meanings. Indeed history-making is abundantly fertile. As we have seen, stories and things made to happen beget more stories and things made to happen, so that while 'history itself' might be empty, history-making is a swarming, irresistible fecundity.

Often the stories produced in and by history-making are, like civi-lisation itself, 'precious. An artifice – so easily knocked down – but precious' (240). As Decoste observes, this celebration of civilisation does not equate to an Atkinson-like faith in progress, but rather, a belief in process. Civilisation is equated with ceaseless inquiry:

> for this artifice that keeps the void at bay is, for Crick, itself a process and not a final destination. The civilization that must be husbanded and ceaselessly renewed is, indeed, the operation of inquiry itself,

that which refuses to foreclose, with whatever degree of violence or finality, on the question why. (Decoste, 2002: 397)

And what the tentative, provisional, ultimately unverifiable stories do is teach that 'by forever attempting to explain we may come, not to an Explanation, but to a knowledge of the limits of our power to explain' (108). For Tom this is valuable knowledge. Accepting 'the burden of our need to ask why' (108) prevents the mistaking of reality for the building of empires.

Historical inquiry thus takes a shape not dissimilar to the movement Keith Tester ascribes to the 'will to know' in *The Life and Times of Post-Modernity* (1993). He says, 'the will to know implies the transcendence of any fixed and evidently formal identities. It implies not certainty, but relentless movement; it implies not the safe havens of ascription but, instead, the never ending and never consummated struggle for achievement'. He contrasts this to the 'will to certainty' which 'implies the creation and imposition of fixed identitie's. The will to certainty asserts the centrality of the human, the 'will to know makes the human small and perpetually peripheral' (Tester, 1993: 55).

Fittingly, then, there are direct parallels between Tom's method of historical inquiry and his 'testament' to the value of education:

It's not about empty minds waiting to be filled, nor about flatulent teachers discharging hot air. It's about the opposition of teacher and student. It's about what gets rubbed off between the persistence of the one and the resistance of the other. A long, hard struggle against a natural resistance ... I don't believe in quick results, in wand-waving and wonder-working ... but I do believe in education. (239)

And what gets rubbed off in the opposition of history-making and reality, order and chaos, is fear itself, leaving behind the 'vital force' (51) necessary for embracing life. Thus, whereas Elias posits the desire for 'history itself', and as a child Tom desired the Grand Narrative, what the novel actually dramatises is the desire for the process of historical inquiry, for historical recollection governed by curiosity.

In *Waterland*, romance *is* the counter-discourse of curiosity. This counter-discourse subverts, disrupts and interrupts history-making's pursuit of order and finality of meaning. It is, therefore, the favoured mode of historical inquiry, the favoured genre, too, for history-telling. Yet, curiosity is not, primarily, a hermeneutic or investigative tool but, like its double romance, is primarily desire. The novel positions this desire as an alternative to the realist project of remembering history in order to come to terms with the past, to put it behind us, and so foreclose it. Committed to an (anti) representation of 'reality' as absence, meaninglessness, but also to the value of seeking historical knowledge, to re-membering the past in our stories, rather than foreclose history or pronounce its end, *Waterland* refigures history as fecund excess, a compelling, even imperative force that begets knowledge, even if that knowledge is provisional and limited. The excessive histories and stories it comprises are depicted as fertile, not futile.

4
(Dis)Possessing Knowledge: A. S. Byatt's *Possession: A Romance*

> The work of the human mind, with its meandering and its logical and fantastic inventions, was literature's field of observation until first natural and social philosophy, then, in the last century, specialized scientific disciplines dispossessed literature of them.
>
> (Safir, Margery Arent, *Melancholies of Knowledge*, 1999)

> Tell me you know – and that it is not simple – or simply to be rejected – there is a truth of Imagination.
>
> (A. S. Byatt, *Possession: A Romance*, 1990)

In April 1992, in an article for *Newsweek* entitled 'Don't Undo Our Work', Margaret Thatcher claimed that during her terms as prime minister 'we reclaimed our heritage' (Thatcher, 1992). As we have seen, her platform after 1984 was built upon the slogan of 'Victorian values', a catchphrase that concealed an expansive programme for quite revolutionary change behind the reassuring visage of a return to old-fashioned values and an all-but-lost national heritage. Her campaign fed into a wider cultural anxiety over the preservation of the nation's legacies, centring upon the tangible relics of the past such as antiques, country houses, and 'period' homes. These homes were opened to the public but, consonant with New Right ideology, now charged an entrance fee. Similarly, industrial museums multiplied but also charged for admission. As Harold Malchow observes, 'English Heritage, if it could not be shunted into the private sector, was expected to pay its way, to impose admission charges' (Malchow, 2000: 201). In short, English heritage was to become a commodity, preferably one bought and sold by the private entrepreneur.

As Thatcher's idea of 'reclamation' perhaps unwittingly suggests, this obsession with Victorian collectibles, and with the preservation of stately homes, invokes the idea of heritage as property. 'History' becomes its tangible objects, which are bought and sold to decorate homes, or to boost tourism. The past becomes a possession.

A. S Byatt's neo-Victorian novel *Possession: A Romance* (1990) engages the idea of the past as a possession in order to re-centre the literary text as a medium for cultural memory. It tells two stories that become increasingly entangled as the novel progresses. A contemporary storyline, set in Thatcher's Britain in the 1980s, depicts the developing professional and personal relationship between two Victorianist literary scholars who join forces to discover the truth about the relationship between the poets they study. Roland is an underemployed scholar who, though trained in poststructuralism, approaches the work of the fictional Victorian poet Randolph Henry Ash primarily as a textual critic. Maud is a more established scholar of some renown in the field of feminist psychoanalytic criticism. She is also a descendant of the object of her study, the (also fictional) Victorian poet Christabel LaMotte. Set in the mid-Victorian period, the novel's second storyline gradually reveals the textual and then carnal affair between Ash and LaMotte. This gothic plot, which incorporates adultery, lesbianism, suicide, illegitimacy, frigidity, and the possibility of infanticide, disrupts the intellectualised climate of the twentieth-century storyline which in turn culminates in an extraordinarily sensational grave robbery.

Within its overarching structure of Romance *Possession* borrows from gothic, as well as its Victorian derivative, sensation fiction, the novel with a secret.[1] The novel deploys a notion of sensation which incorporates both a cerebral and visceral response to interrogate and undermine the division of knowledge between (rational, factual) science and (emotional, fictional) literature, and to resituate literature as a valuable, and valued, mode of knowledge. It does this by placing an intellectually eclectic Victorian period in opposition with a 1980s present characterised by professionalised readers and specialised, demarcated knowledge. Against the painstakingly methodological reconstructive work performed by its literary critics, the novel refigures the relationship between past and present as that between the literary text as medium and an ideal reader who is willing not only to possess the text, but also to be possessed by it, to allow its voices to speak. It is a relationship not of ownership, nor even primarily of intellectual knowledge. Rather, it is a relationship of desire. Byatt therefore establishes the metaphor of the romance, the relationship of lovers, to explicate this model of knowledge. The novel suggests that in an age governed by scientific truths, desire is the disruptive excess that cannot be accounted for nor fully explicated by science. Against dismissals of *Possession* as nostalgic and conservative I suggest that its formulation of sensation as a conjunction of the critical and emotional faculties shifts focus from postmodernism's critique of historical representation to explore instead the creative possibilities arising from an imaginative, affective relationship to the past. In this the novel anticipates subsequent neo-Victorian fiction and its interest in the ways in which the past *can* be remembered in the twenty-first century.

I

Seeking to resituate literature as a mode of knowledge, Byatt seeks a time when the literary text did play a more central, and valued, role in propagating knowledge. She locates this time in the Victorian age, which she depicts as something of an Eden of intellectual endeavour. Her Victorian era exists prior to the specialisation of the intellectual discourses. It is peopled by poets, artists, diarists, historians and mythologists, many of whom are also amateur botanists and scientists. Her Victorian poet, Ash, is both poet and natural scientist, and literally embodies the coexistence of literary and scientific pursuits through the use of standard literary devices for portraying the romantic hero, combined with the language of the nineteenth-century pseudo-science of phrenology, to give him flesh for her late-twentieth-century reader (273–4). His poetry, too, is a fusion of religious belief, pagan mythology, history and science, which attempts to both discover and communicate truths that, he believes, are not accessible through only one of these means. Ash considers himself connected to the figures of the past and he seeks not only to understand them, but also to connect with them and, importantly, to allow them a sort of life after death, a power to speak through his language (395). For Ash, history and science unite in this task: 'the Historian and the Man of Science alike may be said to traffic with the dead [... They] have heard the bloodless cries of the vanished and given them voices' (104). It is in these terms that Ash understands his own historiographic pursuits, and links himself, as a poet, to both the Historian and the Man of Science, claiming that through his poetry he has 'lent [his] voice to and mixed [his] life with those past voices and lives' (104). Like Michelet, Ash invokes the Biblical raising of Lazarus as a metaphor for the power of the imagination to resuscitate the figures from the past (168). This image of the text as medium finds its fullest representation in Ash's likening of the literary text to the Victorian figure of the spiritualist medium. When the medium, Mrs Lees, tells Ash 'I have no power to summon spirits. I am their instrument; they speak through me, or not, as they please, not as I please', he responds with 'they speak to me too, through the medium of language' (395). As Elisabeth Bronfen argues, for Ash, 'a human being can be kept alive beyond the constraints of the body's mortality, namely as long as a belief in the power of the imagination remains' (Bronfen, 1996: 123).

It is this belief in the power of the imagination that is lacking in the characters that inhabit Byatt's contemporary storyline. Whereas literary resuscitations of the past, whether in the public discourse of poetry or the ostensibly private forms of diaries and letters, enrich Byatt's Victorian age, her late-twentieth century is cluttered with impersonal, dense and scholarly works that obscure and obfuscate rather than explicate and enliven the past. Knowledge is specialised and demarcated between disciplines, and the study of literature has become professionalised. Her scholars read Ash's texts not, primarily, to allow their voices to speak, but to produce complex analyses of them, to take intellectual possession of them. The texts become objects upon which to practice their sophisticated tools for reading. These tools are portrayed as those of science. Byatt's amusing parody of twentieth-century literary scholarship represents it as plagued by its subjugation to categorical and methodological imperatives; by each critic's overwhelming commitment to practices that are depicted as more scientific than literary and thus unsuited to the critic's task, rendering their knowledge flawed. Thus, James Blackadder models himself on the naturalist, adopting an exacting, 'stringent' scholarship (10) that paralyses and keeps him working on his *Complete Poems and Plays of Randolph Ash* for more than twenty years. His minute fidelity to identifying the possible sources of each poetic image drains Ash's text of its language, its poetry, and makes Blackadder's own text full of footnotes that 'engulfed and swallowed the text' (28). Striving for a nineteenth-century scientific objectivity, Blackadder buries Ash with footnotes and then erases himself: 'Much of his writing met this fate. It was set down, depersonalised, and then erased. Much of his time was spent deciding whether or not to erase things. He usually did' (300). Blackadder demonstrates the 'death wish' identified by George Levine in *Dying to Know* (2002). Levine argues that there is a connection in western culture between knowledge and death, which he approaches via the idiom 'I'm dying to know'. This idiom has two meanings. The first is 'a passion for knowing so intense that one would risk one's life to achieve it; and second, a willingness to repress the aspiring, desiring, emotion-ridden self and everything merely personal, contingent, historical, material that might get in the way of acquiring knowledge' (Levine, 2002: 2). This second meaning is the legacy of the Platonic tradition but was revitalised in the nineteenth century through the empiricist imperative of objectivity as the necessary counterpart to knowledge.

In contrast to Blackadder but also adopting scientific models, the most successful literary scholars are the deconstructionists, Lacanian psychoanalysts, Marxists and feminists; those who undertake what Louise Yelin calls 'hypertheoretical critical writing' and 'voyeuristic dilettantism and connoisseurship' (Yeelin, 1992: 39). Scholars who do not adopt such methodologies, especially those who undertake what is considered to be old-fashioned textual criticism, such as Beatrice Nest, whose work on the journal of Ellen Ash resists the tools of feminist scholarship, do not share the pecuniary or scholarly success of those who do.[2] The literary-critical establishment, in an age that privileges scientific methodology, privileges in turn these exacting theoretical modes. In *Postmodern Postures* Daniel Cordle positions structuralist and psychoanalytic criticism as postmodern schools that 'at least aspire to inclusion in the scientific box. In these accounts literature itself may be separated from science, but literary criticism becomes a "science" of literature, studying literary artifacts much as scientists study nature' (Cordle, 2000: 31). Aspiring to the scientific, literary criticism carves for itself a role in the production of knowledge in an age characterised by the ascendency of scientific epistemology (Silver, 1998) and by the 'sciencing' of the humanities (Safir, 1999: 4). Yet for Byatt it does so at the expense of the vitality of the text itself. Texts written, as Ash says, for 'the singing of the language itself' (132), are subjected to a pseudo-scientific methodology and cannot mediate historical knowledge; the voices of the past cannot come alive and take possession of the present. The literary text becomes a dead relic, one of Mortimer Cropper's artefacts or 'History to hold in your hand' (100).

Ash's poem, 'The Great Collector,' neatly summarises Cropper's character. With an array of colourful and shiny artefacts of the past placed before him, the collector beholds them, greedy and grasping:

> And then his soul was satisfied, and then
> He tasted honey, then in those dead lights
> Alive again, he knew his life, and gave
> His gold to gaze and gaze (92)

Like this collector, Cropper seeks to know the past through possession of its objects and dead relics. His Ash scholarship prioritises a kind of literary tourism; he walks in the poet's footsteps on the journeys he took and possesses any object he touched, some of which, like Ash's watch, Cropper keeps on his own person. Ash's texts, including his correspondence, become more of these relics to be possessed. The novel ties Cropper's acquisitiveness to his American nationality. A current of anxiety circulates throughout the novel about the loss, during a period of economic decline for England, of English cultural artefacts to rich Americans, like Cropper, who, having purchased them, return with them to their own country. The physical description of Cropper dwells upon his nationality, so that he even purses his lips 'in American, more generous than English pursing' and he has 'American hips, ready for a neat belt and the faraway ghost of a gunbelt' (95). John J. Su observes that this evocation of the 'mythos of the Wild West' links his national identity 'to the threat he represents to the other characters in the novel' (Su, 2004: 684), the threat that he will appropriate and remove national artefacts. This anxiety centres ultimately upon the clandestine correspondence of Ash and LaMotte, and the fear that Cropper will purchase it and remove it from England. Blackadder, in his attempts to prevent this, comes up against the inscrutability of Thatcher's economics:

> Blackadder had written to every public body he could think of who might be concerned with the Ash-LaMotte correspondence. He had lobbied the Reviewing Committee on the Export of Works of Art, and had requested an interview with the Minister for the Arts, which had resulted in a dialogue with an aggressive and not wholly gentlemanly civil servant, who had said that the Minister was fully apprised of the importance of the discovery, but did not believe that it warranted interfering with Market Forces. It might be possible to allocate some small sum from the National Heritage Trust. It was felt that Professor Blackadder might attempt to match this sum from private sponsorship or public appeal. If the retention of these old letters in this country is truly in the national interest, this young man appeared to be saying, with his vulpine smile and slight snarl, then Market Forces will ensure that the papers are kept in this country without any artificial aid from the state. (398)

England is implicated in these transactions, and if the novel parodies acquisitive America then it also excoriates the compliance of Thatcher's England. It is clear, in the novel, that the small sums Blackadder might cobble together from different sources are no match for Cropper's seemingly bottomless chequebook, and that it is this chequebook that determines what is in the national interest. Or, rather, which nation's interests are served. As Blackadder rather dryly observes, 'Mortimer Cropper had a direct line to infinitely more powerful Market Forces than he himself' (399). A nation that devotes 'an occasional five minutes on the Arts on *Events in Depth*' (399) is not economically committed to holding on to its artistic heritage.

Here an implicit distinction is drawn between the attempt to retain the material artefacts of one's own cultural heritage, and coveting the artefacts that, in this case, belong to another nation. The manuscripts are depicted as belonging almost spiritually to England, being a part of its 'national story' (404), and so as naturally belonging in that country. Cropper's attempt to gain the manuscripts is depicted as an almost fraudulent lechery, the appropriation of an inheritance that is not his own, nor his country's.

Yet whether they are whisked away to the United States or remain in England, the letters face the same potential fate, that of becoming dead relics. The building that houses the Stant collection, in the United States, and the British Museum, in England, are rendered similarly in the novel, as mausoleums for dead relics. The British Museum's dome evokes a tomb 'which, however high, held, [Roland] felt, insufficient oxygen for all the diligent readers, so that they lay somnolent like flames dying in Humphrey Davy's bell-jar as their sustenance was consumed' (26). Furthermore, in this building the 'Ash Factory' (which itself suggests an impersonal relationship to the texts) is located in the basement, exemplifying the prioritisation of objects over living texts. The building that houses Cropper's Stant collection, too, is a sterile place in which to display such objects, not to resuscitate living texts. Although it is in the middle of a desert it has 'the finest conditions and purified air, controlled temperature and limited access, only to accredited scholars in the field' (96–7). Neither building promotes an engagement with the text; in these structures the text cannot mediate and resuscitate the past in the body of the reader.[3]

II

In order for her image of the literary text as medium to be effective, it is necessary for Byatt to posit the existence of an ideal reader against the analytical reading made by her twentieth-century literary critics. This reader is one who not only possesses the text, in the sense of knowing it and understanding it, but who also engages with the text as medium, allowing him or herself to be possessed by it. Engagement with the text as medium opens up the possibility of being possessed by the past it mediates. The novel exploits the multiple meanings of the term 'possession' to mobilise its image of the literary text as medium.[4] The term refers to the active form 'possessing', which is implicated in the approach of Byatt's literary academics, whose attempts at appropriation bleed the text of its vitality. It also refers to the more passive state of 'being possessed' and implies a relinquishing of authority and ownership. Or, as Maud puts it, '[a] possession, as by daemons' (492). In the opening scene of the novel when Roland discovers two unfinished letters from Randolph Ash to a woman he later identifies as Christabel LaMotte, he is not only 'shocked' and 'thrilled' but also 'seized by a strange and uncharacteristic impulse', prompting him to steal the letters, 'these living words', from the British library (6, 8). In fact, the possession of Roland, by the texts of the Victorian, Ash, began much sooner than his discovery of the letters. He explains that Ash's poems 'were what stayed alive, when I'd been taught and examined everything else' (55). Yet this possession has been stifled by his own act of possession, his attempts to achieve mastery over Ash's texts, so that now his curiosity 'was a kind of predictive familiarity, he knew the workings of the other man's mind, he had read what he had read, he was possessed of his characteristic habits of syntax and stress' (130). Ash's letters to LaMotte disrupt this comfortable, restricted curiosity, and Ash metamorphoses, in the light of this new knowledge, from 'a man whose life seemed to be all in his mind', to a passionate, urgent man who lived also in his body. Confronted by Ash's lively and pressing voice, Roland is forced to abandon his pleasure in the fact that this man that produced work of 'ferocious vitality and darting breadth of reference' seemed to live 'so peaceable, so unruffled a private existence' (8). Importantly, in the face of this, Roland lets go of the knowledge he possesses of Ash and allows himself to become possessed by this new voice.

Similarly, early in her career, Maud chose to focus upon LaMotte because of a particular poem that took possession of her in her own childhood, and became 'a kind of touchstone' (53). As an adult Maud employs a particularly scientific, psychoanalytical, mode of literary criticism to distance herself from texts, emotions and, in fact, people, claiming 'you can be psychoanalytic without being personal!' (211). After she joins Roland in his pursuit of Ash and LaMotte's affair she reconnects with her earlier sensations; the purloined letters are 'alive' (56). For Maud, possession culminates when she and Roland are in LaMotte's room and she summons up a piece of the Victorian woman's poetry and thus divines the hiding place for the letters. In contrast to Roland who, at this stage, is 'being uselessly urged on by some violent emotion of curiosity – not greed, curiosity, more fundamental even than sex, the desire for knowledge', Maud allows herself to become possessed by the poetry and begins to recite it, 'chill and clear ... a kind of incantation' (82). As Bronfen argues, it is as if LaMotte wanted 'to make sure that justice would be done to her, even if she would have to let one century go by ... [and so] exerts a spectral influence on her descendent Maud' (Bronfen, 1996: 132). Maud's renewed possession by the text begets new knowledge of the author, which forces Maud to revise her scholarship. Furthermore, by allowing herself to reconnect with the text as medium, and so become possessed, Maud gains access to knowledge of her own ancestry. Since Maud is descended from both Ash and LaMotte, this final letter, as Bronfen observes, eventually reaches its destination. 'After a century it finds in Maud and through Maud a resuscitation' (ibid.).

Again, the text as medium is integral. Not just the poem about the dolls but LaMotte's final, undelivered letter to Ash, which Ellen Ash neither reads nor burns but buries with her husband. In this way Ellen helps to facilitate the haunting and even, in some sense, prophesies it:

> I want them to have *a sort of duration*, she said to herself. A demi-eternity.
>
> And if the ghouls dig them up again?
>
> Then justice will perhaps be done to *her* when I am not here to see it. (462)

Ellen's use of the term 'demi-eternity', to describe the kind of persistence she grants to Ash and LaMotte, suggests an afterlife, but of an aborted, 'sort of', kind. In fact, the letter that Ellen keeps also grants the recognition of their persistence in the figure of Maud, who, descended from each, gives them a 'sort of' embodied duration, the demi-eternity of the progenitor. Maud likens this to 'Daemonic' possession: 'I feel they have taken me over' (505).[5] Physical characteristics of her ancestors persist in Maud's own body (504), which becomes a medium through which LaMotte and Ash continue to have an existence. As Tatjana Jukić puts it, 'Maud simultaneously historicizes her self and incarnates history' (Jukić 2000: 84).[6] If Maud is revealed as embodying the memory of Ash and LaMotte, then the reader has been aware throughout of intricately crafted recurrences and patterns which increasingly connect not only the work of the two Victorian scholars, but also the two storylines, so that Byatt's twentieth century characters are (often unconsciously) influenced by the Victorians in a number of ways.[7] For example, throughout the novel images of green, white and gold link Christabel (274), the Princess in the glass coffin (63), Melusine and Maud (38–9), making them recall each other physically and psychologically. Thus, while we can, in a sense, separate out the two storylines at the level of plot, symbolically they are increasingly entangled by this web of imagery and by complex repetitions and allusions. This is particularly important for understanding the relationship between present and past as it is represented in the novel. The novel does not conceptualise the past as distinct, and separate from the present, but rather as entangled and entwined. For the novel, the Victorians continue to have an embodied afterlife today, as part of our cultural memory, mediated in part by the imaginative texts they have left behind them, which continue to shape the present.

Since it is the text that is the privileged medium of the past Roland only embodies the ideal reader when, toward the end of the novel, he realises that as he comes closer to possessing the truth of Ash's life, he feels distanced from Ash himself. His attempts to possess the end of the story, and thus Ash himself, are self-defeating. This realisation leads him back to Ash's text as medium. He reads, not searching for allusions to other texts, nor hunting for hints about Ash's life, but enjoying a reading in which he can again hear the language sing. It is an epiphanic moment that restores to Roland 'the days of his innocence', when he 'had been not a hunter but a reader' (469–70). It is a reading that, we are told, 'is violently but steadily alive' (470), engaging both 'sensuous alertness and its opposite, the pleasure of the brain as opposed to the viscera – though each is implicated in the other, as we know very well, with both, when they are working' (471).[8] His is a 'sensational' reading – one that appeals to and evokes the appetites and emotions at the same moment that it engages the reason and intellect. In her discussion of the 'neo-sensation' novel Kelly Marsh argues that the appeal to sensation in the antecedent genre of Victorian sensation fiction undermined the notion that reason governed (particularly men's) actions and suggested that there were visceral truths, as well as intellectual ones. The sensation novelist ventured the idea that sensation was a strong motivating force, exploring its effects and evoking it in their readers (Marsh, 1995: 109). She notes that the term 'sensation' is 'vexed', but traces Thomas Boyle's etymological pursuit of it which finds that the two meanings of the term given in the Oxford English Dictionary are paradoxical, evoking two

contradictory senses: 'of "cognition" and "emotion" at the same time ...
The physical urge and the mental intent overlap, leaving open the
possibility that there is no convenient way of separating the body and
the mind' (Boyle, 1989: 199 qtd. in Marsh, 1995: 112). Although this
moment of reading, combining body and mind, marks Roland's birth as
a poet (see Hennelly, 2003: 459), it is not a 'modernist epiphany' that
transforms him into Ash as he is takes his place in the Great Tradition
(see Buxton, 2001: 215 and Bronfen, 1996: 128). Rather, Roland has
become the ideal reader, no longer privileging his pseudo-scientific,
theoretical approach to literature but engaging both intellectually and
emotionally with the text-as-medium as it takes possession of him. The
effect is that he moves beyond the postmodern problematisation of
language: 'the ways in which it *could* be said had become more interesting that the idea that it could not'. This is not a *rejection* of his
knowledge that 'language was essentially inadequate' (473). Rather, it
is a willingness to live with this knowledge while making an 'interesting effort of the imagination' (254) to cross the gap between signifier
and signified; to believe that not knowing everything is not the same
as knowing nothing. Of the various reconstructions of Ash in word and
image, including his own, he reflects: 'All and none of these were Ash
and yet he knew, if he did not encompass, Ash' (473).

   This conjunction of the intellectual and the visceral capacities in the
ideal reader complicates the text's apparent excoriation of the literary
academy. Jackie Buxton argues that the 'ideological component' of
Possession is Byatt's 'rejection of criticism – or at least of certain kinds
of criticism' (Buxton, 2001: 101). Indeed, as a novelist, Byatt seems to
want critics to keep their hands off the language of her text, to reassert
the authority of the Author. However, Byatt is also a literary critic and a
reader and her text seems split between the authority of the author and
the power of the reader, and critic, to make meanings.[9] It is Roland's
and Maud's exhaustive knowledge of the Victorian poetry that enables
them to infer that LaMotte accompanied Ash on his Yorkshire expedition long before they can prove it. Their training and practice as literary
critics facilitates their tracing of images, words and cross-references in
each poet's work (252, 266). 'Literary critics make natural detectives',
observes Maud (237).[10] If Byatt's novel ruthlessly satirises the literary
academy – as undoubtedly it does – its most substantial pleasures are
nonetheless reserved for members of precisely that academy. Yelin
writes that for literary critics generally and Victorianists in particulary,
the novel 'entices us with its depiction of scholarship as a detective
game ... and it flatters us by offering us the pleasures of recognizing the

intertextual allusions and revisionary rewritings out of which it is made' (Yelin, 1992: 38). As the stellar sales of the novel suggests, enjoyment of the novel is not dependent upon a detailed knowledge of the Victorian period and its poetry, and of the language, tools and styles of different schools of literary criticism. However, familiarity with these certainly enhances its satire and increases its appeal.

For Byatt's primary textual strategy is to evoke an affective response in her reader. Throughout *Possession* Byatt cultivates the reader's desire for her text to both illustrate and embody a mode of knowledge is one that, in contrast to more scientific modes, appeals firstly to the senses and the emotions in order to cultivate the 'sensual alertness' accomplished in Roland's epiphanic reading. In this way Catherine Belsey describes desire as 'a state of mind which is also a state of body, or which perhaps deconstructs the opposition between the two' (Belsey, 1994a: 3). *Possession* does not resist, or refuse, representation of the past. By avoiding the more overtly self-referential, anti-mimetic techniques which distance the reader from the text and elicit a primarily cerebral response, Byatt's more conventional narrative techniques, and her use of the romance mode as the overarching structure of the novel, enable her to romance her readers, to seduce them. Ventriloquising Victorian romance, Byatt suggests that *Possession* is meant to recall 'the kind of book that people used to enjoy reading when they enjoyed reading' (qtd. in Rothstein, 1991). She builds desire for the text into the fabric of her own novel which, far from univocal, refers, primarily, not to an external, historical reality, but to other texts: myth, history, fairytales, literary criticism, Victorian poetry and other writings. Indeed, this film of citation is dramatised: Maud 'cited Cropper, citing Ash' (252). Flaunting its own fictiveness, this textual promiscuousness, I would suggest, over-determines the literary text as a means to know the past. Specifically, the intertextuality of *Possession* is a significant means through which it mediates cultural memory since it constantly evokes the memory of other texts. This idea has recently been taken up more fully in relation to Byatt's oeuvre by Lena Steveker, who describes the *Possession* as 'a memory-bank – or, in other words, a literary space of memory – that constantly draws on British cultural memory through its manifold intertextual references' (Steveker, 2009: 109). In addition to mediating a certain image of the Victorian period for the contemporary reader, then, *Possession* also becomes a mnemonic space in which literary texts belonging to Britain's canon are remembered: '*Possession* is engaged in a double movement: not only does it draw on British cultural memory by constantly referring to the Victorian Age, but it also contributes to the construction of this memory by creating an image of that of epoch' (ibid.: 123).

III

Thus, via its textual promiscuousness, memory of, and desire for literary texts is produced and reproduced in the novel, generating an excess that Diane Elam has labelled 'characteristic' of the Romance (Elam, 1992: 1). This citational excess continually elicits the reader's desire for the text while also engaging the intellect in an endless process of reaching back for additional meanings. The proliferation of intertexts not only makes reading the novel an exciting detective game, which engages both the intellect and the emotions. It also makes reading an endless process of reaching back for additional meanings, imitating the process of knowledge that, Elam argues, typifies postmodernism. The extensive use of citation, allusion and metaphor ensures that Byatt's text and reader continue to embody the mode of knowledge that she seeks to elucidate.[11] Reading is as Peter Brooks describes it in *Reading for the Plot*:

> a form of desire that carries us forward, onward, through the text. Narratives both tell of desire – typically present some story of desire – and arouse and make use of desire as dynamic of signification. Desire is in this view like Freud's notion of Eros, a force including sexual desire but larger and more polymorphous. (Brooks, 1984: 37)

Through producing desire in her reader for her text, Byatt's own novel thus embodies the model of knowledge it elucidates.[12] It takes the shape of a mystery; unfolding little by little it installs in her reader the desire for an ending exemplified in the Ash poem that begins the chapter in which the Victorian storyline ostensibly ends. This poem figures curiosity in similar ways to its depiction in *Waterland*, as an unceasing desire to know more:

> ... We must know
> How it comes out, the shape o' the whole, the thread
> Whose links are weak or solid, intricate
> Or boldly welded in great clumsy loops
> Of this bright chain of curiosity
> Which is become our fetter. So it drags
> Us through our time – 'And then and then and then',
> Towards our figured consummation. (476)

Byatt's twentieth-century characters believe they possess the whole story when they find LaMotte's final letter to Ash in the grave. Yet in a postscript, a piece of writing accessed by Byatt's reader but not by her characters, the encounter between Maia and Ash, in which he recognises her as his daughter, is disclosed. Byatt's reader is therefore privy to information undisclosed to her fictional literary critics, emphasising that it is reading, and not analysis, literary biography or sleuth work alone that accesses the living past. Byatt's own readers, *as readers*, are awarded fuller knowledge of the story. The integrity and value of the literary text – in this case her own – and its power to arouse interest in, and provide knowledge of, the past is affirmed.

Catherine Belsey observes that, in many romances, it is the unfulfilled quality of desire that ensures its appeal. Her comments about desire in *Gone with the Wind* apply also to *Possession*:

> by withholding closure, by continuing to tease, elude and frustrate, *[it]* succeeds in sustaining the desire of its central character and of the audience simultaneously. Narrative strategies and plot converge, not on an immobilized happiness which fails to satisfy, but on end-less indeterminacy, which is also the condition of desire itself. (Belsey, 1994a: 41)

Byatt ensures the continuing desire of her reader for her text by resisting a coherent, whole ending that ensures the continued happiness and love of Roland and Maud. The novel closes on them triumphant in their love-making but also having to negotiate their love from different sides of the world. Intimately related to the visceral response of the sensational reading, it is desire that comes to characterise the romance between an ideal reader and the text-as-medium.

Byatt develops the respective romances between her two couples as a metaphor for this relationship of textual desire because this relationship, as it emerges in the novel, requires a continual dialogue of mutual possession. The lover must both possess the beloved and be possessed. This model of romantic relationship is naturalised in Ash's mythic rewrite of the creation story in which a situation of mutual possession becomes the primordial state of relationship between man and woman who work '[i]n recognition and in sympathy' (242). And it is this model of mutual possession that shapes Byatt's representation of the affair between the Victorians Ash and LaMotte. Each describes the other as their centre: the place, as LaMotte writes, 'where I have been coming to. Since my time began. And when I go away from here, this will be the mid-point, to which everything ran, before, and *from* which everything will run' (284). Byatt contrasts Ash's love for, and interest in, LaMotte to the objectifying gaze exemplified in Wordsworth's poem about the solitary reaper. Ash reflects:

> the poet had heard the enchanted singing, taken in exactly as much as he had needed for his own immortal verse, and had refused to hear more. He himself, he had discovered, was different. He was a poet greedy for information, for facts, for details. Nothing was too trivial to interest him; nothing was inconsiderable ... so now his love for this woman, known intimately and not at all, was voracious for information. He learned her. (277)

Ash is depicted as one who seeks to know LaMotte, not because such knowledge would enable him to possess her, but for the sake of the knowledge itself. And LaMotte, who had feared the possession by a man, which romantic relationships seemed to mean in her culture, is depicted as enjoying the mutual sympathy and recognition that exists between Ash and herself. Indeed, she is freed from feminine conventions and at liberty to join in his pursuit of knowledge: 'she helped prepare his specimens, and scrambled indomitably over rocks to obtain them ... the crinoline cage and half her petticoats left behind, with the wind ruffling the pale hair' (285). It is during this period that LaMotte is most productive in her own intellectual and creative work, beginning what will become her most famous poem, *The Fairy Melusina*, written in what was considered the masculine form of the epic. Their love is imaged as a partnership, a mutual possession, each of the other. It is figured as a union also of the intellect and emotion, mind and desire.

However, this naturalised state of mutual possession is embattled with the culture in which it finds itself. If *Ragnarök* represents this primeval relationship of mutual understanding between man and woman, it also prefigures its trammelled existence in a wider world. As Ask and Embla 'step forward on the printless shore', their hands clasped,

> Behind them, first upon the level sand
> A line of darkening prints, filling with salt,
> First traces in the world of life and time
> And love, and mortal hope and vanishing. (242)

Ash's imagery unites love and hope with death and loss. Expansive promise is soon marred by the world of objects, the world as resistance.

In the Victorian storyline of *Possession*, the conventional dichotomy between science and art, as modes of knowledge, is inflected also through gender, along the same lines as the conventional dichotomy of rational masculinity and irrational femininity that we saw in the previous chapter of this book. Scientific rationalism, realism and reason are aligned with masculinity, whilst illusion, emotion, make-believe and all that lies outside the masculine domain are identified with the feminine. In this Victorian world that privileges the rational and, therefore, the masculine, women are objects, possessions:

> Know you not that we Women have no Power
> In the cold world of objects Reason rules,
> Where all is measured and mechanical?
> There we are chattels, baubles, property,
> Flowers pent in vases with our roots sliced off
> To shine a day and perish. But you see
> Here in this secret room all curtained round
> With vaguest softnesses, all dimly lit
> With flickerings and twinklings, where all shapes
> Are indistinct, all sounds ambiguous,
> Here we have Power, here the Irrational,
> The Intuition of the Unseen Powers
> Speaks to our women's nerves, galvanic threads
> Which gather up, interpret and transmit
> The unseen Powers and their hidden Will.
> This is our negative world, where the Unseen,
> Unheard, Impalpable, and Unconfined
> Speak to and through us – it is we who hear,
> Our natures that receive their thrilling force. (410)

Denied access to the world of masculinised knowledge, women, in Ash's poem *Mummy Possest*, must inhabit an-other space, and other knowledges. In his reference to 'our negative world', Ash points to the story Christabel evokes in her poetry of the City of Is. Drawn from Breton mythology, the City of Is is a female, underwater city that is 'the obverse of the male dominated technological industrial world of Paris – or Par-is as the Bretons have it. They say that Is will come to the surface when Paris is drowned for its sins' (134). Byatt's Leonora Stern describes the female world of Is as 'in-formed by illogic and struc-tured by feeling and in-tuition' (245), counterpart to, but distanced from, the world dominated by masculine reason and logic. This kind of world-in-reverse is appropriated by Ash for his re-creation of the world of the spiritualists:

> Where power flows upwards, as in the glass ball,
> Where left is right, and clocks go widdershins,
> And women sit enthroned and wear the robes,
> The wreaths of scented roses and the crowns,
> The jewels in our hair, the sardonyx,
> The moonstones and the rubies and the pearls,
> The royal stones, where we are priestesses
> And powerful Queens, and all swims with our will. (410)

Expected, in their culture, to hope for marriage, and yet resistant to the dependence it entails, LaMotte and Blanche Glover form a self-made City of Is, a space where they can be committed to scholarly pursuits and spared the ignominy of becoming possessions: 'a place wherein we neither served nor were served ... But we were to renounce the outside World – and the usual female Hopes (and with them the usual Fears) in exchange for – dare I say Art ... ' (187).

For LaMotte, this chosen way of life precludes the kind of disruption that Ash represents. 'LaMotte' means 'the castle' and to Ash she seems 'distant and closed away, a princess in a tower' (277), although she describes herself as 'circumscribed and self-communing ... not like a Princess in a thicket, by no means, but more like a very fat and self-satisfied spider in the centre of her shining Web ... ' (87). To LaMotte, Ash represents a force that would violate the bastions of this existence and she writes to him 'I cannot let you burn me up' (194). LaMotte's resistance to Victorian cultural norms places her in an oppositional relationship to Ash from the beginning of their acquaintance. As a male he is immediately cast in the role of possessor, seeking to possess.

And it is in this role that LaMotte recasts Ash when she finds that she is pregnant and she begins to look upon her time with Ash as an abandonment of her ideals and characterises the whole time as awash with loss. She rewrites their relationship in terms of the story of the Little Mermaid, 'who had her fishtail cleft to please her Prince, and became dumb, and was not moreover wanted by him. "The fishtail was her freedom," she said. "She felt, with her legs, that she was walking on knives"' (373–4). The romance between Ash and LaMotte, beginning as a mutual possession, is revised in terms of male domination and female subjugation.

IV

Yet this narrative both fits and does not fit. It captures some truth of their story, but not the whole of it. What is denied in this rendering of the story is their mutual pleasure in reciprocal possession; their joint delight in 'trusting *minds* which recognised each other' (501). Ash challenges her revision of their story, saying: 'think over what we did together and ask, where was the cruelty, where the coercion, where Christabel, the lack of love and respect for you, alike as a woman and as intellectual being?' (456).

In her final letter to him, LaMotte acknowledges that although Ash threatened and ultimately destroyed her self-possession and solitude he did so 'meaning me nothing but good' (502). Her refusal to either contact Ash or tell him about their child, and her retreat into her pain and pride, is figured in the novel as a rejection of mutual possession, in favour of self-possession. It is symbolically rectified in the novel not only by LaMotte voluntarily seeking forgiveness and revealing the information that she withheld, but also by her relinquishing self-possession once more. And not only to Ash, but also to his wife: 'I write under cover to your wife – who may read this, or do as she pleases with it – I am in her hands – but it is so dangerously sweet to speak out, after all these years – I trust myself to her and your goodwill' (500).

It is only as Ash nears death that she can again affirm 'we loved each other – *for* each other – only it was in the end for Maia' (502). Their child, born of those moments in which each found the centre of life in possession, each by the other, becomes a literal embodiment of the life that inheres in mutual possession. So, too, does their grandchild, who 'is a strong boy, and *will live*' (503). Witnessing the life that has come of their relationship, LaMotte once again asserts the mutuality of their love, and can see Ash not in his role of usurper and despoiler, but as the man she has known, loved and been loved by.

Byatt's Victorians, who believe in love and write and speak their own copiously, provide a contrast with her contemporary characters Roland and Maud. The sterility of the texts produced by the contemporary scholars is matched by the nullity of their sex lives. For Roland and Maud, love is something they theorise about, a 'suspect ideological construct' in which they cannot believe in any personal way. They are 'theoretically knowing' about desire and sexuality, and possess a sophisticated, scientific vocabulary to describe 'phallocracy [...] punctuation, puncturing and penetration, polymorphous and polysemous perversity' (423), and so on. However, it is their very cerebral, theoretical knowingness that leaves them poorly equipped to respond to desire in their own lives. It is as if knowledge of desire and sex has replaced the sensation itself, in just the same way as knowledge about texts and about reading had replaced the pleasure of the actual experience. Their dependence upon a scientific vocabulary and mode of knowledge to understand desire has squeezed out the feeling associated with it. Desire is the subversive element that cannot be contained by intellectualising scientific constructions of it. As Roland observes, 'I think all the *looking-into* has some very odd effects on desire' (267).[13] He and Maud are left with an absence of desire, or, more accurately, a desire for absence. Their identical wish is 'to have nothing. An empty clean bed. I have this image of a clean empty bed in a clean empty room, where nothing is asked or to be asked' (267).

Roland and Maud's romance develops in silence, as if their vocabulary, so loquacious for dealing with matters of sex and sexuality, cannot find the words to express their feeling for each other: 'they took to silence. They touched each other without comment and without progression. A hand on a hand, a clothed arm, resting on an arm. An ankle overlapping an ankle, as they sat on a beach, and not removed' (423).

The language they use to describe sex and sexuality, and the ideological construct that stands for love, is characterised by what is almost violence. Roland, and especially Maud, guard their solitude, their autonomous selves, jealously, and do not wish to sacrifice this to the other. They associate love with sex, and sex with being a possession. It is this that they resist:

> it was important to both of them that the touching should not proceed to any kind of fierceness or deliberate embrace. They felt that in some way this stately peacefulness of unacknowledged contact gave back their sense of their separate lives inside their separate skins. Speech, the kind of speech they knew, would have undone it ... (424)

Unable to speak their love, their gradual willingness to relinquish self-possession and open themselves to the other is signified by the scene in which Roland convinces Maud to let down her hair. Maud's long, blonde hair, worn tightly wound up and concealed beneath a scarf, is symbolic of her autonomy and independence. The passage in which she unravels it is figured as a kind of answer to the feminist poem that LaMotte had written a hundred or more years earlier. Angered by Ash, LaMotte rewrites the Rapunzel fairytale, replacing the prince who climbs to Rapunzel with a hairy ogre whose 'black claws go clutching / Hand over Hand / What Pain goes thrilling/ Through every strand!' (35).

In Maud, the fairytale is again rewritten to include the agency of the female in giving the prince the means to reach her. It is Maud who unwraps her hair for Roland, signifying her willingness to allow him to reach her emotionally.

The passage is connected to that in which Ash and LaMotte first make love, and not only because it ends the preceding chapter. The two scenes are also connected because for most of the novel this scene stands in the place of a sex scene between Roland and Maud. The release of Maud's hair from its tightly bound turban is a metaphorical undressing that prefigures LaMotte's discarded crinoline and petticoats in the following chapter (283). The scene begins slowly, and builds momentum steadily, until Maud is shaking her head 'faster and faster'. It invokes 'a moving sea', drawing upon conventional representation of female orgasm (272). This rhythm and these images, together with the 'scarlet blood' that Maud sees, make the metaphor more explicit and anticipate the following scene in which Ash finds traces of blood on his thighs after he and LaMotte have made love for the first time (284). Indeed, Mark Hennelly Jr. calls Maud's turban her 'figurative virginity belt' (Hennelly, 2003: 451).

Byatt thus reverses what might be expected of representations of sexuality in the Victorian era and the late twentieth century. On the one hand, she draws the Victorians as frank and relatively uninhibited in their sexuality, whilst on the other, she creates twentieth-century characters whose relationship proceeds slowly, mutely, and with little physical contact.[14] The verbal expression of Roland and Maud's growing love for each other occurs only after they accept that this sensation must coexist with their knowledge that love is a construct, emplotted by Romance as a system (425). Roland's confession of love recognises this paradox: 'they reject the scientific lens through which they view it. Roland's rejection of Leonora Stern's Lacanian-inflected literary criticism, 'But I don't want to see through her eyes ... I just don't' (254), becomes a rejection of the science-based methodologies in which he is trained. Instead, he and Maud embark upon 'an interesting effort of imagination to think how they (Ash and LaMotte) saw the world', to share Ash's interest in the 'origin of life. Also the reason we are here' (254). This attempt to see the world through the eyes of Ash and LaMotte overflows into the way that they see each other and their growing sense of responsibility for each other.

The verbal expression of Roland and Maud's growing love for each other occurs only after they accept that this sensation must coexist with their knowledge that love is a construct, emplotted by Romance as a system (425). Roland's confession of love recognises this paradox: 'I love you ... It isn't convenient. Not now I've acquired a future. But that's how it is. In the worst way. All the things we – we grew up not believing in. Total obsession, night and day. When I see you, you look alive and everything else – fades. All that' (506). His avowal of love acknowledges that all such declarations must always be citations but also that in his quotation he has, as Umberto Eco puts it, 'succeeded, once again, in speaking of love' (Eco, 1984: 32–3). In the dialogue of mutual possession so integral to the novel's representation of reading and loving it is the imagination that holds in tension theoretical knowingness and the desire that subverts it. The ways in which love can be spoken becomes more interesting than the ways in which it cannot.

Ventriloquising Ash and LaMotte enables Roland and Maud to relinquish some of their self-possession in order to take possession of the other, and be possessed in turn. This is represented by the scene in which they make love. It is figured as both possession and dispossession, and the language Byatt uses signifies death as well as life. Or, more specifically, a life that inheres in death:

> in the morning, the whole world had a strange new smell. It was the smell of the aftermath, a green smell, a smell of shredded leaves and oozing resin, of crushed wood and splashed sap, a tart smell, which bore some relation to the smell of bitten apples. It was the smell of death and destruction and it smelled fresh and lively and hopeful. (507)

Byatt's use of sex as a vehicle for characterising Roland and Maud's mutual possession captures the paradox of life coexisting with death, of self-possession cohabiting with dispossession. In this novel, love destroys autonomy and self-possession, and yet it is also somehow necessary to the individual, and much desired. Or, as Belsey writes, 'desire is inevitable ("necessity") Christabel calls it, twice ... and at the same time dangerous – beyond the pleasure principle, destructive, angry, *"a wrecker,"* as Maud puts it' (Belsey, 1994b: 696). Love, in this romance, embodies the paradox of 'possession' itself; it involves possessing the beloved, but at the same time, being possessed, possession and dispossession. Bronfen, too, observes that in the novel 'to take possession in love need not always mean that the beloved is reduced to an object of possession' (Bronfen, 1996: 132).

This is the lesson that Roland and Maud must learn. They must rethink, or, more precisely, re-*feel* the theoretical position they have adopted as postmodern lovers as well as postmodern scholars. Just as in their scholarship their theoretical brilliance gives way to a more personal reading, so their sophisticated understanding of love gives way to a personal investment in each other. In their romance, as in their reading, Roland and Maud learn to respond emotionally as well as intellectually. They allow themselves to feel desire for the text, and also for each other. The same faculties that make them good readers at the end of the novel, will, it is hoped, make them good lovers.

When Maud and Roland finally make love, it is not until Roland has first discovered that Maud looks like Ash. As Bronfen points out, 'their sexual union is thus also the complete eroticisation of (Roland's) scholarly relationship to his desired object of academic research' (Bronfen, 1996: 132). As he takes possession of Maud's body, and is possessed by hers, Roland joins himself to Ash's progeny and thus takes full possession of Ash himself. I argue that this is also the consummation of Byatt's metaphor that makes the ideal lover stand in for the ideal reader to symbolise the mutual possession of reader and text in a relationship that involves a conjunction of both the cognitive and emotional, or desiring, faculties.

That is, it marks the consummation of the metaphor and thus the intermingling of its two sides. For the two models of possession, that between the reader and the text, and that between the lovers, do not remain discrete. Rather, they become intertwined, and so contribute to the conjunction of the theoretical and the practical, the intellectual and the sensate. As Bronfen describes it, the hermeneutic search becomes knotted to love, 'the relationship between the two Victorian lives and the two Victorian archives that Roland and Maud come to explore, enmesh a carnal with a textual dialogue' (ibid.: 117). On the one hand there are the poems which, when read with the knowledge of the affair, seem to document it. On the other hand there is the carnal dialogue, the affair itself, which is bodily and sensual but also clandestine. The two are inveterately intertwined so that one cannot exist without the other. This intermingling of the carnal and textual is re-enacted by Roland and Maud a century later as, Bronfen argues, they 'enter into an academic and a romantic correspondence, where in the end one cannot be distinguished from the other' (ibid.: 118).

Reviews and critics are divided over whether *Possession* can be called postmodern.[15] I agree with Buxton's suggestion that Byatt's use of literary techniques labelled 'postmodern' need not suggest 'a wholesale celebration of postmodernism per se' (Buxton, 2001: 101). *Possession* is, indeed, 'deeply suspicious' of postmodernism (ibid.: 102). What interests me is Buxton's refusal to see the novel as subversive of, or challenging to, postmodernism. Buxton flags the possibility, in Hutcheon's formulation of postmodernism, of 'a postmodernist challenge to postmodernism itself' but refuses to find this 'politics of resistance' in *Possession* because of what she takes to be its regressive nostalgia (ibid.: 98). It is in a foot-noted aside that, I believe, Buxton approaches the crux of the novel's relationship to postmodernism and articulates a third possible position, even if she then places it under erasure. She playfully asks whether Hutcheon would 'consider *Possession doubly* metafictional? Does its com-plicity and critique of postmodernism itself make it *post*-postmodern?' (ibid.: 104). Byatt's comparatively realist narrative, which does not resist or refuse representation of the past, but revels in its textual construc-tion of a seductive fictional world, acknowledges the inadequacies of language but asserts its power to nonetheless seduce the reader. Though the novel is in part flavoured by nostalgia for more traditional notions of authorial authority and linguistic stability, it ultimately shifts the site of representation to the imaginative, indeed imagined, space of desire created between the text and the ideal reader. Her nostalgia is for Ash's ability to confront the ascendancy of scientific Truth and still assert the truth produced in and by the imagination, though this faith in imagi-nation is attributed only to Ash and not to the period as a whole (168–9). The meaning produced is unstable and changes from reader to reader and, indeed, reading to reading. Moreover, the structuring nostalgia of *Possession*, for the Victorian period itself, which allows Byatt to rep-resent her model of sensational reading and mutual possession, does not paint the entire period with its gloss. Byatt does not shy away from representing the limitations and failures of the period in her portrayal of LaMotte, or from contrasting this with the advantages of the present via her representation of (contemporary) Val and (Victorian) Blanche as textual doubles with widely different fates.[16] The novel's fascination with the period is undoubtedly affective but it finds both continuity and discontinuity between the two historical moments, attempting to map the present in relation to its past. In this it anticipates the formulation of a critical, productive nostalgia as a tool for mapping present identities in scholarly debates of the last two decades since the novel's publication.

Indeed, Susanne Becker positions *Possession* on 'the threshold between postmodern thought and new forms of more realist representation' marking a more general cultural shift 'beyond postmodernism before the new millennium' (Becker, 2001: 18).[17] Byatt's self-conscious realism anticipates critiques and modifications of postmodernism's approach to history in the new formulations of realism in more recent neo-Victorian fictions, especially the 'new(meta)realism' of the faux-Victorian novel which, as we shall see in the following chapter, shares historiographic metafiction's problematisation of history but eschews its metafictional techniques, remaining 'resolutely silent' about its fictionality (Kohlke, 2004: 156). Rather than establishing a univocal meaning or truth about the past, on the one hand, or privileging the problematisation of representing history, on the other, neo-Victorian fictions today are primarily concerned with exploring the manifold ways in which the past *can* be (provisionally) remembered and represented. Like Roland's 'materially engaged' reading in Lynn Wells' analysis of *Possession*, the affective relationship to history produced and performed by these novels 'takes into account the representational crisis of his age, but is not longer constrained by it' (Wells, 2002: 687). In this light, Byatt's novel, which wrests the production of historical knowledge from historians, literary critics, and collectors, and places it in the joined hands of the literary text and the ideal reader appears strangely prescient. Her romance of mutual possession between the text and an ideal reader recentres literature as a sensational epistemology that can acknowledge the limits of representation and of historical knowledge and yet nonetheless assert with Ash 'the truth of Imagination', which is 'not simple – or simply to be rejected' (169).

5

'Making it seem like it's authentic': the Faux-Victorian Novel as Cultural Memory in *Affinity* and *Fingersmith*

> A forgotten past is encountered again in fantastic literature. The recounting of that past heals an occluded memory.
>
> (Renate Lachmann 'Cultural Memory and the Role of Literature', 2004)

> The spirit-medium's proper home is neither this world nor the next, but that vague and debatable land which lies between them.
>
> (Sarah Waters, *Affinity*, 1999)

If *Possession* asserts the 'truth of the imagination', then *Affinity* (1999) and *Fingersmith* (2002) harness this truth to invent a genealogy of lesbian desire that exists only as shadows at the margins of Victorian literature and history. In contrast to *Waterland* and *Possession*, each of which constructs a contemporary frame for its representation of the Victorian period, *Affinity* and *Fingersmith* are examples of faux-Victorian fiction; novels written in the Victorian tradition that refuse to self-reflexively mark their difference from it in the characteristically parodic mode of historiographic metafiction. These novels revive Victorian novelistic traditions, offering themselves as stylistic imitations of Victorian fiction. Yet what they imitate they also re-imagine and extend: What would the Victorian novel have looked like had it represented other voices? By depicting female homosexuality in the Victorian period, Waters 'puts the weight of historical precedent behind lesbian existence' (Kohlke, 2004: 65). However she uses the mnemonic power of literature to do it.

Rather than represent the process of constructing the past, highlighting the limits of historical representation whether in history or fiction,

Waters silently inserts her depiction of nineteenth-century female homosexuality into our cultural memory of Victorian fiction. In order to invent a genealogy of lesbian desire, Waters mobilises literary forms that were considered typically feminine; Victorian gothic and sensation fiction were each associated with women as readers, writers and characters. And each created a fantastic space where cultural anxieties, especially those pertaining to gender ideals and sexuality, could be creatively explored. Linked to the representation of transgressive women, and to the depiction of female sexuality, these genres are perhaps the most likely sites where a lesbian tradition could have been voiced or, in fact, may have been voiced in muted, displaced ways. Deploying the easily recognisable tropes of gothic and sensation fiction, and extending their field of representation to include the representation of female homosexuality, Waters' use of Victorian narrative strategies and generic conventions provides a structure within which her invented 'history' can be written, remembered, and communicated as cultural memory. In this way a genealogy of female homoeroticism is mapped on to our sense of Victorian literary and cultural history.

I

The primary narrative strategy of the faux-Victorian novel is simulation; it imitates the stylistic and formal properties of the Victorian novel without overtly drawing attention to the temporal location of its production in the present through the use of distancing devices like contemporary frames (*Waterland* and *Possession*) or an intrusive, ironic narrator (*The French Lieutenant's Woman*). In contrast to the ironic distance that characterises historiographic metafiction the faux-Victorian novel silently imitates: it never draws attention to its status as 'fake'. Rather, it renders its own role in mediating Victorian fiction invisible, effacing its difference from its Victorian antecedent. Thus, *Affinity* and *Fingersmith* might in part function, like *Possession*, as 'imaginary museums' in which readers can view, and remember, past texts (Steveker, 2009: 112), but their references to Victorian literature, such as Henry Mayhew's work on prisons, or Elizabeth Barrett-Browning's poetry, are always made diegetically, as reading material for the characters. As such, they serve to anchor the text in the Victorian present it represents rather than establish distance and difference. For the faux-Victorian novel, imitation becomes an 'authenticating strategy': we 'believe' or 'yield to' the image of the Victorian period it offers because we recognise it from Victorian fiction.[1]

In *Nostalgic Postmodernism* (2001), Christian Gutleben criticises the faux-Victorian novel as a nostalgic celebration of 'the Golden Age of the English novel', suggesting that its 'imitative frenzy cannot but suggest a lack of originality' (Gutleben, 2001: 84). Gutleben notes that '[t]he retrieval of a well-known world, albeit fictional, undeniably bestows pleasure, the pleasure of recognition deemed by Aristotle to be universal' (ibid.: 41), but he approaches this with suspicion, asking: 'What type of pleasure is the recreation of an exclusively Victorian world intended to provide? Whatever the answer, the element of nostalgia, of love of the past, of conservatism clearly cannot be excluded' (ibid.). In fact, Waters has said that her novels are, in part, 'a celebration of the Victorian novel itself' (Dennis, 2008: 46), which suggests this 'love of the past'. Like Byatt, Waters suggests her fascination with Victorian pastiche lies partly in sheer narrative pleasure in 'thrilling plots'. She contrasts these with the 'arid' fiction of the 1990s and suggests that the faux-Victorian novel 'allows for this ... celebration of narrativity, that other sorts of literature just weren't allowing' (ibid.: 46). Thus, while Waters' novels are informed by twentieth-century scholarship, her research is simultaneously the ghostly, absent presence within the novel, and the spirit medium, effacing itself to conjure an apparitional Victorian narrative. As Cora Kaplan observes, '[t]heory and literary criticism underpins these narratives as generic emphasis in settings, in themes: it does not parse the narrative for us, or cut it up into bite-sized lessons' (Kaplan, 2007: 114) in the characteristic style of the historiographic metafiction. Rather than creating ironic distance, Waters' novels are more 'earnest' (Ciocia, 2007: 4) in their use of Victorian literary styles. If Waters' novels do nostalgically evoke the golden age of the Victorian novel in their narrative style, this can be understood as a positive formulation that performs the critique Svetlana Boym identifies as 'off-modern', which 'confuses our sense of direction; it makes us explore sideshadows and back alleys rather than the straight road of progress' (Boym, 2001: xvii). Speaking with the voice of the Victorian novel enables Waters to cast its gaze upon people and practices it marginalised or silenced.

Asked in an interview about whether there is evidence of lesbian desire in the Victorian period, Waters replied: 'it's tricky. There isn't really much in the way of novels and stuff like that ... you have to look for evidence of lesbian life. You have to look at other sorts of things, like medical writing or diaries, letters, and poetry to a certain extent ... ' (Waters, 2002). In an article with Laura Doan, Waters writes about the problem of historical invisibility for contemporary women who seek historical models of same-sex love: 'The suppression or absence of lesbian activity from the historical record, on the other hand, has limited the constituency across which a lesbian genealogy might be traced, and made it difficult for women to imagine themselves as participants in an unbroken tradition of same-sex love' (Doan and Waters, 2000: 12–13). Doan and Waters discuss a number of contemporary lesbian historical novels that work toward inventing this genealogy, arguing that such texts exemplify the 'political charge of lesbian imagining' (ibid.: 15). Fiction, here, is far from being reserved for entertainment. The aim of these novels is not to accurately depict the past in deference to history's authoritative discourse, but rather to *invent* a past that links to the present: Lesbian imagining 'recruits the reader into a community of shared lesbian interests understood to extend across history, and across the border separating history from fiction'. Moreover, since evidence is scarce, 'it offers fantasy and wishful thinking as legitimate historiographical resources, necessary correctives or missing links to the impoverished lesbian archive. In this way, these novelists echo Monique Wittig's famous plea that we should "[m]ake an effort to remember, and failing that, invent"' (Doan and Waters, 2000: 15).

Understood this way, the contemporary lesbian historical novel is an act of memory in the present, in which the past is 'modified' and 'redescribed' (Bal, 1999, vii) through invention and imagination. Here, the needs of the present are firmly privileged since this project 'take[s] its authority from the imperatives of contemporary lesbian identities' (ibid.: 13). While they are not the subject of Doan and Waters' article, Waters' own novels participate in this politically charged imagining. *Affinity* and *Fingersmith* imagine how lesbian desire might have been experienced in the Victorian period. Each text also imagines the way such desire might have inhabited the interstices between official records and legitimised knowledge, and so remained invisible to these discourses. It is not, therefore, historical accuracy that Waters courts in her novels. Rather, proceeding through invention, she pursues the *illusion* of authenticity. Discussing her use of pastiche she suggests: 'Part of the thing of it is making it *seem like* it's authentic ... to imagine the sort of history that we can't really recover' (Waters, 2002, emphasis mine).

In order to achieve this semblance of authenticity, Waters turns to Victorian fiction. When describing her writing strategies, she emphasises not her research but the importance of immersing herself in Victorian literature, particularly the novels, to enable her to 'write in a form, in an idiom, that seems to me to belong to the period' (Dennis, 2008: 47). So effective is Waters' 'Victorian' voice that, writing about *Affinity* specifically, M. L. Kohlke suggests that because it gives voice to taboo areas of

Victorian culture, it 'seems to reflect Victorian reality more comprehensively and thus more authentically than "genuine" Victorian literature' (Kohlke, 2004: 156). However, Waters' novels do not enact history's 'obfuscation of its own narrativity' (Kohlke, 2004: 165) so much as revel in the voice of fiction, its power to invent, to materialise, and to communicate a truth of the imagination. This, of course, is the confidence trick of the faux-Victorian novel. By a fictional sleight of hand, it makes something imagined *seem* like something remembered. In *Affinity* the spirit medium, Selina Dawes, reveals some of her tricks for 'materialising' messages from the dead but teasingly asks: 'Did it make the spirits less true?' if she sometimes helped them seem visible (168).

II

The faux-Victorian novel relies upon the mnemonic power of literature, and the mnemonic function of genre, to perform this sleight of hand. Victorian literature both forms part of the content of our cultural memory of the Victorians and functions as a medium of cultural memory (see Steveker, 2009: 107).[2] That is, we remember Victorian literature as part of the aesthetic production of Victorian culture, but when we read the literary texts themselves they inform the way we think about the Victorian world beyond the text and, in turn, shape the way that we remember it today. By eliding its difference from the Victorian novel, the faux-Victorian novel attempts to enter this memory of Victorian literature and culture in order to revise and extend it. Like all literary texts, it 'inscribes itself in a memory space into which earlier texts have inscribed themselves. It does not leave these earlier texts as it finds them but transforms them in absorbing them' (Lachmann, 2004: 172). That is, the faux-Victorian novel enters and absorbs the mnemonic space inscribed by Victorian fiction itself. Indeed, the extent to which it does this is indicated by the way in which Waters' novels have been dubbed 'Vic Lit', or '"Victorian" fictions' (Kaplan, 2007: 8, 110); they perform the Victorian and in the process both absorb and become absorbed by it, as though in the act of quotation the faux-Victorian novel becomes the thing itself. Renate Lachmann argues that this process of re-inscription, absorption and transformation occurs primarily through intertextual references 'to entire texts, to a textual paradigm, to a genre, to certain elements of a given text, to stylistic device, to narrative technique, to motifs, etc.' (ibid.: 173). For Lachmann, intertextuality *is* the memory of a text. By invoking Victorian literature Waters remembers – and re-members – this novelistic tradition *and* the extra-textual reality with which we associate it. Moreover, as we shall see, in addition to 'remembering' Victorian literature more generally, Waters' novels also 'remember' Victorian gothic and sensation novels specifically, using the force of generic conventions to shape our response to what we read.

John Frow argues that the structuring effects of genre play an active role in the production of meaning: they 'shape and guide' our knowledge and, in fact, 'genres actively generate and shape knowledge of the world' (Frow, 2005: 10, 2). In contrast to *Possession*, in which Byatt announces her use of Romance, Waters' novels silently perform the generic conventions of gothic and sensation. Eve Kosofsky Sedgwick identifies gothic as a highly conventionalised genre: 'you know the important features of its *mise en scène*: an oppressive ruin, a wild landscape, a Catholic or feudal society. You know about the trembling sensibility of the heroine and the impetuosity of her lover. You know about the tyrannical older man' (Sedgwick, 1986: 4). Her repetitious appeal to what we already 'know' suggests the way that the genre has worked its way into our cultural memory so that we bring to it certain expectations. Genres are mutable, and academic scholarship has splintered 'gothic' into various categories – 'imperial', 'female', 'postcolonial', 'lesbian', 'queer', 'feminist', 'postfeminist', and so on – in an attempt to account for its variety. Nonetheless, if gothic has dispersed in academia, it is still the case that readers (and perhaps many more film goers) identify particular texts and films as participating in the gothic because of their use of a set of tropes. To those identified by Sedgwick we could perhaps add the use of dark, eerie settings, the tight plotting of mysterious, possibly criminal events, the terror of entrapment and imprisonment, and sometimes the inclusion of supernatural elements that may or may not be explained rationally at the end. Gothic explores the underside of Enlightenment rationality, things that are to mysterious or too terrible to be explained and, as a result, depicts psychological discomfort and even disintegration (Botting, 2006).

Gothic and sensation, although usually distinguished from each other, do share traits in common and *Affinity* and *Fingersmith* draw on both.[3] Sensation fiction derives in part from gothic, reworking some of it tropes in a modern, urban setting. Waters borrows from the sensation novels of Wilkie Collins and Mary Elizabeth Braddon her melodramatic and twisting plots, which revolve around a central secret that is not revealed until the end and, in light of which, the reader's knowledge of what came before is transformed. A 'generic hybrid', the sensation novel typically combined 'realism and melodrama, the journalistic and the fantastic, the domestic and the romantic or exotic' (Pykett, 1994: 4).

Described this way, the sensation novel begins to appear similar in form to historical fiction, though the sensation novel was always set in the reader's present. Gothic and sensation are each structured by a realism that is punctured at various moments by an excess characteristic of more fantastic modes. The traditional historical novel suppresses the fantastic, and yet its appearance in contemporary historical novels suggests its productive possibilities for historical recollection. Indeed, Lachmann suggests that by testing the bounds of realism and creating 'alternative worlds', the fantastic mode offers productive possibilities for writers seeking to give voice to vanished or silenced elements of the past:

> That which had been silenced regains its voice, that which was made invisible recaptures its shape and that which was buried is disinterred. The fantastic thus operates as a mnemonic device that makes the forgotten or repressed reappear in the guise of an imagery by which the 'real' is connected with the unknown. (Lachmann, 2004: 173)

By staging a confrontation between the 'forgotten, unfamiliar and unseen', and the real (that is, 'an officially legitimated view of reality'), the fantastic displaces 'taken-for-granted categories of presence and rep-resentation' (ibid.: 173–4). In this way the fantastic mode embeds within itself a critique of official versions of historical reality, but this critique also, simultaneously, uses the aura of the 'real' attached to these versions to lend legitimacy to its representation of 'other', excluded elements. Waters' use of recognisable generic conventions that incorporate the fantastic mode provides a structure onto which we, as readers, map the unfamiliar image of Victorian lesbian desire. The generic structure makes it assimilable to our cultural memory of the Victorians. As Astrid Erll and Ansgar Nünning suggest, 'through narrative forms and genre patterns, previously pre-narrative and unformed experiences are sym-bolized, organized, and interpreted *and thereby become memorable.* Genres are a constitutive element of our memory' (Erll and Nünning, 2005: 274, emphasis mine).

A number of critics make links between gothic and queer narratives (see Fincher, 2007; Haggerty, 2006; Palmer, 1999).[4] In fact, Paulina Palmer attributes the appeal of gothic for writers and readers of lesbian fiction to 'its inscription of excess', as well as its 'strongly female focus, its ability to question mainstream versions of reality, and the fact that certain motifs associated with it (such as the double and "the unspeakable") lend themselves especially well to lesbian appropriation and recasting' (Palmer, 2004: 120). Similarly, writing about the male homosexual gaze in gothic fiction of the Romantic period, Max Fincher connects the very narrative properties of gothic with a queer perspective:

> the formal characteristics of Gothic writing, such as its Chinese-box narrative structures, its multiple narrators and interrupted stories, invite a circuitous reading attitude. Such a roundabout approach stands as a symbol of how we can read Gothic writing at the level of narrative as intimately related to the 'perverse' or 'wayward'. Gothic stories never follow a 'straight' course, a fact that in itself makes them queer. (Fincher, 2007: 4)

In *Affinity* the 'twisting passages' of Millbank (7) symbolise the 'twisting' of Margaret's thoughts (30) and, ultimately, the 'twistings' of her desire for Selina (251, 272). They are the circuitous, indirect and shadowy approach to materialising the voices, actions and subjectivities vanished or suppressed from the historical record; Waters' narratives do not take a 'straight' path either.

In *Affinity* Margaret's and Selina's diary entries are twisted together despite the fact that they do not share a temporal or spatial location. The diary form is often utilised in gothic fiction since its partial view builds narrative suspense. Although, as journals, they appear to promise interiority and authenticity, Selina's and Margaret's narratives are characterised by evasion and equivocation. In these journals, as in gothic narratives generally, 'ambivalence and uncertainty obscure single meaning' (Wolfreys, 2002: 3). In Margaret's case, her diary attempts to repress and contain her lesbian desire rather than express and reveal it. Indeed, this appears to be Margaret's intention for her journal, to hide her transgressive thoughts even from herself: 'I mean this writing not to turn me back upon my own thoughts, but to serve, like the chloral, to keep the thoughts from coming at all' (70). The twisting passages of Millbank are mirrored in the twisting of Margaret's heart and of the narrative itself; we learn about Margaret's past in snippets and inferences as she records them in her journal. The journal we read also partially reveals a prior journal, now burnt, which had her 'heart's blood in it' (70). The burnt journal is a spectral presence, the present mark of the absence, not only of itself but of the passion between Margaret and Helen that it recorded. As Sarah Parker observes, the burnt journal is the ghostly double of the one read (Parker, 2008: 9). Thus, despite her attempts to conceal it, Margaret's diary increasingly becomes the record of her transgression: 'Now I can see that my heart has crept across these pages, after all. I can see the crooked passage of it' (241).

The equivocations and evasions of Selina's diary are designed to conceal the truth about her reputed spiritualist powers and the uses to which she puts them. Waters' narrative maintains the ambiguity throughout until, in the final pages, we understand Selina to be a fraud and her circles an opportunity to explore her same-sex desires and, potentially, to defraud heiresses. And yet, even after she has defrauded Margaret and Ruth Vigers has been revealed as the 'naughty' Peter Quick, the characteristic slipperiness of Selina's narrative makes it difficult to 'read' her. Whereas Kohlke remains unsure about the extent of Selina's duplicity for example (Kohlke, 2004), Jenni Millbank suggests we feel 'sly admiration for her ingenuity' (Millbank, 2004: 166), and Jeanette King raises the possibility that Selina may have believed in her own powers, whether they were true or not, as a result of the pressure placed upon her by her benefactor, Mrs Brink (King, 2005: 89). Moreover, the text leaves open the possibility that Selina did have feelings for Margaret, but as Stephen speculates, 'fell foul of some sort of influence' (99), in the form of Ruth. Certainly, a passage from Selina's diary appears to suggest that Ruth is domineering and possibly coercive, even menacing, so that Selina cries (174–5). Ruth makes Selina pray 'May I be used' and proclaims 'my medium must do as she is bid' (261). Ruth's control may also extend to Selina's journal. Ruth is present as Selina writes some of the entries, suggesting that the diary may perform for Ruth rather than reveal Selina's interiority. Since Ruth also reads Margaret's journal, and passes information from it to Selina, Ruth passes in and out of the two diaries in a double sense, both as a figure barely glimpsed at the edge of the narrative frame (and yet ultimately the centre of it) and as the reader hovering at the edge of the page.

Victorian novels with multiple narrators typically explain how the various documents were compiled in their present form; they have a material presence within the world of the text. For example, Bram Stoker's gothic classic, *Dracula* (1897), explains that Mina compiled and typed the narrative (Stoker, 1993: 302) and, as we shall see, in *The Woman in White*, Hartright edits and arranges the various accounts (Collins, 1999: 9). However in *Affinity* the existence of these diaries cannot be accounted for diegetically. Lucie Armitt and Sarah Gamble observe that since Selina's journal is not physically present in the novel, in contrast to Margaret's which is kept in a drawer in her bedroom, 'it lacks a clear locus and sense of being in the possession of a named reader, [and therefore] it "floats" above the rest of the narrative, seemingly unshackled in space, despite being tied to time' (Armitt and Gamble, 2006: 154). Suggesting that when we step back, we realise that only Ruth could be in possession of the journal they astutely ask: 'The question is, do we possess her reading, or does she possess ours?' (ibid.). This points to the fact that we, of course, are also the readers hovering at the edge of the page of each diary, and, in turn, raises the puzzling question, unaccounted for in the narrative, of *how* we come to read these diaries. As we have seen, Selina's diary is never physically accounted for and Margaret's, we discover, is burnt, down to its very last page (348). Within the novel itself, these texts leave no discernible trace; they, like the desire they record, exist only in Waters', and her readers', imagination.

What the novel suggests, then, is that Waters has materialised the diaries for us so that they may retrospectively inhabit and expand the Victorian literary tradition, materialising experiences rendered invisible by the historical record. In fact, this is dramatised for us in the novel. When Margaret Prior first visits Millbank Prison in her role as Lady Visitor, she casts off convention and, instead of reading to the prisoners from the Bible, determines that she will listen to the women tell their own stories (22). The response of one of the wardens indicates the extent of Margaret's subversiveness: 'She looked at me then and said nothing' (22). Indeed, the convict women share in this silence: they have all but lost the ability to tell their stories, stumbling over their words (39). Or, rather, the legal system has made them tell their stories, and has coopted and told their stories for them, so many times that they seem divorced from the women themselves: 'the telling has made a kind of story of it, realer than memory but meaning nothing. I wish I could tell her that I know what such a story feels like' (40). Margaret knows what this feels like because she has witnessed the rewriting of her passionate history with Helen into a heteronormative narrative allows Helen to pass as an ideal of Victorian womanhood:

> 'Helen attended Mr Prior's lectures,' [Mrs Prior] said, 'and, Margaret meeting her there, she was brought to the house. She was always a great guest of ours after that, and always a favourite with Mr. Prior. Of course, we did not know – did we Priscilla – that it was all on Stephen's account that she came here. – You must not blush, Helen dear!' (102)

It is significant, here, that Helen's blush becomes an ephemeral sign which we are asked to read in the light of two contestatory explanations, and that Margaret's agency, as well as her passion, is entirely written out. Her role in bringing Helen to the Prior's residence is written into

the passive voice and her relationship to Helen obscured in a patriarchal narrative of fatherly friendship with Mr Prior and heterosexual
romance with Stephen. Reiterated enough times, it passes as truth, even
to Margaret who is notably not asked to corroborate the fiction: 'I have
heard the story told that way so many times, I am half-way to believing it myself' (103). Here, as for the women in the prison, memory
is oppositional to history; indeed, history – the officially legitimated
stories – replaces memory and comes to be seem more real. Waters
offers her neo-Victorian novels as a means to reverse this trajectory,
using fiction's power to imagine worlds as a means to reinvest these
alternative, silenced memories with a sense of reality. Her fictions are
a space inhabited by these memories; unreal, lacking the authority
bestowed by the law and by History, but nonetheless imbued with
meaning. Thus, Waters marginalises History from the outset of the novel
when, meaning to create a history of Millbank such as her father might
write, 'a book that was only a catalogue, a kind of list' (241), Margaret
finds that her father's preoccupation with dates, statistics and, tellingly,
with men and their concerns, is ill-fitted for telling the stories of the
women whom she is to visit at Millbank, the lives of whom the masculine narratives of the legal and penal system have already sifted and
classified: 'Villainous women, society has deemed them ...' (11). The
women's memories, their own, displaced, versions of their stories, are
excesses that masculinist history must excise for its 'straight' narrative.

Margaret herself describes her 'queer nature' that set her 'at odds with
the world and all its ordinary rules' (315–16). As the 'all' here implies,
Margaret's 'queerness' is not restricted to her sexuality. Margaret is an
intelligent woman who enjoys research and intellectual pursuits. While
her father was alive she could legitimately assist him but her intelligence
now marks her as transgressive of feminine norms (Caroll, 2007: 6):
'But people, I said, do not want cleverness – not in women, at least ...
it is only ladies like me that throw the whole system out and make it
stagger' (209). The two years since her father's death have also marked
her as a spinster, a category that, as Rachel Caroll notes, 'constructs
Margaret's difference as heterosexual failure; the agency potentially at
work in a refusal of gendered heterosexuality is rewritten as an inability
to accept a natural destiny' (Caroll, 2007: 5). In the Reading Room at
the British Museum Margaret realises that those 'who do not know me,
call me "madam" now, I noticed, instead of "miss". I have turned in two
years, from a girl into a spinster. There were many spinsters there to-day,
I think – more certainly, than I remember. Perhaps, however, it is the
same with spinsters as with ghosts; and one has to be of their ranks in

order to see them at all' (58). The categorising impulse that designates Margaret a failure within the heteronormative economy has no difficulty in naming the problem: Margaret is not simply an 'unmarried woman': she is a 'spinster'. It is the process of naming, or categorising Margaret's failure that renders her spectral.

In contrast, Margaret's lesbian desires resist categorisation and, as such, threaten her with spectrality of another order, that of the unnameable: 'we can see Margaret escaping "neat" definitions, defying categorisation; finding herself in an underworld of her own unnameableness' (Llewellyn, 1999: 210) since the narrative occurs, as we know from the dated diary entries, in 1873 and 1874, prior to the construction of homosexuality as an identity – distinct from homosexual acts or desire – in sexological discourses of the later nineteenth century (see Foucault, 1976). Terry Castle points to the silence surrounding the very existence of female homosexuality ascribed to the Victorian period, suggesting that 'behind such silence, one can detect an anxiety too severe to allow for articulation'. In literary representation, then, lesbian desire is displaced onto the figure of the ghost, the disembodied, decarnalised, 'apparitional lesbian' (Castle, 1993: 6). Yet the spectral metaphor which renders the lesbian immaterial becomes, in the hands of the lesbian writer, a means by which 'the lesbian body itself returns' (ibid.: 46–7). In *Affinity* and *Fingersmith* the spectral lesbian, while remaining spectral to the historical record, is given flesh in the world of the text.

Affinity is ambiguous about the extent of Margaret's knowledge about her own desire. On the one hand, presented with the knowledge that the Millbank women are sometimes given to 'palling-up' Margaret is 'disturbed ... to find that the term had *that* particular meaning and I hadn't known it' (67). On the other, although she does not recognise the term, she recognises the meaning behind it. Moreover, while we only gain glimpses of her prior relationship with Helen through apertures in Margaret's diary, she does record that she taunts Helen with the memory of their kisses which, she suggests, haunts her bed (204). Moreover, Helen responds by suggesting that she hadn't been brave enough 'not for what [Margaret] wanted' (ibid.), which seems to imply at the very least that Margaret had wanted Helen to resist marriage and children too and maintain some kind of passionate friendship with her. What is important here for the invention of a tradition of female homosexuality, however, is that Waters resists anachronistically attributing a lesbian identity, as we understand it today, to either Margaret or Selina. Rather, in the continuum she establishes between home, prison and séance, she constructs several spaces in which lesbian desire takes on multiple and diverse forms and in which, as a result, female homosocial bonds are subjected to varying degrees of surveillance.

In *Affinity*, Millbank Prison, with its 'ghastly towers and yellow walls' (75) and its 'dreadful *clamour*' of gates 'swung on grinding hinges, and slammed and bolted' and even the empty passages that 'echo with the sounds of other gates, and other locks and bolts, distant and near' (10), rises out of the London pall with dramatic effect, a reworking of the eighteenth-century gothic castle that now houses a panoptic machine, and stands, moreover, in the middle of London. Nestled on the banks of the Thames, it can be seen from the top floor of Margaret's wealthy home in Chelsea (342). Its gothicism affects Margaret's nerves. Upon her first visit she notes that one must 'walk along a narrowing strip of gravel, and feel the walls on either side of one advancing' (8), and she is afraid that Mr Shillitoe is 'in league' with her mother, 'and means to keep me on the wards' (29). If this is our first glimpse of Margaret's incipient hysteria, it is also the first intimation of the continuum the novel constructs between home and domicile. Its two primary settings, the prison and the middle-class home, are constructed as sites governed by a pervasive, disciplinary panopticism which attempts, but ultimately fails, to police a series of socially constructed boundaries.

The boundary between prison and home is unstable and must be reiterated, insisted upon: 'Your place is here. Your place is here ... You are not Mrs Browning, Margaret – as much as you would like to be. You are not, in fact, Mrs Anybody. You are only *Miss Prior*. And your place – how often must I say it? – Your place is here, at your mother's side' (252). The prison seeps into the home via Margaret's thoughts (30), dreams (32) and the eagerness of dinner guests or sordid details of her prison visits (32, 97). The boundary between prison and domicile is permeated also by Ruth, who conducts a regular traffic of letters, objects and information between them. It is Margaret herself who performs the final collapse of the boundary between the two when, in Ruth's vacated room, 'a room that held *nothing*, like the cells at Millbank, a room that had made nothing a substance, a texture, or a scent' (341), she repeats or doubles the breaking out she has witnessed at Millbank, ripping sheets with her teeth, breaking the bowl and beating the jug, tearing clothes (342) in a frenzy of pain at Selina's duplicity. Moreover, the panopticism of Millbank is replicated in the surveillance of Margaret in her upper middle-class home, in what Jenni Millbank calls a 'continuum of imprisonment' (Millbank, 2004: 174). The watchful gaze permeates the novel, implicating Margaret (102) Helen (101) and Selina (117) and, in the clearest link to the disciplinary structures of

Millbank, Margaret's mother: 'careful as I have been – still and secret and silent as I have been in my high room – [Mother] has been watching me, as Miss Ridley watches, and Miss Haxby' (223). The continuum of imprisonment, from prison to domicile, is epitomised by Margaret's near slip, when she almost calls one of the matrons 'Mother' (267) and by her recurring vision of her own ongoing imprisonment, in which she sits beside her gaoler mother wearing the 'mud-brown dress' that is the Millbank uniform (274).

Having suggested a continuum between prison and middle-class home, the novel then links both to the spirit medium's séance. When Selina is in 'the darks' Margaret imitates her experience, crouching in the darkest corner of her closet, feeling her corset bind her tight: 'Then I knew where I was. I was with *her*, and close to her, so close ... I felt the cell about me, the jacket upon me. And yet I seemed to feel my eyes bound, too, with bands of silk. And at my throat there was a velvet collar' (257). Here, in her own home, Margaret feels as though she is in Selina's place in the prison and then, seamlessly, or simultaneously, also takes her place in the spirit medium's cabinet. The séance, like the prison, is 'a female world-within-a-(patriarchal)-world' (Millbank, 2004: 161) governed by its own rules and with its own cultural features. It is a site where the transgression of one set of boundaries – criminal/legal, this world/the next world – invites the transgression of other boundaries. The prison and the séance each emerge as transgressive of heterosexual boundaries or, more specifically, exist as spaces in-between heteronormative behaviour and its shadowy, unnamed and unnameable other. Waters has suggested in an interview that because it emphasised the spirit over the body, spiritualism 'offered gay members a different discourse of gender and sexuality' (qtd. in Parker, 2008: 10). Thus, the women who come to the sittings 'think kisses from Peter Quick don't count' (218) and Selina terrifies Margaret with the image of her father's spirit unclothed and sexless in the spirit world (210). A 'naughty' spirit, Peter Quick flirts with the women present while ignoring or mocking the men. Whereas the isolation of Millbank makes the women's 'palling-up' a necessarily disembodied practice, the flirtation in the séance and, even more, the private sittings, imbue spiritualism with a *frisson* of ambiguous sexual energy. The sittings are a space in which young women come to be 'developed'. They receive Peter's kisses and undress and embrace Selina, all the while ascribing to a doctrine of sexlessness in the spirit world. As Tatiana Kontou observes, this is, most of all, a theatrical space, in which Selina finds 'a way of expressing or, more accurately, *performing* her passion for Ruth' (Kontou, 2009: 195, original emphasis). The novel suggests that the discourse of spiritualism may have provided Victorian women with both a space and a language with which to speak the unspeakable. The spiritualist notion of 'affinity' provides Margaret with words to identify and communicate her desire. Selina tells her that 'we are the same, you and I. We have been cut, two halves, from the same piece of shining matter. Oh, I could say, *I love you* ... But my sprit does not love yours – it is *entwined* with it. Our flesh does not love: our flesh is the same, and long to leap to itself. It must do that, or wither! *You are like me'* (275). She then adds a more carnal emphasis: 'Now you know why you are drawn to me – why your flesh comes creeping to mine, and what it comes for. Let it creep, Aurora. Let it come to me, let it creep' (276). Yet despite Selina's protestations against mere love, Margaret responds more conventionally: 'I love you, and I cannot give you up' (280).

As much as the novel maintains the dramatic tension, refusing to reveal Selina's fraudulence until the final pages, Margaret's dark ending is gothically prefigured at several places in the narrative, not least in Selina's claim 'you are like me'. Here Selina is only voicing what Margaret has believed she has felt, and even seen. Glimpsing Selina's plait of hair, placed on her own pillow by Ruth, Margaret is 'frozen in fright', believing that she is looking at herself. The doubling of Margaret and Selina portends Margaret's death, as an encounter with the gothic doppelgänger must. She awakens after this encounter with herself/Selina 'as one might wake from death, still gripped by darkness, still sucked at by the soil' (258). Again, after she has a vision of her doubled, future self as an ageing spinster with her querulous mother for company, Margaret recalls a story her father was told as a boy and repeated to her: 'invalids should not gaze at their own reflections, for fear their souls would fly into the glass and kill them' (202). Margaret is an invalid herself, dosed with chloral and laudanum for her 'nervous disorder'. Immediately after Selina has claimed their affinity – itself a doubling declaration – and Margaret has responded with her declaration of love, this image redoubles: 'then I saw her eye, and it was black, and my own face swam in it, pale as a pearl. And then, it was like Pa and the looking-glass. My soul left me – I felt it fly from me and lodge in her' (280). Selina becomes Margaret's mirror image here, but rather than reflect Margaret back to herself she subsumes her. Selina must devour Margaret to gain her own freedom, both literally, from Millbank, and figuratively, from English conventions. Margaret is the means by which she can flee to Italy and live the life Margaret wants for herself. Parker observes that while Margaret 'remains very much stuck inside the Gothic narrative,

Selina Dawes evolves beyond the traditional Gothic plot. Although she receives a realist explanation at the novel's conclusion, Selina seems still to elude the narrative itself; the personal account of her crime remains frustratingly ambiguous' (Parker, 2008: 10).

For this is invented, but not alternative, history. And this is not a narrative of liberation. Waters' fiction does not project a fairytale world of lesbian desire that managed to thrive despite the odds – unless we wish to locate this story with Selina and Ruth. Seeking to invent a tradition of lesbian desire, Waters does not flinch from the knowledge that for many, perhaps most Victorian women, this would have been a painful reality in a culture committed to its impossibility. Moreover, while lesbian desire is central to the novel, it is clearly positioned within a matrix of other constraints, particularly those of class and gender, which prove, for Margaret, insurmountable. *Affinity* gives us 'a Victorian dystopia: its narrative spirals downward into a fugue of depression along with its middle-class protagonist, portraying at every class level a female world of large and small tyrannies and injustices, where even the women who escape are bound together by forms of domination and submission' (Kaplan, 2007: 112).

Although she invents, rather than restores, Waters works within the knowledge we do have – that lesbian desire was hidden, silenced, perhaps violently excised, so that there is no trace – and replicates this in her novels. When Margaret burns her diary she performs the excision of lesbian desire from the record. Or, as Kohlke puts it, by dramatising Margaret's 'collusion in her own silencing as both historian and historical subject, *Affinity* enacts the moment when 'transgression is disciplined and silence re-imposed' (Kohlke, 2004: 162). The novel dramatises and embodies lesbian desire, giving it a fleshly form and portrays, too, its excision from the historical record, the reason for its invisibility.

While Selina and Ruth escape to Italy, Margaret realises her future lies in imprisonment, either within Millbank or within her life as a spinster, or at the bottom of the Thames. She chooses the Thames. As readers we accept this dramatic ending, have been schooled to half-expect it, according to the conventions of the gothic. Paradoxically, the fictional apparatus works to authenticate Margaret's sense of her options, as well as to legitimise her choice. With her diary burnt, she leaves behind only her letter to Helen, which explains her decision to run away with Selina, though without mentioning her name or naming her desire. Fittingly, this leap towards her double, which must also presage death, reads equally as a suicide note. Margaret's queer desire is written out of history and sinks without a trace.

III

I have positioned *Affinity* largely in relation to gothic, though it should become clear in what follows that it also draws upon the sensation novel, a genre partly derived from gothic. Particularly, each of these genres was closely connected to representing transgressive women; women who did not conform to Victorian ideals of feminine domesticity, especially its governance of female sexuality. What was particularly shocking about the Victorian sensation novel was that it combined the transgressive elements of gothic romance with literary realism. This was the genre's defining feature: 'the violent yoking of romance and realism, traditionally the two contradictory modes of literary perception ... The sensation novel ... strains both modes to the limit, disrupting the accepted balance between them' (Hughes, 1980: 16). Like the Fens in *Waterland*, the depiction of Briar in *Fingersmith* shifts between fairytale and realism, signalling the blend of romance and realism. Gentleman first describes it with fairytale inexactness as 'a certain out-of-the-way sort of house, near a certain out-of-the-way kind of village, some miles from London' (23), then rather more dramatically as 'a damnable place: two hundred years old, and dark, and draughty, and mortgaged to the roof – which is leaky by the way' (24). It is Sue that speaks its more prosaic reality: 'They lived west of London, out Maidenhead-way, near a village named Marlow, and in a house they called Briar' (33). Yet, when Sue first sees Briar both the fairytale and the mundane vanish as it rises gothically, 'vast and straight and stark out of the woolly fog, with all its windows black or shuttered, and its walls with a dead kind of ivy clinging to them, and a couple of its chimneys sending up threads of a feeble-looking grey smoke' (57).

The conjunction of realism and romance was performed in the way sensation fiction drew upon the sensational journalism of the 1860s. In its use of newspaper descriptions of crimes and courtroom dramas for its complex plots, the genre, as I described above, was a hybrid of the documentary and the fantastic, of fact and fiction. This hybridity provoked particular anxiety because of the genre's representation of femininity. Women featured prominently in the genre as characters and as its authors and readers: 'Many, perhaps most, of the reviewers' objections to the genre, and their anxieties about it, derive from their perception of it as a form written by women, about women and, on the whole, for women', both in terms of the 'fast women it depicted and because of the kinds of female experience it portrayed' (Pykett, 1992: 32). One of the features that distinguishes it from gothic is its representation of women as implicated in the crimes it portrays: 'For whatever reasons, the heroine of the sensation novel has become enmeshed in a sordid tangle of crime, blackmail, and seduction; she has become a participant, however unwilling, as well as merely a victim' (Hughes 1980: 44). Sensation novels, Pykett argues, 'transformed the representation of women' (Pykett, 1992: 32). Women in sensation novels were often not only 'improper' but downright criminal, as Mary Elizabeth Braddon's eponymous heroine, Lady Audley, exemplifies. The genre's depiction of transgressive, even criminal, women meant that it was charged with being paradoxically 'both characteristically feminine, and profoundly unfeminine, or even anti-feminine'. Since there was disbelief attached to its representation of women and women's experiences, a sense that here it violated reality, the genre was often seen as a failure of realism (ibid.: 33).

The devil was in the detail. As we saw in Chapter 4, critics objected to the way these novels depicted and dwelt upon bodily urges and sensations: 'the proliferation of sensuous detail and the detailed representation of physical sensation' (Pykett, 1992: 34). In particular, the sensation novel focused this detail on the female body, which it presented seductively, and on women's sexual response: 'In this respect sensation novels were doubly transgressive. They did not simply portray women as sexual beings; they also dwelt on the details of women's sexual response in a "very fleshly and unlovely record"' (ibid.: Pykett quotes Victorian novelist Margaret Oliphant). The sensation novel read women's bodies and *'produced a reading in the body'* (Pykett, 1992: 35). It acted on the nerves and replicated the desires it represented in the bodies of the women who read them. In fact, since women comprised much of the sensation novel's readership, Pykett argues that the effect of the highly sexualised narratives that invited the readers' gaze to linger on the female body is 'a representation of female sexuality as voyeuristic spectacle, which offered *both* male and female readers pleasurable images of female erotic power' (Pykett, 1992: 101, emphasis mine). In what follows I want to suggest that Waters harnesses the transgressive power of a genre associated with female flesh to re-embody the spectralised figure of the lesbian.

Like *Affinity*, *Fingersmith* performs the sensation novel's inscription of the domestic sphere as a site of danger characterised by threatened and actual incarceration, typical of urban gothic and sensation narratives. The novel draws heavily upon Wilkie Collins' *The Woman in White* (1860) in which a young heiress, Laura Fairlie, is robbed of her identity and wrongfully committed to an asylum by her husband. As Jenny

Bourne-Taylor argues, Collins' novel 'breaks down any stable division between the resonances of "home" and "asylum" as places of safety and danger' (Bourne-Taylor, 1988: 99). This permeable boundary is literally transgressed in *Fingersmith*, which doubles the asylum and the manor house, so each is a spectralised form of the other. Whereas Briar is rendered as a gothic stronghold, the asylum in which Sue is confined used to be 'an ordinary gentleman's house', with pictures on the walls, rugs on the floors. Upon realising that 'now it had been made over to madwomen' Sue finds that 'somehow the idea was worse and put me in more of creep than if the place had looked like a dungeon after all' (408). What Sue is yet to realise – or, at least, is yet to confide to the reader – is that her own home, at Lant Street, is also a place of danger. She has misinterpreted Mrs Sucksby's close care for her and her apparent refusal to 'put a price to' her (11). If Mrs Sucksby appears to be 'careful' (13) of Sue for seventeen years it is because she covets her fortune. Sue must neither marry nor come to harm, nor be charged with thieving and imprisoned. The fact of her imprisonment is made visible when Sue and Maud are switched, and Maud is actually incarcerated at Lant Street.

It is in Maud that home and asylum are most strongly linked since an asylum is her home until she is eleven. By the time her uncle claims her it has so shaped her understanding that she believes there must be lunatics hidden away at Briar (184). There are no lunatics, only cruel servants and Mr Lilly who is characterised by a kind of monomania, an obsessive single-mindedness about his Index of pornography. Maud links her uncle's 'cruel patience', and his perverse monomania, to that displayed by the women at the madhouse, observing that '[h]ad they been gentlemen and rich – instead of women – then perhaps they would have passed as scholars and commanded staffs' (194). Recognising that this 'dark' mania fills her uncle's house Maud says 'I cease struggling at all, and surrender myself to its viscid, circular currents' (194). Whipped, locked in the icehouse and psychologically tormented by her uncle and his staff, it is here, in her home at Briar, that she is transformed into a 'curiosity', discussed in 'the shady bookshops and publishers' houses in London and Paris' (224). Scratching a hole in the yellow paint that covers the windows of her uncle's study and peering out, Maud describes herself as 'like a curious wife at the keyhole of a cabinet of secrets. But I am inside the cabinet, and long to get out ... ' (204, ellipsis in original).

This situation casts Maud as the archetypal gothic heroine, locked away with an oppressive, patriarchal figure who 'keeps her close' (25). Sue, encouraged by Gentleman, 'reads' her in this way throughout her first narrative: 'She was an infant, a chick, a pigeon that knew nothing' (66). She reads her this way, and encourages the reader to do likewise, right up until the final line of the first part of the book when she addresses her own, and the reader's, mistake: 'You thought her a pigeon. Pigeon my arse. That bitch knew everything. She had been in on it from the start' (173). Addressing the reader in this way emphasises that we, too, have been reading Maud in terms of a set of narrative conventions. The discovery, as Maud begins her own narrative, that she is cruel, wilful and tormenting rather than docile and sweet shifts our terms of reference. Now Sue, because she is docile and sweet and easily led, switches places with Maud, literally and figuratively, to become the heroine locked away for convenience in a private asylum. In this doubling and switching of Sue and Maud, the passive, gothic heroine is transformed into the woman of sensation, victimised by an overbearing patriarchal figure but also criminally implicated herself. Both Sue and Maud are willing to dupe and incarcerate the other. Maud seeks freedom from her uncle's tyranny; Sue attempts to please her pseudo-mother, Mrs Sucksby. She, too, is responding to tyranny, though it differs in kind. In contrast to the conventional sensation novel, neither *Affinity* nor *Fingersmith* offers the example of ideal(ised) femininity as a moral compass to guide our responses to the heroines. All Waters' central female characters are flawed in ways that make it difficult to decide where and how to apportion blame.

While the three first-person narratives that make up the novel, communicated by characters within the story itself, make the narrative structure appear similar to that of *Affinity*, these, unlike diaries, are retrospective accounts of the novel's action. The suspense and mystery imparted in Sue's and Maud's narratives results not from the narrators' position in the middle of events as they unfold but rather from their position beyond the end of the novel's plot. They already know the whole story. Jenny Bourne-Taylor's observation about narrative construction in *The Woman of White* holds true for *Fingersmith*: 'each individual utterance gains meaning from the way it has been placed in the chain, which is presented as continual progression but is in reality a continual, contradictory process of reappropration and redefinition' (Bourne-Taylor, 1988: 100). The very form of the sensation novel thus installs a 'hermeneutics of suspicion' (Cvetkovich, 1992: 72) and *Affinity* and *Fingersmith* embody the very process of reading for shadows that I attributed to the lesbian historical novelist, including Waters, above. As Waters immersed herself in Victorian literature she read it for the shadows at the margins of the page, hypothesising the possibility of a lesbian reader and/or writer. Waters comments that when she read a lot of Victorian pornography while preparing to write her first neo-Victorian novel, *Tipping the Velvet* (1998), she became curious about whether women secretly, invisibly produced or read it:

> I was interested in thinking about what that might offer me, as a modern lesbian feminist writer; but also thinking about [it] historically, how pornography might have worked for the women who read it or the women who wrote it, the women who were involved in the business side of it, women in the sex industry. (Dennis, 2008: 43–4)

Since there is no evidence pointing toward any specific female-authored Victorian pornography this remains a matter to 'speculate about' (ibid.: 44); these imagined readers and writers remain spectral until Waters brings them to novelistic life.

Waters positions her own readers in this way, reading for shadows. We read Sue's carefully constructed account perhaps barely glimpsing the intensity of Maud's feelings for Sue. Upon reading Maud's account of the same events we necessarily revise our first reading in the light of new knowledge and a different perspective. Upon a second reading, we recognise intimations of Maud's feelings in Sue's narrative. Each narrative is quite coy, particularly when describing their sexual encounter. Each attributes more agency to the other woman (141–2; 282–3). Again, Waters is careful not to anachronistically attribute a lesbian identity to Maud and Sue. Maud suggests that her own recognition of desire comes when Gentleman recognises it within her: 'in his face I see how much I want her' (274). Whereas Mariaconcetta Costantini argues that Sue's and Maud's love story 'is opposed by a corrupted, hypocritical society' (Constantini, 2006: 18), a reasonable assumption about the representation of lesbian desire in a (faux)Victorian novel, it is rather more notable that they really meet with no resistance. Gentleman, who may be homoerotically inclined too, is only amused, or perhaps even mildly titillated (276, 277), provided this unexpected shift will not disrupt his plot. What Constantini describes as Waters' 'lesbian militancy' is difficult to detect in the novels themselves. She suggests that Waters' protagonists are rather too knowing about their lesbian identity. However, in *Fingersmith*, in which she has no lesbian models to follow, Sue struggles to recognise the nature of her feelings for Maud:

> But, here was a curious thing. The more I tried to give up thinking of her, the more I said to myself, 'She's nothing to you', the harder I tried to pluck the idea of her out of my heart, the more she stayed

there ... It was as if there had come between us, without my knowing, a kind of thread. It pulled me to her, wherever she was. It was like – *It's like you love her*, I thought. (FS: 136)

Thus, at first Sue can only interpret her feelings for Maud through a heteronormative frame. When they make love, Maud colludes in this displacement, as they cast their sexual encounter in terms of her immi- nent wedding night and her feigned lack of sexual knowledge. Sue tells Maud that her body, which is responding to Sue's touch, 'wants Mr Rivers' (Gentleman). Maud, too, throughout her narrative, cannot interpret Sue's actions toward her. She thinks that Sue's diffidence indi- cates that she knows that Maud is plotting against her (279).

As our narrators, Sue and Maud are, like Margaret and Selina, 'at once reliable and unreliable' (Bourne-Taylor, 1992: 100). Indeed, in the sensation novel multiple narrators perform the same function as the diarist: 'suspense and excitement are generated and maintained by the way that the reader's view is limited at any one time to the per- spective of each individual narrator whose testimonies are at once reliable and unreliable, and whose means of making sense of the world needs to be continually questioned' (Bourne-Taylor, 1992: 100). However, as I have suggested, their accounts are retrospective and so deliberately foreshadow and misinterpret events in a way that diary narratives cannot. When Sue describes her first meeting with Mr Lilly, she claims that 'to describe him as I saw him then, is to tell everything' (75) but of course her description of him, then, fails to 'tell' the most important aspect of Mr Lilly because it refuses to disclose the nature of his library. Indeed, Sue, particularly, addresses us as readers, drawing us in and around to her way of seeing things: 'You are waiting for me to begin my story. Perhaps I was waiting, then. But my story had already started – I was only like you, and didn't know it' (14). She provides clues throughout her narrative that this is part of a much more com- plicated plot: 'We were thinking of secrets. Real secrets, and snide. Too many to count. When I try now to sort out who knew what and who knew nothing, who knew everything and who was a fraud, I have to stop and give it up, it makes my head spin' (110). And throughout her narrative she repeats the phrase 'I thought' (130, 116, 175) to mark out the difference between her knowledge 'then' during the events them- selves, and 'now', which is the temporal location of her writing.

This sense of multiple temporal locations as sites of different types of knowledge is complicated further in Maud's own narrative which, in contrast to Sue's, uses present tense, though the account is clearly retrospective: 'I have said it was my uncles' custom, occasionally to invite interested gentlemen to the house, to take a supper with us and, later, hear me read. He does so now' (205). Maud's account creates the impression that she, and we, are in the midst of events. It also, perhaps, heightens our sense of her confusion when Gentleman takes her to Lant Street and she begins to understand the true author of the plot in which she had thought she had agency. We shrink, as she shrinks, from Mrs Sucksby as she 'wets her lips', and we struggle, as Maud struggles, to interpret Mrs Sucksby's gaze which is 'terribly close and eager' (312). The present tense adds to the immediacy of sensation, particularly at the moment when the secret of Maud's parentage is elliptically, but dramatically, revealed: 'all at once I see her face – the brown of her own eye, and her own pale cheek – and her lip, that is plump and must, I understand suddenly, must once have been plumper ... she wets her mouth. "Dear girl," she says. "My own, my own dear girl". She hesitates another moment; then speaks, at last' (392). Whereas Sue's narrative creates suspense by foreshadowing later knowledge, Maud's is dramatic and immediate. Like Margaret's and Selina's narratives, there is no explanation as to how we come to have these narratives, why Sue and Maud wrote them and for whom. Diegetically they do not exist. While this novel does not explore spiritualism as *Affinity* does, these narratives, too, appear as materialised spirits, conjured by Waters.

As I've suggested above, this contrasts with the preamble to *The Woman in White* which emphasises the inability of the legal and judicial system to detect and prosecute all crimes and offers the unfolding narrative as a pseudo-legal document in one such case. Moreover, in contrast to Laura Fairlie whose narrative does not number among the assembled accounts, though she is at the centre of the plot, Maud and Sue tell us the entire story in their own words. This is in part facilitated by the key difference between the Victorian and the neo-Victorian texts. The Victorian sensation novel is the proto-detective novel; a male figure such as Walter Hartright (*The Woman in White*) or Robert Audley (*Lady Audley's Secret (1862)*) typically becomes obsessed with disclosing secrets, righting wrongs and, ultimately, restoring (patriarchal) order with the zeal of the monomaniac. As the closest relative to both Sue and Maud (as Sue's biological uncle and Maud's guardian), Mr Lilly would conventionally be the most likely figure to adopt this role. However his monomania is directed elsewhere and he exhibits no interest at all in recovering Maud. The detective figure is notably missing from this version of the sensation novel. There is no 'heart-right' man to pursue the truth and rectify wrongs on behalf of the heroines, demonstrating 'what a Woman's patience can endure, and what a Man's resolution can achieve' (Collins, 1999 (1860): 9).

I want to suggest that it is the very absence of the male protector/ detective figure that *enables* Maud's and Sue's happy ending. With no man to act as father/brother/husband and pursue justice on their behalf (and indeed, no one to pursue justice against, since Mrs Sucksby and Gentleman are both dead), Maud and Sue are beyond the patriarchal gaze and, as such, are free to create a female space that exists outside the order provided by law. Significantly, when Sue returns to Briar at the end of the novel, the great clock which tolls regularly through-out the novel while Maud and Sue live there under the authority of Mr Lilly, has ceased to chime. Sue notes: 'It seemed quieter inside the walls, than it had been before – quieter, and queer' (538). The use of 'queer' here reinforces the idea that the clock had symbolised norma-tive, patriarchal, masculinised time, as well as taking the measure of Mr Lilly's tyranny. In the absence of the chiming clock, the silence con-firms Sue's impression that '[i]t seemed like a house not meant for people but for ghosts' (538). She is right. She moves through the house mak-ing 'no sound, and might have glided – as if *I* were ghost. The thought was queer' (540). Here the novel links lesbian desire to its apparitional status but construes this in a positive light. It is Sue's and Maud's very invisibility, their utter lack of men to act on their behalf and restore order, that enables them to reunite in the newly feminised space of Briar. If, as Pykett argues, the cottage beside the Thames in which Lady Audley finds herself exiled as punishment for her crimes at the end of *Lady Audley's Secret* is a world purged of the 'improper feminine of illegitimate desire, passion and French novels' (see Pykett, 1992: 105), then this sensational trajectory for the transgressive woman is rewritten at the end of *Fingersmith*. The Thameside cottage becomes a dilapidated Thameside mansion, and it, too, is a 'private feminized space'. However, in contrast to the cottage, it is a space in which the 'improper' feminine reigns, along with illegitimate desire, passion and French (though not only French) pornography. Whereas Victorian sensation novels tended to domesticate the improper feminine, in *Fingersmith* the improper feminine becomes the new domestic. And while the gothic space of the manor house is, in Briar's disintegration and its sense of being out-of-time, perhaps even *more* gothic, it has been reclaimed as a site for this tradition of lesbian desire. The novel closes upon Maud and Sue having rejected their inheritance – and thus the model of reproductive heteronormativity on which it relies – in favour of earning their own income producing pornography. At this moment Sue and Maud literally embody the female readers of Victorian pornography that Waters had imagined as accessing and using pornography for the own ends. If we are to take the fact of Sue's authorship of two of the retrospective narratives seriously, then becoming a producer of pornography has taught Sue to read and write. This is particularly empowering because, earlier in the novel, her inability to do either contributes to her entrapment; she cannot discover that Maud is less innocent than she seems since she cannot discover the nature of Mr Lilly's books (69) and when locked in the asylum or inability to write exacerbates Dr Christie's impression that she is mad (430).

Waters has suggested that in *Fingersmith* she 'wanted to take all the classic scenarios and tropes of sensation fiction and to take a different path through them, pursuing lesbian attraction, and making them mean different things' (Waters, undated). She uses the generic structure of sensation fiction, associated with the depiction of 'improper' femininity to give flesh to the apparitional lesbian of the historical record and literary tradition. At the same time, she dramatises the very process by which lesbian desire becomes invisible to history and fiction. Diegetically, Sue and Maud are ghosts made flesh, their desire sensuously depicted. Extra-diegetically they are the invisible women whose lesbian desires can only be – and yet must be – conjectured.

Thus, Waters exploits the 'generic repertoires' (Wesseling, 1991: 18) of gothic and sensation as an authenticating strategy for her faux-Victorian fiction. Her use of popular Victorian genres that are associated with transgressive women – and transgressive representation of women's sexuality – creates a space in which a tradition of lesbian desire in the Victorian period can be invented. Perhaps paradoxically, given that the gothic is often associated with demonising transgressive sexuality, and the sensation novel with domesticating it, the play of difference and similarity (Jones, 2009: 129) between Victorian and neo-Victorian uses of these genres creates as a space in which Waters can sympathetically explore how lesbian desire might have been experienced prior to its essentialisation by late-Victorian medical discourse. In both *Affinity* and *Fingersmith*, offering no diegetic explanation for the existence of these first-person accounts of same-sex desire consolidates the sense that Waters offers her narratives as spectral additions to our cultural memory of the Victorian, transforming and extending it by focusing on invisible desires and practises. Her novels ventriloquise Victorian gothic and sensation fiction, grafting the representation of lesbian experience onto their generic structure and transforming it, in order to make this invented history memorable. In this way, Waters' novels participate in the 'political charge' of lesbian imagining, inventing memory where none exists.

6

'The alluring patina of loss': Photography, Memory, and Memory Texts in *Sixty Lights* and *Afterimage*

[I long] to have such a memorial of every being dear to me in the world. It is not merely the likeness which is precious in such cases – but the association and the sense of nearness involved in the thing ... the fact of the very shadow of the person lying there fixed forever! It is the very sanctification of portraits I think – and it is not at all monstrous in me to say, what my brothers cry out against so vehemently, that I would rather have such a memorial of one I dearly loved, than the noblest artist's work ever produced.

(Elizabeth Barrett Browning in a letter to
Mary Russell Mitford, 1843)

Photography is an elegiac art, a twilight zone ... All photographs are *memento mori*. To take a photograph is to participate in another person's (or thing's) mortality. Precisely by slicing out this moment and freezing it, all photograph's testify to time's relentless melt.

(Susan Sontag, *On Photography*, 1977)

Writing about historical recollection and material culture, Elizabeth Edwards asserts that 'photographs are perhaps the most ubiquitous and insistent focus of nineteenth- and twentieth-century memory' (Edwards, 1999: 221). It is fitting, then, that many contemporary historical novelists return to the Victorian origins of photography to explore history, memory and the Victorian era.[1] They dramatise the value that attaches to photography as a memorial medium, its promise, as Elizabeth Barrett Browning suggests in the epigraph above, to erase distance, to

143

cheat time, and allow access to the past, the resuscitation of the dead. Their novels return to the inception of photography in the early Victorian period when it was greeted as a ghostly medium that could supplement memory, function as time's receptacle, and pledge to remember in the face of loss. This chapter examines Gail Jones' *Sixty Lights* and Helen Humphreys' *Afterimage*, which exemplify the way in which, for many neo-Victorian novels, memory, history and fiction come together in the trope of the photograph. Employing a lexicon of haunting and spectrality to represent the photographic medium, *Sixty Lights* and *Afterimage* are concerned with recognising the persistence of the past in a present cut off from linear models of inheritance and memory, symbolised by the dead mother. Ghostliness becomes a metaphor for a past both lost and, paradoxically, perpetuated, endlessly returned or repeated in the present. The mediums for this haunting are photographs, maps, bodies and, importantly, novels and stories. Contrary to the prevailing notion that we can only know the past through its documentary traces, these novels deploy the ghostly figure of photography in order to posit the persistence of the past as uncanny repetition and as embodied memory.

Significantly, the novels use the language of spectrality to also position themselves as revenant. They resuscitate, or, to use Hilary Schor's evocative phrase, 'ghostwrite' (Schor, 2000) Victorian literary texts and mediate Victorian culture in the present. This chapter connects the vocabulary of photography as a memorial and ghostly trace with that of memory discourse, particularly as it is deployed by scholars such as Patrick Hutton and Pierre Nora. Particularly, it makes use of the distinction between history as willed recollection, and memory as unconscious repetition, to explicate the novels' exploration of the persistence of the past and the ways in which we can recognise it. The chapter closes by considering the implications of these historical fictions as 'memory texts' (Jones, 2005) arguing that they are not, primarily, concerned with metafictional or metahistorical reflections. Rather they offer us shards of the Victorian past, a family album of images and repetitions, mimicking the features of memory as it is depicted in the novels. These novels invoke the Victorian past as a cultural memory, our heritage and inheritance, and the origin of features of our own, contemporary culture, in which the period continues to exist as repetition.

I

When it emerged on the Victorian scene, photography was greeted with excitement and widespread enthusiasm, stemming from its promise of objectivity, its capacity for verisimilitude. Eschewing the narratives of photography's origins which focus upon the invention of chemical and technological processes,[2] Geoffrey Batchen attributes the invention of photography to the desire for objective knowledge, a desire that, by the nineteenth century, had become a social imperative.[3] The camera's mechanical 'eye' functioned as a guarantee of its objectivity, establishing what Scott McQuire has called its 'aura of neutrality' (McQuire, 1998: 124) and inveterately tightening the knot which had connected seeing and knowing for centuries.[4] The unerring camera stands in place of the erring human subject, guarantor of authenticity and accuracy. As Helen Groth suggests, 'the photographic image appeared to manifest the mimetic ideal of the arrested moment rendered transparent by the observer's gaze' (Groth, 2003: 7). This 'transparency' implies that the photograph provides knowledge beyond its own image, that image and understanding are coeval and power accrues to the photograph as an unauthored representation.

Such was the power of a medium professed to be 'synonymous with fidelity' (McQuire, 1998: 13) that histories of photography have often described its advent in terms of a transformative rupture. For example, McQuire argues that 'the invention of the camera marks a threshold beyond which representation is itself irreversibly transformed' and that 'belief in a mimetic power *beyond all previous jurisdiction* constitutes the camera's codex' (ibid). And Roland Barthes discusses the advent of photography as an epistemic rupture that transformed the individual's relationship to history in similar terms to those deployed by Hayden White in discussing the impact of the French Revolution and Napoleonic wars. As we saw in Chapter 1, these events are thought to have transformed history into a mass experience and to have prompted the realisation that the individual is intimately affected by history. For Barthes, photography transformed the perception of history so that it no longer took 'the form of myth' but was granted 'evidentiary power' via the camera's lens (Barthes, 1984: 87). Photography was invested with the capacity to stand in the place of individual memory and substantiate events. It made history visible to the ordinary individual. Moreover, Barthes interprets the democratising effect of photography upon portraiture, formerly the privilege of the wealthy, as granting each individual the capacity to see 'oneself (differently from in a mirror): *on the scale of History*' (ibid.: 12, emphasis mine).

The nineteenth-century invention and popularisation of photography complicates and transforms thinking about historiography, too. The photograph's intimation of unmediated knowledge and absolute veracity, its perceived incapacity to lie, promised itself to positivist history's project of depicting the past 'as it really happened', pledging to provide ultimate representation and authentication for the historical record. Indeed, photography held this promise well into the second half of the twentieth century, even as challenges to the assumed objectivity of historiography were beginning to emerge in history theory. Writing about his own discovery of nineteenth-century photographs as historical sources, Raphael Samuel observes that, for himself as for other social historians during the 1960s and 1970s,

> the discovery of photography was over-determined ... It corresponded to the search for 'human' documents ... It also seemed to answer to our insatiable appetite for 'immediacy', allowing us to become literally, as well as metaphorically, eyewitnesses to the historical event. It also promised a new intimacy between historians and their subject matter, allowing us if not to eavesdrop on the past ... at least to see it, in everyday terms, 'as it was'. (Samuel, 1994: 319–20)

Samuel argues that the discovery of these seemingly transparent historical sources revitalised the nineteenth and twentieth centuries as research interests for historians. Green-Lewis, too, partly attributes our current fascination with the Victorians to their continuing visibility in photographs: 'The Victorians are visually real to us because they have a documentary assertiveness unavailable to persons living before the age of the camera' (Green-Lewis, 2000: 31).

For the idea of the photograph as unauthored, as pure image, is one that slides easily into the idea of the photograph as an object that stands in for that which it represents. More than a mirror, the photograph, because of its 'invisible umbilicus joining image and referent' (McQuire, 1998: 15), was, and is, conflated with its object: 'a photograph stood not only for but occasionally as the very object itself (Green-Lewis, 1996: 61–2). Indeed, more than having its eye 'fixed on the past' (Barthes, 1984: 87), the photograph is thought to inhere the past in a unique way. In a sense this is obvious; the actual material photograph did originate in a moment in the past. However, the 'symbiotic connection' (McQuire, 1998: 13) between the photograph and its object pledges a more direct access to the past. The medium of the photograph grants its subject, to return to A. S. Byatt's phrase, a 'demi-eternity'. As Roland Barthes observes, 'the realists do not take the photograph for a 'copy' of reality, but for an emanation of *past reality*: a *magic*, not an art' (Barthes, 1984: 88).

This depiction of photography as magical is present in some of the earliest reviews of the medium. Thus, one English reviewer, writing for *The Athenaeum* in 1839, called its effects 'perfectly magical' (qtd. in McQuire, 1998: 13). Mary Warner Marien argues that in the earliest stories of photography's origins the technology that made the science of photography possible is couched in mythical, magical language, making of photography a mysterious and hybrid form. She gives the example of stories about Louis Daguerre in which accident, or fate, becomes a character. Daguerre receives a vision of the camera obscura during a dream and a spoon in his cupboard is darkened by mercury fumes overnight. These serendipitous accidents, or fateful events, become as important to Daguerre's role in the invention of photography as his technological successes engendered by hard work and scientific knowledge and experimentation. Such stories, suggests Marien, 'pitch mystery, magic, and alchemy against banal technological accounts of photography's advent' (Marien, 1997: 54).[5] Green-Lewis calls this 'realism's romance with photography', and suggests that in a culture dominated by realism and the desire to reveal, the depiction of photography as magical allowed it to be romanced as the ultimate in proof, as unbiased truth (Green-Lewis, 1996: 9–10).[6]

It is the photograph's association with perfect representation that, for Linda Hutcheon, makes it attractive to historiographic metafiction. In *The Politics of Postmodernism* (1989) she links fiction and photography since 'both forms have traditionally been assumed to be transparent media which paradoxically could master/capture/fix the real'. She argues that in historiographic metafiction photographic models become metaphors for 'the related issue of narrative representation – its powers and its limitations', particularly for the telling of history (Hutcheon, 1989: 39).

However, this focus upon the camera's perceived capacity for representational veracity elides the other capacity for which photography was enthusiastically welcomed and celebrated in the nineteenth century. The magic attributed to photography also allowed it to be romanced as a memorial. Barrett-Browning's celebration of the photograph as 'the very shadow of the person lying there fixed forever' is echoed in the late twentieth century by Susan Sontag, for whom the photograph is 'something directly stenciled off the real, like a footprint or a death mask ... never less than the registering of an emanation'. More than realist representation, here the photograph contains the 'trace' of its subject, is a 'material vestige' (Sontag 1977: 154). More than correspondence, the photograph inheres its subject. As Green-Lewis argues, 'photographs, after all, have sometimes been perceived not as simply telling the truth so much as being a part of it, physical traces of passing moments' (Green-Lewis, 1996: 5).

The photograph as a representational medium has been used for classification, historical knowledge, for surveillance, and as a witness. The photograph as a memorial medium establishes an affective relationship to its object, and functions as a souvenir. It promises time arrested, loss restored, home returned. Or, as Kate Flint describes it, the photograph promises 'the continuation of the past into the present ... the poignant hope of an impossible endurance' (Flint, 2003: 534).

Interestingly, historians' discovery of old photographs seems also to have corresponded to the emergence of memory in historical discourse in the last decades of the twentieth century, in which memory becomes an affective metahistorical category contrasted with a problematised history. Samuel identifies a flood of books from local and community presses, and from the public libraries, which opened up the old photographs from family albums to public view, and calls these 'We Remember' books, instead of 'personal history' or 'local history' books (Samuel, 1994: 321). Indeed, photography merges the conventional antinomies of history and memory in a unique way, by effacing the gap between past and present, public and personal. As Groth puts it, the photograph enables 'the simultaneous experiencing of past and present in a single encounter with a frozen moment in time' (Groth, 2000: 32).[7] And this is true whether the past is recent, or several generations previous. The photograph positions us as observers of scenes and events even if they occurred before our birth. By offering up history to our sight, it gives it to us as memory, as though we had, indeed, witnessed and experienced it. This is especially the case because of the materiality of the photograph. Framing a photograph for display, placing it in an album or carrying it on one's person suggests a relationship to the photograph's object and imparts a sense of its being one's own memory. As Edwards observes, the photograph is 'deemed significant as a bearer of memory'. Photographs 'can be handled, framed, cut, crumpled, caressed, pinned on a wall, put under a pillow, or wept over'. Indeed, she notes that the display of photographs in albums, in framed collections or on top of televisions and mantelpieces lends the form 'shrine-like qualities', and that Victorian photograph albums were bound to look like family bibles or devotional books, with relief leatherwork and metal clasps' (Edwards, 1999: 226). The photograph produces an affective relationship to its object, even if that object is a past not personally experienced. In this sense, photographs do indeed function, as

Edwards suggests, as 'surrogate memory' (ibid.: 222). Moreover, when the photographs' object is history, the Victorian past, for example, history becomes personalised; the past is established in a particular, affective, relationship to the present. History becomes memory.

It is the photograph's perceived capacity to fix the fleeting moment, to remember it, that is the focus of *Sixty Lights* and *Afterimage*. The staging of the Victorian emergence of photography in these novels signals a foregrounding not, primarily, of a problematics of representation, as Hutcheon's category of historiographic metafiction suggests, but of memory discourse, invoking its vocabulary of presence and restoration: 'as much as the photograph marks a site of irreducible absence', McQuire observes, 'it is frequently the talisman signaling the possibility of return' (McQuire, 1998: 7). In these novels, as in other examples of neo-Victorian fiction, photography is invoked as a memorial, or shrine, and as a tool to combat transience and loss. As the fictionalised Charles Dodgson reflects in Katie Roiphe's *Still She Haunts Me* (2001), the photograph promises that 'everything that flickered could be made permanent' (Roiphe, 2001: 8).[8] Photography becomes a vehicle for exploring the attempt to restore the past via word and image.

II

Set in the early 1860s, *Afterimage* tells the story of a young Irish orphan, named Annie Phelan, who works as a maidservant for the Dashell household. Eldon Dashell reads books and makes maps while his wife Isabelle is an amateur pictorial photographer, modelled loosely on Victorian photographer Julia Margaret Cameron. The novel explores the merits of reading, cartography and photography as media for image-making and examines their respective capacities to restore the past, to offer a means of return. Annie, who befriends and beguiles Eldon while becoming Isabelle's muse, is caught between the conflicting possibilities represented by Eldon and Isabelle, and stories and photographs, respectively.

The novel links photography to death. Eldon gives Isabelle her camera after their third stillborn baby (54) and Isabelle, formerly a painter, is reborn as a photographer. In Isabelle's mind, the birth of her children and that of her photographs are linked. She thinks of her babies in terms of 'their blood-slick bodies, slippery as fish, having swum from their dark ocean out into a light that killed them' (99), and, when developing her photographic image, '[s]he has to let it go into darkness and then she has to believe it will return ... It swims under the light in the glasshouse, limpid, the dull colour of blood seen through the water' (135). This memory makes processing, or birthing, her photographs acts of faith in the face of potential loss:

> it is at this moment that the image is truly gone. She cannot make it stay. She has to let it go into darkness and then she has to believe it will return. It takes so much strength from her, to believe this. To believe that it still lives, that it will flutter towards her ... It swims under the light in the glasshouse, limpid, the dull colour of blood seen through the water. (135)

The novel embraces images of imminent loss, so that even the garden at the end of summer, although still in full bloom, signals only imper-manence, erasure and the plea for remembrance:

> it is this time of year, the moment even, when the garden is most fully alive. It is the moment right next to the one where everything begins to die. Flowers lose their hold on the air, curl inward, hold their small, dry, rattling thoughts to themselves. *Don't forget me. Don't forget me* ... A garden in winter is a state of oblivion. (133–4)

Yet photography is not, chiefly, a means for Isabelle to immortalise a moment she does not wish to forget. Hers are not souvenirs of people and events she wishes to hold onto but pictorial photographs with which she seeks to immortalise her artistic vision. Isabelle's pictorial photographs are of other people's stories, or of abstract sentiments. Annie poses for her as Guinevere, Ophelia, Grace, Humility, Faith and the Madonna. Seeking refuge in telling other people's stories, instead of her own, Isabelle does not pursue photography as a means to restore her dead children or her lost childhood friend, yet her pictures are, nonetheless, memorials to the grief engendered by these losses.

Her photographs are a means for Isabelle to push away the thought of her dead children, 'she wants to forget them. She wants to cancel their image entirely' (123), by literally producing new ones. Through art she seeks to assert her control over loss: 'what she can create. What she can control. Life is accidental. Art is thick with purpose' (133). In her photographs, Isabelle seeks 'the vision [she] had, made flesh. It is a work of art, her art. It is a miracle' (38). Isabelle fears that what she can create will melt away, or die, as her children did. "Art is like light', she says. She almost says, like *Love*. 'Isn't it? Always burning with the same brightness, no matter how long we've been gone from the room?'

Isabelle opposes art, which is permanent, to nature, which is ephemeral, always threatening loss and destruction (85, 133).

The novel's protagonist, Annie, also seeks control through photography, first as a model for Isabelle's portraits and then, briefly, as a photographer herself. As a maid habituated to being inconsequential and overlooked, Annie rejoices in the attention that Isabelle lavishes upon her when she models (153). Accustomed to having no control over her life and circumstances, she rejoices, too, in the moments when she realises she has rearranged her pose and so has changed the photograph, resisted Isabelle's control (127). When she photographs Isabelle, the sense of control is more palpable: 'she had been in command of four and a half minutes. This world, for that time, had been hers and she had never felt such a sense of possibility for herself, a sense that she was someone apart from what she did, that she was real' (97). When Annie looks through the lens, at the way it delimits and truncates the scene before her she thinks 'it is a small enough world ... that it can be easily controlled. That is something to want' (226).

Throughout the novel, photography is associated with this kind of controlled seeing, which is not necessarily linked to knowing: 'Isabelle Dashell has looked so hard at Annie Phelan and has never once seen her at all' (346). Isabelle's pursuit of photography as a memorial of her own vision, as the creation of layers of images to paper over the more painful images that threaten to surface in her memory, is associated with a kind of death or, at least, is depicted as something divorced from life. 'What if art is not the greater power? What if art is an excuse to hide from life?' wonders Isabelle in one of her less assured moments (133). This possibility is foregrounded by the scene that frames the novel, providing its introduction and then, from a different perspective, its conclusion. A young boy, with fiery wings strapped to his body, leaps from the high window of Isabelle's burning house and flies through the air. At the beginning of the novel, it is rendered as the boy's memory of the event, much later in life, when he has grown into a man. Dressed as an angel for one of Isabelle's pictorial photographs, he had been admiring himself in the mirror when the house caught fire and rapidly burned. He remembers that Annie rescues him by throwing a mattress to the ground below and holding him over the edge of the window sill. 'I've got you, she says. And then she lets him go' (1). It is a moment when he is rescued from death and falls back into life. At the end of the novel, when this scene is repeated from Isabelle's perspective, as she watches from below, we know that while Annie has been in the house rescuing the boy, and Eldon has been attempting to rescue Annie,

Isabelle locked herself in her dark room, away from the house and wilfully oblivious to the cries and screams that filter through to her. Again, the scene is motion, capturing only the boy's flight through the air, not his landing: 'it is the falling moment. Unrecorded' (248). To Isabelle it represents life, and her inability to create anything other than still life:

> it is the perfect photograph, and she has missed it. This is what she has always feared. That she will not be able, no matter how she wills it or orchestrates it, to create an image as pure and true as this. That what she does is not really about life, about living. It is about holding on to something long after it has already left. Like grief. Like hope. (248)

Sixty Lights, too, is a novel coloured and shaped by death and grief. Its protagonist is, like Annie, an orphan and migrant. The novel tells the story of Lucy Strange's brief life and, like *Afterimage*, explores the potential of words and images to restore loss. In *Sixty Lights* Lucy, like Isabelle, becomes a photographer to assuage loss. In this novel, photography is also associated with death, but it becomes, too, a celebration of life. Lucy's philosophy is built upon the notion of photographic seeing, which is a 'celebration of the lit-up gaze' (142).[9] It echoes Barthes' assertion that 'the Photograph is never anything but an antiphon of "Look," "See," "Here it is"' (Barthes, 1984: 5). Lucy exemplifies this philosophy of photographic seeing well before she is introduced to photography. Photography crystallises what she has already begun in her notebook, in which she records 'special things seen', aware that the act of recording them confers a special status upon ordinary people, places and occurrences. Lucy's passion for photography stems from the desire to hold onto that which would otherwise be neglected or forgotten, those images that are overlooked because they are apparently commonplace: 'the commandment of ordinary things to look, and the countervailing sense of the world's detachment, troubled and distressed her. Lucy wondered how she might tell this, or to whom' (83). Photography lends significance to the otherwise unremarkable. It grants permanence to the otherwise forgettable. The act of photographing asserts the significance of the ordinary.[10] Although, like Isabelle, Lucy considers herself an artist, her photographs are of the people and places she encounters in life. Lucy comes to think of photography as 'a shrine', 'of objects inverted, of death defeated. She thought too of the glass plates that held the envisioned world – in eight by ten inches – returned to itself, as an act – surely – as an act of devotion' (154). Elsewhere in the novel the photograph 'is another form of love, is it not, the studied representation? It is devotional. Physical. A kind of honouring attention. I think of photography – no doubt absurdly – as a kind of kiss' (200).[11]

Jones has said that Lucy's philosophy of seeing was inspired, in part, by Sei Shōnagon's *Pillow Book*. Shōnagon was a Japanese courtier in the eleventh century, whose philosophy held:

> what we should notice are the things that 'make the heart beat faster' and that we should drag them away from what Sontag calls 'the relentless melt of time'; this awful sense that everything's dissolving into a dark space behind us as we live, that there's a beauty in securing one little image … that's enough, that those moments of attention are what aesthetic experience is about and what makes life meaningful. (Jones, 2005)

Connected to the securing of one little image, one that makes the heart beat faster, photography is linked with life and meaning, and also with light, the 'diffuse and glimmering light, [Lucy] has seen inherent in wet collodion and silver-nitrate photographic prints. … It is the light of memory, and of the earliest petals of gardenia. It is the blurred aura, perhaps, between concealment and unconcealment' (46).

Jones invokes the Victorian understanding of the photograph as recovery, as return, in contrast to contemporary theory about photography that links it to melancholy, loss and death. In a novel about the Victorian period which contains relatively few specific references to it, she borrows from the era the excitement attaching to an emerging medium that, in Jones' words, Jones invokes the Victorian notion of photography as memorial, when it 'seemed not to be about loss but to be about recovery … Photography, at a particular moment in its history, must have seemed so life-affirming, so much to return us to the real rather than take it away from us' (ibid). This desire, to return to the real, is what Green-Lewis calls the 'will to authenticity' which, she argues, 'may be understood in part as a desire for that which we have first altered and then fetishized … most frequently experienced and figured as a desire, or a sickness for home' (Green-Lewis, 2000: 43).

In both *Sixty Lights* and *Afterimage* it is the body of the mother that becomes the focus of this nostalgia for origins, the figure for the real and the symbol of a lost past. Each novel is infused with dead and irretrievable mothers; each of the characters' mothers has died or is irrevocably absent. The trope of the dead mother is a self-conscious appropriation of a device familiar to Victorian fiction. Indeed, in *The Maternal Voice in Victorian Fiction: Rewriting the Patriarchal Family* (1997), Barbara Z. Thaden, refers to the 'long litany of dead mothers in nineteenth-century fiction'. And Carolyn Dever argues that in Victorian fiction the dead mother 'motivates a formal search for "origins" ... And symbolically, in fictional worlds, the crisis of maternal loss enables the synthesis of questions of originality, agency, erotic and scientific desire' (Dever, 1998: xi–xii).[12]

In *Sixty Lights* and *Afterimage* the loss of the mother symbolises the loss of history. It is an ungrounding, or displacement and disruption of identity. In *Camera Lucida* (1980), Barthes makes our notion of history, that traditional manifestation of groundedness, inextricable from the mother's body. In a passage aptly headed 'History as Separation' he 'is History not simply the time when we were not born? ... that is what the time when my mother was alive before me is – History' (Barthes, 1984: 64, 65). This foreshortens our sense of what history is, and brings the more recent past into its purview. It is also makes the maternal body a symbol of history, as it is in Jones' and Humphreys' novels. Moreover, Barthes cites Freud's observation of the maternal body: that there is no other place of which one can say with so much certainty that one has already been there (ibid.: 53). This makes of the maternal body the original origin, the home *par excellence*, and, in Barthes' phenomenology, the quintessential photograph, since the photograph's *noeme* is, for Barthes, 'That-has-been' (ibid.: 7).

When the newly-orphaned Lucy stands aboard the ship bound for England, several years before her introduction to photography, she desires a tool that will return her not, primarily, to her lost, Australian, home but to her dead mother. Separating lovers, who use mirrors to locate each other in the crowd, grant Lucy a glimpse of the technology that will promise such a return. We are told:

> it was the woman who was leaving. She tilted her oval mirror to catch at the sun and a young man, diminishing, answered from the shore. Lucy was transfixed. This was what she wanted, a photosensitive departure. Light trained by glass to locate and discover a face, a beam to travel on, a homing device, a sleek corridor through the infinity of the sky itself. (77)

Of course light, trained by glass to locate a face, is the essence of photography. And the face that Lucy seeks, the photograph she longs for, is that of her mother. The reference to a homing device signals

Lucy's disorientation, that without the grounding force of her mother she is cut loose, and cannot orient herself to a home irrevocably gone.

The novel makes the mother's body the centerpiece of its portrayal of loss and potential restoration by introducing Lucy's mother almost entirely in terms of her physicality: 'her belly was enormous'; 'this rather heavy irascible woman, almost entirely immobile'; 'appearing as if some artist had tinted her face pink'; 'her bare swollen feet'; and, importantly, 'the fan that now rested against her face, obscuring it' (6, 7). Lucy's pregnant mother, soon to die in childbirth, is already slipping away from Lucy, ungrounding her: 'the fan imprints itself on Lucy's heart, for it is from this day that her life enters the mode of melodrama, and this little partition between them, of such oriental blue, will register for ever the vast distances that love must travel' (7). This moment is the first time that Lucy really experiences her mother as separate and unreachable, obscured. The maternal body symbolises not only Lucy's past but also her continuity with it. The death of this body disrupts Lucy's sense of connectedness, her sense of history.

Following her mother's death, Lucy searches for the suggestion of her amongst the belongings she has left behind. These objects, contained in a hatbox, are 'a little amnesiac circle: everything was lost and without association. Nothing summoned her mother's face. Nothing was intelligible' (45–6). Her mother is a 'hieroglyph' (70), a mystery that resists decoding.

> [Lucy] becomes, at this very moment, one whose mission it is to unconceal. This is the moment, aged eight, Lucy becomes a photographer. And every photographic ambition will turn on the summoning of a face and the retrieval of what is languishing just beyond vision. (46)

While Lucy's longing for origins is clearly nostalgic, the novel makes this a productive and creative force, rather than a conservative or regressive one. Severed from her maternal origins, Lucy embraces photography as a tool for memory, an instrument to combat imminent, intractable loss and the ungrounding of identity. For Lucy, as for Barrett Browning, the photograph promises proximity, the erasure of time and distance. Barrett Browning's words, quoted in the epigraph to this chapter, encapsulate the idea of photography as a resurrection of past persons or places, not merely representing them but, in an important sense, re-presenting them, or re-membering them, restoring them to a time and place in which they no longer exist.

Yet in *Sixty Lights*, the photograph of the mother has never been taken, it exists only in, and as, Lucy's desire for it. Kerwin Klein identifies the photograph as a familiar trope in contemporary memory discourse. He describes the way certain objects, such as archives, statues and museums *become* memory:

> ideally, the memory will be a dramatically imperfect piece of material culture, and such fragments are best if imbued with pathos. Such memorial tropes have emerged as one of the common features of our new cultural history where in monograph after monograph, readers confront the abject object: photographs are torn, mementos faded, toys broken. (Klein, 2000: 136)

The untaken photograph of Lucy's mother becomes the quintessential imperfect memory, imbued with pathos: it is not torn, but rather eternally absent. It symbolises not only the promise of restoration but also its cruel negation. Her mother's face 'could not be willed into vision' (70).[13]

Similarly, there is no photograph of Annie's mother in *Afterimage*. Annie is further displaced from the maternal body, and therefore from history, because, unlike Lucy, she has no conscious memory of it. She was a baby when she was separated from her mother. It is in Annie's dreams that the maternal body asserts its significance. Annie dreams that she is again an infant, being passed back to her mother: 'the relief of this, of finally having her mother back, is such a huge feeling it bursts out of her body, out of her skin, makes Annie cry out loud when, at last, her mother takes her in her arms' (125). And yet, elusive as a ghost, her mother remains just out of vision: 'she was almost there. She had almost seen her mother's face' (125).

The description of Annie's response to this recurring dream produces it as a ghostly presence in her life; it haunts her: 'she is afraid to fall asleep, afraid to fall into her dream of the road. The sound of the shovels and axes chipping at the hard ground is already playing in her head, a rattling, somber tattoo, like the sound of bones knocking together' (58). This road, which features so prominently in Annie's haunting dreams, is a symbol of her dislocation, her disconnectedness from history. The English government had famine victims, including Annie's mother, father and brothers, work on public relief schemes, building roads. When there were enough roads they continued building them. However, these roads were truly excess, they went nowhere and connected nothing: 'it was not for anything, did not tie this place to that. No one could ever walk down it expecting to get to the next village' (51).

After she shares the story with him, this image of this road to and from nowhere haunts her employer, Eldon, too. Indeed, it haunts the novel itself as a symbol of dislocation of time and place, the disruption of a linear sense of time, the continuum of past, present and future. In a novel obsessed with 'distance. Position. How to find your way back when where you are depends on where everything else is' (47), the road to and from nowhere symbolises disorientation and displacement. With no connection to her past, cut off from her origin in the maternal body, Annie is as a traveller on this road that offers no hope of return. Moreover, Annie reflects that as a maid, she is unlikely to ever marry or have children, stunting, afresh, the maternal line: 'the future is more of the same. No, the future is less, and the same' (85). Disconnected from her past, Annie also has no future.

Cut off from the maternal body, but desirous of a reunion with it, indeed haunted by it, *Sixty Lights* and *Afterimage* explore the inherence of the past in the present via a series of images of, and metaphors for, haunting. Whereas in *Afterimage* the use of haunting is restricted to Annie's dreams, *Sixty Lights* explores the notion of ghostly haunting more fully. Lucy is jealously convinced that her brother Thomas, who sleepwalks, 'otherworldly and implacably absent ... communes with ghosts' (105), particularly those of her parents. Thomas' feeling about these visions captures the characteristic indeterminacy of the spectral figure: 'it was something that would follow him all his life, like having the wrong person's shadow, like carrying an aberration of presence' (95). The liminal figure of the ghost, which exists in a space between presence and absence, and is perhaps only a trick of the light or of the mind, is an aberration of presence. It is not the restoration of what is lost.

The trope of the ghost is a familiar one in contemporary fictional returns to the Victorian era. Indeed Rosario Arias Doblas argues that the prevalence of the use of ghostliness and hauntings as a metaphor for the presence of the past makes the 'spectral' novel a 'subset' of the neo-Victorian novel (Doblas, 2005: 88). In Liz Jensen's *Ark Baby* (1998) a Victorian ghost literally inhabits the same space as the contemporary characters. Having lived in the house herself, when alive, she now haunts it in death (Jensen, 1998). Christian Gutleben observes that the ghost literally interacts with the modern characters, thus establishing a sort of hyphen between the past and present' (Gutleben, 2001: 190). However, the figure of the ghost is actually a disruption of linear time. The link it establishes between past and present is not so much a hyphen, bridge, or other linear form, but is rather a repetition. Or, more precisely, it is repetition with a difference. As Nick Peim suggests, 'the spectre is *revenant*, a past figure that keeps coming back, disrupting the smooth logic of time' (Peim, 2005: 75).

The spectre is an evocative metaphor for the past, as 'the *nothing-and-yet-not-nothing* and the *neither-nowhere-nor-not-nowhere* that none-theless leaves a trace in passing and which has such a material effect' (ibid.: 140). Indeterminacy and incompletion are embedded in the figure of the spectre. The materiality of the ghost is illusory and always already under erasure. As Peim argues, 'the authenticity of the spectre is always questionable – a function of the gap between its partial nature and the full version it claims to represent' (ibid.: 77). This makes the figure of the ghost an apt metaphor for textual representation. Colin Davis explores the way in which Jacques Derrida's formulation of *hauntologie*, or 'hauntology' has been productively adopted in literary criticism to explore the use of ghosts and hauntings in fiction: 'hauntology sup-plants its near-homonym ontology, replacing the priority of being and presence with the figure of the ghost as that which is neither present nor absent, neither dead nor alive' (Davis, 2005: 373). As Derrida asserts in an interview given in 2005, 'in a certain way every trace is spectral' (Derrida, 2001: 44).

This seems especially true of the photographic trace, which as Barthes suggests, always contains 'the return of the dead' (Barthes, 1984: 9). Yet Barthes' phenomenology of photography also suggests the contradictory notion, that 'every photograph is a certificate of presence' (ibid.: 87). Like the spectre, the photograph, it seems, occupies a strange space between presence and absence, loss and return. The photographic image is truly revenant. Green-Lewis calls this the 'absolute and paradoxical present of the photograph', observing that, as the subjects of the earli-est photographs we have, the Victorians continue to exist for us in this way, 'always there yet gone forever; both in, and out, of history; always already dead – and yet still alive' (Green-Lewis, 2000: 31).

While *Afterimage* and *Sixty Lights* each employ the language of haunting, and *Sixty Lights* in particular raises the possibility of spectral visitations through both Thomas and the spurious spiritualist Madam Esperance, the notion of the past as revenant is largely elaborated via the ghostly medium of photography. Rather than the actual figure of the ghost, it is the ghostliness of photography that becomes a metaphor for the revenant past. In *Sixty Lights* Neville greets the spiritualist's luminous image, supposedly the ghost of his dead sister, with the whispered word 'ectoplasm' (94). He believes 'it is ectoplasm ghosts are composed of' (92), and which Madame Esperance can summon. Barthes deploys the same language to describe photography. He writes that upon their inception, photographs must have seemed, 'like the ectoplasm of "what-had-been": neither image nor reality, a new being, really: a reality one can no longer touch' (Barthes, 1984: 87). This word, ectoplasm, entwines the ghostly image and the photograph as images of an aberrant, or 'hauntological' presence.

Ectoplasm resonates throughout the novel, connected to other luminous evocations of presence, shiny, viscous substances and fluids such as the blood and vernix smeared on the newborn baby, (163), blood, a throbbing heart (144) and bioluminescent sea algae (110). These are incandescent, but ephemeral, emanations. They are 'auratic', but not solid (142). Invoking presence, they are also inextricably linked to the lustre of loss, intuitively visible to Lucy and Thomas as they leave their childhood home when, 'without turning to look, they knew that behind them everything was already coated with the alluring patina of loss. It shone as it receded, like embers in a dying fire, and held for evermore the smouldering glint of their pasts' (75).

The aberrant presence of a ghost, like the photograph itself, *is* this alluring patina; the film, or gloss that attaches to loss itself, making it paradoxically beguiling, mesmeric, even as it is painful. Indeed, first glimpsed in sharp relief against the dark ocean, 'silvery threads of light in a thin film' (110), 'bioluminescence' becomes, for Lucy, a symbol of unexpected light, of ethereal presence amidst implacable absence. It is inextricably linked to 'still moments in time, moments arcane, seductive, trivial, breathtaking, that waited for the sidelong glance, the split-second of notice, the opening up of an irrefutable and auratic presence' (142).

Suggesting restoration and return, this ghostly patina is, importantly, not always visible, indeed it comes most often by accident, unexpectedly. Lucy's pursuit of light is the adult manifestation of her fantasy as a child, of 'casting out every threatening and mystifying shadow' (11). Part of Lucy's journey into adulthood (and this is, after all, a self-conscious reworking of the Victorian *Bildungsroman*) includes the recognition and acceptance of the shadows, as well as the light. For 'the world is like this, don't you think?', Lucy asks, '[m]arked, and shadowed, and flecked with time' (146). As Jones describes it in an interview, '[Lucy] comes to realize that images can't do everything. There are losses that cannot be recovered' (Jones, 2002 5).

The most significant resonance of this is that there are recesses of memory, that are always obscured by shadow, like her mother's face, which is 'so vague it might be a wet footprint, shimmering thin as breath, transient as a sundial shadow, poised on the very edge of complete disappearance' (73). It cannot be 'willed into vision ... called, or fabricated' (70). The shiny, ethereal substances that are metaphors for the photograph are also, paradoxically, like the shiny surface of a mirror. As Jennifer Green-Lewis observes:

> no effort, however extraordinary, will ever yield access to a photo-graph and permit the viewer, Alice-like, to climb through its frame into another world. Quite apart from the irony contingent on our every encounter with the paradox of the photograph, and at odds with photography's promise of interiority and penetration, is the hard surface of mirror images that will not melt into air. (Green-Lewis, 2000: 31)

The photograph is spectral; like the ghost, it 'represents what is not there: a present mark coincides with absent presence' (Peim, 2005: 77). The photograph's 'mark' might be a promising patina but it is also the hard surface of the mirror image. The photograph remains a trace, such as Hutcheon refers to when she suggests 'we only have access to the past today through its traces – its documents, the testimony of witnesses, and other archival materials. In other words, we only have representa-tions of the past from which to construct our narratives or explanations' (Hutcheon, 1989: 55).

III

Against the unyielding image, the incapacity for willed recollection, *Sixty Lights* and *Afterimage* each posit as time's receptacle, not the photo-graph, whose 'absent presence' must always produce a strange mixture of ethereality coupled with impenetrable surface, but the body itself, which is the fundamental home to memory. The lexicon of spectrality is transferred to the body, which becomes a medium for the repetition of the past, its unbidden persistence in the present.

For *Afterimage,* the notion of embodied memory, or corporeal his-tory, is a question that is posed. Annie wonders if her body holds the memory of her voyage across the sea to a new life in England (115, 116). The novel raises the possibility that her dreams of the road that goes nowhere, and of her mother taking her in her arms, are memories held by her body, that these dreams are, in fact, repetitions of actions Annie has performed. Moreover, Annie's body is itself a memory object: 'Annie is the record of her family. She is the cairn they left, what remained for the world to see after they had gone' (149). Faced with the absence of a photograph of her mother she realises that 'the one thing above all others that she wants to know about her is what she looked like'. And yet, 'this is the one thing she can never know. What her mother looked like, and if Annie looks like her.' However, in the absence of a visual image, Annie's body allows her some knowledge of her mother:

> all she can really imagine of her mother is the work she did. Annie cannot guess what it is her mother would have been thinking on that road in Ireland, or even what she would have been wearing, but Annie does know what the labour would feel like. The roughness of the stone would rub hands raw and bleeding. The body stooping and lifting would make the back ache and force the body to move stiffly to accommodate the pain. Looking up would hurt. (94)

The novel thus effaces the conventional link between seeing and knowing, and the conventional epistemological function of the photography, by privileging the body as the means to knowledge. Eldon, for example, 'has to touch something to make it real, to really see it' (111). When Eldon shows Annie an image of Ireland, her 'motherland', in the form of a map, she, too, attempts to learn it physically, 'puts her finger down, gently, on Kilkee and traces the fogged outline of the Loop head' (111). In this way the map itself, the very paper on which it is drawn, returns to Annie (imperfectly, incompletely) the home she does not recall ever seeing in a tangible form. Later that evening Annie performs her own, rudimentary, cartography, drawing the map of Ireland, from memory, into the cover of her Bible. It is, in place of a photograph, her act of devotion. It is also her act of ownership. Drawing the lines is an act of connecting herself to her home, the place she cannot consciously remember, of claiming it as her own history. She places the map face down on her chest, hoping that the shape of Ireland 'will melt into her skin' (116).[14] Having no memory of it, she seeks, in this way, to embody her homeland.

The question posed by *Afterimage* is explored more explicitly in *Sixty Lights*. In this novel, in place of a photograph of her mother, which is doubly absent because never taken, it is Lucy's body that returns her mother's face to her. When she shows a black paper silhouette of her mother to her lover William Crowley, he observes that she has her mother's profile so that, to Lucy, 'at that instant, they were alchemically fused: she was the bright-lit original for her mother, the shadow' (118). Here Lucy embodies the photograph that she so desires. The alchemic fusion of Honoria and Lucy at this moment both invokes and reverses the photograph, whose lit-up gloss depends upon the shadowy negative.

Honoria's face is continued in and by Lucy's own. Lucy's own body remembers that of her mother.

The idea of embodied memory is exemplified by Lucy's fascination with the elongated lobes on a statue of the Buddha, 'a reminder', Isaac tells her, 'of his life as a prince, when he wore pendant earrings. Before Enlightenment, that is. Before he became the Buddha.' Lucy thinks of this as 'the way the body carries small signatures of its former selves. Small telltale markings' (125). Thus, when she thinks of William she thinks of 'the vulnerable area at the back of his thighs ... a pale screen of skin, petal-looking in its texture' and he becomes not the uniformed, confident, and ultimately unfeeling man she has known 'but a man who carried, as it were, the flag of his own childhood. And though she knew now of his definitive meanness and duplicity, she wanted to preserve him thus, in continuity with this quality of unremarked softness' (127). The body is engraved by time, etched with past experience. In this sense memory is carried with us bodily, not so much remembered as 'membered', or embodied.

Opposed to willed recollection and reconstruction, embodied memory is a repetition, and is therefore linked to Pierre Nora's more authentic 'memory', rather than the artificial 'history' (see Nora, 1989: 15). Manifesting this idea of embodied memory is the unconscious repetition of various bodily actions and gestures across generations in the novel:

> how often, [the novel asks] in what small or gifted or implausible moments, do we replay what our parents knew, or did? How often do we feel – in another generation – what they imagined was sequestered in their own private skin? (119)

The novel suggests that we repeat, bodily, the actions, recollections and images of previous generations, and that this creates links between us. When Lucy stands on board the ship as it enters the harbour in Bombay, it resembles Sydney Harbour as it appeared to her mother as she entered it years before: 'Lucy could not have known that she experienced arrival as her mother did: with just the same arousal of spirit, with the same quickening of the heart, like a small fish leaping' (119). Lucy is the unwilled, and indeed unconscious, medium that repeats her mother's experience. This pattern is repeated in the closing passage of the novel when Lucy's daughter, Ellen, opens the door upon Thomas in his unleashed grief, repeating the moment, the 'wedge of disclosure' (9), when Lucy, in her childhood, similarly came upon her father in his grief. In a sense the novel ends as it began, with a small child grieving her dead mother, and witnessing, too, the debilitating grief of another who loved her. Moreover, Ellen 'looked exactly, Thomas thought, as Lucy had as a small child' (247). The effect is to suggest that Ellen, like Lucy before her, embodies the presence of her mother and that the past will persist in the present in the form of repetitions, fragmented images and unbidden memories. These are Hutton's 'habits of mind', the 'moment of memory through which we bear forward images of the past that continue to shape our present understanding in unreflective ways' (Hutton, 1993: xx–xxi).

The intergenerational repetition of her mother's experience also suggests the connection between storyteller and listener envisioned by Walter Benjamin in describing his notion of the aura:

> it is not the object of the story to convey a happening *per se*, which is the purpose of information; rather, it embeds it in the life of the story-teller in order to pass it on as experience to those listening. It thus bears the marks of the story-teller as much as the earthen vessel bears the marks of the potter's hand. (Benjamin, 1994: 19 qtd. in Geyer-Ryan, 1994: 19)

In *Sixty Lights* and *Afterimage* the mark of the storyteller proves, like the photograph, to be the mark of the ghost. In these novels, then, as in *Possession*, the novel becomes a medium of the past, allowing its voices to speak. As we saw in Chapter 1, Julien Wolfreys suggests that the textual trace is always the medium for spectral encounters (Wolfreys, 2002: 140).

This has particular resonance in the novel because initially, shifted from her home across the world to London with only her brother as a link with her old life, Lucy experiences a profound sense of disruption to her personal narratives. Without her mother to embody them, the stories her mother told her as a child threaten to become meaningless:

> what shall Lucy do with her inheritance of story? Now she is left with a repertoire of exasperating desire, of hokum, memory, nonsense and tall-tale, that she has siphoned into herself as a stream of chill water. These stories fill her with an amorphous dissolving feeling. (73)

However, when Lucy is eighteen, she discovers the reading of novels as 'a séance of other lives into her own imagination', a 'metaphysical meeting space – peculiar, specific, ardent, unusual' (114). Through reading, Lucy 'learnt how other people entered the adventure of being alive' (114). Her experience of reading helps her to understand her desire to search out the connections 'that knitted the whole world' (114). The novel, rather than the photograph, becomes the medium of experience.

More importantly, through reading, Lucy rediscovers, or re-members, her mother's early stories, which come flooding back to meet her. These stories form the 'purest geometry of connections' (114) between Lucy and her mother. They return her mother to Lucy in small slices: 'a tone of voice, the feminine scent of gardenia' (115). It was like,' Lucy thinks, 'something swaying just in and out of vision' (115).

Furthermore, Lucy's reunion with Molly Minchin, her mother's friend and midwife, also returns her to her mother. Lucy tells Isaac of the association, in her mind, of Molly with her parents' death, so that upon first seeing her years later, 'it was as if the long-past sprang phantom-like to confront me: I was afraid of a whiff of death, of some wound, or corruption, of something dark which would fly up like a bat and scratch at my face' (201). Yet Molly has known her parents, especially Lucy's mother, and can tell many stories about them: 'I tried for so long to forget my parents, but think now that Molly's company is meant to return me to them. She has a fine collection of stories and a loving presence' (201). Word-images, rather than photographic ones, mediate the past for Lucy. In this way, *Sixty Lights* shares the privileging of storytelling in both *Waterland* and *Possession*. It explicitly makes storytelling, and especially the novel, a medium of the past by making reading a séance of Lucy's mother's life into her own. Where the photograph is impenetrable surface, the story allows communion with, and transmission of, the past, as the spiritualist does at a séance.

Indeed, word-images, or stories, both anecdotal and novelistic, also embody memory and perform the devotional, memorialising function of photography. Jones has made this link elsewhere, attributing the 'emblazoning gesture' to both writing and photography, and claiming that it is 'central to all writing ... as light is central to photography. The wish to ennoble what is fragile, pitiable, mortal, vulnerable' (Jones, 2006). Lucy's record of 'Photographs Not Taken' and 'Special Things Seen' are as important to the novel as her photographs. Indeed, they are itemised more fully than the photographs which suggests they might even be privileged. Lucy does not distinguish between the images she records in her diary and those she records with her camera. Each represent 'a whole empire of images to which she felt affinity and loyalty.

Her diary would compel attentiveness. Would claim these images. Would set her formally agape' (178).

Like the shards of a mirror in the opening pages of *Sixty Lights*, which continue, in the face of death, loss and grief, to hold the world, offering it up, not whole and complete, but as slices (3–4), memory and its surrogates, photography and writing, do retrieve images from the melt of time, but only in fragments. 'This was memory as an asterix [*sic*]. The glory of the glimpse. The retrieval of just enough lit knowing to see [the] way forward' (115). While Lucy learns to celebrate these moments if not of retrieval then at least of truncated remembrance, of diffuse light, the use of the word 'asterisk', which is most often used to mark omissions or footnotes in a text, signals here all that cannot be brought into vision. An asterisk is as the ghostly trace, 'the present mark of an absent presence' (Peim, 2005 79). For each memory there is a shadow archive of lost moments and forgotten features.

Having posited both stories and the body as fragmented, imperfect, media of memory, *Sixty Lights* and *Afterimage* link these more explicitly by suggesting that the novel itself can stand in the place of, or embody, memory. Following Lucy's death, Thomas feels 'suspended in a kind of absent-minded grief' (248) and wonders if it is possible 'to summon as an after-image on the surface of the retina some image-memory that has lain, pristine and packed away, unglimpsed since early adulthood?' (58). Yet this summoning of a photograph-like image, stored as memory, is not granted him within the novel. Rather, it is his re-reading of *Great Expectations*, 'saturated by memories' (249) of reading it with his uncle and sister nearly a decade earlier that finally unlocks Thomas' grief (249). Re-reading *Great Expectations* enables Thomas to re-member the sister and uncle he once read it with. Re-reading it is his act of devotion to them, consolidating and celebrating the geometry of connections that still joins them. In the absence of both Neville and Lucy, *Great Expectations* holds, or embodies, this, their collective memory.

This idea of the story as a medium, channelling the past and forming a geometry of connections with present, is also dramatised by *Afterimage*. Eldon lends Annie books, which become a shared image-repertoire between them, a collective memory, or shared experience, siphoned from the accounts they read. Annie reads with a 'feverish passion for words' that recalls Roland's epiphanic reading at the end of *Possession*. She reads 'with the same bursts of clandestine intensity that one would use to pursue an illicit encounter' (17). When Annie reads Eldon's books about John Franklin's expedition to the Arctic, they stand in for a shared history between them, one which is placed alongside Eldon's actual shared history with Isabelle: 'he looks across at Annie, suddenly so grateful that she knows this about Franklin, that she knows some of what he knows of the expeditions. Isabelle, in all their married life, has never once read the same books he has, has never shown the slightest interest in doing so' (151).

Annie's reading also provides her with an image-repertoire that she shares with Franklin's men, who died almost before she was born. Having read that among the possessions found with the remains of Franklin's men was a copy of the novel *The Vicar of Wakefield*, Annie reads it, and tries to imagine what the story's litany of calamities would have meant to the men, reading it in the context of their own disaster: 'were they able to do as the line in *The Vicar of Wakefield* said, the line that Annie stumbled over and then went back to again. *Read our anguish into patience*' (157, emphasis in original).

Moreover, the narratives of arctic exploration provide Annie with the images she needs to re-member her own past, to understand her own family's experience. They provide her with some, imaginative, knowledge of that which eludes her conscious memory: what it was like to be starving to death, as her family did, during the Irish famine. Annie reflects that in the same year that Franklin and his men were dying on their Arctic expedition, her family were dying in Ireland. Annie is transfixed by the realisation that, at the same point in history, her parents suffered the fate ascribed to the members of Sir John Franklin's expedition to the arctic: '*they fell down and died as they walked along*. On a road, in Ireland. On the shifting, unsteady pans of ice in northern Canada. At almost the same time' (149).

Although reading about and reimagining the fate of the members of Franklin's expedition enables Annie to imagine the fate of her own family, to affectively assimilate that which she has not experienced, it is the *recovery* voyages of Leopold McClintock, in 1858, that are more important to the novel's larger theme of memory and retrieval. Reading the account of McClintock's voyages to discover what had happened to the Franklin expedition prompts Annie to wonder, for the first time, whether the story she has been told is what really happened to her family:

> and why, thinks Annie, holding *The Voyage of the 'Fox' in the Arctic Seas* against her chest, why have I never questioned Mrs. Cullen's account of my family's death? Why could I not believe, as Jane Franklin believed and kept believing, that out there, against all odds,

there was perhaps one who made it through alive. One person. One soul. (150)

For Annie, who has spent her life in England being asked to forget her Irish history, the very fact of the McClintock voyages raises the possibility, for the first time, of retrieving a different version of her own past, of recovering a survivor from her among her own family (150).

McClintock's voyages become a motif for historical recollection in the novel, so that it casts the project of salvaging the past, of imaginatively re-mapping previous journeys, as fruitful. Eldon who, as a boy, had wanted to be part not of Franklin's original, mapping, expedition, but of McClintock's recovery expedition, observes: 'they have mapped more of Canada's Arctic in looking for Franklin than was ever mapped by Franklin himself' (143). The goal of the recovery expedition, as it is imaged in McClintock's voyages, is not actually the past, but the journey itself:

> Annie is surprised by McClintock's book. She had thought that an expedition that had set off in search of Franklin would spend the time sailing towards the Arctic pondering what might have happened to Franklin and his men, imagining their possible fate. But McClintock doesn't even mention Franklin for the first half of the book. Instead, he talks about what he's seeing and experiencing, as though he's on his own scientific survey of the Arctic. (148)

McClintock's journey makes some discoveries about the fate of the Franklin expedition but questions remain. 'All the dead weren't found' (150). McClintock leaves a record of his own discoveries and explorations under the cairn at Point Victory, added to material the Franklin Expedition had left. 'Because it was his voyage, thinks Annie, closing the book. John Franklin was just as much a place as Cape Farewell or Point Victory, something to head towards, something to take bearings from, but truly the journey was McClintock's' (150).

Thus, like *Waterland*, *Afterimage* emphasises the importance of the *process* of historical inquiry, the telling of stories, over the meanings produced, which are always provisional. It privileges journey over destination. Curiosity is also privileged, as it is in *Waterland*. This is explicated not only through the privileging of storytelling, but also through Eldon's map-making. The theme map that Eldon's employer wants him to make goes against Eldon's belief in the value of the journey: 'to mark down the mineral deposits in South America relegates the map to a mere guide. Exploration loses its edge of curiosity and becomes only a reason for exploitation' (46). The theme map emerges from the belief that 'there is nothing left to show of the world. Nothing new' (25). For Eldon, the map's central function is to offer a means of return: 'the simple purity of the act of making the map, so that the map-maker would find his way back to where he was, so that others could find their way there' (46). When Eldon shows Annie the map of Ireland it transforms her thinking about it, making it a place of potential return. Previously, all her thoughts of home have been tied to that single, endless road her family died building. Thus, Annie 'looks down at the map and is surprised that Ireland is not long and thin, loping off the top of the page into distance' (110). The map of Ireland joins with McClintock's story in Annie's mind and together they enable her to take command of her own recovery expedition: 'she will go back to Ireland herself, back to County Clare, to try and find out what happened to her family. Eldon would like that' (247).[15]

Annie's decision to leave involves a symbolic rejection of photography. For much of the novel, Annie has been caught between Isabelle and Eldon, and therefore, between photography on the one hand and reading and storytelling and cartography on the other. The novel dramatises a contest over knowledge, between photography and the older art forms of cartography and books. For Isabelle, the contest between these epistemologies is characterised as that between a 'living piece of art' and 'dusty old maps' (44). Photography is associated with 'the future' (44, 198), and yet, for the novel, this makes it imperfect as a memorial to, or of, the past. Whereas photography is a fixed image, map-making, for the novel, represents a journey: Eldon observes, 'a photograph is always a destination. It's not concerned with getting there, but being there ... To look at a photograph ... is always to have arrived' (112). Annie responds with her own assertion that 'your map ... is better than a photograph' (112).

The suggestion that the photograph is not a journey but a destination, a kind of truncated or aborted narrative, is also taken up in *Sixty Lights*. For, despite their celebration of photography, through each novel there also runs a critique of the image, the intimation of an alternative, negative, trajectory for the medium. In *Sixty Lights* this takes the form of a tension between image and narrative as ways of knowing which is never satisfactorily resolved. It relates to the different types of meaning-production these perform. The novel takes as an epigraph to its second section Walter Benjamin's assertion that 'knowledge comes only in flashes', which informs, too, its notion of photographic seeing.

These flashes seem to 'fit' Lucy's knowledge of the world as a series of random events, actions and objects:

> unable to reason her profound sense of discrepancy in the world ... and the cloudy abstractions they brought in their wake, she decided she would know the world by its imagistic revelations. Seen this way, London presented a venerable randomness, by which, eventually, Lucy was won over. (86)

Lucy is most attracted to image when it remains evocative but imprecise. She saw a magic-lantern show of

> a Chinaman in a peaked hat, carrying two buckets on a stick. This last image she cherished because it connected in some way with her father, but she did not dwell on the significance of something so imprecise. Instead she rejoiced in the arbitrariness of all she had seen. (88)

Yet not all 'imagistic revelations' provide knowledge in the novel. Whereas 'not diversion, but knowing was the gift that story gave her' (114), the reverse is true of images that are made into narrative. Thus, there are magic lantern shows that produce 'enthralment' (108), the patrons 'surrendered to visions fantastical' (248). Here the magic lantern shows possess 'the weird Medusa power ... people lassooed [*sic*] willingly into vitreous fictions ... improbable conjunctions and fabulous spectacles' (233). They are linked to Madame Esperance's projections as luminous but spurious lies. Jones suggests:

> I wanted a certain scepticism about how the photograph was used ... this technology rapidly became used as a narrative form, as a form of deception and as a form of a different kind of pleasure. So, rather than recollection or recovering the real, it became a form of pleasurable fraudulence. (Jones, 2005)

In fact, Lucy's introduction to photography in the novel, and our own, foregrounds its fraudulent use. She visits the photographer's studio with Isaac, the man to whom she travelled as a potential wife, but whose relationship to her is soured by her pregnancy to another man. The visit is an effort, on Isaac's part, to project the image of them as a legitimate couple 'before – as he so indelicately put it – her shape betrayed her – an image, he said, that would help later on and might even serve as consolation to the future child' (139). The photographer's studio is a 'little world of props and false objects' (139), drawn together to construct an 'immaculately posed' (140) image.[16] The result, for Lucy, is at odds with her image of herself. It has elided some part of herself, making her less substantial, so that 'it seemed plausible that the rumour was true: that the camera removed some human quotient or iota with each image it took' (140). Gazing at a photograph of herself for the first time, Lucy experiences the characteristic dissonance between herself and her photographic image, and foresees the effect of this image, which will outlive her: 'people will look at this image when I am dead; it will stand in for me, for ever, just as my mother's austere paper cut-out – all stasis and reduction – now cruelly betokens her' (141). Lucy distinguishes between the studio photographer's immobilising 'seeing-eye coffin,' which 'sedated and mortified all he saw' and her camera which, she felt, 'discerned the capability of all things, all ordinary things, to be seen singly and remarkably' (141). That is, to be seen as unique, and not forced to fit a particular narrative.

The tension between knowledge-as-narrative and knowledge-as-image is dissolved at the end of the novel. Here, narrative unravels and becomes image. Or rather, the verbal and visual merge together as a series of memories that repeat for Lucy, unbidden. Lucy is dying at the age of twenty-two, drowning in tubercular fluid, and Violet's voice, reading Wilkie Collins' novel, *The Woman in White,* floats in and out of Lucy's consciousness. '[In] her mind, now, the novel unplaited and reversed. The mysterious encounter with the woman in white, an enigma drifting out of the darkness with no identity and purpose, seemed to her especially poignant and compelling, and the end, not the beginning, of any story' (243). As the narrative moves on, for Lucy the story is reduced to the single, luminous image of the woman in white: 'she was transfixed, perhaps self-indulgently, by this single, strange sign ... ' (243). Rather than a lesson in how others greet death, this seems more of the séance into her self of the experience of becoming a ghost, a hieroglyph, an image. The narrative of *Sixty Lights,* which has been, throughout, more a series of images than a linear, continuous narrative, dissolves further into flashes, using the images and metaphors that have been associated with the ethereal photograph throughout. Lucy is described as 'disembod[ied]', 'incandescent', 'ectoplasm' (244–5), until finally:

> the image slides suddenly away, into shiny nothingness ... Special things seen, and memories, and photographic prints, all converged to this quiet, private point. She tilted the glass. She was still

anticipating images. She was still anticipating, more than anything, an abyss of light ... (246)

Curiously, since she has so yearned for a photograph of her own dead mother, Lucy refuses her family, including her daughter, an image of herself before she dies. She leaves behind only two photos of herself:

> one was the ghost image, which the family could not quite bring themselves to dispose of, and the other was a studio photograph, taken in Bombay, in which Lucy stood posed beside Isaac Newton. She looked like a stranger, like a Mrs Newton, like someone unknown to them all. She was wearing unfamiliar clothes and had alien eyes. As her real face faded, slowly and imperceptibly, this false portrait would begin in sinister fashion to replace her. (248)

Thus, the photograph taken with Isaac, an example of photography used in the service of narrative, designed to create and propagate the legitimising story that they are a married couple, functions, after Lucy's death, as she envisioned it would, to fix her in an identity that she never embodied in life. The ghost image is of Lucy who, while being photographed with Thomas, Violet, Ellen and Mrs Minchin, moved during the exposure so that she 'appeared in print as blurred and residual' (236). In this picture Lucy almost literally embodies the figure of the ghost. 'Clearly I am meant from now on to be a partickler ghost' (236), she says.[17] Or, we might say, as she dies, that she is meant to be an asterisk, or present mark of an absent presence.

Rather than the photograph, then, which provides no memorial of Lucy, the novel returns to the idea of embodied, or re-membered memory. Thus, for Jacob, it is not a photograph that will reconnect him to Lucy, but the Indian Miniature, given to Lucy by Isaac and in turn gifted to Jacob. Jacob, an artist, finds the painting 'childish, inept', and yet, 'something in the face of Radha subtly evoked Lucy's face. She had an intractable self-possession and a whispering gaze' (248). His fingers repeat Lucy's own touch years before, when Isaac had first given her the miniature and remarked on the beetle wings. Rubbing his own finger on them, Jacob 'felt his own heart respond: some mystery of after-life momentarily possessed and moved him. In the absence of likeness there remained this trace of a touch, this memento of something actual but wholly unpictured' (248).[18]

This idea that objects other than photographs can hold memory through the medium of touch, through contact with the body, is a possibility that Isabelle ponders in *Afterimage*. She reflects that there is no one else to remember her in relationship to her childhood friend, and first love, Ellen:

> no one is thinking of us. We no longer exist to anything in the world. Maybe, in that forest there's a tree that remembers your touch when you stood there, close against it, waiting for me, over twenty years ago. Maybe that patch of bark you laid your hand on is now farther up the tree than I could reach. (96)

In addition to suggesting that objects might hold a memory of touch, this passage also stresses the importance of collective memory. It suggests that if there is no one to share a memory of what is lost, then the loss is felt afresh. Isabelle lost Ellen during childhood but the realisation that there is no one to remember them together, since her parents have now died, produces a second loss. Similarly, when Eldon dies, Isabelle feels it as a loss not only of Eldon, but of the memory he embodied:

> he was a place she had been that still glows dimly in the memory of her flesh. Now that he has died he has taken their whole shared past with him and she is left ... What is she to do with her understanding of him? ... And what about her? Will anyone ever know Isabelle again, as long and as well as Eldon did? He has remembered her, so she doesn't have to ... the truth is that Eldon's death means also that Isabelle will never be as she was, will not exist as strongly as before. (238)

This adds a further resonance to the notion, in each novel, of embodied memory. It is not only that the past inheres in individual bodies, but that memory is held collectively by bodies, and the death of the body necessarily involves a loss of memory too. This, in turn, threatens erasure. Isabelle becomes ghostly.[19]

IV

Each novel thus posits the need for communal recollection, a community of witnesses to cultural memory. And, in each novel, this takes the form of a community of readers. For, while they share thematic concerns such as historical recollection as a process, the importance of curiosity and of story-telling, and the text as a medium for historical recollection, *Sixty Lights* and *Afterimage* are configured differently to *Waterland* and

Possession, in which literary critics and historians construct a narrative of the Victorian past, deciphering traces left for the historical record and examining historical texts such as letters and diaries. Rather than represent the writing of the past, they explore the *reading* of it. *Sixty Lights* and *Afterimage* primarily mimic the action of memory, recurring and redoubling as a series of hallucinated images which re-member the Victorian period. With its sixty chapters that read as sixty snapshots, some apparently unrelated to the others, *Sixty Lights* is akin to an album of photographs, or a collection of memories, offering images that are partly obscured by shadow, flecked with time, coloured by loss, in keeping with Lucy's personal philosophy. The implication of the novels' depiction of reading as the siphoning of other experience is that *Sixty Lights* and *Afterimage* offer the Victorian era as the séance of another experience, another time, into ourselves. Indeed, through the notion of embodied and inherited memory, they offer the Victorian era as part of our heritage, and inheritance; the Victorian period is written into our cultural memory.

Thus, more than she invokes 'history', 'metahistory' or 'historiographic metafiction', Jones identifies her novel a 'memory text' (Jones, 2005). This can be understood in the same sense that Edwards calls photographs 'memory texts', suggesting that the circulation of photographs establishes and maintains links between groups and individuals, overcoming distance, for example, and enabling distant family members to participate in special moments and rituals. 'They reinforce networks and identity built on the memory to which they relate, positioning individuals vis-à-vis the group, linking past, present and perhaps implying a future.' By offering her novel as a memory text, Jones attempts to establish these connections between the Victorian era and our own. Or, in the vocabulary of her novel, to prompt the recognition that there are 'sight-lines, image tokens, between people and people, between people and objects and words on a page, that knit[s] the whole world in the purest geometry of connections. One simply ha[s] to notice. One ha[s] to remark' (114).

One way she does this is by allowing her text to mediate, or resuscitate, Victorian novels. In both *Sixty Lights* and *Afterimage*, the incorporation of well-known Victorian fictions as reading material for the protagonists – notably Charlotte Brontë's *Jane Eyre,* which also features in Humphreys' text, but also *Great Expectations* and Wilkie Collins' *The Woman in White,* among others – creates an image-repertoire that we share with the characters. Reading becomes an act of communal recollection not only between ourselves and our contemporaries, but also between ourselves and our Victorian ancestors, mediated by the Victorian novel itself. In this way, the use of Victorian novels in the contemporary texts acts as Groth suggests photography did for Victorians such as Barrett Browning, 'in the interests of thickening the connective tissue of memory' (Groth, 2003: 10).[20] Jones calls these links and connections 'acts of imaginative transfer', an 'aesthetic mobilisation by which we connect with the irreducible otherness of the beloved' (Jones, 2006) or in this case, the Victorian past. Georges Letissier's discussion of the 'refraction' of the English canon in 'post-Victorian' fiction elucidates this notion of Victorian novels as a repertoire of images we share not only with our contemporaries but with the Victorians themselves. Moreover, it points, too, to the way in which the Victorian novels become 'source-texts' for contemporary fiction:

> refraction ... is used in physics to designate the phenomenon by which a ray of light, or an electromagnetic wave is deflected from its previous course in passing out of one medium into another of different density. When metaphorically applied to literature, it would imply that the source-text – the composite Victorian corpus – has been passed on, through reading, to a contemporary filtering consciousness, which in its turn produces its own mediated version of the original. Such refracting process is all the more complicated as it implies both reading as personal activity ... and simultaneously, reading as a collective experience. (Letissier, 2004: 112)

Both *Sixty Lights* and *Afterimage* position the Victorian era as antecedent to, and persistent in, our own culture. In an interview with Jeffrey Canton, Humphreys suggests that she 'was interested in this particular time because, in a sense, it's the beginning of our time. The birth of photography is the beginning of our modern, image-obsessed world' (Canton, 2000). *Sixty Lights*, too, suggests certain continuities between the birth of photography in the Victorian era and features of our own, visual, culture. It establishes connections between the Victorian past and our own by making Lucy a visionary, able to predict the future uses of photography, including x-rays and ultrasound technology, the cinema and television (233). Lucy also foresees critical commentary upon these visual technologies. She explains to Jacob her aestheticism, 'what she call[s] art-in-the-age-of-mechanical-reproduction' (239), using Walter Benjamin's phrase (Benjamin 1968b), and Jacob reflects that 'she spoke like someone who was watching history unfold' (218). While this appears to invoke an evolutionary relationship between the Victorian period and our own, the specificity with which Lucy foresees us evokes the logic of the ghost; suggests the disruption of linear time, the aberrant presence of the Victorian in our culture. In a photographic reversal, that is, Lucy is able to *see us*. For Jacob, it is as though 'unbidden, he had glimpsed Lucy in another realm' (218). The distance between past and present is elided.

Indeed, both novels have been criticised in reviews for psychological anachronism. For Susan Elderkin, Lucy is too modern, 'eerily ahead of her time' and the portrait of the period is unconvincing: 'references to Dickens and pink bonnets come as a surprise' (Elderkin, 2004). For Ion Martea, the novel 'fails to bring the insight into the period the author had intended to deliver' (Martea, undated review). Humphreys, too, has been criticised for creating an anachronistic heroine. Andrea Barrett observes that Annie 'reshapes Isabelle's thinking about proper representations of women' and, therefore, Annie 'can seem both too good to be true and anachronistic, her character shaped by class and gender issues that belong to our time and not hers' (Barrett, 2001). For Elderkin, Martea and Barrett these anachronisms represent chronological and historiographical confusion and a serious failing in an historical novel. However, I would argue that the use of anachronism contributes to the sense that the Victorian past continues to exist in uncanny forms today; it suggests its absent presence.

The sense of linear disruption is consolidated in *Afterimage* through the immediacy of its present tense. It suggests a kind of afterlife, or, more properly as Humphreys' title suggests, an 'afterimage', a picture that continues to be visible, in altered form, after its original has vanished. It is memory, seeking to hold onto the transient and, in the process, transfiguring it. These novels proceed as memory does for Benjamin, in fragments, connecting events according to 'resemblances' or 'correspondences' (Benjamin, 1968a: 211). They offer themselves as aberrant repetitions of the Victorian period, suggesting that what is important is not that the past is accurately known, or fully understood or made sense of, but that it is remembered in fractured form, as shards of memory. Jones suggests that 'words and images do not have achieved reparation within them, what they have are the gestures towards reparation' (Jones, 2006). Like Lucy's notebook of 'Special Things Seen', the historical novel becomes, here, a kind of shrine, a 'kind of honouring attention' (200).

Thus, a scene in *Sixty Lights* in which Lucy sees a gaslit street in London '*remade* in a quivery film of light' provides a model for thinking about memory and historical recollection in the novel. Moreover, it provides a model for thinking about Jones' project as an historical novelist or, as she might put it, the author of a memory text. The novelist casts light upon aspects of the Victorian period. This light does not simply illuminate, but, like London's gaslight, *remakes* that which it touches. Just as Lucy is 'bound to this contradiction between the material and its ethereal incarnation in light' (186), so the historical novel does not so much materialise past actuality as recast it in, and as, light. Invested in re-membering the Victorian period, in its imaginative re-creation in and through word-images, *Sixty Lights* and *Afterimage* offer themselves as the (transfigured) repetition of the Victorian in contemporary culture.

Like Lucy and Annie, we are positioned as readers and, like them, we trace references from text to text, not in order to reconstruct the past but to re-member it, as a séance of another time and experience into our own. Finally, then, it is Annie who ties together reading as an act of historical recollection, an embodied memory that returns us to the past. She ponders questions of reference, wondering, 'What is to be believed? Is the true story the story that is made or the story that is forgotten?' (69). The experience that she imagines for herself, gleaned from books she has read, might be as 'true' as the experience itself, she thinks: 'perhaps what can be imagined is somehow a stronger truth because it inhabits you, is you, becomes you. It happens from the inside out' (67). As Lyn Jacobs observes in her article about Jones, this is 'the power of the 'cherished image': the way in which, when *re-embodied* by the reader, intensities of experience are distilled and/or re-invested with "symbolic" meaning' (Jacobs, 2006, 192, emphasis mine).

Thus, in *Sixty Lights* and *Afterimage* the Victorian past is offered to us, via a series of references to popular Victorian novels, photographs, fashion, events and landmarks, as an afterimage, a picture that we continue to see, albeit in 'ghosted' form. The novels are themselves repetitions of the Victorian period, mediums for its haunting presence. Their exploration of Victorian photography, cartography, and reading foregrounds memory discourse, with its vocabulary of loss, but also of retrieval. These novels write the Victorian period into our cultural memory, and suggest that the period has left myriad traces embodied in texts, images and other material, if ephemeral, forms. Rather than focus upon the problematisation of historical representation, *Sixty Lights* and *Afterimage* utilise the spectrality of the photograph as a means to explore the uncanny repetition of the Victorian past in the present, and to focus upon the possibility of recovery, the attempt at reparation, even if that which is restored amounts only to the aberrant presence of the ghost. Each posits the historical novel as one means through which the Victorian past can be remembered, if not restored, through the power of language.

Conclusion: 'What will count as history?'

> The Victorian past has come to uncanny life in contemporary fiction.
>
> (Hilary Schor, 'Sorting, Morphing and Mourning', 2000)

This book has traced the re-creation of the Victorian era in recent historical fictions, focusing on novels by Graham Swift, A. S. Byatt, Sarah Waters, Helen Humphreys and Gail Jones. It has argued that that these fictions deploy the vocabulary of Victorian strategies of history-making and recollection in order to re-member the period as part of our cultural memory. These fictions, together with other cultural and political evocations of the period, explore both our continuity with, and difference from, our Victorian forebears, and formulate our relationship to the period as a series of repetitions which produce both the shock of recognition and the fright of estrangement. They naturalise and celebrate the desire for historical recollection and are themselves evidence of the continuing longing for cultural memory today.

I have suggested that throughout the twentieth century, and into the twenty-first, the Victorian period has proved remarkably amenable to rewriting. As we have seen, whether it has been produced as ancestor or as 'other', celebrated as superior or denigrated as inferior to contemporary culture, the Victorian period has played a central role in our representations of ourselves, to ourselves. A period that can be cast in terms of its elegance, propriety, and imperial grandeur and, equally, in terms of its squalor, poverty, discrimination and humanitarian neglect, offers ample resources for praise or censure, emulation or disclamation. Together, the contemporary returns to the Victorian era in fiction, history, politics and popular culture produce multifarious and sometimes contradictory images of the period. They write and rewrite the Victorian period, but in so doing, they remember it, and perform the important work of shaping and producing cultural memory.

This book has added to the critical discussion of neo-Victorian fiction a focus on which particular images of the Victorian period they produce and to what ends. It has particularly highlighted the novels' representation of Victorian strategies of history-making. In *Waterland,* the era is governed by the exigencies of progress, particularly technological advancement, enabling ambitious, forward-thinking entrepreneurs to cast themselves as servants of the future. Yet this stereotypically Victorian image of faith in progress is undermined by a counter-narrative of doubt in progress and the desire for return. In *Possession,* the desire for return is no longer subjugated and instead becomes the defining feature of the era. Byatt's Victorian period is characterised by wide-ranging intellectual endeavour motivated by the desire to mediate the past, to make dead voices speak, whether through its fossilised remains or through poetic ventriloquism. *Affinity* and *Fingersmith* appropriate the conventionally feminine forms of Victorian gothic and sensation, genres not normally associated with the historical but which sought to represent Victorian culture to itself, in order to invent a history of lesbian representation in literature. In *Sixty Lights* and *Afterimage* the desire to make dead voices speak transforms into the desire to cheat the obliterating action of time and death by creating permanent images, though words and writing, as defences against forgetting. Thus, one of the period's important technological inventions, the photograph, is proclaimed as 'the future' but is, paradoxically, inextricably linked to the past via the yearning for memory-made-permanent.

While each novel highlights diverse aspects of the Victorian period and different strategies for historical recollection, what they have in common is the depiction of the period as one that looked back, desirous of a means to 'fix' memory, indeed, to materialise it. In *Possession, Affinity, Fingersmith, Afterimage* and *Sixty Lights,* the literary text is depicted an important medium for materialising the past. Texts written in the Victorian era and, in slightly different ways, contemporary texts that return to it, write the Victorian period into our cultural memory and continue to re-member it in new contexts and for a variety of purposes today. Dramatising Victorian strategies of recollection and celebrating the text-as-medium enables these writers to lay a claim to representing the past in a climate of historiographical crisis. It enables them to suggest, too, that in addition to textual traces, the past persists in the form of embodied memory and in repertoires of shared images that form and inform our historical consciousness. Furthermore, each novel utilises its representation of the Victorian period to dramatise and promulgate the desire for historical recollection as fundamental to human experience.

I have attempted, in both the theoretical foundations and the textual analyses, to suggest that history, fiction and historical fiction, together with memory, are mutually implicated, although conventionally distinct, discourses that each lay a (more or less contested) claim to historical representation. My account of historical fiction's relationship to 'official' histories has argued that the genre has always been supplementary and revisionary of official history in ways that problematise the notions of objectivity and reference. Adding to the critical discussion of these novels by positioning them in relation to their generic heritage, I have also suggested that contemporary recreations of the Victorian period elaborate and extend the theoretical approaches to contemporary historical fictions that remain influential today. The first, Linda Hutcheon's account of 'historiographic metafictions' as the representative genre of postmodernism, foregrounds the problematisation of historical reference, and reads these texts in terms of their deployment of self-reflexivity, irony and complicitious critique to question the very possibility of historical knowledge. The second theoretical approach, Amy J. Elias' conception of 'metahistorical romance', foregrounds the romance elements of these fictions in order to posit their desire for 'history itself'; history as unproblematic presence and locus of Truth.

The texts discussed here challenge Hutcheon's opposition of nostalgic recuperation versus a critical engagement with the past signalled by the pattern of complicity and critique. Emerging amidst a broader cultural fascination with the period, their very evocation of the Victorian era makes nostalgia a structuring principle of these texts, yet this does not negate their critical engagement with the past they represent. Indeed, contrary to Christian Gutleben's assertion that a nostalgic text *cannot* be subversive (Gutleben, 2001: 218), it might be the case today that the cultivation of nostalgia to critically engage the past is not only possible, but constitutes a potentially more subversive approach to historical recollection today. As Jennifer Green-Lewis persuasively suggests, the academic formulation of nostalgia that

dismiss[es] it as reactionary and politically suspect, a combination of poor history and narcissistic imaginings ... forgets the postmodern complexities of history and indeed threatens a new essentialism by inferring a retrievable, primary past to be subverted or erased by the falsification of nostalgic imagination. (Green-Lewis, 2000: 44)

I have suggested that re-presenting (making present) and representing (creating a portrayal of) the Victorians fold together in these novels. The resultant representation of the past is not an invocation of history as presence/Being/Truth, as Elias' account suggests. Rather, in these novels, the depicted past is a ghostly, aberrant presence, 'nowhere as such, and yet everywhere; and yet everywhere different' (Wolfreys, 2002: 140). The ghost marks disappearance. Having no presence of its own, its meaning derives only from those attributed to it in the present. As Hilary Schor claims in the epigraph above, 'the Victorian past has come to *uncanny* life in contemporary fiction' (Schor, 2000: 235, emphasis mine).

This book has demonstrated the centrality of the figure of the ghost in these fictions as a metaphor for both the persistence of the past and our relationship to it today. Reversing the conventional image of the beckoning ghost returning to make a claim upon the present, in these fictions the ghost does not reach out to us, rather we seek it out, conjure it up. Our very desire to remember produces both Victorian texts and contemporary fictionalisations of the period as mediums through which we remember the past. By suggesting some of the meanings that the spectre accrues in these fictions, and by pointing to the prevalence of ghostly metaphors in neo-Victorian novels, this book has laid the groundwork for further investigation of the uses of spectrality in these fictions. One productive avenue to explore would be a comparison of the use of the spiritualist movement in contemporary fictions and their Victorian counterparts. If the use of the supernatural opens up a space for discussing the illicit and unsayable in Victorian fictions, for example, does it continue to function this way in contemporary uses of the Victorian supernatural?[1] Are we and the Victorians haunted by the same ghosts?

Yet in an age of historiographical crisis which, paradoxically, proliferates historical representation in histories, fictions, politics, literary and cultural criticism, in advertising, fashion, home furnishings and on websites, it is not only 'history itself', that is the spectral figure. Rather, this commingled obsession with and scepticism toward history produces the question 'what will count as history?' as the ghost that haunts contemporary culture.

Historical fictions can, perhaps, be considered some of the many '*competing* narratives' that Hayden White envisages as forming, together, intellectually engaged and rigorous accounts of the past (White, 1999:

28).[2] White's discussion of the narrative properties of even traditional histories highlights the way in which the question of what will count as history is often contested over the question of generic appropriateness. For White, all narrative histories are subject to generic considerations; the same facts can be shaped into a variety of generic forms, and the same facts accrue different meanings, depending upon whether they are given a tragic, comic, or epic structure (ibid.: 29–30). He argues that while some genres are considered more appropriate to the telling of particular events – he points to the often unarticulated stipulation that 'a serious theme ... demands a noble genre, such as epic or tragedy, for its proper representation' – there are actually many genres that can produce meaningful versions of the same events. White takes Art Spiegelman's *Maus: A Survivor's Tale* (1972, 1973–1991), which uses the form of a comic book to present the events of the Holocaust, as an example of the successful deployment of a 'low' genre to produce 'a particularly ironic and bewildered view of the Holocaust ... one of the most moving narrative accounts of it that I know of, not least because it makes the difficulty of discovering and telling the whole truth about even a small part of it as much a part of the story as the events whose meaning it is to discover' (ibid.: 31).[3] Although White's persuasive argument about the value of a variety of genres in the telling of history focuses upon traditional histories, it points, too, to the ways in which historical fictions, and even counterfactual histories, can play a role in producing meaningful, competing narratives of past events despite, or even because, of their particular generic, and figural, properties.

In the last few decades, the proliferation of fictional accounts of the Victorian period, when considered in relation to each other and to other constructions of the period by historians, politicians and cultural critics, form a textured, diverse, and at times contradictory picture of a period that continues to fascinate the contemporary imagination. These accounts revise and contest each other, so if the period is always written and rewritten, a palimpsest, its meaning is also never fixed. In *Waterland's* terms, these constructions and reconstructions of the Victorian period ensure that our histories of the era are continually dredged. They serve to remind us of the fictiveness, that is, the constructedness, of all the significations that we ascribe to it.

Thus, the question of what will count as history continues to hover, contested. In fact, because of the problematisation of narrative as a means for representing past reality, which has highlighted, too, the shared conventions of historical and fictional narratives and elided their discursive differences, history and fiction appear again, in some way, as they were in the eighteenth century, united as branches of rhetoric in an effort of understanding. This is a not a coming full circle, an arching backward, or a regression, but rather a distorted repetition. In contrast to the eighteenth-century understanding, the question is not which discourse most effectively provides access to history, conceived as unproblematic presence. In an age that treats the narratives of history and fiction as more or less ideologically suspect versions of the past, the question becomes, will anything count as history? Posed another way, this is the question raised by Fredric Jameson and others and addressed in the Introduction to this book: can contemporary culture think historically at all? Instead of being more or less authentic ways of accessing the meaning of the past, history and fiction today are alike engaged in exploring the ways in which the past can be meaningfully produced in an age that has problematised the very notion of historical reference.

Neo-Victorian novels, such as those by Swift, Byatt, Waters, Humphreys and Jones, emerge from, contribute to and dramatise a continuing desire for cultural memory today. Acknowledging that arriving at a final, complete version of the past is impossible and, indeed, undesirable, these novels shift the aim and focus of historical recollection from the production of an accurate account of past events to the always-unfinished *process* of remembering. In doing so, they participate in what Jerome de Groot has called the 'historical imaginary'. Like other forms of non-academic history 'they reflect the complexity of contemporary cultural and social interface' (De Groot, 2009: 6). Thus, historical novelists continue to explore the creative possibilities of their own role in historical recollection. The re-presentation of the Victorian era in these novels celebrates the potential of the literary text as an act of memory. Its imaginative re-creation stems from a desire to re-member the period as part of our shared history, our cultural memory, and asserts both continuities and discontinuities between Victorian culture and our own. The novels examined here propose that the persistence of the Victorian era today takes the form of repetitions and restructurations, through embodied memories, both personal and collective, and, importantly, through the manifold meanings that we continue to attribute it in our cultural, political, historical and literary discourses. These novels return to Victorian vocabularies of history, memory and loss in order to recast historical inquiry as desire, to avow the enduring importance of historical recollection. The very prevalence of contemporary historical fictions today is witness to this desire and its importance, and suggests, too, that the field of literature can productively contribute to ongoing debates about what will count as history. In an age charged with the inability to think historically, these historical novels exploit their generic heritage as modes of historical recollection to explore the ways in which it is still possible, desirable and necessary to re-present the past.

Notes

Introduction

1 Select examples include the following: On the cholera epidemic: Iain Sinclair's *White Chappell Scarlet Tracings* (1987) and Matthew Kneale's *Sweet Thames* (1992). On the Crimean War: Beryl Bainbridge's *Master Georgie* (1997). On the invention of photography: Lynne Truss' *Tennyson's Gift* (1996), Robert Solé's *The Photographer's Wife* (1999), orig. pub. *La Mamelouka* (1996), Helen Humphreys' *Afterimage* (2000), Ross Gilfillan's *The Edge of the Crowd* (2001), Katie Roiphe's *Still She Haunts* Me (2001), Fiona Shaw's *The Sweetest Thing* (2003), and Gail Jones' *Sixty Lights* (2004). On the race to control the Nile: Robert Solé's *The Photographer's Wife* (1999). On Colonialism: David Malouf, *Remembering Babylon* (1994), Peter Carey's *Jack Maggs* (1997) and Tobsha Learner's *Soul* (2006). On the discovery of fossils: John Fowles' *The French Lieutenant's Woman* (1969) and Graham Swift's *Ever After* (1992). On spiritualism: Michèle Roberts' *In the Red Kitchen* (1990), and Sarah Waters' *Affinity* (1999). The crisis of faith engendered by science: Graham Swift's *Ever After* (1992). On the emergent discipline of psychiatry: Sebastian Faulks' *Human Traces* (2005). On the new city: Iain Sinclair's *White Chappell Scarlet Tracings* (1987), Sheri Holman's *The Dress Lodger* (1999) and, in an Australian context, A. L. McCann's *The White Body of Evening* (2002). On consumerism: Fiona Shaw's *The Sweetest Thing* (2003).
2 A. S. Byatt's *Possession: A Romance* in 1990, Peter Carey's *The True History of the Kelly Gang* in 2001 and *Oscar and Lucinda* in 1988.
3 Green-Lewis' reference to the 'look' of the period may resonate with Jameson's indictment of the glossy images that stand in for the 'substance' of the historical past (Jameson, 1985: 118), but given that her discussion is concerned with Victorian photographs and visual technologies, it seems more likely that the use of 'look' is simply reflective of her own interests and concerns.

1   Memory Texts: History, Fiction and the Historical Imaginary

1 In the *Waverley* novels, she argues, this pressure is manifest in Scott's slow beginnings and speedy conclusions, which must grapple with historical expectations.
2 Writing in 1937, Lukács mirrors this concern, praising Scott's invention of figures that never 'fall psychologically outside the atmosphere of the age'. For Lukács, this is an important part of what separates Scott from the 'pseudo-historical' novels of the earlier centuries, since those novels 'simply equated naively the world of feeling of the past with that of the present', and establishes him as the founder, and leading example, of the historical novel. Nonetheless, he finds it necessary to trace, in the thought of Hegel and

Goethe, a philosophical defence of 'necessary anachronism' which, in Scott, 'consists, therefore, simply in allowing his characters to express feelings and thoughts about real, historical relationships in a much clearer way than the actual men and women of the time could have done. But the content of these feelings and thoughts, their relations to their real object, is always historically and socially correct. The extent to which this expression of thought and feeling outstrips the consciousness of the age is no more than is absolutely necessary for elucidating the given historical relationship' (See Lukács, 1962: 60, 61, 63).

3 For more on Scott and Hegelian dialectical evolution see Lukács, (1937) 1962. For an elaboration of Foucault's archeological model of historical inquiry see Foucault, 1977.

4 For Janik, Hutcheon's category of historiographic metafiction does not adequately describe novels such as Graham Swift's *Waterland* or A. S. Byatt's *Possession* or those by Peter Ackroyd, Julian Barnes and Kazuo Ishiguro, which have been defined by many scholars (some of them by Hutcheon herself), as examples of her genre. 'Indeed, these novels transcend the categories into which we have lately come to divide contemporary fiction.' He argues that these novels belie the neat allotment of twentieth-century literature into one of three categories: modernism, antimodernist realism and postmodernism, suggesting, rather, that they display, and exploit, characteristics of each (Janik 1995: 161–2).

5 Rody usefully describes this complicated notion of rememory: '... a "rememory" (an individual experience) hangs around as a "picture" that can enter another's "rememory" (the part of the brain that "rememories") and complicate consciousness and identity. "Rememory" as trope postulates the interconnectedness of minds, past and present ... For Sethe as for her author, then, to "rememory" is to use one's imaginative power to realize a latent, abiding connection to the past. "Rememory" thus functions in Morrison's "history" as a trope for the problem of imagining one's heritage' (Rody 1995: 101).

6 Indeed Rosario Arias Doblas argues that the prevalence of the use of ghostliness and hauntings as a metaphor for the presence of the past justifies the naming of the 'spectral' novel as a 'subset of the neo-Victorian novel' (Doblas, 2005: 87).

2 Contemporary Victorian(ism)s

1 This is an image of the Victorian era utilised by Matthew Kneale in his novel *Sweet Thames* (1992), in which he draws Felicia Lewis, a stereotypically puritanical Victorian in whose own home 'the dark dullness of colour and the hangings modestly concealing every table and chair leg well reflect[ed] the prudish natures of its inhabitants' and who, the narrator conjectures, 'was offended that the legs of the chairs and tables [in his home] were not modestly concealed behind hangings' (Kneale, 1992: 64, 17). In *Inventing the Victorians* (2001), historian Matthew Sweet devotes several pages to debunking this as myth and, indeed, asserting its American, not British origins. 'Whatever the case,' he argues, 'the synecdochic relationship that now exists between Victorian sensibilities and the clothed piano leg is wholly fraudulent.

It persists, however, because the story is useful as a way of dismissing the Victorians' experience as less honest, less sophisticated, less self-cognizant than our own' (see Sweet, 2001: xiii–xv).

2 Despite what appears, here, as a tendency to flatten the two eras, and make them continuous, Armstrong's analysis also points to the differences between them, the ways in which the Victorian era cannot be considered continuous with our own.

3 My examination here is necessarily selective. For a more comprehensive discussion of the variety of ways in which the twentieth century has engaged with the Victorian past see Miles Taylor's edited collection of essays *The Victorians Since 1901* (Taylor, 2004).

4 This phrase was first attributed to Thatcher's platform by Brian Waldon in an interview in 1983, although Thatcher had invoked the period in service of her politics as early as 1977 (Thatcher, 1983a).

5 Bailin takes this phrase from the website *Wings and Roses*, which sells period garments for everyday wear (see www.wingsandroses.com). Her argument, here, is itself perhaps implicated in nostalgia for the Victorian, producing the period as having a somehow more authentic relationship to its past than we do to ours today.

3 A Fertile Excess: *Waterland*, Desire and the Historical Sublime

1 This multiple definition, ostensibly taken from the dictionary, which is, as Alison Lee argues, 'the ultimate self-referential text' (Lee, 1990: 41) together with the second epigraph, from Charles Dickens' *Great Expectations*, also foregrounds the question of reference in a complicated way. The novel's treatment of the Victorian era is referenced to a Victorian novel, suggesting that fiction of the period is an important source for its own depiction of the Victorian period and for the shape of the novel itself. As we shall see in more detail in Chapter 6, the use of Victorian novels as intertexts in neo-Victorian fiction foregrounds the way in which the Victorian period has entered our cultural memory via multiple sources, including its own fictions, and continues to be read, to function and to have meaning. For more detailed analyses of *Great Expectations* as a sub-text see Landow (Landow, 1990) and Lee (Lee, 1990: 41).

2 Price's use of the term 'history,' instead of 'world' here points to a further resonance of the 'End of History'. This refers to a sense of crisis in the discipline of history prompted by the challenge to the grand metanarratives of history, and to historiography itself, posed by postmodernism and discussed, for example, in Francis Fukuyama, *The End of History and the Last Man* (New York: Free Press, 1992). Fukuyama argues that capitalism had reached a stage of global consensus with the fall of communism. This ended the clash of civilisations that Hegel determined as the evolutionary pattern of history and, therefore, ended history. The End of History is given further resonance in *Waterland* via curricular cutbacks at the hands of Thatcherite economics and at the hands of fictional headmaster Lewis who, as we shall see, views history as an irrelevance.

3 Indeed, as we shall see, the novel's themes also perform this rejection of linear history. In the dramatisation of abortion and incest, instead of birth, the novel brings paternity, and the notions of linearity, continuity and progress on which it rests, to an abrupt end. As Rufus Cook observes, 'whatever else might be said about them, experiences involving incest and abortion, murder and suicide and child-abduction, all have to do in one way or another with the mysteries of origin and end' (Cook, 2004: 4).

4 While I am arguing here that there are some similarities between Tom's 'reality' and Elias' 'History', 'the postmodern historical sublime' or 'history itself' there is an important difference which stems from the rather loose and elusive way that Elias deploys her terms. These terms seem to refer at once to an Absence, but also, paradoxically, to a Truth which beckons, and which is a depository of meaning separate from our attempts at meaning-making. Tom's concept of reality takes in Elias' notion of the absence of over-arching meaning, but his reality is always other than the events of the past, which are conjoined in the novel to history-writing as familial exercises.

5 In fact in one of Tom's ruminations about the French Revolution, it happens for no other reason than that his school-children 'should have a subject for [their history] lessons' (16).

6 Swift's *Ever After* makes explicit this theme of historiography as artificial, as other than fundamental meaning, or reality. Here, it is connected with plastic and other synthetic products (lauded by Sam Ellison, entrepreneur of plastics, as 'substitoots'), and opposed to all 'naturally occurring substances' such as rock. See Graham Swift, *Ever After* (London: Pan Books, 1992). For a more detailed discussion of this theme, see Holmes (Holmes, 1996).

7 This litany of cause and effect forms a pattern, hubris, which the novel ultimately discredits as falsifying since, for it, there is no over-arching pattern to the histories and stories told. For Hanne Tange this passage is evidence that 'history has been regressive rather than progressive' (see Tange, 2004: 82). However it seems clear that Tom is not advocating this either, which is equally as dependent upon a supra-historical view. Meaning and pattern are not found, but constructed, produced in and by narrative. The novel does support, however, a model of historical inquiry, a Foucauldian archaeology of descent, which depicts these stories and things made to happen not according to strict cause and effect but as multiplicities that came into being against each other. This does not happen according to a pattern or plan but as the effect of a multiplicity of history-making jostled together.

8 My reading of the Here and Now here converges with deCoste's reading of it 'as, in effect, a glimpse of Crick's real'. DeCoste usefully argues that Swift uses the 'Here and Now' to contrast 'history as meaningful Maia, as narrative fiction, and the real as a chaotic, semantic void' (Decoste, 2002: 381). However he fails to situate the Here and Now at the cusp of making history on the one hand, and empty reality on the other, tending, rather, to conflate it with the real, or let it stand in for it as another metaphor, in a way that the novel does not. The failure to note that the Here and Now results from history-making has significance for his reading of reality in the novel, which, as we shall see, cannot retain the sense of 'semantic void' that he, following Tom, attributes to it. An articulation of reality, the Here and Now is, for DeCoste,

the moment when the nullity of reality rises up against history and takes it back to itself. Indeed, the real is associated, for Decoste, 'not simply with the death of meaning but with more concrete deaths, more material destruction, as well' (ibid.: 382). I want to suggest that this attributes to reality a materiality, design and an intention that the novel is not supported by the novel.

9   This can be seen has his playing out, on a smaller scale, the course of narrative history that Decoste observes in the novel on a larger scale. Tending to insist on final answers without appeal, on stable but restricted definitions of the meaning of things, the narrativisation that fuels the making of history carries with it, too, the desire to simplify, finalise, and even brutally exclude. In its fulfilment of such narrative desires, history works to bring forth apocalyptic conflagrations to burn away that which does not conform to the answer sought, the 'proper' end of the story' (ibid.: 390).

10   As we have already seen, Tom also provides two explanations, one mythic and the other more realist, for Ernest Atkinson's actions in the novel.

11   Focusing on the evocation of a 'fairy-tale place', Hanne Tange argues that the description of the Fenland setting does not place the Fens in the wider context of the map of England, and that this is to emphasise the marginality of the locale, claiming 'no initial attempt is made to place this landscape on the map of England, for the rest is of little significance'. I agree that the Fens are represented as somewhat insulated from a British centre. And, moreover, that Tom's ultimate relocation to London marks, in some sense, a commitment to national history. However, the introduction, so early in the novel, of the precise geography of the Fens does seem to attempt to place the Fens on the map of England, and this is important to the depiction of 'making history', in all its resonances, in the novel (see Tange, 2004: 78).

12   Indeed, Brewer and Tillyard assert that Swift's novel attempts to be 'a universal story of the human condition' (Brewer and Tillyard, 1985: 50). My reading of the novel aligns human nature with natural history and therefore identifies it as a category of the real, in opposition to history, stories and making things happen. It therefore counters Decoste's association of the real with 'inhumanity', because of the death and destruction he attributes to the real (Decoste, 2002: 395).

13   Cooper, too, notes that Tom 'maps her desirability' in these terms. For Cooper, Mary is 'stereotyped and essentialized as a kind of 'eternal feminine' ... less a character than a placeholder or conduit for desire: a dioramic sequence of paradises lost' (Cooper, 1996: 385).

14   See also Pamela Cooper's argument that 'in Ernest's passion for Helen the trajectory of imperialism is reversed; its expansive energies are redirected towards an interior space of desire, neither subjective nor objective, but abject: the body of the daughter' (Cooper, 1996: 380).

15   Indeed Brewer and Tillyard argue that the novel traffics in the 'cult of naturalness', what they call 'the notion of "naturalness" as somehow both better and more real' and which 'has become one [of] the most tiresome clichés of the modern age' (Brewer and Tillyard, 1985: 51). The novel certainly does seem to support this reading, although it is countered, as we shall see, by Tom's own belief in the value of artificial history and the civilisation it supports and makes possible.

4   Dispossessing Knowledge: A. S. Byatt's *Possession: A Romance*

1   In this I take my cue from Kelly A. Marsh who uses the term 'neo-sensation novel' to designate a number of contemporary historical fictions (see Marsh, 1995).

2   However, they are treated rather sympathetically by Byatt, who in some way, validates the work of Beatrice Nest, who had wanted to study Ash because she fell in love with him, even to the point of placing a photograph of him in her home 'where those of a father or lover might have stood' (477). The personal connection with her subject that is suggested by the photograph most approximates 'resuscitation' as Ash describes it, and contrasts with the impersonal style of the other critics. Significantly, it is the critically naïve Beatrice Nest who comes closest to guessing at the truth about Ash and LaMotte prior to the discovery of the letters, by recognising that Ash addresses a real woman in his poetry, and not a feminine ideal (113). Moreover, in contrast to the collector Mortimer Cropper, Nest is correct in surmising that Ellen burnt many letters (219) and, importantly, she is right in her assessment of Ellen's journal, that something is 'omitted' (221) and that she wrote it to 'baffle' (220). Ellen herself notes that in her journal the truth of her life is 'carefully *strained*' (461) and that 'it was both a defence against, and a bait for, the gathering of ghouls and vultures' (462).

3   Depicting the buildings that house archival materials in this way complicates Suzanne Keen's use of *Possession* as exemplificative of her category of 'romances of the archive', which 'have scenes taking place in libraries or in other structures housing collections of papers and books' and in which 'scholarly and amateur characters seek information in collections of documents' (Keen, 2001: 3), by suggesting that these places are not conducive to attaining knowledge, at least of the kind that Byatt celebrates and elucidates. While Keen's reference to scholarly research as 'intellectual questing' intimates Byatt's model for knowledge by implying something of the visceral as well as the cerebral, her discussion needs to be elaborated to focus the role that the text itself plays in *Possession*, its importance in unearthing 'the secrets and hidden truths that can be ferreted out of archives' (ibid.: 28). While Keen's focus remains upon the scholarly act of 'ferreting out' such truths, the novel is also preoccupied with the limitations of this 'documentarism' and pursuit of 'hard facts' (ibid.: 3), and accords the text a more central role in the attainment of knowledge.

4   For an excellent discussion of the many multiple meanings of possession and dispossession in the novel see Hennelly (Hennelly, 2003: 449ff).

5   This idea that the past persists in the present through bodily inheritance is explored further in Chapter 6 of this book in relation to *Sixty Lights* and *Afterimage*, each of which suggest that the body itself has a memory and is thus a medium for the past, holding onto it and bestowing upon it an endurance.

6   Jukić observes that in Emma Tennant's *Tess* (1993) and Isabel Colegate's *The Summer of the Royal Visit* (1991), lineage is similarly used to establish a link with the Victorian past. 'In each case', she argues, 'the contemporary narrators, in their accounts of Victorian circumstances, affirm their credibility

by claiming to be the authentic descendants of the Victorians whose stories they tell' (Jukić, 2000: 84). I would argue that for Tennant's and Colegate's novels, as for those studied in this book at length, the notion of embodied memory goes further, to suggest not only credibility in storytelling, but the actual persistence of the past in bodily signs and repetitions.

7   Some of the novel's motifs include thresholds, fountains, baths, gardens, glass stones and, importantly, the multiple meanings of 'possession', and many more. For a fuller discussion of these repeating patterns see Henelly (Henelly, 2003).

8   Hennelly pertinently suggests that at this moment, when Roland hears Ash's voice and his language comes alive for him, he becomes Ash's 'poetic descendant ... [and] inherits Ash's unified sensibility in an intrapsychic sense' (Henelly, 2003: 459). This adds a further resonance to the notion of the text as medium, allowing the voices of the past to haunt the present, and, indeed, to take possession.

9   The ideal reader of the novel thus approximates Byatt's hopes for her own efforts as critical reader: 'I do believe that if I read *enough*, and carefully enough, I shall have some sense of what words meant in the past, and how they related to other words in the past, and be able to use them in a modern texts so that they do not lose their relations to other words in the interconnected web of their own vocabulary' (Byatt, 2000: 177).

10   Their textual analyses do, however, sometimes lead them to the wrong conclusion, as when they take LaMotte's poem about spilt milk (381–2) to mean that her child was still-born (422). Literary critics might be 'natural' detectives, but they are not infallible.

11   Indeed, as Buxton has pointed out, the swift critical and popular success of *Possession*, which saw it win major literary awards and enter its eighth print run within months of its first publication, suggests that its title 'uncannily prophesied its readerly effect' (Buxton, 2001: 89).

12   Katherine Coyne Kelly notes that 'rather than a description of reading, *Possession* ... is an *enactment* of reading' (Kelly, 1996: 95).

13   This is an echo of the idea raised in Fowles' *The French Lieutenant's Woman*, in which the narrator muses that 'by transferring to the public imagination what they left to the private, we are the more Victorian – in the derogatory sense of the word – century, since we have, in destroying so much of the mystery, the difficulty, the aura of the forbidden, destroyed also a great deal of the pleasure' (Fowles, 1992: 234). The colonisation of desire at the hands of science in the nineteenth century is also discussed by Catherine Belsey who suggests, similarly to Byatt and Fowles, that 'in the process of scientific analysis something slipped away. What is arbitrary, paradoxical and elusive, subjected to explanation and measurement, becomes drab and clinical' (Belsey, 1994a: 11).

14   Byatt does, however, include a more stereotypical depiction of Victorian sexuality in the figure of Ellen Ash who, made to wait twelve years to marry Ash, is unable to consummate her marriage (456–60). Matthew Kneale's *Sweet Thames* also invokes this image of the Victorian woman in Isobella Jeavons, who is also unable to consummate her marriage, despite being the consummate wife and helpmeet in all other respects. Yet whereas Byatt retains the image of a Victorian woman so thoroughly protected and innocent that she

is unable to enjoy physical intimacy, Kneale's heroine is revealed to have been marred by the incestuous attentions of her father, from whom her marriage to Joshua is her attempt at escape (Kneale, 1992).

15 See, for example: Hulbert, 1993; D'Evelyn, 1990; Heron, 1990; Thurman, 1990. For examples of criticism that approaches the novel as postmodern see Belsey, 1994b; Bronfen 1996; Wells, 2002. For the suggestion that its postmodern techniques are used to conservative, and not postmodern, ends see Holmes 1994; Buxton, 2001; Yelin 1992.

16 As Richard Todd argues, the film of citation, repetition and textual doubles that connect the Victorian past with the 1980s present allows us to compare Val, for whom the realisation that she is 'superfluous' enables her to leave Roland and form a new relationship with Euan, and Blanche, for whom the realisation ends in her tragic suicide (see Todd, 1994).

17 Becker cites Judith Butler's centring of the body in her aptly titled *Bodies that Matter: on the discursive limits of sex* (1993) and the collection of essays *Emotions in Postmodernism* (1997) as examples of 'developments in both the critical and a larger cultural discourse that *Possession* so joyfully anticipates' (Becker, 2001: 29).

5 'Making it seem like it's authentic': The Faux-Victorian Novel as Cultural Memory in *Affinity* and *Fingersmith*

1 I have adapted this from Julie Sanders' discussion of the authenticating strategy of the historical novel more generally: 'But historical fiction is a wide umbrella term. It can, for example, include novels or plays which choose to locate themselves in the "past", known or otherwise, providing contextual details of that "past" as an authenticating strategy: we "believe in" or yield to the events of such novels or plays partly because the background detail is so accurately drawn' (Sanders, 2006: 138).

2 See Erll and Nünning, 2005 and Lachmann, 1997, 2004. Much of this work is emerging from Germany. Lena Steveker provides a very interesting and informative account of the work of some German scholars, including Jan Assman and Aleida Assman and Astrid Erll, who have worked toward theorising the role of literature in performing cultural memory, using her own translations from the German (see Steveker, 2009).

3 The monomaniacal pursuit, which followed clues based on sensation, intuition and emotion more than calculated, rational inquiry, is what distinguished these early proto-detective figures from the later, rational detective figure epitomised by Sherlock Holmes a few decades later.

4 Recently there have also been some interesting and productive links made between gothic and queer theory (see for example Rigby, 2009).

6 'The alluring patina of loss': Photography, Memory, and Memory Texts in *Sixty Lights* and *Afterimage*

1 As we saw in Chapter 2, some examples of neo-Victorian fictions that concentrate on the emergent technology of photography include Lynne Truss'

Tennyson's Gift (1996), Robert Solé's *La Mamelouka* (1996) trans. *The Photographer's Wife* (1999), Ross Gilfillan's *The Edge of the Crowd* (2001), Katie Roiphe's *Still She Haunts Me* (2001), Fiona Shaw's *The Sweetest Thing* (2003) and Susan Barrett's *Fixing Shadows* (2005).

2 John Tagg, for example, explicates photography's origins with reference to the emergence of particular technologies, observing that the 'experimental initiatives which resulted in the invention of photography itself were situated at the point of convergence of a variety of scientific disciplines, involving optics, the chemistry of light-sensitive salts, the design of lenses, and the precision engineering of instruments' (Tagg, 1988: 40).

3 He situates the invention of photography against a broader crisis of the subject/object relationship which, by the early nineteenth century, he argues, had been problematised: 'intellectuals across Europe and its colonies have begun to question the presumed separation of observer and observed, locating all acts of seeing in a contingent and subjective human body. The observer is no longer imagined to be the passive and transparent conduit of God's own eye but now is regarded as someone who actively produces what is seen ... ' Batchen argues that photography became an imperative because 'what had to be invented ... was an apparatus of seeing that involved both reflection and projection, that was simultaneously active and passive in the way it represented things, that incorporated into its very mode of being the subject seeing and the object being seen' (Batchen, 2001: 22).

4 See, for example, Hannah Arendt's claim that 'from the very outset, in formal philosophy, thinking has been thought of in terms of seeing' (Arendt, 1978: 110–11).

5 Sandra Goldbacher's 1998 film concerned with the Victorian invention of photography, *The Governess*, participates in this mythologising of photography's origins. It credits a young governess, played by Minnie Driver, with discovering that saline is the necessary ingredient for making the photographic image permanent after she serendipitously cries salt tears over an image.

6 This magical imagery is adopted by *Afterimage* in references to photography as 'alchemy' (117), 'something she has conjured up' (15). In *Sixty Lights* photography is 'magic and illusion' (177), a part of 'visions fantastical' (248), the camera is a 'black-magic box' (154).

7 In fact, Kate Flint describes the Victorian experience of memory in terms similar to those used by Groth to describe photography. She observes that in the Victorian period 'the very nature of memory' was thought to be constituted by the 'elision of past and present' (Flint, 2003: 529).

8 Roiphe's novel explores the relationship between Charles Dodgson, also known as Lewis Carroll, and his most famous photographic subject, Alice Liddell. As the title suggests, it, too, invokes the ghostly aspect of photography.

9 At the end of A. S. Byatt's 'Morpho Eugenia,' Captain Papagay professes a similar notion, that 'as long as you are alive, everything is surprising, rightly seen' (Byatt, 1993: 160).

10 Later in the novel Lucy appears to register a negative effect of this capacity when she muses on the ubiquity of images and the difficulty of discerning between them on behalf of her daughter: 'how does one direct the vision of small children or assert which image is important or which inconsequential? Perhaps this can only be known by one's self' (198). This appears, at times,

to be a problem for the novel itself, which draws all things into its aesthetic of the ordinary. As Ken Gelder remarks 'there is not a critical bone in Jones's novel, which lends its aesthetic consent to pretty much everything it comes across' (Gelder, 2005: 36).

11 Edwards notes that the display of photographs, in albums, in framed collections or on top of televisions and mantelpieces lend the form 'shrine-like qualities' (Edwards, 1999: 233).

12 The trope is also utilised in other neo-Victorian novels such as Michèle Roberts' *In the Red Kitchen* (1990), in which Hattie King is, like Lucy and Annie, an orphan who feels lost and displaced; and Graham Swift's *Waterland* (1983), in which the protagonist and his wife are each motherless.

13 Similarly, in Sebastian Faulks' neo-Victorian novel, *Human Traces* (2005), Jacques' mother dies following childbirth and he has 'no memory of his mother, he could not revive her ... there was not so much as a daguerreotype of the first Madam Rebiere' (Faulks, 2005: 8). Faulks deploys imagery that is similar to both Humphreys' and Jones' to describe the way that Jacques' mother is an elusive, ephemeral and only partially glimpsed image: 'An 'impression', on wax or metal, was draughtsmanship from which accurate images, unlimited in number, could be taken. His mother was something much vaguer, beyond even the abstract grasp of memory, yet still present, still an entity in his mind, a glimpse of life withheld' (ibid.: 9).

14 This action, of trying to make the map melt into her skin, to make herself literally embody Ireland, is reversed later in the novel when the maps that they have laid Eldon's burned body upon 'has become a blotter for the ink of his dissolving body. His flesh has divided counties and formed tiny islands in the sea. The seepage from his body has permanently altered the maps beneath him ... He has been granted his wish ... He has made his map of the world' (240).

15 Indeed, Eldon makes his own journey of recovery and retrieval when he learns that Annie is still inside his burning house and he goes back in to rescue her. When he realises that he is suffering from smoke inhalation he thinks: 'But it is alright ... He has done his best. He has gone back for a member of the expedition. He has been his bravest self. It has been a long journey. He is home' (232). His words are echoed by Annie when, after Eldon's death, she reflects on her own act of bravery during the fire. She, too, entered the burning building to rescue the boy Isabelle has 'borrowed' from a neighbour for her photograph. 'Eldon would have been proud that Annie had rescued the boy from the fire. She had behaved in a loyal way to those in her charge. She had been a good member of the expedition' (246). Each has commanded a recovery expedition. It is the journey, not the destination, that is important.

16 Fiona Shaw's *The Sweetest Thing* (2003) also represents a first encounter with a photographer's studio in this way, as a room 'full of things out of place,' listing many and varied props and backdrops for the construction of images that purport to be 'real' (Shaw, 2003: 16). As we saw in Chapter 2, this text explores the exploitative possibilities of photography more fully.

17 The reference is to a family joke shared between Thomas, Uncle Neville and herself in their early days together in London when they had read *Great Expectations* together. This reference to Hamlet's father's ghost, filtered through Dickens' novel, marks the moment when Lucy and Thomas see that

Neville carries their mother in/with him as an embodied memory, 'and they looked at each other reassured and with instinctive understanding' (85).

18 Jacob is a painter, and he, too, '[yearns] to create an artwork that summons one, just one, sure and precise memory, immediate as a photograph'. The memory he wishes to retrieve is one of his (now deceased) father standing in a doorway, 'his face bright, alive' (216). Thus, the exploration of images as acts of devotion, cheating death, is continued in him. He, like Isabelle in *Afterimage*, is attracted to art because he 'learned as a young boy that nothing was fixed but art' (203).

19 Similarly, in Faulks' *Human Traces*, as Jacques' brother Olivier retreats inside himself, disconnecting from the world that Jacques inhabits and listening only to mysterious voices inside his head, he takes the memory of their mother with him: 'now, as Olivier travelled further into his own world, he took with him Jacques's last chances of ever making contact with his mother's memory' (Faulks, 2005 11). It is this knowledge that, in part, spurs Jacques' determination to become a psychiatrist, desperate to understand the disease that afflicts his brother and for which, in the nineteenth century, there is no name.

20 Suzanne Keen argues, too, that Peter Ackroyd's fictions and biographies (several of which reimagine the Victorian past) act similarly, so that 'the present in which we live becomes in Ackroyd's handling a palimpsest of imagined pasts, recovered not for the sake of historical accuracy or revisionist narrative (though he sometimes achieves these goals along the way), but to heighten the sense of connection, continuity, tradition and repetition' (Keen, 2001: 130).

Conclusion: 'What will count as history?'

1 Rosario Arias Doblas has posed one answer to this question by suggesting that contemporary spectral novels are 'a textual space for fictionalising what is absent from the historical record', including women and, particularly, lesbianism, in Sarah Waters' novels, for example (see Doblas, 2005). One could speculate that if the 'spectral' novel allows women to enter history, it might function similarly for postcolonial texts.

2 White takes up Saul Friedlander's use of the term 'competing narratives' to refer to the epistemological and ethical difficulties raised by the proliferating representations of Nazism and the Final Solution in the narratives of history, fiction, film, museums and memorials and various other media. Friedlander used the term in a memo to participants in a conference that gave rise to the collection of essays published in *Probing the Limits of Representation: Nazism and the 'Final Solution,'* edited by Friedlander in 1992.

3 Originally published serially, first for underground comic *Funny Animals* (1972) and then in *RAW* magazine (1973–1991), Art Speigelman's comic strip is also published as *Maus: A Survivor's Tale* (New York: Pantheon, 1986).

Select Bibliography

Primary sources

Ackroyd, Peter. 1983. *The Last Testament of Oscar Wilde*. London: Penguin.
_____. 1987. *Chatterton*. London: Penguin.
Atwood, Margaret. 1996. *Alias Grace*. New York: Doubleday.
Bainbridge, Beryl. 1998. *Master Georgie*. London: Abacus.
Braddon, Mary Elizabeth. 1987 (1862). *Lady Audley's Secret*. Oxford: Oxford University Press.
Buxton, James. 1997. *Pity*. London: Orion.
Byatt, A. S. 1991. *Possession: A Romance*. London: Vintage Books. Original edition, London: Chatto & Windus, 1990.
_____. 1993. 'Morpho Eugenia.' In *Angels and Insects*. London: Vintage.
Carey, Peter. 1997. *Jack Maggs*. St Lucia, Queensland: University of Queensland Press.
_____. 1988. *Oscar and Lucinda*. Brisbane: University of Queensland Press.
_____. 2000. *The True History of the Kelly Gang*. Brisbane: University of Queensland Press.
Carr, Caleb. 1994. *The Alienist*. New York: Random House.
Carter, Angela. 1984. *Nights at the Circus*. London: Chatto and Windus.
Collins, Wilkie. 1999 (1860). *The Woman in White*. London and New York: Penguin.
Doctorow, E. L. 1998. *The Waterworks*. Sydney: Pan Macmillan. Original edition, 1988.
Drabble, Margaret. 1987. *The Radiant Way*. London: Weidenfeld and Nicolson.
Eco, Umberto. 1984. *Postscript to The Name of the Rose*. Translated by W. Weaver. Orlando: Harcourt Brace Jovanovich.
Falkner, John Meade. 1991. *The Lost Stradivarius*. Oxford and New York: Oxford University Press. Original edition, 1895.
Faulks, Sebastian. 2005. *Human Traces*. London: Hutchinson.
Fowles, John. 1992. *The French Lieutenant's Woman*. London: Pan Books. Original edition 1969.
Frazier, Charles. 1997. *Cold Mountain*. London: Hodder and Stoughton.
Fruttero, Carlo, and Franco Lucentini. 1994. *The D Case, or the Truth About the Mystery of Edwin Drood*. London: Chatto and Windus.
Gibson, William, and Bruce Sterling. 1991. *The Difference Engine*. New York: Bantam Books.
Gilfillan, Ross. 2001. *The Edge of the Crowd*. London: Fourth Estate.
Glendinning, Victoria. 1995. *Electricity*. London: Hutchinson.
Holman, Sheri. 1999. *The Dress Lodger*. London: Hodder and Stoughton.
Humphreys, Helen. 2001. *Afterimage*. London: Bloomsbury. Original edition 2000.
Jensen, Liz. 1998. *Ark Baby*. Woodstock, New York: Overlook Press.
Jones, Gail. 2004. *Sixty Lights*. London: Harvill Press.

Kneale, Matthew. 1992. *Sweet Thames: A Novel*. London: Sinclair-Stevenson.
Learner, Tobsha. 2006. *Soul*. Sydney: Harper Collins.
Lee, Vernon. 1890. The Wicked Voice. In *Hauntings: Fantastic Stories*. London: William Heinemann.
Lively, Penelope. (1991) 1992. *City of the Mind*. Harmondsworth: Penguin.
Malouf, David. 1994. *Remembering Babylon*. London: Vintage. Original edition 1993.
Martin, Valerie. 1990. *Mary Reilly*. London: Doubleday.
McCann, A. L. 2002. *The White Body of Evening*. Sydney: Flamingo.
Morrison, Toni. 1987. *Beloved*. London: Chatto and Windus.
Rhys, Jean. 2000. *Wide Sargasso Sea*. London: Penguin. Original edition 1966.
Roberts, Michèle. 1990. *In the Red Kitchen*. London: Methuen.
Roiphe, Katie. 2001. *Still She Haunts Me*. London: Review.
Shaw, Fiona. 2003. *The Sweetest Thing*. London: Virago.
Sinclair, Iain. 1998. *White Chappell Scarlet Tracings*. London: Granta Books. Original edition 1988.
Solé, Robert. 1999. *The Photographer's Wife*. Translated by J. Brownjohn. London: Harvill. Originally published as *La Marmelouka* (1996).
Soueif, Ahdaf. 1999. *The Map of Love*. London: Bloomsbury.
Starling, Belinda. 2007 (2006). *The Journal of Dora Damage*. London, New York and Berlin: Bloomsbury.
Stephanson, Neal. 1995. *The Diamond Age*. New York: Bantam.
Stoker, Bram. 2003 (1897). *Dracula*. London: Penguin.
Swift, Graham. 1991 (1983). *Waterland*. London: Picador.
_____. 1992. *Ever After*. London: Pan Books.
Tennant, Emma. 1993. *Tess*. London: Harper Collins.
Tóibín, Colm. 2004. *The Master*. Sydney: Picador.
Truss, Lynne. 1996. *Tennyson's Gift*. London: Penguin.
Waters, Sarah. 1998. *Tipping the Velvet*. London: Virago.
_____. *Affinity*. 2000 (1999). London: Virago.
_____. *Fingersmith*. 2003 (2002). London: Virago.

Films

Frears, Stephen (director). 1996. *Mary Reilly*.
Gyllenhaal, Stephen (director). 1992. *Waterland*.
LaBute, Neil (director). 2002. *Possession*.
Goldbacher, Sandra (director). 1998. *The Governess*.
Sax, Geoffrey (director). 2002. *Tipping the Velvet*.

Secondary sources

Anderson, Perry. 1998. 'Foreword'. In *The Cultural Turn: Selected Writings on the Postmodern 1983–1998*, edited by F. Jameson. London and New York: Verso.
Anonomous. 1843. Photogenic Drawing, or Drawing by the Agency of Light. *The Edinburgh Review* (January): 154.
Appleby, Joyce, Lynn Hunt, and Margaret Jacob. 1994. *Telling the Truth About History*. New York and London: W. W. Norton.
Arendt, Hannah. 1978. *The Life of the Mind*. New York: Harcourt Brace Jovanovich.

Armitt, Lucie, and Sarah Gamble. 2006. 'The haunted geometries of Sarah Waters' *Affinity'*. *Textual Practice* 20 (1): 141–59.

Armstrong, Nancy. 1999. *Fiction in the Age of Photography: The Legacy of British Realism*. Cambridge, Massachusetts and London, England: Harvard University Press.

_____. 2000. 'Postscript. Contemporary Culturalism: How Victorian Is It?' In *Victorian Afterlife: Postmodern Culture Rewrites the Twentieth Century*, edited by J. Kucich and D. F. Sadoff. Minneapolis and London: University of Minnesota Press. 311–26.

Assmann, Jan. 1995. 'Collective Memory and Cultural Identity'. *New German Critique* 65: 125–33.

Bailin, Miriam. 2002. 'The New Victorians'. In *Functions of Victorian Culture at the Present Time*, edited by C. L. Krueger. Athens, Ohio: Ohio University Press. 37–46.

Baker, John F. 1996. 'A. S. Byatt: Passions of the Mind'. *Publisher's Weekly* 243 (21): 235–6.

Bal, Mieke. 1999. Introduction. In *Acts of Memory: cultural recall in the present*, edited by M. Bal, J. Crewe and L. Spitzer. Hanover: University Press of New England. vii–xvii.

Barefoot, Guy. 1994. '*East Lynne* to *Gas Light*: Hollywood, Melodrama and Twentieth-Century Notions of the Victorian'. In *Melodrama: Stage, Picture, Screen*, edited by J. Bratton, J. Cook and C. Gledhill. London: British Film Institute. 95–105.

Barrett, Andrea. 2001. Catching the Light. Review of *Afterimage*, by Helen Humphreys. *The New York Times*, April 15. http://query.nytimes.com/gst/fullpage.html?res=9CO4E3DC123EF936A25757COA9679C8B63.

Barthes, Roland. 1957. *Mythologies*. Translated by A. Lavers. London: Paladin Grafton.

_____. 1984. *Camera Lucida: Reflections on Photography*. Translated by R. Howard. London: Fontana Paperbacks. Original edition 1980.

_____. 1986. 'Historical Discourse'. In *The Rustle of Language*. New York: Hill and Wang. Original edition 1967.

_____. 1997. *Image, Music, Text*. Translated by S. Heath. London: Fontana.

Basbanes, Nicholas A. 1999. 'The More Things Stay the Same'. *Biblio* 4 (1): 10.

Batchen, Geoffrey. 2001. *Each Wild Idea: Writing, Photography, History*. Cambridge, Massachusetts and London, England: MIT Press.

Baudrillard, Jean. 1983. 'The Orders of Simulacra'. In *Simulations*. New York: Semiotext(e).

_____. 1995. *The Illusion of the End*. Cambridge: Polity Press.

Becker, Susanne. 1999. *Gothic Forms of Feminine Fictions*. Manchester and New York: Manchester University Press.

_____. 2001. 'Postmodernism's Happy Ending: *Possession!*' In *Engendering Realism and Postmodernism: Contemporary Women Writers in Britain*, edited by B. Neumeier. Amsterdam and New York: Rodopi. 17–30.

Beer, Gillian. 2000. *Darwin's Plots: Evolutionary Narrative in Darwin, George Eliot and Nineteenth Century Fiction*. 2nd edn. Cambridge: Cambridge University Press. Original edition 1983.

Belsey, Catherine. 1994a. *Desire: Love Stories in Western Culture*. Oxford, UK and Cambridge, USA: Blackwell.

_____. 1994b. 'Postmodern Love: Questioning the Metaphysics of Desire'. *New Literary History* 25 (3): 683–705.

Benjamin, Walter. 1968a. 'The Image of Proust'. In *Illuminations*, edited by H. Arendt. New York: Schocken Books.

_____. 1968b. 'The Work of Art in the Age of Mechanical Reproduction'. In *Illuminations*, edited by H. Arendt. Glasgow: Fontana. Original edition 1936.

Bennett, David. 1990. 'Postmodernism and Vision: Ways of Seeing (At) The End of History'. In *History and Post-Modern Writing*, edited by T. D'haen and H. Bertens. Amsterdam: Rodopi. 257–9.

Berger, James. 1997. 'Trauma and Literary Theory'. *Contemporary Literature* 38 (3): 569–82.

Berger, John. 1972. 'Understanding a Photograph'. In *The Look of Things: Selected Essays and Articles*, edited by N. Stangos. London, UK and Victoria, Australia: Penguin Books. Original edition 1959. 178–82.

Bernard, Catherine. 1997. 'A Certain Hermeneutic Slant: Sublime Allegories in Contemporary English Fiction'. *Contemporary Literature* 38 (1): 164–83.

Beum, Robert. 1997. 'Gertrude Himmelfarb on the Victorians and Ourselves'. *Sewanee Review* 105 (2): 260–6.

Bodnar, John. 1992. *Remaking America: Public Memory, Commemoration, and Patriotism in the Twentieth Century*. Princeton, New Jersey: Princeton University Press.

Botting, Fred. 2008. *Gothic Romanced: Consumption, gender and technology in contemporary fictions*. London and New York: Routledge.

_____. 1996. *Gothic*. London and New York: Routledge.

Bourne-Taylor, Jenny. 1988. *In the Secret Theatre of the Home: Wilkie Collins, sensation narrative and nineteenth-century psychology*. London and New York: Routledge.

Boyle, Thomas. 1989. *Black Swine in the Sewers of Hampstead: Beneath the Surface of Victorian Sensationalism*. New York and London: Viking Penguin.

Boym, Svetlana. 2001. *The Future of Nostalgia*. New York: Basic Books.

Bradford, Richard. 2007. *The Novel Now: Contemporary British Fiction*. Malden, Massachusetts: Blackwell.

Bradley, James. 2004. Humanity in Focus Through a Camera Lens. Review of *Sixty Lights*, by Gail Jones. *The Age*, 21 August, 4.

Brewer, John, and Stella Tillyard. 1985. 'History and Telling Stories: Graham Swift's *Waterland*'. *History Today* 35: 49–51.

Bronfen, Elisabeth. 1996. 'Romancing Difference, Courting Coherence: A. S. Byatt's *Possession* as Postmodern Moral Fiction'. In *Why Literature Matters: Theories and Functions of Literature*, edited by A. Rudiger and L. Volkmann. Heidelberg: Winter. 117–34.

Brooks, Peter. 1984. *Reading for the Plot: Design and Intention in Narrative*. Oxford: Clarendon.

Bullen, J. B. 1997. 'Introduction'. In *Writing and Victorianism*. New York: Longman. 1–13.

_____. ed. *Writing and Victorianism*. London and New York: Longman.

Burgin, Victor. 1982. 'Introduction'. In *Thinking Photography*. London and Basingstoke: Macmillan.

Burton, Anthony. 2004. 'The revival of interest in Victorian decorative art and the Victoria and Albert Museum'. In *The Victorians since 1901: Histories, representations and revisions*, edited by M. Taylor and M. Wolff. Manchester and New York: Manchester University Press. 121–37.

Bury, J. B. 1956. 'The Science of History'. In *The Varieties of History from Voltaire to the Present*, edited by F. Stern. New York: Meridian. Original edition 1902. 209–23.

Buxton, Jackie. 2001. 'What's love got to do with it?': Postmodernism and *Possession. Contributions to the Study of World Literature* 110: 89–104, 165–88.

Byatt, A. S. 1991a. 'People in Paper Houses: Attitudes to "Realism" and "Experiment" in English Post-war Fiction'. In *Passions of the Mind*. London: Chatto and Windus.

_____. 1991b. 'Robert Browning: Fact, Fiction, Lies, Incarnation and Art'. In *Passions of the Mind: Selected Writings*. London: Chatto and Windus. 29–71.

_____. 2000. 'True Stories and the Facts in Fiction'. In *On Histories and Stories*. London: Chatto and Windus. 99–122.

Cadava, Eduardo. 1997. *Words of Light: Theses on the Photography of History*. Princeton, New Jersey: Princeton University Press.

Canton, Jeffrey. 2000. 'The Winds of Change: Victorian Snapshot Captures Culture in Transition'. Review of *Afterimage*, by Helen Humphreys. *Eye Weekly*.

Cardinal, Roger. 1992. 'Nadar and the Photographic Portrait in Nineteenth-Century France'. In *The Portrait in Photography*, edited by G. Clarke. London: Reaktion Books. 6–24.

Carroll, Rachel. 2007. 'Becoming My Own Ghost: Spinsterhood, Heterosexuality and Sarah Waters' *Affinity*'. *Genders* 45. http://www.genders.org/g45/g45Carroll.html

Castle, Terry. 1993. *The Apparitional Lesbian: Female Homosexuality and Modern Culture*. New York: Columbia University Press.

Chandler, James. 1998. *England in 1819: The Politics of Literary Culture and the Case of Romantic Historicism*. Chicago and London: University of Chicago Press.

Chapple, J. A. V. 1986. *Science and Literature in the Nineteenth Century*. Edited by A. Pollard, *Context and Commentary*. London: Macmillan.

Chase, Malcolm, and Christopher Shaw. 1989. 'Dimensions of Nostalgia'. In *The Imagined Past: History and Nostalgia*, edited by C. Shaw and M. Chase. Manchester and New York: Manchester University Press. 1–17.

Chatman, Seymour. 1978. *Story and Discourse: Narrative Structure in Fiction and Film*. Ithaca and London: Cornell University Press.

Ciocia, Stephania. 2007. 'Queer and Verdant': The Textual Politics of Sarah Waters's Neo-Victorian Novels. *Literary London: Interdisciplinary Studies in the Representation of London* 5 (2). www.literarylondon.com

Clancy, Laurie. 2004. 'Selective History of the Kelly Gang'. Review of *The True History of the Kelly Gang*, by Peter Carey. *Overland* 175: 53–8.

Colley, Ann C. 1998. *Nostalgia and Recollection in Victorian Culture*. Basingstoke, UK and New York: Macmillan and St. Martin's – now Palgrave Macmillan.

Collingwood, R. G. 1946. *The Idea of History*. Oxford.

Connerton, Paul. 1989. *How Societies Remember*. Cambridge: Cambridge University Press.

Constantini, Mariaconcetta. 2006. '"Faux-Victorian Melodrama" in the New Millenium: The Case of Sarah Waters'. *Critical Survey* 18 (1): 17–39.

Cook, Pam. 2005. *Screening the Past: Memory and Nostalgia in Cinema*. London and New York: Routledge.

Cook, Rufus. 2004. 'The Aporia of Time in Graham Swift's *Waterland*'. *Concentric: Literary and Cultural Studies* 30 (1): 133–48.

Cooper, Pamela. 1996. 'Imperial Topographies: The Spaces of History in *Waterland'*. *MFS: Modern Fiction Studies* 42 (2). 371–96.

Cordle, Daniel. 2000. *Postmodern Postures: Literature, science and the two cultures debate*. Aldershot: Ashgate.

Crosby, Christina. 1992. 'Reading the Victorians'. *Victorian Studies* 36: 63–74.

Curthoys, Ann, and John Docker. 2005. *Is History Fiction?* Michigan: University of Michigan Press.

Cvetkovich, Ann. 1992. *Mixed Feelings: Feminism, Mass Culture, and Victorian Sensationalism*. New Brunswick, New Jersey: Rutgers University Press.

Dale, Peter Allan. 1989. *In Pursuit of a Scientific Culture: Science, Art, and Society in the Victorian Age*. Madison, Wisconsin: University of Wisconsin Press.

Dames, Nicholas. 2001. *Amnesiac Selves: Nostalgia, Forgetting, and British Fiction 1810–1870*. Oxford and New York: Oxford University Press.

Davis, Colin. 2005. 'Etat Present: Hauntology, Spectres and Phantoms'. *French Studies* LIX (3): 373–9.

Day, Gary. 1998. 'Introduction: Past and Present: the case of Samuel Smiles' *Self Help*'. In *Varieties of Victorianism: The Uses of a Past*. London and New York: Macmillan. 1–24.

De Certeau, Michel. 1988. *The Writing of History*. Translated by T. Conley. New York: Columbia University Press.

Decoste, Damon Marcel. 2002. 'Question and Apocalypse: The Endlessness of *Historia* in Graham Swift's *Waterland'*. *Contemporary Literature* 43 (2): 377–99.

De Groot, Jerome. 2009. *Consuming History: Historians and Heritage in Contemporary Popular Culture*. London and New York: Routledge.

Demos, John. 2005. 'Afterword: Notes From, and About, the History/Fiction Borderland'. *Rethinking History* 9 (2/3): 329–35.

Dennis, Abigail. 2008. '"Ladies in Peril": Sarah Waters on neo-Victorian narrative celebrations and why she stopped writing about the Victorian era'. *Neo-Victorian Studies* 1 (1): 41–52.

Derrida, Jacques. 1980. 'The Law of Genre'. *Glyph* 7.

_____. Derrida, Jacques. 1983. 'The Principle of Reason: The University in the Eyes of Its Pupils'. *Diacritics* 13 (3): 2–20.

_____. 1994. *Specters of Marx: the state of the debt, the work of mourning, and the new international*. Translated by P. Kamuf. New York: Routledge. Original edition, Derrida, Jacques. Spectres De Marx. Paris: Galilee, 1993.

_____.1996. *Archive Fever: A Freudian Impression*. Translated by E. Prenowitz. Chicago: University of Chicago Press.

_____. 2001. *Deconstruction Engaged: the Sydney Seminars*. Sydney: Power-Publication.

D'Evelyn, Thomas. 1990. A Book About Books. Review of *Possession: A Romance*. *Christian Science Monitor*, 16 November, 13.

Dever, Carolyn. 1998. *Death and the Mother From Dickens to Freud: Victorian Fiction and the Anxiety of Origins*. Edited by G. Beer and C. Gallagher. Vol. 17, *Cambridge Studies in Nineteenth-Century Literature and Culture*. Cambridge, UK: Cambridge University Press.

D'haen, Theo, and Hans Bertens, eds. 1995. *Narrative Turns and Minor Genres in Postmodernism*. Amsterdam: Rodopi.

Doan, Laura, and Sarah Waters. 2000. 'Making up lost time: contempo-rary lesbian writing and the invention of history'. In *Territories of desire in queer culture: Refiguring contemporary boundaries*, edited by D. Alderson and L. Anderson. Manchester and New York: Manchester University Press. 12–28.

Doblas, Rosario Arias. 2005. 'Talking with the Dead: Revisiting the Victorian Past and the Occult in Margaret Atwood's *Alias Grace* and Sarah Waters' *Affinity*'. *Estudios Ingleses de la Universidad Complutense* 13: 85–105.

Docherty, Thomas, ed. 1993. *Postmodernism: A Reader*. New York: Harvester Wheatsheaf.

Edwards, Elizabeth. 1999. 'Photographs as Objects of Memory'. In *Material Memories*, edited by M. Kwint, C. Breward and J. Aynsley. Oxford, New York: Berg. 221–36.

Elam, Diane. 1992. *Romancing the Postmodern*. London and New York: Routledge.

_____. 1993. 'Postmodern Romance'. In *Postmodernism Across the Ages*, edited by B. Readings and B. Schaber. New York: Syracuse University Press. 216–37.

Elderkin, Susan. 2004. My Brilliant Career. Review of *Sixty Lights*, by Gail Jones. *Guardian*, September 25. http://books.guardian.co.uk/reviews/generalfiction/0,6121,1312167,00.html

Elias, Amy 2001. *Sublime Desire: History and Post-1960s Fiction*. Baltimore and London: Johns Hopkins University Press.

_____. 2005. 'Metahistorical Romance, the Historical Sublime, and Dialogic History'. *Rethinking History* 9 (2/3): 159–72.

Erll, Astrid, and Ansgar Nünning. 2005. 'Where Literature and Memory Meet: towards a systematic approach to the concepts of memory used in literary studies'. In *Literature, Literary Memory and Cultural Memory*, edited by H. Grabe. Tübingen: Gunter Narr. 261–94.

Evans, Eric. 1997. *Thatcher and Thatcherism*. Edited by E. Evans and R. Henig, *The Making of the Contemporary World*. London and New York: Routledge.

Ferris, Ina. 1991. *The Achievement of Literary Authority: Gender, History, and the Waverley Novels*. Ithaca and London: Cornell University Press.

Fincher, Max. 2007. *Queering Gothic in the Romantic Age: The Penetrating Eye*. Basingstoke and New York: Palgrave Macmillan.

Fitting, Peter. 1991. 'The Lessons of Cyberpunk'. In *Technoculture*, edited by C. Penley and A. Ross. Minneapolis: University of Minnesota Press.

Flegel, Monica. 1998. 'Enchanted Readings and Fairy Tale Endings in A. S. Byatt's *Possession*'. *English Studies in Canada* 24: 413–30.

Fleishman, Avrom. 1971. *The English Historical Novel: Walter Scott to Virginia Woolf*. Baltimore and London: Johns Hopkins University Press.

Flint, Kate. 1997. 'Plotting the Victorians: Narrative, Post-Modernism, and Contemporary Fiction'. In *Writing and Victorianism*, edited by J. B. Bullen. London: Longman. 286–305.

_____. 2003. 'Painting Memory'. *Textual Practice* 17 (3): 527–42.

Flynn, Thomas. 1994. 'Foucault's Mapping of History'. In *The Cambridge Companion to Foucault*, edited by G. Gutting. Cambridge, UK and New York and Melbourne, Australia: Cambridge University Press. 28–46.

Foley, Barbara. 1986. *Telling the Truth: The Theory and Practice of Documentary Fiction*. Ithaca: Cornell University Press.

Foucault, Michel. 1970. *The Order of Things: An Archaeology of the Human Sciences*. London: Tavistock Publications. Original edition *Les Mots et les choses*. Éditions Gallimard, 1966.

____. 1972. *The Archaeology of Knowledge*. Translated by A. M. Sheridan Smith. London: Routledge. Original edition *L'Archéologie du savoir*. Éditions Gallimard, 1969.

____. 1976. *The History of Sexuality: An Introduction*. Translated by R. Hurley. Vol. 1. London: Penguin.

____. 1977. 'Nietzsche, Genealogy, History'. In *Language, Counter-Memory, Practice*. Ithaca, New York: Cornell University Press. 139–64.

____. 1988. 'Power and Sex'. In *Michel Foucault: Politics, Philosophy, Culture, Interviews and Other Writings 1977–1984*, edited by L. D. Kritzman. New York and London: Routledge. 110–24.

Fradenburg, Louise, and Carla Freccero. 1996. 'Caxton, Foucault, and the Pleasures of History'. In *Premodern Sexualities*, edited by L. Fradenburg and C. Freccero. New York and London: Routledge. xiii–xxiv.

Friedlander, Saul. 1993. *Memory, History, and the Extermination of the Jews of Europe*. Bloomington: Indiana University Press.

Fuery, Patrick, and Nick Mansfield. 2000. *Cultural Studies and Critical Theory*. 2nd edn. Oxford, UK and New York: Oxford University Press. Original edition 1997.

Fukuyama, Francis. 1992. *The End of History and the Last Man*. New York: Free Press.

Frow, John. 1997. *Time and Commodity Culture: Essays in Cultural Theory and Postmodernity*. Oxford: Clarendon Press.

____. 2005. *Genre*. NewYork: Routledge.

Gaille, Andreas. 2001. 'The True History of the Kelly Gang at Last!' Review of *The True History of the Kelly Gang*, by Peter Carey. *Meanjin* 3: 214–19.

Gardiner, John. 2004. 'Theme-park Victoriana'. In *The Victorians Since 1901: Histories, representations and revisions*, edited by M. Taylor and M. Wolff. Manchester and New York: Manchester University Press. 167–80.

Gasiorek, Andrzej. 1995. *Post-War British Fiction*. London, New York, Sydney and Auckland: Edward Arnold.

Gearhart, Suzanne. 1984. *The Open Boundary of History and Fiction: A Critical Approach to the French Enlightenment*. Princeton, New Jersey: Princeton University Press.

Gelder, Ken. 2005. '"Plagued by Hideous Imaginings": The Despondent Worlds of Contemporary Australian Fiction'. *Overland* 179: 32–7.

Geyer-Ryan, Helga. 1994. *Fables of Desire: Studies in the Ethics of Art and Gender*. Cambridge: Polity Press.

Gilmour, Robin. 1993. *The Victorian Period: The Intellectual and Cultural Context of English Literature, 1830–1890*. Edited by D. Carroll and M. Wheeler, *Longman Literature in English Series*. London and New York: Longman.

Giobbi, Giuliana. 1994. 'Know the Past: Know Thyself. Literary Pursuits and the Quest for Identity in A. S. Byatt's *Possession* and in F. Duranti's *Effetti Personali*'. *Journal of European Studies* 24 (93): 41–54.

Gitzen, Julian. 1995. 'A. S. Byatt's Self-Mirroring Art'. *CRITIQUE: Studies in Contemporary Fiction* 36 (2): 83–95.

Gottlieb, Anthony. 1995. Why Can't We Behave. Review of *The De-Moralization of Society*, by Gertrude Himmelfarb. *The New York Times on the Web*, February 19. http://www.nytimes.com/books/home/

Green, Anna, and Kathleen Troup. 1999. *The Houses of History: A Critical Reader in Twentieth-Century History and Theory*, edited by A. Green and K. Troup. New York: New York University Press.

Green-Lewis, Jennifer. 1996. *Framing the Victorians: Photography and the Culture of Realism*. Ithaca and London: Cornell University Press.

_____. 2000. 'At Home in the Nineteenth Century: Photography, Nostalgia, and the Will to Authenticity'. In *Victorian Afterlife*, edited by J. Kucich and D. F. Sadoff. London and Minneapolis: University of Minnesota Press. 29–48.

Groth, Helen. 2000. 'A Different Look: Visual Technologies and the Making of History in Elizabeth Barrett Browning's *Casa Guidi Windows*'. *Textual Practice* 14 (1): 31–52.

_____. 2003. *Victorian Photography and Literary Nostalgia*. Oxford: Oxford University Press.

Gutleben, Christian. 2001. *Nostalgic Postmodernism: The Victorian Tradition and the Contemporary British Novel*. Edited by T. D'haen and H. Bertens, *Postmodern Studies*. Amsterdam and New York: Rodopi.

Haggerty, George. 2006. *Queer Gothic*. Urbana and Chicago: University of Illinois Press.

Hall, D. E. 1999. 'The production of Victorian culture and Victorian cultural studies: Introduction'. *Nineteenth Century Prose* 26 (1): 1–11.

Hamilton, Paul. 1996. *Historicism*. London: Routledge.

Hardt, Hanno, and Bonnie Brennen. 1999. 'Introduction'. In *Picturing the Past: Media, History, and Photography*, edited by H. Hardt and B. Brennen. Urbana and Chicago: University of Illinois Press. 1–10.

Harlan, David. 2007. 'Historical fiction and the future of academic history'. In *Manifestos for History*, edited by K. Jenkins, S. Morgan and A. Munslow. London and New York: Routledge. 108–30.

Hassan, Ihab. 1987. *The Postmodern Turn: Essays in Postmodern Theory and Culture*. Columbus: Ohio State University Press.

Hayes, Julie C. 1998. 'Fictions of Enlightenment: Sontag, Suskind, Norfolk, Kurzweil'. In *Questioning History: The Postmodern Turn on the Eighteenth Century*, edited by G. Clingham. Lewisburg: Bucknell University Press. 21–36.

Hayles, N. Katherine, ed. 1991. *Chaos and Order: Complex Dynamics in Literature and Science*. Edited by D. N. McClosky and J. S. Nelson, *New Practices of Inquiry*. Chicago and London: University of Chicago Press.

Heilman, Ann, and Mark Llewellyn. 2004. 'Hystorical Fictions: Women (Re)Writing and (Re)Reading History'. *Women: A Cultural Review* 15 (2): 137–52.

Hennelly, Mark M. Jr. 2003. ''Repeating Patterns' and Textual Pleasures: Reading (in) A. S. Byatt's *Possession: A Romance*'. *Contemporary Literature* 44 (3): 442–71.

Heron, Liz. 1990. Fiction. Review of *Possession: A Romance*. *Times Educational Supplement*, 6 April, 26.

Hewison, Robert. 1987. *The Heritage Industry: Britain in a climate of decline*. London: Methuen.

Himmelfarb, Gertrude. 1995. *The De-Moralization of Society: From Victorian Virtues to Modern Values*. New York: Alfred A. Knopf.

Hirsch, Marianne, and Valerie Smith. 2002. 'Feminism and Cultural Memory: An Introduction'. *Signs* 28 (1, Gender and Cultural Memory): 1–19.

Hobbs, Jerry R. 1990. *Literature and Cognition*. Stanford: Center for the Study of Language and Information.

Hodge, J. 1993. 'Darwin Metaphor: Nature's Place in Victorian Culture'. *Biology & Philosophy* 8 (4): 469–76.

Holdsworth, Nadine. 1998. 'Haven't I Seen You Somewhere Before? Melodrama, Postmodernism and Victorian Culture'. In *Varieties of Victorianism: The Uses of a Past*, edited by G. Day. London and New York: Macmillan. 191–205.

Holmes, Frederick M. 1994. 'The Historical Imagination and the Victorian Past: A. S. Byatt's *Possession*'. *English Studies in Canada* 20 (3): 319–33.

_____. 1996. 'The Representation of History as Plastic: The Search for the Real Thing in Graham Swift's Ever After'. *ARIEL: A Review of International English Literature* 27 (3): 25–43.

_____. 1997. *The Historical Imagination: Postmodernism and the Treatment of the Past in Contemporary British Fiction*. Victoria, B.C.: University of Victoria.

Holton, Robert. 1994. *Jarring Witnesses: Modern Fiction and the Representation of History*. New York and London: Harvester Wheatsheaf.

House, Humphrey. 1955. 'Are the Victorians Coming Back?' In *All In Due Time: The Collected Essays and Broadcast Talks of Humphrey House*. London: Rupert Hart-Davis. 75–93.

Hughes, Winifred. 1980. *The Maniac in the Cellar: Sensation Novels of the 1860s*. Princeton, New Jersey: Princeton University Press.

Hulbert, Ann. 1993. 'The Great Ventriloquist: A. S. Byatt's *Possession: A Romance*'. In *Contemporary British Writers: Narrative Strategies*, edited by R. E. Hosmer Jr. New York: St. Martin's Press – now Palgrave Macmillan. 55–66.

Hunt, Lynn. 1989. 'Introduction: History, Culture, Text'. In *The New Cultural History*. Berkeley: University of California Press.

Hunt, Tristram. 2001. Revisiting the Age of Victoria. *The Australian Financial Review*, 25–28 January, 6–7. 1–22.

Hutcheon, Linda. 1984. *Narcissistic Narrative: The Metafictional Paradox*. New York and London: Methuen. Original edition 1980.

_____. 1988. *A Poetics of Postmodernism: History, Theory, Fiction*. New York and London: Routledge.

_____. 1989. *The Politics of Postmodernism*. London and New York: Routledge.

Hutton, Patrick. 1993. *History as an Art of Memory*. Hanover and London: University Press of New England.

Huyssen, Andreas. 2000. 'Present Pasts: Media, Politics, Amnesia'. *Public Culture* 12 (1): 21–38.

Iggers, Georg G. 1997. *Historiography in the Twentieth Century: From Scientific Objectivity to the Postmodern Challenge*. Middletown, Connecticut: Wesleyan University Press.

Irish, Robert K. 1998. '"Let Me Tell You": About Desire and Narrativity in Graham Swift's Waterland'. *MFS: Modern Fiction Studies* 44 (4): 917–34.

Iser, Wolfgang. 1974. *The Implied Reader*. Baltimore: Johns Hopkins University Press.

Jackson, Rosemary. 1981. *Fantasy: The Literature of Subversion*. London and New York: Methuen.

Jacobs, Lyn. 2006. 'Gail Jones's "light-writing": Memory and the Photo-graph'. *JASAL* 5: 191–208.

James, Henry. 1865. 'Miss Braddon'. *The Nation* (9 November): 594.

Jameson, Fredric. 1985. 'Postmodernism and Consumer Society'. In *Postmodern Culture*, edited by H. Foster. Port Townsend, US and London, England: Pluto Press.

_____. 1988. 'Cognitive Mapping'. In *Marxism and the Interpretation of Culture*, edited by C. Nelson and L. Grossberg. Urbana and Chicago: University of Illinois Press.

_____. 1991. *Postmodernism, or, The Cultural Logic of Late Capitalism*. London and New York: Verso.

_____. 1998. *The Cultural Turn: Selected Writings on the Postmodern 1983–1998*. London and New York: Verso.

Janik, Del Ivan. 1989. 'History and the "Here and Now": The Novels of Graham Swift'. *Twentieth Century Literature* 35 (1): 74–88.

_____. 1995. 'No End of History: Evidence from the Contemporary English Novel'. *Twentieth Century Literature* 41 (2): 160–89.

Jeffrey, Francis. 1817. 'Review of *Waverley*, by Sir Walter Scott. *The Edinburgh Review* 28: 216.

Jenkins, Alice, and Juliet John. 2000. *Rereading Victorian Fiction*. Basingstoke: Macmillan – now Palgrave Macmillan.

Jones, Gail. 2005. Interview by Lyn Gallacher. *Books and Writing*, Radio National, March 27, 2005. http://www.abc.net.au/rn/arts/bwriting/stories/s1330197.htm

_____. 2006. 'Images and Longing: The Insufficiency of Language'. Paper read at Love and Desire: Literature and the Intimate Conference, 23–24 September, at The National Library of Australia. http://www.nla.gov.au/events/loveand-desire/program.html

Jones, Norman. 2007. *Gay and Lesbian Historical Fiction: Sexual Mystery and Post-Secular Narrative*. New York and Basingstoke: Palgrave Macmillan.

Jones, Timothy G. 2009. 'The Canniness of the Gothic: Genre as Practice'. *Gothic Studies* 11 (1):124–33.

Joyce, Simon. 2002. 'The Victorians in the Rearview Mirror'. In *Functions of Victorian Culture at the Present Time*, edited by C. L. Krueger. Athens, Ohiho: Athens University Press. 3–17.

Jukić, Tatjana. 2000. 'From Worlds to Words and the Other Way Around: the Victorian Inheritance in the Postmodern British Novel'. In *Theme Parks, Rainforests and Sprouting Wastelands: European essays on theory and performance in contemporary British fiction*, edited by R. Todd and L. Flora. Amsterdam and Atlanta, Georgia: Rodopi. 77–88.

Kakutani, Michiko. 1994. Books of the Times; Witness Against Postmodernist Historians. Review of Himmelfarb, Gertrude, On Looking Into the Abyss. *The New York Times on the Web*, March 1, http://www.nytimes.com/books/home/.

Kansteiner, Wulf. 2002. 'Finding Meaning in Memory: A Methodological Critique of Collective Memory Studies'. *History and Theory* 41 (2): 179–97.

Kaplan, Cora. 2007. *Victoriana: Histories, Criticisms, Fictions*. Edinburgh: University of Edinburgh Press.

Kearney, Richard. 1988. *The Wake of Imagination: Toward a Postmodern Culture*. Minneapolis: University of Minnesota Press.

Keen, Suzanne. 2001. *Romances of the Archive in Contemporary British Fiction*. Toronto: University of Toronto Press.

Kellner, Douglas, ed. 1989. *Postmodernism/Jameson/Critique*. Washington DC: Maisonneuvre Press.

Kelly, Kathleen Coyne. 1996. *A. S. Byatt*. Edited by K. E. Robie. Vol. 529, *Twayne's English Author Series*. New York: Twayne.

Kermode, Frank. 1967. *The Sense of an Ending: Studies in the Theory of Fiction*. New York: Oxford University Press.

———. 1968. 'Novel, History and Type'. *Novel* 1 (3): 231–8.

Kiely, Robert. 1993. *Reverse Tradition: Postmodern Fictions and the Nineteenth Century Novel*. Cambridge, Massachusetts and London: Harvard University Press.

King, Jeanette. 2005. *The Victorian Woman Question in Contemporary Feminist Fiction*. Basingstoke and New York: Palgrave Macmillan.

Klein, Kerwin Lee. 2000. 'On the Emergence of Memory in Historical Discourse'. *Representations* 69: *Grounds for Remembering*: 127–50.

Knight, David. 1986. *The Age of Science: The Scientific World-view in the Nineteenth Century*. Oxford and New York: Basil Blackwell.

Knoepflmacher, U. C., and G. B. Tennyson. 1977. *Nature and the Victorian Imagination*. Los Angeles and London: University of California Press.

Kohlke, M. L. 2004. 'Into History through the Back Door: The "Past Historic" in *Nights at the Circus* and *Affinity*'. *Women: A Cultural Review* 15 (2): 153–66.

———. 2008a. 'Introduction: Speculations in and on the Neo-Victorian Encounter'. *Neo-Victorian Studies* 1 (1): 1–18.

———. 2008b. 'Sexsation and the Neo-Victorian Novel: Orientalising the Nineteenth Century in Contemporary Fiction'. In *Negotiating Sexual Idioms: Image, Text, Performance*, edited by M.-L. Kohlke and L. Orza. Amsterdam and New York: Rodopi. 53–77.

Kontou, Tatiana. 2009. *Spiritualism and Women's Writing From the Fin de Siècle to the Neo-Victorian*. Basingstoke and New York: Palgrave Macmillan.

Krueger, Christine L. 2002. 'Introduction'. In *Functions of Victorian Culture at the Present Time*. Athens, Ohio: University of Ohio Press. xi–xx.

Kucich, John, and Dianne F. Sadoff. 2000. 'Introduction: Histories of the Present'. In *Victorian Afterlife: Postmodern Culture Rewrites the Nineteenth Century*. Minneapolis and London: University of Minnesota Press. ix–xxx.

Kunow, Rüdiger. 1996. 'The Return of Historical Narratives in Contemporary American Culture'. In *Ethics and Aesthetics: The Moral Turn of Postmodernism*, edited by G. Hoffmann and A. Hornung. Heidelberg: Universitätsverlag C. Winter. 255–74.

LaCapra, Dominick. 1985. *History and Criticism*. Ithaca: Cornell University Press.

———. 1998. *History and Memory After Auschwitz*. Ithaca, New York: Cornell University Press.

Lachmann, Renate. 1997. *Memory and Literature: Intertextuality in Russian Modernism*. Minneapolis and London: University of Minnesota Press.

———. 2004. 'Cultural memory and the role of literature'. *European Review* 12 (2): 165–78.

Lalvani, Suren. 1996. *Photography, Vision, and the Production of Modern Bodies*. Edited by H. A. Giroux, *SUNY Series, INTERRUPTIONS: Border Testimony(ies) and Critical Discourse/s*. Albany: State University of New York Press.

Landow, George P. 1990. 'History, His Story and Stories in Graham Swift's *Waterland*'. *Studies in the Literary Imagination* 23 (2): 197–211.

Lee, Alison. 1990. *Realism and Power: Postmodern British Fiction*. London and New York: Routledge.

Lehmann-Haupt, Christopher. 1990. Books of The Times; When There Was Such a Thing as Romantic Love. Review of *Possession*, by A. S. Byatt. *The New York Times*, October 25. http://query.nytimes.com/gst/fullpage.html?res=9C0CE2D D143CF936A15753C1A966958260

Leighton, Angela. 2000. 'Ghosts, Aestheticism, and "Vernon Lee"'. *Victorian Literature and Culture* 28: 1–14.

Leonard, Elisabeth Anne. 1998. '"The Burden of Intolerable Strangeness": Using C. S. Lewis to See Beyond Realism in the Fiction of A. S. Byatt'. *Extrapolation: A Journal of Science Fiction and Fantasy* 39 (3): 236–48.

Letissier, Georges. 2004. 'Dickens and Post-Victorian Fiction'. *Postmodern Studies* (35. Refracting the Canon in Contemporary British Literature): 111–28.

Levenson, Michael. 1992. 'Ever After'. Review of *Ever After*, by Graham Swift. *The New Republic* 206 (25): 38–40.

Levine, George, ed. 1987. *One Culture: Essays in Science and Literature*. Madison, Wisconsin: University of Wisconsin Press.

_____. 1988. *Darwin and the Novelists: Patterns of Science in Victorian Fiction*. Cambridge, Massachusetts and London: Harvard University Press.

_____. ed. 1993. *Realism and Representation: Essays on the Problem of Realism in relation to Science, Literature and Culture*. Madison, Wisconsin: University of Wisconsin Press.

_____. 2002. *Dying to Know: Scientific Epistemology and Narrative in Victorian England*. Chicago and London: University of Chicago Press.

Levine, Phillipa. 1986. *The Amateur and the Professional: Antiquarians, Historians and Archaeologists in Victorian England 1838–1886*. Cambridge and New York: Cambrige University Press.

Ley, James. 2004. Celluloid Path to Enlightenment. Review of *Sixty Lights*, by Gail Jones. *Sydney Morning Herald*, September 4, 10.

Liu, Alan. 1989. 'The Power of Formalism: The New Historicism'. *ELH* 56 (4): 721–71.

Llewellyn, Mark. 2004. '"Queer? I should say its criminal!": Sarah Waters' *Affinity*'. *Journal of Gender Studies* 13 (3): 203–214.

Lloyd, Genevieve. 1993. *The Man of Reason: 'Male' and 'Female' in Western Philosophy*. London and New York: Routledge.

Loesberg, Jonathan. 1986. 'The Ideology of Narrative Form in Sensation Fiction'. *Representations* 13 (Winter): 115–38.

Loomis, Chauncey C. 1977. 'The Arctic Sublime'. In *Nature and the Victorian Imagination*, edited by U. C. Knoepflmacher and G. B. Tennyson. Berkley, Los Angeles and London: University of California Press. 95–112.

López, Marta Sofía. 2000. 'Historiographic metafiction and resistance postmodernism'. In *Theme Parks, Rainforests and Sprouting Wastelands*, edited by R. Todd and L. Flora. Amsterdam and Atlanta, Georgia: Rodopi. 195–214.

Lord, Geoffrey. 1997. 'Mystery and History, Discovery and Recovery in Thomas Pynchon's *The Crying of Lot 49* and Graham Swift's *Waterland*'. *Neophilologous: An International Journal of Modern and Mediaeval Language and Literature* 81 (1): 145–63.

Lowenthal, David. 1985. *The Past is a Foreign Country*. Cambridge, New York: Cambridge University Press.

_____. 1998. *The Heritage Crusade and the Spoils of History*. Cambridge: Cambridge University Press.

Lubenow, William C. 2004. 'Lytton Strachey's *Eminent Victorians*: the rise and fall of the intellectual aristocracy'. In *The Victorians Since 1901: Histories, representations and revisions*, edited by M. Taylor and M. Wolff. Manchester and New York: Manchester University Press. 17–28.

Lukács, Georg. 1962. *The Historical Novel*. Translated by H. Mitchell and S. Mitchell. London: Merlin. Originally published as *Der historische Roman* (1937).

Lyotard, Jean-François. 1984. *The Postmodern Condition: A Report on Knowledge*. Translated by G. Bennington and B. Massumi. Minneapolis: University of Minnesota Press. Original edition 1979.

Macintyre, Stuart, and Sean Scalmer, eds. 2006. *What If?* Melbourne: Melbourne University Press.

MacKay, Carol Hanbery. 2001. *Creative Negativity: Four Victorian Exemplars of the Female Quest*. Stanford, California: Stanford Unviersity Press.

MacKinnon, Kenneth. 1992. *The Politics of Popular Representation: Reagan, Thatcher, AIDS, and the Movies*. London and Toronto: Associated University Presses.

Maidment, B. E. 2005. '*Mr Wroe's Virgins*: the "other Victorians" and recent fiction'. In *British Fiction of the 1990s*, edited by N. Bentley. London and New York: Routledge. 153–66.

Malchow, Howard L. 2000. 'Nostalgia, "Heritage", and the London Antiques Trade'. In *Singular Continuities: Tradition, Nostalgia, and Identity in Modern British Culture*, edited by G. K. Behlmer and F. M. Leventhal. Stanford, California: Stanford University Press. 196–214.

Malik, Rachel. 2006. 'The Afterlife of Wilkie Collins'. In *The Cambridge Companion to Wilkie Collins*, edited by J. Bourne-Taylor. Cambridge: Cambridge University Press. 181–93.

Mansel, H. L. 1863. 'The Sensation Novel'. *London Quarterly* 113–14: 251–67.

Marcus, Steven. 1966. *The Other Victorians: A Study of Sexuality and Pornography in Mid-Nineteenth Century England*. London: Corgi Books. Original edition 1964, 1965.

Marien, Mary Warner. 1997. *Photography and its Critics: A Cultural History, 1839–1900*. Cambridge: Cambridge University Press.

Marsden, Gordon, ed. 1990. *Victorian Values: Personalities and Perspectives in Nineteenth-Century Society*. London and New York: Longman.

Marsh, Kelly. 1995. 'The Neo-Sensation Novel: A Contemporary Genre in the Victorian Tradition'. *Philological Quarterly* 74 (1): 99–123.

———. 1997. The Sensation Novel Then and Now. Ph.D. Dissertation, Pennsylvania State University.

Martea, Ion. *Sixty Lights*. Review of *Sixty Lights*, by Gail Jones. *Culture Wars*. http://www.culturewars.co.uk/2004–02/sixty.htm (accessed 2004).

Marwick, Arthur. 1970. *The Nature of History*. London and Basingstoke: Macmillan Press.

Maynard, John, Adrienne Auslander Munich, and Sandra Donaldson. 1993. *Victorian Literature and Culture*. New York: AMS.

Maynard, Patrick. 1997. *The Engine of Visualization: Thinking Through Photography*. Ithaca and London: Cornell University Press.

McGowan, John. 2000. 'Modernity and Culture, the Victorians and Cultural Studies'. In *Victorian Afterlife: Postmodern Culture Rewrites the Nineteenth Century*, edited by J. Kucich and D. F. Sadoff. Minneapolis and London: University of Minnesota Press. 3–28.

McHale, Brian. 1987. *Postmodernist Fiction*. New York and London: Methuen.
_____. 1992. 'Postmodernism, or the Anxiety of Master Narratives'. Review of Linda Hutcheon, *A Poetics of Postmodernism: History, Theory, Fiction*. (1988). Linda Hutcheon, *The Politics of Postmodernism* (1989). Fredric Jameson, *Postmodernism, or, the Cultural Logic of Late Capitalism* (1991). *Diacritics* 22 (1): 17–33.
_____. 2003. 'History Itself? Or, the Romance of Postmodernism'. Review of Amy J. Elias, *Sublime Desire: History and Post-1960s Fiction*. Baltimore and London: Johns Hopkins University Press, 2001. *Contemporary Literature* 44 (1): 151–61.
McKinney, Ronald H. 1997. 'The Greening of Postmodernism: Graham Swift's *Waterland*'. *New Literary History* 28 (4): 821–32.
McQuire, Scott. 1998. *Visions of Modernity: Representation, Memory, Time and Space in the Age of the Camera*. London: Sage Publications.
Millbank, Jenni. 2004. 'It's About *This*: Lesbians, Prison, Desire'. *Social and Legal Studies* 13 (2): 155–90.
Miller, Andrew H. 1995. *Novels behind Glass: Commodity Culture and Victorian Narrative*. Cambridge: Cambridge University Press.
Mink, Louis O. 1978. 'Narrative Form as a Cognitive Instrument'. In *The Writing of History: Literary Form and Historical Understanding*, edited by R. H. Canary and H. Kozicki. Madison, Wisconsin: University of Wisconsin Press. 129–49.
Morris, Pam. 2003. *Realism*. Edited by J. Drakakis, *The New Critical Idiom*. London and New York: Routledge.
Morrison, Jago. 2003. *Contemporary Fiction*. London and New York: Routledge.
Nile, Richard. 2006. Facts Set the Truth Free. *The Australian Literary Review*, December 6, 18.
Nora, Pierre. 1989. 'Between History and Memory: Les Lieux de Mémoire'. *Representations* 26: *Memory and Counter Memory*: 7–24.
Onega, Susan. 1993. 'British Historiographic Metafiction in the 1980s'. In *British Postmodern Fiction*, edited by T. D'haen and H. Bertens. Amsterdam and Atlanta, Georgia: Rodopi. 47–61.
_____. and Christian Gutleben. 2004. *Refracting the Canon in Contemporary British Literature and Film*. Edited by T. D'haen and H. Bertens. Vol. 35, *Postmodern Studies*. Amsterdam and New York: Rodopi.
O'Neill, Patrick. 1994. *Fictions of Discourse: Reading Narrative Theory*. Toronto, Buffalo, London: University of Toronto Press.
Orr, Linda. 1986. 'The Revenge of Literature: A History of History'. *New Literary History* 18: 1–22.
Pacey, Arnold. 1983. *The Culture of Technology*. Cambridge, Massachusetts: MIT Press.
Palmer, Paulina. 1999. *Lesbian Gothic: Transgressive Fictions*. London and New York: Cassell.
_____. 2004. 'Lesbian Gothic: Genre, Transformation, Transgression'. *Gothic Studies* 6 (1): 118–30.
_____. '"She began to show me the words she had written, one by one": Lesbian Reading and Writing Practices in the Fiction of Sarah Waters'. *Women: A Cultural Review* 19 (1): 69–86.
Parini, Jay. 1990. Unearthing the Secret Lover. Review of *Possession*, by A. S. Byatt. *The New York Times*, October 21, 9.

Parker, Sarah. 2008. '"The Darkness is the Closet in Which Your Lover Roosts Her Heart": Lesbians, Desire and the Gothic Genre'. *Journal of International Women's Studies* 9 (2): 4–19.

Peim, Nick. 2005. 'Spectral Bodies: Derrida and the Philosphy of the Photograph as Historical Document'. *Journal of Philosophy of Education* 39 (1): 67–84.

Phelps, Guy. 1988. 'Victorian Values'. *Sight and Sound* 57 (2): 108–10.

Phillips, Louise. 1996. 'Rhetoric and the Spread of Thatcherism'. *Discourse and Society* 7 (2): 209–41.

Pickering, Michael, and Emily Keightley. 2006. 'The Modalities of Nostalgia'. *Current Sociology* 54 (6): 919–41.

Powell, Katrina M. 2003. 'Mary Metcalf's Attempt at Reclamation: Maternal Representation in Graham Swift's *Waterland*'. *Women's Studies* 32 (1): 59–77.

Pritchard, William H. 1984. 'The Body in the River Leem'. Review of *Waterland*, by Graham Swift. *New York Times Book Review* 89 (March 25): 9.

Pultz, John. 1995. *The Body and the Lens: Photography 1839 to the Present*. New York: Harry N. Abrams.

Pykett, Lyn. 1992. *The 'Improper' Feminine: The Women's Sensation Novel and the New Woman Writing*. London and New York: Routledge.

_____. 1994. *The Sensation Novel: From The Woman in White to Moonstone*. Plymouth: Northcote.

Ranke, Leopold von. 1973. 'Introduction to *The History of the Latin and Teutonic Nations*'. In *Ranke, the Theory and Practice of History*, edited by G. G. Iggers and K. von Moltke. New York: Irvington Publishers. Original edition 1824. 55–9.

Rauch, Alan. 2001. *Useful Knowledge: The Victorians, Morality and the March of Intellect*. Durham and London: Duke University Press.

Raymond, Meredith B., and Mary Rose Sullivan, eds. 1983. *The letters of Elizabeth Barrett Browning to Mary Russell Mitford, 1836–1854*. 3 vols. Vol. 3. Waco, Texas: Armstrong Browning Library of Baylor University.

Richards, Thomas. 1990. *The Commodity Culture of Victorian England: Advertising and Spectacle, 1851–1914*. Stanford, California: Stanford University Press.

_____. 1993. *The Imperial Archive: Knowledge and the Fantasy of Empire*. London: Verso.

Ricoeur, Paul. 2004. *Memory, History, Forgetting*. Translated by K. Blamey and D. Pellauer. Chicago and London: University of Chicago Press.

Riddell, Peter. 1989. *The Thatcher Decade: How Britain Has Changed During the 1980s*. Oxford, UK and Cambridge, US: Basil Blackwell.

Rigby, Mair. 2009. 'Uncanny Recognition: Queer Theory's Debt to the Gothic'. *Gothic Studies* 11 (1): 46–57.

Rigney, Ann. 2004. 'Portable Monuments: Literature, Cultural Memory, and the Case of Jeanie Deans'. *Poetics Today* 25 (2): 361–96.

_____. 2007. 'Being an improper historian'. In *Manifestos for History*, edited by K. Jenkins, S. Morgan and A. Munslow. London and New York: Routledge. 149–59.

Rody, Caroline. 1995. 'Toni Morrison's *Beloved*: History, "Rememory," and a "Clamor for a Kiss"'. *American Literary History* 7 (1): 92–119.

Rorty, Richard. 1987. 'Science as Solidarity'. In *The Rhetoric of the Human Sciences: Language and Argument in Scholarship*, edited by J. S. Nelson, A. Megill and D. N. McClosky. Madison, Wisconsin and London: University of Wisconsin Press. 38–52.

Rosenbaum, Ron. 2000. 'Now the Play's the Thing, Once Again'. *The Australian Financial Review* (Friday 15 September).

Rosenstone, Robert A. 1995. *Visions of the Past: The Challenge of Film to Our Idea of History*. Cambridge, Massachusets and London: Harvard University Press.

Roth, Michael S. 1995. *The Ironist's Cage: Memory, Trauma and the Construction of History*. New York: Columbia University Press.

Rudwick, Martin, J. S. 1985. *The Great Devonian Controversy: The Shaping of Scientific Knowledge among Gentlemanly Specialists*. Chicago and London: University of Chicago Press.

Safir, Margery Arent. 1999. *Melancholies of Knowledge: Literature in the Age of Science*. New York: State University of New York.

Samuel, Raphael. 1992. 'Mrs Thatcher's Return to Victorian Values'. In *Victorian Values: A Joint Symposium of the Royal Society of Edinburgh and the British Academy December 1990*, edited by T. C. Smout. Oxford: Oxford University Press. 9–30.

_____. 1994. *Theatres of Memory*. Vol. 2, *Past and Present in Contemporary Culture*. London and New York: Verso.

Scanlan, Margaret. 1990. *Traces of Another Time: History and Politics in Postwar British Fiction*. Princeton: Princeton University Press.

Schliefer, Ronald, Robert Con Davis, and Nancy Mergler. 1992. *Culture and Cognition: The Boundaries of Literary and Scientific Enquiry*. Ithaca: Cornell University Press.

Schor, Hilary M. 2000. 'Sorting, Morphing and Mourning: A. S. Byatt Ghostwrites Victorian Fiction'. In *Victorian Afterlife: Postmodern Culture Rewrites the Ninteteenth Century*. Minneapolis and London: University of Minnesota Press. 234–51.

Sedgwick, Eve Kosofsky. 1986 (1976). *The Coherence of Gothic Conventions*. London and New York: Methuen.

Scott, Walter. 1887. 'Essay on Romance'. In *Essays on Chivalry, Romance, and the Drama*. London: Frederick Warne. 65–108.

Seixas, Peter. 2004. 'Introduction'. In *Theorizing Historical Consciousness*, edited by P. Sexas. Toronto, Buffalo, London: University of Toronto Press. 3–24.

Seldon, Anthony, and Daniel Collings. 2000. *Britian Under Thatcher, Seminar Studies in History*. Essex: Longman.

Shaffer, Elinor S., ed. 1998. *The Third Culture: Literature and Science*. Edited by W. Pape. Vol. 9, *European Cultures: Studies in Literature and the Arts*. Berlin, New York: Walter de Gruyter.

Shaw, Christopher, and Malcolm Chase, eds. 1989. *The Imagined Past: History and Nostalgia*. Manchester and New York: Manchester University Press.

Shiffman, Adrienne. 2001. '"Burn What They Should Not See": The Private Journal as Public Text in A. S. Byatt's *Possession*'. *Tulsa Studies in Women's Literature* 20 (1): 93–106.

Shiller, Dana. 1997. 'The Redemptive Past in the Neo-Victorian Novel'. *Studies in the Novel* 29 (4): 539–61.

Shinn, Thelma J. 1995. '"What's in a Word?": Possessing A. S. Byatt's Meronymic Novel'. *Papers on Language and Literature* 31 (2): 164–83.

Shuttleworth, Sally. 1998. 'Natural History: The Retro-Victorian Novel'. In *The Third Culture: Literature and Science*, edited by E. S. Shaffer. Berlin and New York: Walter de Gruyter. 253–68.

Silver, Brian L. 1998. *The Ascent of Science*. New York, Oxford: Oxford University Press.

Smith, Amanda. 1992. 'Graham Swift: The British Novelist Grapples with the Ambiguities of Knowledge and the Secrets of the Past'. *Publishers Weekly* 239 (10): 43–4.

Smith, Patricia. 1997. *Lesbian Panic: Homoeroticism in Modern British Women's Fiction*. Columbia: Columbia University Press.

Smout, T. C., ed. 1992. *Victorian Values: A Joint Symposium of the Royal Society of Edinburgh and the British Academy December 1990*. Oxford: Oxford University Press.

Sontag, Susan. 1977. *On Photography*. New York: Penguin.

Spencer, Kathleen L. 1992. 'Purity and Danger: Dracula, the Urban Gothic, and the Late Victorian Degeneracy Crisis'. *ELH* 59 (1): 197–225.

Spiegal, Gabrielle M. 2002. 'Memory and History: Liturgical Time and Historical Time'. *History and Theory* 41 (2): 149–62.

Spufford, Francis. 1996. 'The Difference Engine and *The Difference Engine*'. In *Cultural Babbage: Technology, Time and Invention*, edited by F. Spufford and J. Uglow. London, Boston: Faber and Faber. 266–90.

Steinmetz, Horst. 1995. 'History in Fiction: History as Fiction: On the Relations Between Literature and History in the Nineteenth and Twentieth Centuries'. In *Narrative Turns and Minor Genres in Postmodernism*, edited by T. D'haen and H. Bertens. Amsterdam: Rodopi. 81–103.

Stephanson, Anders. 1989. 'Regarding Postmodernism: A Conversation with Fredric Jameson'. In *Postmodernism/Jameson/Critique*, edited by D. Kellner. Washington, DC: Maisonneuvre Press. 43–74.

Steveker, Lena. 2009. *Identity and Cultural Memory in the Fiction of A. S. Byatt*. New York and Basingstoke: Palgrave Macmillan.

Stewart, Garrett. 1995. 'Film's Victorian Retrofit'. *Victorian Studies* 38: 153–98.

Stewart, Susan. 1993. *On Longing: Narratives of the Miniature, the Gigantic, the Souvenir, the Collection*. Durham and London: Duke University Press.

Stout, Mira. 1991. What Possessed A. S. Byatt? *The New York Times Magazine*, 26 May. http://www.nytimes.com/books/99/06/13/specials/byatt-possessed.html?_r=1&oref=slogin

Sturken, Marita. 1997. *Tangled Memories: The Vietnam War, the AIDS Epidemic, and the Politics of Remembering*. Berkeley, Los Angeles and London: University of California Press.

Su, John J. 2004. 'Fantasies of (Re)collection: Collecting and Imagination in A. S. Byatt's *Possession: A Romance*'. *Contemporary Literature* 45 (4): 684–712.

Sussman, Herbert. 1994. 'Cyberpunk Meets Charles Babbage: *The Difference Engine* as Alternative Victorian History'. *Victorian Studies* 38 (1): 1–23.

Sweet, Matthew. 2001. *Inventing the Victorians*. London: Faber and Faber.

Swift, Graham. 1988. Interview with Del Ivan Janik (unpublished).

Tagg, John. 1988. *The Burden of Representation: Essays on Photographies and Histories*. Edited by S. Hall and P. Walton, *Communications and Culture*. Basingstoke and London: Macmillan Education.

Talbot, William Henry Fox. (1844) 1969. *The Pencil of Nature*. Vol. 1. New York: DaCapo.

Tange, Hanne. 2004. 'Regional Redemption: Graham Swift's *Waterland* and the End of History'. *Orbis Litterarum* 59: 75–89.

Tarbox, Katherine. 1996. '*The French Lieutenant's Woman* and the Evolution of the Narrative'. *Twentieth Century Literature* 42 (1): 88–102.

Taylor, Charles. 1984. 'Foucault on Freedom and Truth'. *Political Theory* 12 (2): 152–83.

_____. 1989. *Sources of the Self: The Making of Modern Identity.* Cambridge, Massachusetts: Harvard University Press.

Taylor, Miles. 2004. 'Introduction'. In *The Victorians since 1901: histories, representations and revisions,* edited by M. Taylor and M. Wolff. Manchester and New York: Manchester University Press. 1–16.

Tester, Keith. 1993. 'Nostalgia'. In *The Life and times of Post-modernity.* London and New York: Routledge. 1–5.

Thaden, Barbara Z. 1997. *The Maternal Voice in Victorian Fiction: Rewriting the Patriarchal Family.* New York and London: Garland Publishing.

Thatcher, Margaret. 1983a. *Interview with Brian Waldon.* Janurary 16. London Weekend Television, *Weekend World.* http://www.margaretthatcher.org/speeches/displaydocument.asp?docid=105087

_____. 1983b. *Interview with Peter Allen.* IRN, *The Decision Makers,* April 15, 1983. http://www.margaretthatcher.org/speeches/displaydocument.asp?docid=105291

_____. 1992. 'Don't Undo Our Work'. *Newsweek* (27 April): 14.

Thurman, Judith. 1990. 'A Reader's Companion'. Review of *Possession: A Romance. New Yorker,* 19 November, 151.

Tillotson, Kathleen. 1969. 'Introduction: The Lighter Reading of the Eighteen-Sixties'. In *The Woman in White,* edited by K. Tillotson. ix–xxvi.

Todd, Richard. 1994. 'The Retrieval of Unheard Voices in British Postmodernist Fiction: A. S. Byatt and Marina Warner'. In *Liminal Postmodernisms: The Postmodern, the (Post-) Colonial, and the (Post-) Feminist,* edited by T. D'haen and H. Bertens. Amsterdam and Atlanta, Georgia: Rodopi. 99–144.

Traub, Valerie. 2001. 'The Renaissance of Lesbianism in Early Modern England'. *GLQ* 7 (2): 245–63.

Trevelyan, G. M. 1949. 'Introducing the Ideas and Beliefs of the Victorians'. In *Ideas and Beliefs of the Victorians: an historic revaluation of the Victorian Age,* edited by H. Grisewood. London: Sylvan Press. 15–19.

Trumpener, Katie. 1993. 'National Character, Nationalist Plots: National Tale and Historical Novel in the age of *Waverley,* 1806–1830'. *ELH* 60: 685–731.

Tuck Rozett, Martha. 1995. 'Constructing a World: How Postmodern Historical Fiction Reimagines the Past'. *Clio: a Journal of Literature History and the Philosophy of History* 25 (2): 145–64.

Tuttleton, James W. 1995. 'Rehabilitating Victorian Values'. *The Hudson Review* 58 (3): 388–96.

Uglow, Jenny. 1996. 'Introduction: "Possibility"'. In *Cultural Babbage: Technology, Time and Invention,* edited by F. Spufford and J. Uglow. London, Boston: Faber and Faber. 1–23.

Wallace, Diana. 2005. *The Woman's Historical Novel: British Women Writers, 1900–2000.* New York: Palgrave Macmillan.

Walvin, James. 1987. *Victorian Values: A Companion to the Granada Television Series.* London: André Deutsch Limited.

Waters, Sarah. 1996. 'Wolfskins and Togas: Maude Meagher's *The Green Scamadner* and the lesbian historical novel'. *Women: A Cultural Review* 7 (2): 176–88.

_____. 2002. *A chat with Tipping the Velvet author Sarah Waters* [cited 26/03/08 2008]. Available from http://moviepie.com/filmfests/sarah_waters.html.

Waters, Sarah. Undated. *Her Thieving Hands: interview with Sarah Waters*. Virago [cited 26/03/2008]. Available from: http://www.virago.co.uk/author_results. asp?SF1=data&ST1=feature&REF=e2006111617063697&SORT=author_id&TA G=&CID=&PGE=&LANG=en.

Waugh, Patricia. 1984. *Metafiction: The Theory and Practice of Self-Conscious Fiction*. London and New York: Methuen.

Weeks, Jeffrey. 1989. *Sex, Politics and Society: The regulation of Sexuality since 1800*. 2nd edn. London and New York: Longman.

_____. 1991. 'Pretended Family Relationships'. In *Against Nature: Essays on History, Sexuality and Identity*. London: Rivers Oram Press. 134–56.

Wells, Lynn. 2002. Corso, Ricorso: Historical Repetition and Cultural Reflection in A. S. Byatt's *Possession: A Romance*. *MFS: Modern Fiction Studies* 48 (3): 668–92.

Wesseling, Elisabeth. 1991. *Writing History as a Prophet: Postmodernist Innovations of the Historical Novel*. Amsterdam and Philadelphia: John Benjamin's Publishing Company.

White, Hayden. 1973. *Metahistory: The Historical Imagination in Nineteenth-Century Europe*. Baltimore: Johns Hopkins University Press.

_____. 1978a. 'The Burden of History'. In *Tropics of Discourse: Essays in Cultural Criticism*. Baltimore and London: Johns Hopkins University Press. 27–50.

_____. 1978b. 'The Fictions of Factual Representation'. In *Tropics of Discourse: Essays in Cultural Criticism*. Baltimore and London: Johns Hopkins University Press. 121–34.

_____. 1987a. 'The Value of Narrativity in the Representation of Reality'. In *The Content of the Form*. Baltimore and London: Johns Hopkins University Press. 1–25.

_____. 1987b. 'The Politics of Historical Interpretation: Discipline and De-Sublimation'. In *The Content of the Form: Narrative Discourse and Historical Repesentation*. Baltimore and London: Johns Hopkins University Press. 58–82.

_____. 1999. *Figural Realism: Studies in the Mimesis Effect*. Baltimore and London: Johns Hopkins University Press.

_____. 2005. 'Introduction: Historical Fiction, Fictional History, and Historical Reality'. *Rethinking History* 9 (2/3): 147–57.

Williams, Anne. 1995. *Art of Darkness: A Poetics of Gothic*. Chicago: Chicago University Press.

Wilson, Cheryl A. 2006. 'From the Drawing Room to The Stage: Performing Sexuality in Sarah Waters's *Tipping the Velvet*'. *Women's Studies* 35 (3): 285–305.

Wilt, Judith. 1990. *Abortion, Choice, and Contemporary Fiction: The Armageddon of the Maternal Instinct*. Chicago and London: University of Chicago Press.

Wolfreys, Julian. 2002. *Victorian Hauntings: Spectality, Gothic, the Uncanny and Literature*. Basingstoke: Palgrave – now Palgrave Macmillan.

Yelin, Louise. 1992. 'Cultural Cartography: A. S. Byatt's *Possession* and the Politics of Victorian Studies'. *The Victorian Newsletter* Spring: 38–42.

Young, James E. 1997. 'Toward a Received History of the Holocaust'. *History and Theory* 36 (4): 21–43.

Zamora, Lois Parkinson. 1989. *Writing the Apocalypse: Historical Vision in Contemporary U.S. and Latin American Fiction*. Cambridge: Cambridge University Press.

Index